One-Way Elevator

Henry Pavlak

BLACK ROSE writing

© 2015 by Henry Pavlak

All rights reserved. No part of this book may be reproduced, stored in a retrieval system or transmitted in any form or by any means without the prior written permission of the publishers, except by a reviewer who may quote brief passages in a review to be printed in a newspaper, magazine or journal.

The final approval for this literary material is granted by the author.

First printing

This is a work of fiction. Names, characters, businesses, places, events and incidents are either the products of the author's imagination or used in a fictitious manner. Any resemblance to actual persons, living or dead, or actual events is purely coincidental.

ISBN: 978-1-61296-331-0
PUBLISHED BY BLACK ROSE WRITING
www.blackrosewriting.com

Printed in the United States of America
Suggested retail price $17.95

One-Way Elevator is printed in Calibri

To everyone who pushes the elevator button more than once, believing it makes a difference.

To Ed and Abe,
I wish I had not left you both on the 27th floor.

One-Way Elevator

Preface

We all realize how fragile life is. Each of us lives trying to deal with whatever obstacles are thrown in our path. The fragility is soon forgotten, and the instinct for survival kicks in. Each of us can look back and see the mistakes or the right moves made, but what we usually fail to see is how our actions at one moment can lead to unforeseen consequences in the future. In a story from the Bible, Moses hit the rock three times instead of once questioning his faith in God. As punishment, Moses was not allowed to enter the Promised Land. How many of us hit the elevator button more than once, questioning if it makes a difference? Depending on one's point of view or religious beliefs, everything can be explained by rationalizing that it was either the will of God or just an accident. The only certainty is that each prior action determines what happens in the current moment and the past cannot be changed. The question is, do all paths taken lead to the same point?

Chapter 1

The blood curdling sound of the alarm clock jolted Jim Winters from his dream of running on the beach as the sun's rays were fading and the tide was rising. He slowly rolled out of bed, while his wife Terri remained in her own private dream world.

The steam from the shower only magnified the fog he navigated through each day of his life. Even if he had used cold water, he would still not feel invigorated or energized. Twenty-five years at the same company without much advancement would suck the life out of most people, and Jim was no exception. He dried himself off, except for his stubble-covered face, wiped the fogged mirror with his hand, studied his reflection, and wondered how much longer he could continue his daily grind to New York City. Jim was fifty years old and married for twenty years. He still wondered how a beautiful woman like Terri could be his wife. They had married a week after Terri's graduation from Rutgers.

Lately he wondered how fast all the years had gone by. He quickly calculated that if he averaged eight hours of sleep a night, he had slept nearly seventeen years. "Not much time for living," he mumbled as he covered his face with shaving cream. His forehead displayed a few thin lines that would only multiply and deepen with time. Jim vowed he would never use Botox. He would rather go to Home Depot and buy a small can of spackle and a very fine grade of sandpaper instead. His hair was light brown with a few grey hairs interspersed on each side. Laugh lines played around his mouth, now hidden by the shaving cream. His eyes were set deep, and he always had trouble keeping his sideburns equal and straight. "No wonder I never became a surgeon," he thought as he began removing the daily stubble. He was exactly six feet tall and a trim one hundred and seventy pounds. He never drank much, never smoked, but had a weakness for chocolate. He kept himself in shape by running at least five times a week. His last marathon was many years ago. Although he no longer competed in races, or had the desire to endure the necessary training to run another marathon, he still loved to run. The trophies and medals from all his races were stuffed in a box somewhere in the attic. "I have three meetings today and two of my projects are running late. I can't wait for vacation. Never mind vacation, I can't wait for retirement. That's a depressing thought. It's July 2001, and 2016 seems a thousand years away."

Jim quickly finished shaving, then he put on a pair of beige Dockers and a light blue short-sleeved shirt, took one last look in the mirror, and went downstairs for breakfast. When he returned upstairs to brush his teeth, Terri rolled over and said sleepily, "Good morning. You kept me up all night again with your snoring."

Jim laughed and retorted, "You're still way ahead on keeping me up with your snoring."

Terri threw a pillow at him and yelled, "I don't snore."

Jim swooped the pillow up from the floor, lightly hit her over the head and replied, "One night I'll turn on a tape recorder and we'll see who snores more."

Terri was a middle school language arts teacher, enjoying her summer vacation. She was eight years younger than Jim. She was five-feet seven and a slender one hundred and fifteen pounds. Her short, dark brown hair never seemed mussed, even after a night of sleeping and snoring. Her complexion was light, and her wide brown eyes exhibited no signs of aging. Her nose was thin and a little small for her face, but her mouth was full, and she had an inviting smile that could put anyone at ease.

She rolled over and thought back to the bookstore where she and Jim met. She had been buying a book for one of her college classes, while Jim had just been browsing.

She had approached Jim and said, "I can't wait until I can read what I want."

Jim looked startled but managed a smile. "Sometimes it's easier when somebody tells you what to read, so you don't wander aimlessly like me."

Terri wondered why she had started the conversation, but she followed her instincts and asked, "What do you like to read?"

Looking down at the book in her hand Jim declared emphatically, "Not *Crime and Punishment*."

Terri laughed and responded, "I don't want to read it either, but it's for my literature class."

Jim continued, "I did have to read that years ago. The only way I got through it was to give English names to all the characters."

Terri gave her best smile and said, "Maybe I'll try that too. I'm Terri Matthews."

Jim extended his hand. "Jim Winters. Nice to meet you."

After shaking hands, Jim asked, "So where do you go to school?"

"I'm a senior at Rutgers."

"I graduated from Rutgers."

Jim left out his graduation year on purpose, but in vain.

"What year did you graduate?"

"In 1973."

Terri was initially shocked by the age difference, but quickly recovered and suggested, "Let's have a cup of coffee and you can tell me all about Rutgers in the old days."

Jim ignored the old days comment and eagerly agreed. They sat down at one of the small tables and were encircled by others who were tired of walking the aisles, tired of trying to meet someone in the aisles, or just plain tired.

She could sense Jim was searching for something to keep the conversation going and she was not impressed with his next question. "What's your major?"

"I'm going for teaching."

"What subject?"

"Language arts in middle school. I was going to major in history, but then I figured there weren't too many jobs for a history major, so I switched to teaching. What was your major?"

"Economics. I really had no idea about anything, I knew I could never be a teacher, so I decided finding out how the economy works might be good."

Terri took a sip of her coffee. "Well, was it?"

Jim laughed. "I found out two things. I know how the economy works."

"What's the second thing?"

"That nobody would hire me as an economist."

Terri laughed, "So there were no openings down at the Federal Reserve?"

He shook his head. "It took me a couple of months, but I finally found my first job working for a life insurance company in Newark. The job had nothing to do with economics, except that I knew I was near the bottom of any economic curve."

"Are you still working in Newark?"

"I managed to escape. For the last few years I've been working for a health insurance company in the city. "

"What's your job?"

"I work in the systems department."

"I thought you were an economist, not a programmer."

"I'm neither. I write the specifications that the programmers use to code."

"Sounds like a hard job."

"It is, but it's also interesting most of the time."

***

The age difference was not a factor to Terri, but her parents had a different point of view.

"He's eight years older than you!" yelled her father. "You're still in school and haven't been out in the world. Why would you want to get involved with an older guy?"

Terri retorted, "I don't care about any age difference. I really like him, and we have a lot in common."

"What can you have in common other than the fact that he's close to the same age as some of your professors?"

"You're five years older than Mom, so what are you complaining about?"

"What are you daydreaming about?" Jim asked

"Oh, nothing much. Just trying to force myself to wake up and go for a run."

The love of running was one of the many things they enjoyed, either running alone or together. It was Terri who had convinced Jim to start running. He had gained a few pounds after the wedding and it seemed the more Terri ran, the more Jim ate. One day Terri placed an insurance policy for $500,000 over his bowl of potato chips and asked for his signature.

"Why do I need all this insurance?"

Terri replied, "Because if you keep on gaining weight, you'll have a heart attack by age forty and if I have to be a widow, I want to be rich."

Jim had a tough time starting, but after running for a few months he was able to beat Terri at any distance. When she questioned why he never ran in high school or college, Jim replied without any hesitation, "Because I was lazy."

"I bet you could have gotten a scholarship."

"But then maybe I wouldn't have met you."

Now sitting on his usual train, Jim thought back to his first New York City marathon. It was October, 1983, and he felt apprehensive the morning of the race. Marathon Sunday was a very warm day. He had attended mass on Saturday night and prayed that he would break three hours. Registration for the marathon took place at Fort McHenry in Staten Island. It was a mob scene with a festive atmosphere. There were over 15,000 runners, and he questioned what he was doing there. His legs felt heavy and achy, and for some strange reason, Jim could not stop yawning. It was a beautiful day to watch a race, but not a good day to run. The sun was strong and it was humid. He had his excuse for not breaking three hours. He had memorized what time he should be at almost every mile to reach his goal. Jim had stretched a bit, but he skipped any warm-up sprints, because he knew he needed every ounce of energy to make it to the finish.

When the time came to line up on the Verrazano Narrows Bridge for the start, runners were grouped in sections based on expected finishing times. One section in front was reserved for the elite runners. Then further divisions were made, starting with a section under two hours and thirty minutes, then two hours and forty-five minutes, and so on. Jim went to the three-hour section. In front of him were a few thousand runners and the beautiful span of the bridge. Behind him were thousands more, packed solid across the bridge back to the toll booths. Jim's mouth was dry, and he felt as if he were carrying a ten-pound weight in each hand.

The train clanked and swayed on the track, while Jim continued to reminisce.

The "Star Spangled Banner" played as he sweated in the heat of the day and from the heat of the runners' bodies pushing against him. The President of the Road Runners Club said a few words. Then the Mayor of New York fired the cannon to start the ordeal. The mass of humanity lurched forward, slowly at first and then a little faster. Jim worried about tripping or bumping into someone. If he fell, the thundering herd would trample him. At that moment, the running of the bulls in Pamplona, Spain, seemed like a walk in the park. Jim hit the first mile in over seven minutes. He was already behind his time, but there was no cause for panic. There were twenty-five miles to make up time, and he felt good. At three miles, the sweat poured out of his pores and the sun felt hot. He grabbed two cups at the water stop, drinking one and pouring the other over his head. He reached the five-mile mark exactly at his projected time. With people cheering and urging the runners on, it was fun running through Brooklyn. Jim began praying by saying the rosary. He cruised by the halfway mark in one hour and twenty-three minutes, which was better than a three hour pace, but he knew the last six miles would be the toughest.

Jim was prepared for the 59th Street Bridge at sixteen miles. It was a steep bridge, but this would be where the hill training and stair climbing paid off. Jim started passing runners as he sped up the span, feeling renewed. He picked up the pace on the downhill into Manhattan. The crowd was cheering, but he paid little attention, because he was so focused on the race. Jim was in a zone, but it was a hot zone. The course up First Avenue was all in the sun, which was starting to take its toll. The water Jim was pouring over his head also dripped down to his socks, which were now soaked. The initial blister appeared at about eighteen miles. As the race spread out, Jim he was still ahead of his pace. He started to say the rosary again. The praying kept his mind off the blister, which had now gone forth and multiplied.

About fifty yards ahead was a runner in a white cap. Jim did his best to catch him before finishing a decade of the rosary, reciting the Hail Mary ten times. The runner was keeping a steady pace. When he passed the white-capped runner on the ninth Hail Mary, Jim was shocked to see his hair was all gray, and he must have been in his mid to late fifties. That really shot Jim's ego down a few notches. When he reached the twentieth mile in two hours and ten minutes, someone from the crowd yelled that the winner just crossed the finish line. In a twenty-six mile race, Jim had lost by six miles. His blisters began to hurt more and the thrill of the race was fading fast. He had fifty minutes to cover 6.2 miles. This was going to take a lot of praying. Jim said every prayer he could think of. He also tried to picture where he would be if there were six miles left on a Sunday morning twenty-mile training run. Jim entered Central Park knowing that even if he had to crawl, he would finish the last three miles. There were some hills in the park, which were pretty tough at this point in the race, but in his mind Jim was not in Central Park but heading home. He passed mile twenty-five and glided by the local library. The only sounds he heard were his heavy breathing and blistered feet touching the pavement. At mile twenty-six, in his mind he was at the high school three blocks from his house. He crossed the finish line and walked in the front door of his house. Jim's time was two hours and fifty-five minutes and nineteen seconds. Back to reality, Jim was a little wobbly as he stopped running and walked through the roped lanes at the finish. Jim could not believe it. He had beaten his goal! He was handed a bottle of Pierre water, which he gulped down without coming up for air. His stomach felt like an erupting volcano, and the blisters were excruciating. He was also awarded a medal and a foil sheet the size of a cape to retain the body heat, even though it was seventy-five degrees outside. Proud and sick at the same time, he wrapped the sheet around his body and held the medal tightly as he threw up in a garbage can. Wide World of Sports could have used that scene as its "The Agony of Defeat" clip aired in the opening of each show.

For the next three years, Jim ran the New York City Marathon. His

One-Way Elevator

times improved each year. In 1984, it was two hours and forty-six minutes and in 1985, it dropped to two hours thirty-five minutes and thirty-nine seconds. He placed 289th out of more than 18,000 runners.

The next year, his goal was to finish in two hours and thirty minutes, but he was overconfident going into the race. Three weeks before the race, he placed 25th out of nearly five thousand runners in a 30-kilometer race in Central Park and finished feeling strong. In order to reach his goal, he had to average five minutes and forty-six seconds a mile. The plan was to go out at five minutes and thirty seconds for as long as possible and then hold on at the end. He felt there would be a big enough cushion to hit his projected time, even if he slowed down a little over the last few miles. The first mile, Jim was stuck in a crowd and could not break free. He was a minute behind schedule. He foolishly attempted to make up the time by running the second mile in five minutes. It was also a windy day, and the first eight miles were into the wind. He was near the front of the race without anyone to block the wind. That five-minute mile took more out of him than he thought. Jim was too structured and did not allow for any adjustments based on the race conditions. Unable to settle into a comfortable pace, Jim was pretty drained at ten miles, when he heard a loud cheer from behind. It was one of the top women runners, surrounded by a group of runners blocking the wind for her. He nearly stopped in his tracks as she passed him by. He felt so stupid; he could have hung back and run with her and used the group to block the wind. He was disgusted and angry with himself. No amount of praying could help. Jim finished in two hours, thirty–six minutes and twenty-nine seconds and that was his last marathon.

**

Jim's semi-sleep state was disrupted, when the PATH train pulled into the World Trade Center station. Jim maneuvered through the crowd that reminded him of the marathon on the Verrazano Bridge. "No wonder I'm always so tired. Everyday is like a marathon with no medal at the finish," he thought.

Jim shifted into work mode after swiping his ID card and pushing the turnstile. Jim badly needed his tea and bagel as a crutch to start his day as a systems analyst in his company's information technology department. His job was to work on different projects to write the requirements programmers followed to code changes, so that claims could be correctly processed through the system. It did not sound like a difficult or a high-pressured job, but it was. Constant deadlines had to be met. On most projects, it took several meetings with the stakeholders to determine the objective and set the scope of the project. The next step required Jim and his team to analyze the system to determine the changes needed. Once the changes were identified, then the technical requirements would be written for the programmers. Deadlines for most projects were set before any analysis had taken place, and if the changes turned out to be significant, that is where the problems would start.

Being late on a project was almost like going before the Spanish Inquisition. The standard first question asked was, who is at fault? The usual scapegoat was Jim's systems analysis team. Either the requirements were incomplete, or all the necessary changes were not identified. It did not matter that the unrealistic implementation date left insufficient time for analysis. Nor did it matter that there were also other projects with unrealistic implementation dates scheduled. Jim's company expected all projects to be implemented on time without any problems.

Jim enjoyed analysis, but he hated working in this type of environment. He hated the finger pointing and posturing that took place. At one time he had thought about finding another job, but realized the work culture was probably the same in most companies. Readily accepting responsibility if he or his team caused a problem, Jim chose honesty over playing the finger-pointing blame game. He also treated all his team members — nine other systems analysts and five programmers - as equals, and he earned the respect of both upper management and his team.

When Jim's company announced that all its programming work was to be outsourced to India but the systems analysts would remain in New York, Jim became distressed. He was relieved that he still had a job, but angry that everything came down to dollars and cents. The transition would officially begin in October when his programmers would become employees of IBM for a short period of time. The U.S. programmers would help to train the programmers from India. To Jim this was the same as digging your own grave.

A videoconference had been scheduled so that the staff in India could meet the U.S. staff. Jim did not want to go to the meeting, but he had no choice. He sat in the back of the large conference room and watched intently as the programmers from Bangalore appeared on the large screen.

The senior vice president of Information Technology opened the meeting by singing the praises of the new collaboration with IBM and its professional staff in Bangalore. Outsourcing was necessary, he said, in order to keep up with the competition and keep health care costs down. He admitted that there would be a learning curve, but in the long run the company would see significant savings.

Jim mused, "Significant savings means the programmers here get screwed and lose their jobs."

After a few additional minutes of corporate brainwashing, each person on each continent had to introduce himself or herself and give a brief background and include current, or in the case of India, future job responsibilities. Jim always hated speaking about himself, but he'd played the game. When it was Bangalore's turn, Jim could not hide his prejudice and thought, *I wonder which one is the terrorist.*

As he listened to each IBM programmer enthusiastically speak, he began to realize that each person was only trying to do a job, just like everyone else. The programmer was not to blame for the situation. After the last programmer spoke, Jim felt ashamed about having any thoughts about terrorists and vowed to treat each new programmer as an equal to any other team member.

***

A few weeks later, Jim took a long run. In addition to the training, he used the time to daydream, plan for the future, or just think about things in general. On this particular run he was feeling nostalgic. He had recently read an article about the effects of Agent Orange on the troops in the Vietnam War and the environmental impact.

Thinking about Vietnam triggered a memory of a particular concert he attended back in the spring of 1973. It was a month before graduation from Rutgers, and his friend, Marty, had an extra ticket to see Neil Young. The ticket became available at the last minute because Marty had a fight with his girlfriend, who was a real bitch. Jim did not care that he was second choice. He wanted to tell Marty he should find someone else, because she was a miserable person who treated him as her own personal servant. Jim decided to withhold his commentary until after the concert. He had no job prospects, and he was number forty-six in the draft lottery to win an all-expenses paid tour of the quaint, picturesque country on the South China Sea called Vietnam. Upon graduation, he would lose his college deferment, and with that low number he would have rice paddies, napalm, and pungi sticks in his future, rather than a boring office job. Instead of fighting to stay awake, he would be fighting to stay alive.

Jim was against the war and thought President Nixon and his Secretary of State, Henry Kissinger, were liars and war criminals. Jim first protested against the war after four students were shot and killed by National Guardsmen at Kent State. He angrily blamed the government for the killings more than the soldiers who actually pulled the triggers, because it was the government that had placed the soldiers in a situation that so easily spiraled out of control. Occurring at the end of his freshman year, the Kent State shootings changed his view of government forever. He initially thought that he could never be the one to pull the trigger, but then wondered what he would do if he felt threatened, or panicked.

The next three years had gone by so fast, and then he made the difficult decision that if drafted, he would serve. He knew that despite all its faults, the United States was still the best country in the world. Burning a draft card and running to Canada would not change anything. The only way to make any change was from within.

Jim and Marty walked around the block from Madison Square Garden and smoked the normal pre- concert appetizer. Jim could not remember most of the songs played, but in his mind Neil Young was great.

Near the end of the concert, Neil made a special announcement that the draft was ending. While Neil was blasting his guitar, Congress had voted to end the draft, but to continue blasting Vietnam. The crowd went wild cheering more loudly than for any song Neil had sung that night, which was no affront to his performance, as the crowd consisted of mainly anti-war white college students, who did not want to go to Vietnam, or to join the National Guard as an alternative. Jim remembered his father, who would become angry whenever Jim argued against the war or said he would not go to fight in Vietnam. Of course, Jim only said that because he knew it would upset his father, a World War II veteran who believed that any war the United States was fighting was a just war.

Jim continued his run and his trip down memory lane. There were certain events that defined a generation. In the summer of 1969, there was Woodstock and the moon landing but Jim's main memory was his summer job in the brass factory. When he punched the time clock on his first day of work, Jim felt as if he had traveled back in time to the Industrial Revolution, as if he had stepped into a Charles Dickens novel. The workers had all missed the brass ring of life and by some unseen celestial force found themselves in a stifling factory with the constant hum of machinery, the yelling of orders and excessively loud music.

Working at the brass factory, Jim learned the importance of an education and the importance of not settling for the easy way out. There were class divisions between the brass polishers and the machinists. The brass polishers sat in front of large grinding wheels and held pieces of brass against the spinning wheel for eight hours a day. All the specks of whatever had dulled the brass went flying all through the air. As a result, each polisher had a persistent cough and walked as if the wheel had also ground him down.

The machinists usually operated the same machine each day. Jim's favorite was the drill press, where holes were punched, one at a time, for eight hours every day of the week, every week of the year. The machinists would eat lunch and take breaks with each other, while the polishers would all lumber along with the weight of the world on their shoulders. In economic terms, the machinists made about twenty cents an hour more than the polishers.

Jim would load trucks, fill orders, pack boxes, take inventory, and do just about anything else that was needed. Although treated well, he could never break into one of the established cliques. He worked with his high school friend, Ed, who was also going to college that fall.

There was one job Jim enjoyed somewhat and found almost relaxing. The factory also made vacuum cleaner equipment for pools. The function of this low-tech job was to glue the rubber edge around the bottom of the suction attachment at the end of the vacuum hose. Jim's little enchanted workspace was in the middle of the factory, where he endured sniffing in glue and brass shavings, while the grinding of the polishing wheels and other machinery slowly fried his brain, polluted his lungs and deteriorated his hearing. He began to understand why some people drank and were nasty to everyone.

Jim told himself, "If I had to work here my whole life, I would just place my head directly under the drill press and end it all."

Jim walked out of the factory the Friday before Labor Day, eager to start school. He vowed never to return. This experience gave Jim a new admiration for hard working people and he always thought back to his summer in the brass factory whenever he was disappointed or frustrated by his job.

A few years later, Jim recalled, there had been a strike at the brass factory. The workers held out for ten weeks and wound up with thirty cents an hour over management's original offer. The pay raise did not even cover the money lost by striking in the first place. Jim thought all the workers must have inhaled an excessive amount of brass dust to strike for so little.

During the strike, in order to meet the contractual obligations for the pool vacuum attachments, the gluing of the rubber edges was transferred to a company that trained the mentally and physically challenged to enter the workforce. They did such a good job that even after the strike was settled, the task was permanently outsourced. This little brass factory was years ahead of the rest of the economy in outsourcing jobs. Jim then understood that anyone could be replaced. He also concluded that most jobs were really not so difficult, if one was properly trained and had the right attitude.

Jim also realized that some employees would steal anything, even the brass swords, ships, plaques and ever popular key to the city. There was one employee, Charlie, whose job it was to clean up the shop and keep the inventory of stock in order. The dumpster, where the garbage was emptied, was in the parking lot behind the factory. Sometimes Jim would see Charlie's car parked next to the dumpster. At first he thought nothing of it. Charlie did not speak English well and he would always say, "Charlie, take out the garbage." One day in the storage aisle, Jim saw Charlie placing some brass swords in a large black plastic garbage bag. He looked up and smiled nervously.

Jim stared at him for a moment, returned his smile and said, "Charlie take out the garbage."

Charlie nodded, turned, and made his way to the dumpster by way of his car.

That summer while Jim was busy gluing rubber and inhaling cancer-causing dust particles, Neil Armstrong landed on the moon where he said his famous line, "One small step for man, one giant leap for mankind."

Quite a contrast to, "Charlie, take out the garbage."

That summer there was also a "little concert" in Woodstock, where a few hundred thousand slopped around in the mud while the bands played on. Many of the attendees were farther out in the solar system than Neil Armstrong.

Jim understood the Earth was only a speck in the universe, and he was just a speck on the earth. Scientists estimate that the earth is over four billion years old and the universe ten billion years older than the earth. When Jim was eighteen years old, he wondered if he would ever go to the moon. He also wondered if he would ever exit the Eastern Time Zone.

Finally, that summer Jim learned not only humility, but also compassion for others. The brass factory was where he first realized that each person was simply trying to get by in life as well as possible. At least the brass factory workers were making something, instead of staring at and manipulating numbers on a computer screen. Each person from the factory went home every night with dirt under his fingernails, dust in his lungs, and a weariness from a hard day's work, whereas the workers who sat in front of a computer screen went home with tired eyes and a sense of weariness, with nothing tangible, nothing created that could be held, instead of spiraling with all the other clutter in cyber space.

As Jim finished his run, which ended up a lot longer than originally planned, he wondered, why have all those memories surfaced?

***

It was the last week in August and it was time for a vacation. This year Jim and Terri chose St. Martin. It was a time-share exchange. Terri wanted to try some place new for a change. She loved Hilton Head, but there were so many other places she had never been. If Jim had his way, they would go back to the same place every year, so she was pleasantly shocked when he agreed.

Terri opened Jim's passport and there was no smile on the face looking back at her. Jim's biggest concern was his stomach. He was worried about the drinking water and that he would spend most of his vacation looking out the bathroom window.

In a reassuring voice, Terri proclaimed, "The water at the resort is clean. You can drink bottled water everywhere you go. I'll pack some Imodium, if it makes you feel better."

"You better pack a lot just in case."

"We're gonna have a great time. There are beautiful beaches and there are casinos."

Jim smirked. "Do they have slots in the bathrooms?"

Keith was not thrilled about going either. He was starting high school, and he was at the age where he wanted nothing to do with his parents. If they were going to Hilton Head, he could have brought a friend, but with a flight out of the country, that option was nullified.

About an inch shorter than his father, Keith was on track to be able to look down at him within the next year or two. He had his father's deep-set eyes and smile. Jim wanted him to run track, but Keith thought it was boring. Keith loved basketball, and he was looking forward to playing on the high school team. He had longish blond hair, blue eyes and an angular face. With a complexion almost as white as the sand, he needed a sunscreen with SPF of about one thousand. He was thin without an ounce of fat, despite his big appetite and love of chocolate. Jim would do anything for his son, but he knew he had to let him live his own life and make his own decisions. Raising his own son, he now realized all the sacrifices his parents had made for him.

At Newark International Airport, Jim, Terri and Keith checked their bags, displayed the passports to the security agent and waited in the boarding area. This was the first time Jim and Keith were leaving the country. Terri had been to Paris with her parents when she was younger.

Saint Martin was divided into two sections, one French, the other Dutch. The hotel was on the French side and from the map did not look far away from the airport. During the long flight Jim mostly nodded off to sleep while Terri read and Keith listened to his Walkman. Jim awoke when the captain said to fasten all seatbelts and they would be landing in fifteen minutes. Jim looked out the window and marveled at the random white cumulus clouds alongside the plane and the deep blue water below. After a few minutes the plane slowed down and its wings dipped to make the landing approach.

As the plane descended lower and lower, Jim could see the foam from the waves lick the beach. The plane continued its descent and now Jim could clearly see the faces of the tourists standing in the water looking up at the plane. It almost looked as if the plane would land directly on top of them. The thrust from the engines stirred the water more than any waves and the people turned and retreated closer to shore.

Jim tapped Terri on her shoulder and said, "Take a look at how close we are to the swimmers."

Terri gasped and said, "It looks like the plane will blow them out of the water."

Jim continued, "I wouldn't want to stay at that hotel. I'd have a fit."

Terri agreed and replied, "I bet they don't advertise that in the travel brochure."

After landing, they endured the last humiliation of flying, which was lunging for luggage between two people before it rotated on the carousel out of reach. The car rental pickup was not at the airport. There was a shuttle bus to take them to their luxury car, so they had to maneuver the luggage onto the decrepit, sweltering bus and endure the ten- minute ride. Jim had reserved a compact car, but at first glance, it resembled a clown car from the circus.

"Luckily we don't know anybody here." Keith complained, "I wouldn't be caught dead in that car back home."

Jim glanced at Terri and they both cracked up laughing.

"I don't think that car could even be sold back home," Terri quipped.

The luggage could not entirely fit in the trunk, so Keith had to share the backseat curled up next to two suitcases. When Jim pulled out of the rental lot, he pressed hard on the accelerator, but the car barely responded. He followed the directions to the hotel and barely made it up the ramp to the front entrance, where they unloaded the luggage. Jim then parked the car in an underground lot anxious to check in. When they went to the registration desk, the suite was not ready, but the Concierge gave them tickets for drinks at the outdoor bar and said it should be available in less than an hour.

The hotel lobby was large, spacious and nicely decorated. When they walked out the back exit, Jim was thrilled. There was a large pool with lounge chairs and the beach was only yards away. The ocean displayed its clear multi-shades of blue water.

The outdoor restaurant and bar was to the left of the pool. A large bamboo roof covered the bar, with nearly a dozen tables overlooking the beach. They sat down, and Jim ordered a beer, Terri a pina colada, and Keith an iced tea. When the waiter returned with the drinks, Jim took a long sip and thought to himself, *Life is good.*

He looked at his beautiful wife and son in this tropical paradise and felt totally relaxed. He closed his eyes for a moment to relish the moment, but the sound of an approaching jumbo jet shattered the bliss. He looked up and could read the numbers on the plane's underbelly. He watched as the bathers in the water headed for the beach to get out of the choppy surf caused by the roaring engines.

Jim jumped up and yelled, "This is the beach I saw from the plane. How could we be so stupid?"

The plane appeared to be heading straight into the hotel, but then it veered to the right for the landing on the runway, which to Jim's horror was no more than fifty yards behind him.

"Calm down, Jim. It's just a plane. It's gone now."

"I didn't realize when we took the shuttle that we were going in the opposite direction. We must have almost travelled around in a circle to the front of the hotel."

Keith thought it was cool. "I can't wait to take a picture of the plane coming in over the water."

The concierge came out to announce that the suite was ready. When they went up to the sixth floor, Jim wondered what other surprises were in store. Terri inserted the card into the lock and cautiously entered. They walked down a short hallway into a large living room with a beige couch and two light brown wing chairs. On the opposite wall was a large screen television. The floors were white ceramic tile with a beige floral design. Sliding glass doors opened to a large balcony, with a small table and four chairs on one side and a lounge chair that looked inviting in the opposite corner. The view of the beach and ocean was unobstructed and Jim felt his sense of calm and serenity slowly return.

Inside were two bedrooms. The smaller bedroom had two beds with light blue bedspreads. A deeper shade of blue covered the walls. A ceiling fan was centered between the two beds. A large bathroom was connected with light blue floor tiles and more pale blue tiles halfway up the walls, whose other half was painted an off white. Matching the tiles were the light blue sink and tub with its frosted sliding doors. A modern kitchen large enough to fit a table for six in one corner was separated from the living room by a counter with two stools on each side. Down the hall from the kitchen was the master bedroom, divided into two sections. Upon entering, Jim encountered a sitting area with a small couch and a wing chair with a light floral pattern. A television was on the opposite wall. To reach the second section, one had to step up to another level, which contained a king-sized bed, a dresser with a mirror and another chest of drawers. A large window to the left overlooked the ocean. The master bathroom contained a double vanity granite sink, shower and a Jacuzzi.

Any thoughts Jim had about the poverty on the rest of the island were erased for the moment. Everyone quickly unpacked and changed to go down to the pool, which was shaped like an enormous kidney. It started off at three feet but went to six feet before a rope separated the diving area. There was both a low and a high dive. Reggae music flowed from the speakers, and once Jim had completed a few quick laps around the pool, a lounge chair, book and a beer beckoned.

After a few pages, Jim was about to nod off when his small piece of paradise was invaded by several adults of various ages and at least six screeching children, all under the age of ten. Jim groaned as each of the children screamed and jumped into the pool. Suddenly, the low flying plane did not seem that bad. The plane was gone in a minute, but he knew this latest incursion would last much longer. Keith and Terri were in the pool, but they retreated to the relative safety of the lounge chairs as if the water were suddenly overrun with piranhas.

Terri gave Jim a wary look, but he attempted to maintain his composure.

Calmly picking up his beer, Jim said wryly, "I guess tomorrow there will be a category five hurricane approaching."

Terri sighed. "Despite everything, you have to admit this is one gorgeous place."

"I know. If you just get rid of the planes and most of the people, it really would be paradise."

They looked over at Keith, sleeping with his headphones on, oblivious to the chaos in the water. After a few minutes and several repeated screams for the screeching children to come out of the pool, the water was once again safe for adults. Jim and Terri decided to go in again and take advantage of the momentary lull in the action.

"I'm glad we decided to try something new for a change," Terri mused as she bobbed on one of the pink noodles available to the guests.

"Me too. I can't wait to do some sightseeing tomorrow."

Terri continued bobbing. "I just hope that clown car can make it

One-Way Elevator

up the hills. I read in the tour guide that there are some pretty steep mountain roads."

"I think my lawnmower has a bigger engine."

Jim could sense someone watching and maybe eavesdropping on the conversation. A moment later a man in his forties with black hair and the same height as Jim began a conversation. "I hope the kids didn't annoy you too much?"

Jim looked at Terri and then replied, "No. Not at all. They're just having fun."

The man extended his hand. "I'm Tony Alphonse."

Jim shook his hand. "Jim Winters."

Tony asked, "Where are you from?"

"I'm from New Jersey. How about you?" Jim knew the answer, but he made polite conversation.

"Me, I'm from Staten Island now, but I grew up in Brooklyn."

Jim introduced Terri, and she commented, "This place is beautiful."

Tony dipped his head into the water and then replied enthusiastically, "This is my favorite place. Every year my family and my brother's family come down for two weeks. We own two timeshares so there's plenty of room."

Terri said, "This is our first time here. We usually go to Hilton Head, but this is a nice change."

"The weather is usually good, except for the hurricane a few years ago that hit the island pretty bad. The beach used to be much wider, but the hotel wasn't damaged like some of the others."

One of the kids did a cannon ball into the water and splashed everyone. "Gino," Tony yelled, embarrassed, "if you do that one more time, you're out of the pool for a week." Jim could see that Tony did not take anything from anybody. Tony calmed himself down. "So, Jim, where do you work?"

"I work in the city for a health insurance company in the World Trade Center."

Tony laughed and said, "What a coincidence. I work in the Trade

Center too. I'm with Cantor Fitzgerald. I'm a bond trader. For about fifteen years."

"I work in IT. So you were there for the bombing in 1993?"

"Yeah. The building held up good. It was tough walking down from the 93rd floor."

"I bet it was. We've only been there two years. I guess they lowered the rent after the bombing."

Tony laughed. "I guess so, but it seems like ancient history now. I'm not worried about anything."

Jim said, "When I looked up before and saw that plane coming in, it scared the hell out of me."

"Don't worry about that. You get used to it."

"One wrong turn and the plane could go right into the hotel."

Tony laughed. "I bet you didn't realize, when the brochure said close to the airport, it was really true."

"No, it was quite a surprise. Can't get them for false advertising on that one."

A short, slender woman with black hair and olive skin yelled from the other side of the pool, "Hey, Tony, you watch the kids. I want to relax." From the Brooklyn accent Jim knew it was his wife.

With a look of defeat in his eyes, Tony said, "I guess that's my order to leave. It was nice meeting you. I'm sure we'll see each other during the week."

"Nice meeting you too."

With shoulders slumped, the high-powered bond trader, slowly walked back to his brood.

Jim swam a lap of the pool and then announced to Terri, "I'm due for a nap."

Terri laughingly remarked, "I thought you were a marathon runner and now one lap knocks you out."

Jim splashed her and said, "I can still beat you." He quickly exited the water and ran for the safety of his lounge chair.

Terri came out of the water as if angry and exaggerated her stride. "I'm going to get back at you for that," she teased. "When you least expect it, I'll get my revenge."

One-Way Elevator

Jim laughed and tried to appear serious. "You may think I'm not expecting anything, but it will only be a trick to lull you into thinking you have the upper hand."

Terri sat on his lap and said seductively, "After all these years of marriage, you think you can still fool me? I know what you like."

Putting his arms around her, Jim nodded. "I can't argue with that one."

"Will you two stop it? It's embarrassing." Keith pulled the earplugs out and shook his head in disgust. He stood up. "I'm going up to the beach, where nobody knows who my parents are."

"Just be careful," Terri cautioned, "and don't go out far."

"See ya later." Keith walked away feeling awkward and wishing he had a friend to hang out with.

The vacation flew by. They drove all over the island and visited several beaches. The weather was perfect. The only regret was that Jim never ran into Tony again.

In the late afternoon on their last day, Jim was sitting on a lounge chair on the beach with a book and a bottle of Amstel Light. The beach was nearly empty, and Jim enjoyed the solitude. He was waiting to take a picture of the giant Air France plane that arrived like a hurricane every afternoon around this time. It was another perfect day with a bright blue sky and a light breeze. Two young girls spread out a blanket about fifteen feet away. Jim looked up for a moment but then went back to reading his book. A few minutes later he searched the sky for the plane, but when he looked down, the girls were both topless. They were sitting sideways and Jim felt like a lecherous old man staring at them. It appeared as if they knew but seemed not to mind. Both girls were around twenty years old, and each was very attractive. The blond had long legs, but Jim was concentrating on another part of her anatomy. Jim was not concerned about her height, but her body was perfect. The brunette was shorter, but what she lacked in height she made up with her shapely body. The blonde reached into her bag, removed a tube of sunscreen, opened it, and began applying it to the back of the brunette. Once the back was covered she lay down on her back and the blonde squirted the white cream from the tube over her stomach and each breast slowly rubbing it in. Jim was transfixed by the sultry scene, as if he were watching a porno movie. Jim had to pinch himself to make sure he was not dreaming, but all of a sudden a slap on the side of his head brought him back to his senses.

In an annoyed voice, steaming with sarcasm, Terri raved, "You're a dirty old man!"

Jim was startled but quickly regained his composure. He smiled and his face was red, but not from the sun. "I'm just relaxing, enjoying the beautiful scenery, the blue sky, the water..." he remarked.

Terri interrupted in an angry derogatory tone, "Who are you trying to kid. Your eyes were glued to the little private show right in front of you. Should I get you some dollar bills?"

The look Terri gave, made Jim feel like a level 1 sex offender, who had to stay away from schools, or Girl Scout troops.

The sound of the Air France jumbo jet drowned out further conversation, which was perfect timing. Jim grabbed his camera and took several pictures of the jumbo jet against a deep blue sky. The water rippled and the sand flew as the plane made its descent. Jim was able to snap one picture of the two girls as they stood looking up at the plane. He had to make sure he picked up the pictures after they were developed; otherwise he would be in trouble again. It was late afternoon, and now that he had his picture of the plane, all he wanted to do was to slink away and go take a shower. "I'm going back to the room now," Jim said meekly.

"Go ahead. I'm gonna walk over to the bar and have a drink with that cute young bartender."

Jim did not want to argue on the last day, so he replied, "I guess I deserved that. If I didn't look, there would be something wrong with me."

Terri laughed and relented. "There definitely is something wrong with you, but I still love you."

"I love you too and if that bartender tries anything with you, I'll kick his ass."

"Thanks for caring, but you wouldn't stand a chance against him."

Jim knew she was right. As he turned to walk away he said, "Who am I kidding? I'm too old to fight anybody now."

***

One-Way Elevator

The last night they went to the casino before dinner. About a block from the hotel, the casino was located next door to C C's, an outdoor restaurant with local entertainment. Since one had to be eighteen to enter, Terri stayed with Keith and they walked around outside, while Jim went in alone.

Jim was not much of a gambler, but he stood in front of the roulette table for a few minutes and then decided to play. He took one hundred dollars in chips as his limit. Five minutes later he was out of chips. Jim was disappointed with himself, but he could understand how people could easily get into trouble.

He walked down one of the many rows of slot machines and on the spur of the moment deposited four quarters into one of the brightly lit money holes. The numbers and symbols rolled around and three sevens magically appeared. The bells went off and the quarters started falling into the tray below like manna from heaven. A small group circled, stared, and listened to the coins hit the metal, each one wishing he had selected that machine instead of the one sucking in all the money.

When the music stopped and the coins were tallied, Jim found himself with five hundred and twenty-five dollars. That was the most money he had ever won, except for the time he had picked five out of six numbers in Lotto and won seven hundred and forty-two dollars. He'd played the month and day of his, Terri's and Keith's birthdays. For a moment, he was mad at Terri, because had she been born two days later, he would have won four million dollars.

Jim cashed in his coins and walked out with five one hundred dollar bills, one twenty and a five. Looking dejected, he slowly walked up to Terri and Keith.

Keith asked, "How much did you blow, Dad?"

Jim kept quiet knowing Terri would be next.

"Do we have enough left to eat something before we go home?"

Jim kept his head down, but reached into his pocket and, with a flash and a grin, whipped out the packet of money.

"We're rich," Keith shouted.

"I don't believe it!" Terri exclaimed.

"How much is it, Dad?"

"It's five hundred and twenty-five dollars. So tonight you can even have dessert."

Terri gave Jim a hug. "You're a high roller now."

Jim shrugged. "It was pure luck. I had lost a hundred at the roulette table, and I was walking down the aisle to leave when I decided to play the slots one time."

Jim floated on air into the warm clear night and wished he could stay another week. When they arrived at C C's almost every table was taken. Reggae music erupted from the speakers, and several waiters were scurrying around with trays of drinks and food. The tables formed a semicircle in front of a large wooden stage that was one step above the ground. A long bar to the right of the stage partially obstructed the perfect ocean view. A large hurricane lamp in the middle of each table provided ample light, but the din of the party atmosphere blotted out the sounds of the ocean. Jim never drank mixed drinks, but when Terri ordered a pina colada, Jim ordered one too. They ordered a non-alcoholic one for Keith. Jim was definitely in relaxation mode as Bob Marley wailed, "Jamming" in the background. Jim slurped down his drink before the waitress came back for their order: Fried calamari and mushrooms stuffed with crabmeat for appetizers and another round of drinks. For the main course Jim had surf and turf and Keith and Terri had fillet of flounder.

When the drinks were served, Terri said, "Let's make a toast."

Jim and Keith gave each other a wary look but went along. Terri continued, "Raise your glasses and let's toast to a great vacation on a beautiful island."

Everyone took a sip and then remarkably Keith announced, "I had a great time. Maybe we can come back one of these years."

Jim was surprised, because Keith had been pretty quiet all week.

Terri spoke up. "I would like to come back here too."

Jim replied, "If we do return, I'm not waiting until the last night to go to the casino."

Terri commented, "Maybe you can meet your buddy Tony again?"

Jim swallowed some calamari. "Maybe I'll run into him at the World Trade Center. He was a nice guy, even though his family was a bit loud."

The dinner was excellent. Jim did not want this perfect night to end. The band came on during dessert. There were two singers, a lead and a base guitarist, a saxophone player, and a drummer with regular drums and a set of steel drums. Dessert was a slice of chocolate cheesecake for everyone and another round of drinks. Keith had a sugar high and Jim and Terri were lost in an alcohol-induced zone of impairment.

The male lead singer, tall, in his early twenties with dreadlocks, and a muscular build, wore a leather vest with no shirt, which displayed his well-formed biceps, chest, and rock hard stomach.

The woman was stunning with light brown skin, short hair, and an athletic figure. Her eyes were wide, and her lips were full. She wore a low-cut blue floral dress. Her voice was clear, crisp and intoxicating.

After the fourth song, the female lead singer said, "I need some volunteers to help with the next song. I'm going to walk around and pick a few people from our wonderful crowd."

She walked around the tables with her microphone and selected several, including a woman in her thirties and a college kid. Jim did not want to be chosen. He was usually nervous in front of a crowd. The singer walked near Jim's table and grabbed Jim's hand, but Jim shook his head no.

Turning, she said to the crowd, "He doesn't want to go with me. Don't you think he should go up on the stage?"

Everyone started yelling for Jim to go on stage.

Keith yelled, "Come on, Dad, go up."

Terri told the singer, "Take him. He's all yours."

Jim stood up and the crowd cheered as he was led to the front of the stage.

"Go, Dad!" Keith screamed.

Terri could not remember Jim ever getting up in front of a crowd to sing. There were six volunteers in total, three women and three men. The lead singer asked where each was from. The answers ranged from Maine to Texas with one woman from Paris. When Jim answered, "New Jersey", a few fellow New Jerseyans started cheering and clapping.

The lead singer asked Jim, "Are all people from New Jersey like that."

Jim responded, "Just about."

The audience laughed, and Keith was totally amused by his father.

The group was divided into two - male and female. The volunteers were given instructions and then the music began. The song was a duet about a troubled relationship. When it was time for the chorus, the women sang, "I thought I knew you, but I was wrong."

The male section sang, "I'm going back on the street where I belong."

It was a cute number and by the last verse the couple had made up. The last verse started with, "Come back here where you belong, without you I'm lost, with you I'm strong."

The volunteers sang the last chorus.

"When you're in Saint Martin you have no worries,
When you're in Saint Martin nobody hurries,
When you're in Saint Martin you never say never,
When you're in Saint Martin you want to stay forever."

The volunteers then paired together and to the delight of the crowd began to dance. Jim was swaying with a heavyset older woman from Texas, with platinum blonde hair and a low-cut dress that displayed way too much bouncing cleavage. She was dancing a little too close for Jim's comfort. His face flushed, Jim saw Terri standing with the camera, snapping pictures to hold over his head as blackmail for the rest of his life. When the music stopped, the crowd cheered and each volunteer was forced to take a bow. As compensation for the embarrassment, each one was given a token for a free drink.

When Jim returned to the table, Keith exclaimed, "Dad, you were awesome."

Terri chided, "Did she give you her number?"

With a look of euphoria mixed with embarrassment, Jim laughed and said, "I'm lucky I'm going home tomorrow."

Terri could not help herself. "I can't wait to get home to have these pictures developed."

Jim went along with the kidding. "Fifty years of carefully keeping a

One-Way Elevator

clean image, all ruined on the last day of vacation."

Jim gave his token to a young couple seated at the next table. He knew that one more drink could ruin the rest of the evening and he wanted to clearly recall every moment.

When the plane took off the next morning, Jim regretted leaving. He loved the island and the special time he had shared with his wife and son, but for some reason he could not erase from his mind a picture of the jet crashing into the hotel and crumbling to the ground.

Chapter 2

Nancy Anderson stopped in a drug store a few blocks away from the World Trade Center on her lunch hour. She did not know if she was more nervous than excited as she walked down the aisle to the birth control section and selected one of the boxes containing a pregnancy test.

She was frustrated and said to herself, "If you're picking up one of these, whatever you were using probably did not work." She picked up another brand, compared the two, and continued her internal conversation. "What the hell. I'll take one as a backup to be sure."

Nancy was a well-organized and meticulous planner in every aspect of her life. How could she let this happen? This was no time to have a baby.

She paid for the pregnancy tests and walked into the crowded, sweltering streets, fearful of the most important test she would take in her life.

"How many times have I seen this same scene played out on television shows or the movies? I always thought the characters were acting so stupid, and now here I am playing the stupid part. The only difference is that this is reality. If I am pregnant, what will Phil say? For someone who tries to plan and control every aspect of my life, I've really screwed up this time. I guess screwed is the right word to use. Would it really be such a bad thing? Who am I kidding? We're not married and then how could I ever go to law school?"

She looked down at her flat stomach and could not imagine carrying another life.

"I never had an ounce of fat on me and now I'm going to blow up like the Pillsbury Doughboy."

A blaring horn from a yellow cab brought her back to reality. She had crossed against the light and walked directly into traffic. She jumped back to the relative safety of the sidewalk and had to work hard to control her shaking. "How am I supposed to take care of a baby, when I can't even cross the street?"

When the light changed, she carefully maneuvered over the asphalt and a few minutes later slowly pushed the revolving door of 1 World Trade Center, which was the North Tower. She swiped her identification badge at the turnstile and walked to the elevator bank deep in reflective thought.

"It would be easy to blame everything on Phil, but is he really the root cause? All my planning seemed to go out the window when we met. It was at a Bruce Springsteen Concert. I was tailgating with my girlfriends before the concert and Phil was with his friends in the next car. I was the designated driver, so when this half drunk guy questioned why I wasn't drinking, I should have ignored him. He wasn't obnoxious, or a sloppy drunk and he made me laugh. I wonder if he'll be laughing, if I'm pregnant. When the concert was over, he was leaning on my car door. Before I could say anything, he asked me out. When I hesitated, he began to sing a verse from *Born To Run*.

"In an off key bad Karaoke voice he sang, mixing up the words, 'The Highway's filled with broken heroes on a last chance power drive. We got to get out while we're young. Cause tramps like us, baby we were born to run.'

"I laughed and replied, 'I'm no tramp.'

"He took my hand and began to apologize, saying he never meant to call me a tramp. I was tempted to drive away, but for some reason I gave him my number. That was the best concert I ever went to. At least my baby wasn't conceived in a parking lot after a Springsteen concert."

Nancy had only begun her career in the Human Resources Department in June. She graduated from Rutgers University in Newark with a degree in history, but could not afford to go to Law school, so the plan was to work for a year or two, save up some money and then start her law career. She had been accepted to Columbia University and was so depressed when she had to decline. She already had some loans and could not take on any additional debt.

Nancy had light brown hair and a fair complexion. She was five feet eight inches tall and weighed no more than one hundred and ten pounds. She was one of the few, who could go without using makeup and still appear glamorous. Her brown eyes were wide and her cheekbones were high. Her smile was warm and full, but just a bit too wide in proportion to her face. Although she was thin, she had a seductive figure and an air of sexuality, when she walked. None of the boys in high school ever bothered her, because it was well known and documented that her brother Ronnie was her protector. The word was that if one wanted to live to graduate high school, he did not mess around with Nancy.

Nancy grew up in Hoboken, New Jersey. Ronnie, her only brother, was three years older and a world apart. He was only five feet eight, but weighed almost two hundred and twenty pounds. He had thick, dark black hair and a dark complexion. His eyes were set deep under his thick brow. His constant five o'clock shadow made him appear older than his twenty-five years. He was the spitting image of his father, and a constant reminder to his mother of her ex-husband, Frank, who left her for another woman when she was pregnant with Nancy. Before Nancy was born, she changed her married name of Nataliano back to Anderson.

Whenever anyone would say to his mother that he was the spitting image of his father, she would say, "Yes, I want to spit every time I hear that son of a bitch's name."

When Ronnie was in high school he played middle linebacker on the football team. He was surprisingly fast and nimble on his feet despite his tank like build. He never went to college, but after high school a friend's father was able to find him a job in the local construction union. He became a pipe fitter and made a decent salary. The only problem was that the work was not always steady. To supplement his income, he worked as a bouncer in a local club. He never had any real trouble, and it was a convenient way to meet some women. He did meet quite a few, but they were not the type to bring home to Mom and settle down with. Ronnie was content to be single for the moment, but he did plan to marry and raise a family. He vowed to be a good father to make up for what his father had done to his family.

Mrs. Jane Anderson worked as an English teacher in Hoboken High

One-Way Elevator

School. She loved teaching, but the salary did not go very far after paying the rent and feeding two children. She still lived in the same three-bedroom apartment where Frank had carried her over the threshold on their wedding night. Jane never remarried, because she felt like a failure after being left for another woman. She never wanted to be dependent on anyone again. She was very attractive and had several relationships, but never allowed any to become serious.

Nancy learned at an early age how to help her mother with all the household duties. Nancy and her girlfriend, Janice, would lug the laundry bag around the corner to the local laundromat. They would sit and listen to music with the rumble of the washing machines and humming of the dryers in the background. They would talk about the future and how each would go to college and marry a great guy and live in a big house in the suburbs.

Nancy also became a competent cook. She started by helping her mother in the kitchen, but soon she was able to prepare a meal all by herself. It was nothing fancy, but Ronnie always liked it better when Nancy cooked. Nancy did not take it as a compliment, because she knew that Ronnie did not have a very discerning palate. All one had to do was fill the plate in front of him, and it was gone.

Nancy always wanted to meet her father. She knew nothing about him, and her mother never allowed any conversation with his name. She loved her mother, but she felt that there was a piece missing without her father. She wanted to know him as a person and she also wanted to understand why he left. She never understood why there was no contact, and she was curious to find out what he was doing with his life. Did he remarry? Did he have any other children? If he did, was he now a good father? She never wanted to think about it, but she also wondered if her mother did anything to drive him away. Was it entirely his fault, or was the blame shared between them? She tried to imagine what she would say to her father if they ever met. How would she act? Should she be angry because he left? Should she be happy to finally meet him? Could they ever have any type of relationship? What if she found him and then he told her to go away? In her fantasy, he would see her and immediately feel guilty about leaving and promise to make it up to her.

Then she realized that there was nothing he could do to make up for the lost time. There was nothing to compensate for all the birthdays and special events missed, when he was living his other life. She wondered if he ever thought about her and Ronnie. She did not even know what he looked like now. Her mother had ripped up every picture, but one day Nancy did see a wedding photo that was in an old shoebox in her mother's closet. There was no mistake that Ronnie was his son.

Nancy also helped her mother with the food shopping. They sat together at the kitchen table and clipped coupons. Nancy did not need a home economics class in high school. She could have taught the class. Nancy loved to tally how much they saved after the groceries were put away and all that remained was the register receipt. Nancy dreamed of the day, when she would not have to cut coupons, or go to the laundromat, or spend the hot summers in Hoboken, instead of going on vacation like many of her friends.

When it was time for college, Nancy was accepted to Columbia University and the three other schools she had applied to. At that time, she was interested in journalism, because as a journalist she could travel to many places she had only dreamed of. Her dreams were shattered, because she could not afford the tuition. She reluctantly settled for Rutgers University, where she could commute to from home.

Nancy's second love besides journalism was history, especially United States history. She always fantasized about how she would have acted if she were living during whatever period was being studied. In the American Revolution, would she have been a Whig or a Tory. Would she have been for or against slavery? Would she have supported the North or the South? Would she have protested for the right for women to vote? If she were in college at the time of the Vietnam War, would she have boycotted classes and protested in the street?

The answer to the last question was definitely, "Yes."

She ardently admired the message of Doctor Martin Luther King. She had seen clips of several of his speeches and some of the protests, but it was not until she began to read the full transcripts of the speeches that she understood and fully appreciated his courage.

One-Way Elevator

Would it be any different today if he had not been gunned down in April, 1968? How different would the country be if Robert Kennedy had not suffered the same fate that same year? These were questions she could only speculate on. Those were events that changed the course of the country.

How different would her life have been if her father had not left? Once again, any answer was as elusive as attempting to understand infinity.

In order to pay her college tuition, she worked as a cashier in the same supermarket she shopped in with her mother. She worked almost forty hours a week for minimum wage and was grateful to have the job. The manager of the store was a short, balding man in his late forties. He had a small nose and a small potbelly supported by scrawny legs. He had bags under his eyes and a short beard. Everything about the man was short and undersized, and Nancy speculated that it probably included his penis.

Nancy should have known something was not right, when he first interviewed her for the job. She knew some of the questions were inappropriate for an interview, but she really needed the job, so she was afraid not to answer, or to question his questions. Her impression of Mr. Brandon was that he was a leering man with an inferiority complex who probably could not live within a mile of a school, playground, or anywhere else with kids. He was stuck in his position and had to interview college students, who only needed the job for a short time, and after graduation would probably start at a salary higher than he was making.

After he had finished with the typical questions about job experience, what school she was attending, and what her major was, the questions became too personal for any normal interview.

He grinned like a fighter who had his opponent on the ropes, when he asked, "Do you live with your parents?"

Nancy did not expect that question, but obediently answered, "I live with my mom and my older brother."

"Where's your father?"

She should have walked out at that point, but she needed the job. "My parents are divorced."

"That's too bad. Do you have a boyfriend?"

Nancy finally had the courage to speak up. "I think these questions shouldn't be asked at a job interview."

Mr. Brandon acted as if he was insulted. "I only want to know a little bit about the background of anyone I hire. You'll be spending a lot of time here and I want to know if there's anything that will affect your work."

"He's a lying pig," Nancy thought. She let her displeasure show in her reply. "I'm only going to be at the register, and that's all you have to know."

He stood up. "I'm glad to see you have a backbone and won't take anything from anyone. That's important in your job, because some of the customers can be pretty rude." Nancy knew that was just a cover, but she acted as if she believed him. He then asked, "Do you have any questions?"

She shook her head, feeling that she had not gotten the position.

He walked over to a closet and pulled out a red vest. Mr. Brandon turned around and with an impish smile said, "Well, welcome to Shop Smart. You have the job."

Nancy stood up and in a voice filled with excitement replied, "Thank you, Mr. Brandon. You won't be disappointed that you hired me. I'll work hard."

Mr. Brandon then walked over to her and said, "Let's see if the vest fits."

Instead of handing the vest to Nancy, he held the vest in front of him, so that Nancy had to stand with her back to him and slip her arms through the openings. As she slowly maneuvered her arms, she could feel his hot, stale breath on the back of her neck. He adjusted the vest on her shoulders and applied a little too much pressure with his fingers.

She quickly pulled away, turned around and said, "I think it fits fine." She tried to maintain her composure, but she knew her face was flushed.

Mr. Brandon had no reaction and said, "Come in on Saturday at 9:00, and you can work with one of the experienced cashiers, and then you're on your own."

In a curt voice, Nancy sternly said, "Fine."

One-Way Elevator

His only response was, "9:00 sharp."

Nancy walked out of the small office and through the store, feeling as if she had just been violated.

"Am I any different from a prostitute? I let him close to me because I needed the money." In her eyes there was no difference. From that point she vowed never to let any man take advantage of her.

It was a big adjustment from high school to college. She had breezed through Hoboken High, and now it was a challenge to be expected to work at a different level. She loved her classes, but with the job her free time was almost non-existent. Mr. Brandon never bothered her again and treated her with respect. Maybe he did some checking and found out Ronnie would kill him if he tried anything.

***

In the summer before her senior year, she met Phil. She had other boyfriends, but nothing serious. When she met Phil, after a few dates she knew he was the one. He was six-feet two inches tall, lean and muscular. He treated her like a princess and she loved everything about him, except his job. Phil was a New York City fireman, one of the city's bravest. Nancy did not need him to be brave. She wanted him to be safe and be with her. He had brown wavy hair, brown eyes and a light complexion. His face was thin, and his cheekbones protruded a bit when he smiled. His nose was straight and his jaw more square than round. He kept in shape by going to the gym and running a few miles at least four days a week, depending on his work schedule.

They moved in together, the week after she graduated Summa Cum Laude. Phil's apartment was in Brooklyn not far from the Brooklyn Bridge. It was on the fourth floor in an old but well maintained building. The only drawback was that there were no elevators, but Phil liked to use the steps to keep his legs strong. There were two large bedrooms, a twelve by fourteen foot living room and a kitchen large enough for a small table and chairs. The dark oak hardwood floors in the bedrooms and living room were recently refinished. Light beige tile covered the kitchen floor. The cabinets were light oak, and the appliances were all new stainless steel. There was an added bonus of a dishwasher and a former pantry now proudly displayed a side-by-side washer dryer. Phil loved to cook and he had all the necessary equipment that he could afford from Macy's. There was ample counter space to display his mixer, food processor, and blender. The kitchen table and chairs, toaster, and coffeemaker were also from his favorite store. It was not the typical apartment of a single guy, but Phil was planning for the future.

The living room contained a dark brown couch, a mahogany coffee table, and a light brown recliner. A 32-inch television was in the corner. True to his profession, there were smoke alarms in every room and one in the hallway over the front door. He would usually set off the alarm at least once a week with his cooking. He did not mind, because he had too often seen the results of ignoring fire safety.

Although they had been going out for some time, Nancy had never spent the night at Phil's. She always went home to her mother, because that is what her mother said was the right thing to do. Mrs. Anderson liked Phil, but she was over protective. She knew Phil was a good man and nothing like her ex-husband, but she could not help herself from lumping all men into that one category.

It was almost two weeks before graduation and Nancy was at the apartment. It was late and Phil had to be in work early the next morning. He was annoyed that he had to take her back to Hoboken.

While driving back and stuck at a red light just before the entrance to the Holland Tunnel, Phil turned to Nancy and said, "Why don't you move in with me?"

Nancy was caught off guard and did not know how to respond. The light turned green and she tried deflection as a response. "Why are you asking me now? Is it just because you don't want to drive me home anymore?"

Phil did not smile and in a serious voice said, "I do hate driving you home, but I've been thinking about this for awhile, and now I think it's a good time to do it."

Nancy knew that he was really serious and she felt her mouth go dry and her stomach churn. "This is all kind of sudden for me."

"You're at my apartment most of the time anyway, so why not make it permanent?" Phil kept his eyes on the road, hoping for a positive answer. He had not planned to ask her in the car, but the words just came out.

"What would my mother think?" Nancy finally asked.

"I'm not concerned about your mother. I want to know how you feel about it."

Nancy smiled. "I'd love too."

When they came out of the Holland tunnel on the Jersey side, Phil pulled over, shifted to park, gave her a big kiss and said, "You won't regret it. I love you."

Nancy replied, "I better not regret it. I love you too."

When they reached Nancy's apartment, Phil asked, "Do you want me to come up so we can tell her together?"

Nancy frowned. She now fully realized the enormity of her decision and the impact it would have on her mother.

"No. This is something I want to tell her myself."

She gave him a quick kiss and stepped out of the car. She watched him drive away and was hesitant to turn to make that long trip up the stairs when she knew she would break her mother's heart. She slowly opened the door, but was greeted with silence. Luckily, her mother had already gone to bed and the news would wait until the morning. Nancy tossed and turned and slept in small spurts fearing the rise of the sun like a vampire, except she had no coffin to hide from the light of day. She had nothing to fear from the sun's rays, except she had to face her mother and deliver her announcement.

Nancy could smell the aroma of fresh brewed coffee before she opened her eyes. She could hear the mumbling of the all-news radio station, with traffic and weather every ten minutes. Nancy forced herself out of bed, and when she could delay no longer, walked into the kitchen.

Her mother looked up and said, "Good Morning. What time did

you get in last night?"

Nancy removed a coffee cup from the cabinet and replied, "About 11:30."

"I just missed you. I was pretty tired last night."

Nancy filled her cup with her drug of choice and sat down at the table. She took a sip for courage and said, "I have something to tell you."

Her mother looked up with a worried look on her face. "You're not pregnant are you?"

Nancy laughed. "No. Don't even think that."

"Then what is it?"

Nancy cleared her throat. "I'm going to move in with Phil."

"What do you mean, *move in with Phil*?"

"It means exactly what I said. I'm going to move out of here and in with Phil."

Her mother looked shocked, and there was a trickle of tears slowly meandering down her cheeks.

"But you're not married. You should stay at home until you're married."

"I'm not breaking any rule, by moving out."

Her mother gazed at her with sorrow in her eyes and lamented, "No, but you're breaking my heart."

Nancy felt the pangs of guilt about leaving her mother, but each knew this day was inevitable. Her mother knew time could not be stopped, but if only there were ways to slow it down.

"Phil and I love each other. Maybe we'll get married one day, but for right now living together is what we both want."

"You're also breaking the rules of the church."

Nancy became a bit annoyed at that reference. "Don't bring the church into this. I rarely even go to church anymore."

Her mother softened her tone. "But if you get married, you will have a church wedding?"

"Of course we will. I'm not thinking about that right now."

"All you want to do is leave your mother."

"Mom, I'm only going twenty minutes away. I'll visit you all the time."

"Maybe, but it won't be the same."

Nancy could see that her mother needed some consoling. "You always knew this day would come. I couldn't live with my mother my whole life. You won't be alone. I don't think Ronnie will ever leave."

Her mother laughed. "I think you're right about that."

"It's part of life, Mom."

"True, but there are many parts of life that I don't like."

"Just think, if me and Phil get married, maybe you'll have some grandchildren."

Her mother's face brightened. "That would be nice as long as you're married before you're pregnant."

"Don't worry. We're careful"

Her mother put her hands over her ears and in a high pitched voice shrieked, "I don't want to hear about that."

Her mother relaxed a few moments later and asked, "When are you moving?"

"Right after graduation. I also have a job interview for a company in the World Trade Center coming up. It's an easy commute from the apartment."

"Don't take the job just because it's close. Make sure it's a good job and don't sell yourself short."

"I won't. Remember, I want to go to law school, so I need the money for tuition. That's what my first job is going to be - a way to pay for law school."

"Well speaking of school. I have to get ready to go teach. I need this job to pay the bills."

"Yes, but you know you love your job."

"I do. I feel like I am contributing to society."

"You always have. Look at the two great kids you raised."

Her mother gave a contemplative look and said, "I'm proud of you both," and walked out of the kitchen.

Nancy had a few more classes and then she had to endure the final exams for the last time. She had a hard time concentrating knowing she was definitely going to graduate and move out of the only place she knew as home her entire life, but she forced herself and did well.

The day before graduation, she was on the Path train at 9:00 heading for her interview at the World Trade Center. She wore a dark blue pants suit with two inch black high heels. She stood holding the overhead railing for stability, not risking sitting on something unpleasant, or wrinkling her clothes. Nancy signed in at the security desk, had her picture taken and was handed a temporary identification badge. She swiped her card at the turnstile and rode the elevator up to the human resources department. She walked in and immediately had to fill out a formal application form.

Before she could finish the application, a secretary called her into her prospective boss's office. Nancy was surprised to see that the person behind the desk was not much older than she. All she knew about the job was that it was for a college graduate as a management trainee. The young man stood up from his chair, walked around his desk and shook her hand.

"Hi. I'm Tom Pasternak."

Nancy forced herself to give a firm handshake. "I'm Nancy Anderson. Nice to meet you."

Tom was twenty-seven years old and looked like a model for one of the mannequins at Brooks Brothers. He had thick wavy blond hair. He was six feet three and a forty long suit fit him like a glove. His bright white shirt emphasized his tan face, and his teeth were as bright as his shirt.

When she sat down, he asked her questions about college and what extra-curricular activities she was involved with. Nancy explained that she wrote for the school newspaper, but with her working to pay the tuition, there was no time for anything else. She said she had to pick one thing she liked and concentrate on that.

Tom remarked that he paid his own way through college, so he completely understood. "I think having to work makes you appreciate your education more. It makes you work harder in school, since you know it's your hard earned dollars that are paying."

Nancy nodded her head in agreement.

"Let me explain about the position," Tom said. "It's more an amalgamation of a few jobs into one. We have a company newspaper, but it's not written very well. We need some new blood to write the articles and also conduct interviews etc. You will also be responsible for employee benefit questions and sometimes you will have to contact the insurance companies on their behalf. You will also work

One-Way Elevator

with the benefits team and learn everything there is to know about our health insurance coverage, pensions, vacations etc."

Tom could tell that Nancy seemed a bit overwhelmed. "Does it sound like too much to handle?"

She knew this was the critical question of the interview and tried to appear confident. "It can't be any harder than working forty hours a week while taking eighteen credits, writing on the school paper and graduating with honors."

Tom laughed. "You're the first person, who didn't hesitate to answer that question."

Nancy just sat and grinned.

Tom then asked, "Do you have anything else to add?"

"I'm a fast learner and I know I'm a good writer and I know how to deal with people from my last job. I'm sure it won't take me long to learn all the benefits."

She did not mention her desire to go to law school, although she did feel a bit guilty about lying by omission.

Tom gave her an approving nod. "So do you see any reason why you would not take this job?"

Nancy beamed. "No! Not that I can see."

"In that case, the job is yours."

Nancy almost jumped out of her seat. Her hands dug into her thighs as she tried to remain professional. "Thank you very much Mr. Pasternak."

"Now that you'll be an employee, call me Tom. We still have a few things to work out, like salary and when you will start."

Nancy could not contain her excitement. "I'm not too concerned about the salary. All I want is a chance to prove myself."

"The starting salary is $35,000 with two weeks vacation and after five years it's three weeks. I don't remember the charge for health insurance, but for an individual, it's not much at all."

"That's fine with me. I can start any time after tomorrow, since that's my graduation."

"Since you have to get a blood test and physical, let's say a week from Monday."

"Great. Now I'll really enjoy my graduation."

"I'll let Mary know you have the job, and welcome to the team."

She stood up, shook his hand, and walked out of his office floating on air. She finished her application and filled out the health insurance forms and scheduled her physical.

When she walked outside the World Trade Center, she gazed up and could not believe she would soon be working in one of the most famous buildings in the world. She felt she was rewarded for all her hard work in school and the long hours in the supermarket. There were times she thought it would never end. Now things were happening so fast - graduation, moving in with Phil, and a new job.

She walked around the blocks surrounding the World Trade Center, blending in with everyone who seemed to be in a rush. She looked at some of the faces, even though she knew making eye contact with anyone in the city was a cardinal sin. Most appeared to be stressed and expressionless, except for a few Japanese tourists, who were taking pictures. She hoped never to become like one of the walking dead. She discarded that negative thought, because at that moment she had nothing to worry about and everything to look forward to.

Her mother, Ronnie, and Phil were all working, so her news would have to wait until later. She took the subway up to Macy's and went shopping for her new wardrobe. When she finished, she had three bags filled with blouses, skirts, pants, and a credit card bill that would take a year to pay off. It was one of the only times she remembered shopping without any coupons.

Both her mother and Ronnie were ecstatic about her job. Nancy was afraid that Ronnie would be a bit jealous, but if he was, he hid it well.

When she called Phil and told him the news; after the congratulations, he jokingly said, "Now I guess I can ask you to chip in on the rent?"

***

Graduation day was bright and sunny, and the ceremony was not too drawn out. When the Dean said to the graduates, "Now is the beginning of a new chapter in your life. Remember to always lead an ethical life and always try to make the world a better place," Nancy thought about all the prior chapters that she was happy to leave behind. She had not had much time to think about how to make the world a better place, but maybe when she finished law school, she'd be in a better position.

Nancy was invited to several graduation parties over the next few weeks, but she did not want to have one of her own. That night Phil insisted on taking everyone out to dinner in celebration. Mrs. Anderson knew that Phil would treat Nancy well, but she wished they were married before they lived together. Then she thought, "I stayed at home until I was married and look what happened to me."

They went to an Italian restaurant on Washington Street not far from the Anderson apartment. The restaurant had recently opened and replaced a hardware store that closed, when the owner of forty-seven years retired. They ordered fried calamari and antipasti for appetizers along with a good bottle of wine. After the waitress filled each glass, Ronnie proposed a toast.

"To Nancy. I am so proud of her and I know she is going to go places in her life, but no matter where she is, or what position she has, she will always be my little sister. If she ever needs my help, she knows all she has to do is ask. So congratulations, and let's raise our glasses in honor of her graduation."

Nancy had tears in her eyes, when she leaned over and whispered to Ronnie, "I'll always love you."

***

Nancy did not have much to move other than clothes, some mementos, and pictures. Luckily, Phil had ample closet space in his apartment. The only piece of furniture needed was a new king size bed to replace Phil's double bed frame. They bought the mattress at one of the discount mattress chain stores and the frame from an antique store on the lower east side.

There were a few things that Nancy wanted to change, but she decided to wait until the adjustment period was over. She was second-guessing herself on her first official night sitting alone, while Phil was on duty. She cringed each time she heard a fire engine. Was Phil on that fire engine racing to the scene of a fire? Would he be safe? It never bothered her living in Hoboken, because she knew the engines she heard did not involve Phil. He was the first one in his family to graduate from college, but he kept the family tradition alive by taking the entrance exam for the fire department, instead of applying for a job with his business major. His grandfather was a fireman. His father was a fireman, but his uncle generated a rift in the family by joining the police force. Phil's plan was to work twenty years for the department and then be eligible for a good pension. He could then start a second career at a fairly young age. He was planning to go for his MBA, so he would be more marketable.

Phil's parents lived in Queens. His father was retired and still told stories of past fires, even though he had not held a hose, or climbed a ladder for twenty years. He could have used a little more hair and thirty fewer pounds. He was six feet three, barrel-chested, with his stomach overhanging his belt buckle by more than a few inches. Based on the laws of gravity, his spindle legs should have collapsed under the weight of his torso and his arteries should have exploded from all the alcohol and bad food he consumed.

John McClosky still adored his wife, Betty, after thirty years of marriage. Betty's black hair required no coloring and her pure white Irish skin needed no cosmetic improvements. She was thin, but standing next to her husband, she appeared anorexic. Phil could not help but imagine that if his parents still had sex, his mother had to be on top or risk being crushed. Phil knew it was somewhat perverted to think about that, but sometimes it just popped into his head.

Phil had no intention of becoming one of New York's bravest until his senior year in college. It was in the middle of his last semester, when one had to face the reality that there was no more delaying going out into the real world. It usually caused panic attacks and a strong wish to turn back the clock. Phil had a decent grade point average and he generally liked his courses, but now he had to find a job. With a business degree he was destined to sit in an office behind a desk for eight hours or more a day for the next forty-five years. He would be forced join the living dead that robotically went through life drinking the same coffee from the same coffee shop, squeezing into the same subway and after eyeing a young girl one day, suddenly felt like a pervert, because he was, by that time, old enough be her father.

He still remembered the day he made his announcement. It was during Sunday dinner and his father questioned, in his loud booming voice, "So how are classes going? Are you going to graduate?"

Phil always felt intimidated by his father, even though he knew there was no need to be.

Phil responded, "Everything's going good. I'm all set. I met with my advisor and I have everything in order."

His mother smiled. "That's my boy." She did not want another fireman in the family. She was glad her days of worrying were over.

The next question from his father drowned out any other noise in the room. "So what kind of job are you going for?"

Phil hesitated, looked at his mother and said, "I took the written test for the fire department, and I'm waiting for the results."

His mother dropped her fork. His father slapped him on his back and said, "That's my boy. I was hoping you would come to your senses."

In a pleading voice, his mother said, "How come you didn't discuss it with us? I thought you would have a nice safe job in an office."

"I will, once I put in my time, and then I can start my business career. I plan to get my master's at night."

His mother continued, "Do you really want to risk your life for the next twenty years just for a pension?"

"There are a lot of jobs more dangerous than fighting fires."

"Yes there are," his mother replied in an angry tone, "but you have a choice. The shifts, the stress and the danger take a toll on not only you, but also your whole family."

His father interrupted. "Phil's a big boy now. He can make his own decisions. He wouldn't be doing it, if he didn't think he could handle it."

There were a few times when Phil did not think he could handle it. He vividly remembered when the roof of a two-story house collapsed during a fire and crushed his good friend, Walt. Phil was manning a hose from a ladder, but Walt had gone in to check if everybody was out. There was a sickening feeling in his stomach as he watched the roof cascade into the floor below. It turned out that Walt was the only one inside. Phil had stood ashen faced, while the captain attempted CPR, but it was useless. Walt was thirty years old and the father of two beautiful girls. His wife, Barbara, was a stay at home mom and her whole world revolved around Walt and the kids.

Every firefighter understood the risk before he started, but most were under the delusion that it would only happen to the other guy. Phil realized why his mother was so upset, when he told her. He now understood how she must have worried every day for her husband and now she had to worry for him.

At the funeral, Phil watched the new widow, Barbara and the two girls and wondered if he would feel comfortable risking his life, if he had a family. Could he put his wife through that stress? Could he risk not seeing his children grow up? Would it be fair to his children to grow up without a father?

Ironically it had been his mother who convinced him not to quit and take some time to think about it. He did follow her advice, and then his turning point was when he pulled a little boy out of a burning bedroom. He went in from a ladder through the bedroom window and spotted the five-year-old boy huddled in a corner, crying. He quickly scooped him off the floor and went back out the window. Once it was confirmed that the boy was okay, Phil began to shake. The adrenaline rush had worn off and he realized what he had done. He only had a faint memory of even going into the burning bedroom. He could not describe his feeling, knowing that he had actually saved someone's life. Nothing else he had done in his life could compare to that moment. He then wondered if he had quit would that little boy be dead? He decided that saving other lives was worth the risk.

When he told his parents he was staying, his father said, "Saving someone almost makes up for all the other things you have to deal

One-Way Elevator

with."

His mother said, "I'm glad you made your own decision, because now you won't be second guessing yourself. If you quit, and then didn't like your new career, you would have said, you should have stayed. If this is what you truly want, I can handle a little more worrying."

***

Nancy was living a dream. She loved her job and fit right in with everybody. She was treated with respect and like part of a team, unlike her former position. It did not take long for her to learn all about the benefits, and she truly enjoyed dealing with all areas of the company. She was afraid she would be bored with a desk job, but that was not the only surprise she had. Things were better than she ever thought they could be with Phil. She wondered, if she were pregnant, would it change anything? She wanted to have a baby, but not at this time. First, she was not married. She definitely did not want her child to grow up without a father present. Second, she wanted to finish law school. Third, she was too young. She was just starting out on her own, and she wanted to enjoy life before settling down with a family. She liked having her freedom and the money to do things that she never could before. If she had a baby now, it would almost bring her back to the past with the time constraints and frustrations. Could she work full time and raise a baby? Could she ever go to law school? Would Phil even marry her? She knew Phil loved her, but would he panic and things between them reverse course?

She settled down in her cubicle, checked her messages and then went into the bathroom to confirm her fate. She had not mentioned anything to Phil. She wanted to be sure before she broke the news. She did feel a little nauseous, but she did not know if that was from nerves or her body adapting to its new state.

Luckily all the stalls were empty, so she had a few moments to see if a new life was now within her.

"With all the high tech tools available, here I am peeing on a stick," she thought to herself. Sitting on a toilet bowl in the most famous building in the world, she realized that despite all the advances and new technology, it still all came down to family and relationships. She looked down at the stick and her hand began to shake.

She left the stall and could see the terrified reflection staring back at her. She needed a few moments to calm herself down, so she went to the cafeteria and bought a container of yogurt and a bottle of water. She felt she needed a cup of coffee, but now she had to cut out the caffeine. She was in a fog for the rest of the day, but managed to walk out at five o'clock without anyone noticing any change in her behavior.

She loved going home to her new apartment, but now she dreaded facing Phil. She had no idea how to break the news. Should she go to a doctor first and let him confirm? No, that would only delay it. He deserved to know. She had not seriously thought about marriage, and the subject never came up. She now had to ask herself, did she really want to marry Phil? Would he even propose? If he proposed after he found out, would it be because he really loved her, or out of the pressure of fatherhood?

She stopped on the way home and bought shrimp, rice, asparagus, lettuce, tomatoes, and onions for a salad and a dark chocolate cake for dessert. She had the other ingredients at home for Phil's favorite shrimp dish. It was a little bit spicy, and she hoped her stomach could handle it. She also hoped her stomach could handle her announcement. She worried how Phil would react. Would he be angry or happy? Would he choke on his shrimp in shock, or jump up in excitement? She knew they loved each other and this would be the true test of that young love. Before starting dinner, she took another test to be sure and the results were the same.

"I'm already acting like a little wife," she thought as she carefully set the table. She cleaned the shrimp, cut the asparagus, and followed the recipe, so that Julia Child would be proud.

One-Way Elevator

The door opened and Phil said, "What smells so good? Is that my favorite shrimp dish?"

Nancy turned around from the stove and replied, "Yes it is. How was your day?"

Phil responded, "My day was fine. What's the special occasion?"

"Nothing really. I just felt like making something good tonight."

"I have to be careful I don't gain too much weight with all your good cooking."

Nancy smiled, "I have to watch too."

Phil scoffed in jest, "You don't have to worry about gaining any weight. You can eat anything and still have that great body."

Nancy felt her face flush and asked, "Would you still love me if I were fat?"

Phil gave the standard response, "Of course, I would."

She left the simmering pots and gave him a big hug and kiss.

"Now this is what I like to come home to. A good meal cooked by a beautiful woman."

"Enough with the flattery. Go wash your hands and sit down, before I send you to bed without any dinner."

Phil laughed. "We'll go to bed after dinner."

Nancy played along, "As long as you finish your vegetables."

Nancy placed the food in serving dishes and they sat down to an enjoyable meal, but it was mainly Phil who did the enjoying. Nancy only wondered how to break the news.

"So what's new in the wacky world of human resources?"

"Nothing much, but I'm so thankful that I have this job. I know I have good benefits, especially health insurance."

Phil finished his second beer and second helping and said, "You don't have to worry about health insurance. You're the picture of health."

"You already have your meal, you don't have to flatter me anymore."

"You have me all wrong. I wasn't using flattery to get anything. I really mean it."

Nancy then turned serious, "You never know when you'll need

your health insurance."

"Don't start worrying about me. Actually, the number of fires is down in our district."

Nancy looked down. "I wasn't talking about you."

A look of concern crossed Phil's face. "Then who are you talking about?"

Nancy sipped her water and said, "Me."

Phil looked up with a look of panic on his face. "What's the matter? Is there something wrong?"

Nancy replied, "No there's nothing wrong with me at all."

"Then why are you bringing up health insurance?"

"Because I'll be using my insurance soon."

"If there's nothing wrong with you, then why would you be using health insurance?"

Nancy forced a timid smile and said, "Because I'm pregnant."

Phil ejected himself from his chair, knelt beside Nancy and said, "Are you sure?"

"Yes, I'm sure." Nancy knew that his next response would be the determining factor.

Phil pulled out her chair, grabbed her arms, lifted her out of her seat and gave her a big kiss. "That's great news. I'm gonna be a father!"

Nancy felt relieved and happy. It was like a big weight had been lifted.

She replied in a pitch a few notches above her normal tone, "Yes, we're having a baby."

"When are you due?"

"I think in the beginning of March. I just took the pregnancy test today. I still have to go to the doctor."

Phil sat down on the couch. "I need a few minutes to process all this. I'm still in shock."

Nancy was able to laugh, "How do you think I feel?"

Phil then said, "I thought we were taking precautions?"

"We were, but I guess one of your little guys broke through the defense."

"That's a good way to put it. So this is why the big dinner and no drinking on your part."

In a reflective tone, Nancy said, "I guess we have a lot to think about, but for tonight let's relax and enjoy the moment."

Phil motioned for Nancy to sit next to him. He put his arm around her. "You know I love you, and everything will work out. Don't worry about anything, except having a healthy baby."

"I love you too, but I wasn't sure how you would react to the news."

"You should never doubt me. I only want the best for us."

"Should we tell anybody, or keep it a secret until I start to show?"

Phil thought for a moment. "I think we should keep it between us, until you can't hide it. I think that's best for now. This complicates things, but in a good way. Let's have dessert now and then we can relax and call it an early night."

Nancy laughed, "You're only interested in getting me in bed early, so you can have your favorite desert sooner."

Phil tried to act serious. "You're my favorite dessert."

She pushed him away. "I should make you sleep on the couch. "

Phil's face lit up with a big grin. "I think it's too late for that."

Chapter 3

He sat alone in his office in the North Tower of the World Trade Center. Everyone else was gone, except for the cleaning ladies slowly meandering from office to office, suffering through the daily drudgery, counting down the remaining offices and days until the weekend. Don Parsons turned his leather chair so it faced the window, leaned back and stared at the boat traffic on the Hudson River. Only a few sailboats skimmed across the calm surface on this hot humid mid August evening. It felt like the Santa Anna winds were blowing across a river in New York City, instead of a desert in California. Watching the sailboats always had a calming effect, even though Don never set foot in one. At sixty-four, the Staten Island Ferry, or a large cruise ship was more his speed. Maybe he would finally take a cruise, instead of only thinking about it. He would soon have all the time in the world. One part of him could not wait until September 14th, but another part did not want to rush it. He glanced at the pile of folders on his desk and laughed. He would not miss the constant deadlines, but he would miss the people. Not all, but there were a few.

The easiest way to describe Don Parsons was to use the two-word phrase, "Big Man." He stood six-feet five with a bumper crop of grey hair, which made him look more distinguished than rugged. Despite his size, there was nothing intimidating about Don. He had long ago realized that size did not make the man. His blue eyes had lost some of their sparkle, but his smile was bright and engaging. His nose had not been perfectly straight since the first of four times it was broken years ago. He had a barrel chest and long arms with large hands attached. His legs were long and his size fourteen shoes were extra wide. Small children could use his flip-flops to ride the waves.

He was in the last quarter of his life and he did not know if he was winning or losing. He walked early. He talked early. He did not know what he would have done without football. He was the typical football jock or jerk in high school and college, depending on who was asked. He was a star at Notre Dame, but the Giants cut him after his first season. It was a complicated trade involving three teams and he somehow wound up the odd man out.

The phone rang, interrupting his nostalgic journey. Even before answering, he was pretty sure who was on the other line. It was his wife, Beth.

"What are you still doing there?"

"I'm just getting ready to leave."

"How many times have I heard that one?"

"Too many times, but you won't be hearing it too much longer. What's for dinner?"

In an exasperated voice, Beth replied, "I didn't cook anything. I figured we would order Chinese."

"I'm leaving in five minutes. Order me my usual crispy shrimp and walnuts. See you soon."

Their apartment was in Manhattan on east 23rd street. They'd moved from a large house in central New Jersey after their two children were both married. With the reduction in commuting costs, the rent was not much more than paying taxes and maintaining a large house that swallowed up two people. Don also loved the time he saved not sitting on, or waiting for the train. He never thought he would live in New York City and work in one of the world's most famous buildings. He shut the light off, closed the door, and attempted to piece together the events in his life that led him to this point.

When he reached the lobby and walked into the indoor mall, most of the stores were closed. There were a few remaining tired-looking faces heading home, only to repeat the same routine tomorrow.

It all seemed to go by in an instant. He remembered his high school graduation throwing his cap in the air, and the births of Ryan and Collette. Now they were both married and he was a grandfather. The bomb attack in 1993 was seared into his mind, just like a million other random events from his life.

There were no seats on the subway car, but he managed to secure a space in front of one of the doors.

He saw a soldier in uniform and his thoughts immediately drifted back to his father. His memories of his father were few and faded like an old photo. Don's most vivid memory was when his father was not even present. Don was nine years old and his father was in Europe fighting in World War II. Don had not seen his father for over a year. There was the occasional letter, but Don wanted his father, not some words scribbled on a piece of paper saying, "I'll be home soon." Don did not see the irony at the time, but his father did come home, only it was in a coffin. Don remembered the doorbell ringing and when he ran to open the door, he looked up saw two soldiers staring down at him, each with no expression on his face. He heard his mother crying, before she even reached the door.

She was handed a letter and Don remembered one of the soldiers mumbling, "Sorry," in between his mother's sobs.

At nine years old, Don never thought his father was in danger fighting a war. He was on the good side and only the bad Nazis were killed. It was not long before he realized the letters were not the only thing that had ended.

As the reality sunk in, Don became angry. When he saw his friends, each with his own father, he became angrier. He began to act out at school. He began to pick fights with older students, but the age difference did not matter, because of his size. His mother was devastated by her husband's death and beside herself, because she could not control her son. Don was not interested in sports, but one day he picked a fight with a player on the Pop Warner team. The coach saw Don throw his starting tackle easily to the ground, before he rushed over to break it up. The coach took Don aside and after calming him down, explained how he could throw all the people he wanted on the ground from the other team, so Don agreed to play football.

Once he was able to direct his anger at the football field, he became more controlled at home and in school. His grades improved and his relationship with the rest of the world also improved. It was anyone on the other side of the line of scrimmage, who paid the price. Once he was able to control his emotions, he found life much easier and even somewhat enjoyable. His teammates were his

One-Way Elevator

friends. He no longer was the school bully looking to humiliate someone else in order to feel better about himself. When he entered high school, he was the starting tackle on the varsity football team. He had the most quarterback sacks and the most unassisted tackles in the conference. He was named to the all conference team and the college scouts were already taking notice.

His mother was proud of her son. She kept on thinking how proud her husband would have been watching his son excel on and off the field. Don was also on the honor role, and without the bullying he was one of the more popular students. He also played baseball, but he was only average. He would strike out frequently, but when he connected it was usually over the fence.

He reached the lobby of his apartment at the same time as the Chinese food. Don knew the delivery man, so he paid him and brought the food up himself.

He knocked on the door and in his best fake Chinese accent said, "Delivery."

When Beth opened the door, Don continued the charade and said, "Twenty Two dollar and fifty cent."

Beth played along and said, "That's not my order," and slammed the door in his face.

Don yelled out, "Come on, open up. The food's cold."

Beth opened the door and he knew why he loved her so much. Even after all these years, they could still make each other laugh.

***

Don had been writing his retirement speech a little each day for a few weeks. He wanted to say a lot of things, but then he thought a lot of things are better left unsaid. He had made many friends during his career and had seen countless people come and go, never to be heard from again. He was fortunate to have landed his job in 1958. Not many people spent an entire career at one company. He was crushed when the New York Giants cut him. He knew he had to pick himself up off the turf, but he was not sure what to do. He had ridden the football wave, and now he had wiped out. Back then there were not many teams, but today with all the expansion, he probably could have made it on another team. Also, the pay was not that great, and he began to question how long his body could take the grueling punishment. Football had been his ticket, but now he had to make another adjustment to his life. A business management degree would have to be his new ticket, but then he received some unexpected help. The alumni of Notre Dame are faithful to the football team. When Bob Robinson heard that Don had been cut, he offered him a job. He started as a management trainee and now he was retiring as a vice president with nearly two hundred employees in his department. He started from the beginning of his speech.

"I would like to thank everyone for coming tonight and I have an extremely long list of people to thank for help and support. I'm living proof that the old saying, 'If one door closes another opens,' is true. Another door opened up when I was offered a job here from a Notre Dame Alumni. Football was my first dream. Back in high school and college, this huge body could actually move pretty well. Now I only shuffle along with arthritic knees from being hit too much and from carrying too much weight. When I started back in 1958, the Giants had just cut me and mentally it was like I was laid out on the field from a vicious block. I knew I had to pick myself up and move on. To most of the people I worked with, it did not matter that I was an ex football player, and I soon found that I liked my new job. I do have to admit there were a few times over the years, I did have the urge to throw someone across the table. I'm also sure a few people wanted to see me knocked on the floor. Once I realized that if I worked as hard in my job as I did on the field and I could move up, things started going my way. I now think it was really a blessing to be cut. If I had stayed with the Giants, I would have sat on the bench most of the time and retired after a few years. Who knows where I would have wound up? I know I would not be standing in front of you tonight. If that had happened, I doubt my life would have been as rewarding as I found it here.

"I never expected to stay with the same company, and there were times when I thought about leaving, or worried that I would be asked to leave. I had two rules that I followed that are really pretty simple.

One-Way Elevator

First, I always tried to be a team player. I know all of you here have heard me say that too many times. But it is true. The best way to accomplish anything is by working together. I won't bore you with another football analogy. The second rule I followed was to treat everybody with respect. That way, no matter what happens you can hold your head high.

"I don't know what I'm going to do with all my free time. I'll probably drive my wife nuts, but we've always been a good team. I'll try to travel to all the places I said I was going to go and never made it. I better go quickly, before my knees totally give out. I'll also be able to see more of my children and grandchildren and maybe even learn to relax.

It truly does all go by too fast. I have met so many great people and I have learned so much from everyone. I had a lot of help along the way, and I also tried to help anyone I could. It's not important what your job title is, or how much money you make. It's the little things that are really important and more memorable than any raise or promotion. I learned the most important lesson of my life when I was nine years old and my father was killed in the D Day invasion. When he left to go oversees, I never thought that would be the last time I would see him. So treat your time with your family as precious, because that is the most important thing in life. Now, enough of this philosophical stuff. I'm starting a new chapter of my life, so let's all celebrate and hope it's a long one."

He knew the speech needed some work and maybe it should have a lighter tone. The speech made him think of his father again. Don always tried to be a good father and not spoil his children, but he knew he was more than a little bit guilty. He tried to keep himself in decent shape, but with bad knees it was pretty hard to exercise. He did occasionally watch what he ate and his main goal was to make sure his children had their father around for a long time.

He was fiercely patriotic, since his father had died for his country. It was a way to honor his father more than his country, but he never wanted to join the army, because it would have brought back too many memories. He remembered back to one day, when his office was located on Wall Street and during his lunch hour, he walked into a huge anti Viet Nam war demonstration. There were thousands of young people and a few older citizens mixed in. The nearby streets were closed, and there were police barricades set up to separate the crowd and keep the protestors marching through the streets.

The marchers were chanting, "One, two, three, four, we don't want your fucking war!"

There were several signs floating along with the crowd. They ranged from, "STOP THE WAR, MAKE LOVE NOT WAR" to "LBJ IS A MURDERER."

It was peaceful, but Don saw the look of determination on the faces of the marchers. He had not paid too much attention to the war, other than knowing there were too many deaths fighting for some country he barely knew anything about.

The large majority of the male marchers had long hair and proudly wore bell-bottoms like a uniform. Most of the women also wore bell-bottoms and many included headbands.

Don stopped for a few minutes and watched. There were cops everywhere, ready to jump in at the first sign of any violence. Don laughed to himself and thought, "It's pretty ironic, when a peace march turns violent."

He walked up a few blocks and then he heard some angry shouting. A large group of construction workers crowded behind one of the barricades and was chanting, "U.S.A. ALL THE WAY," while the protestors tried to outdo them with their shouts of, "One, two, three, four, we don't want your fucking war!"

A few other passers-by also joined the construction workers and a minute later, Don found himself standing behind one of the hard hats, with his deep voice bellowing in unison. He studied the determined faces of the protestors and the resolute faces of the opposing crowd and began to wonder, who was right? He ended his chanting and walked along the route of the protestors for a few more blocks.

He began to closely follow the war. He was concerned, when the Viet Cong launched the TET offensive, which marked a turning point in the war. On the television network news, he watched the fighting in the streets of Saigon and wondered if the United States could win this war. He also began reading all the war related stories in the papers.

He did some of his own research and found out how the French had lost Vietnam, and the United States was giving aid to stop the wave of communism in the region. He thought the term "Domino Theory," was a clever way to describe what would happen, if Vietnam fell to the communists. He was surprised when he read that John Kennedy had allegedly approved the assassination of the president of South Vietnam. It was rumored that the CIA was behind the plot. It was a bit ironic that when Kennedy was assassinated, some speculated that the CIA was also behind that plot. He was not sure who was responsible for President Kennedy's death, but there were conspiracy theories that believed the Mafia was involved. Some even called the assassination a coup. He read about all the different conspiracy theories and could not be sure if any were legitimate. He did wonder about Senator Arlen Specter's description of the so-called, "MAGIC BULLET," that went through the president's head and also wounded Governor John Connally of Texas in the chest and wrist before coming to rest in his thigh. If the story was not coming from official sources, he almost would have laughed at how absurd that sounded. Don did think it was kind of shady that Jack Ruby was allowed into the basement of police headquarters with a gun, when Lee Harvey Oswald was being transferred to the county jail. Don was watching television when Jack Ruby jumped out of the crowd of reporters and fired his gun. He was not convinced of a conspiracy, but he knew it was a convenient way to keep someone silent about the truth.

When Martin Luther King and Bobby Kennedy were both shot and killed in 1968, he wondered about the workings of the government and the FBI and the CIA. Don researched some of Dr. King's speeches and came away with a totally different point of view than he had from the mainstream media. He truly stood for non-violence and his desire was racial equality. It was his speech on April 4th, 1967 at Riverside Church in New York City about the war in Vietnam that made the biggest impression on Don. He was mesmerized by the words of Dr. King:

"A time comes, when silence is betrayal. I could never again raise my voice against the violence of the oppressed in the ghettos without having first spoken clearly to the greatest purveyor of violence in the world today – my own government."

When Don saw how Bobby Kennedy reacted and spoke after the King shooting, he had a new respect for the man, who had worked for Joseph McCarthy during his communist witch-hunts. He wondered who was responsible for shooting Martin Luther King. Yes, they say James Earl Ray pulled the trigger, but it was never clear who pulled the strings?

Once Don began to question the media's story, he began to view everything in a new questioning light. When Robert Kennedy was gunned down in the kitchen of the Ambassador Hotel after winning the California primary, Don wondered why the Secret Service led Kennedy through the kitchen. Was it to avoid the crowds in the hotel, or was it to be led into a trap? There were many conspiracy rumors, and once again Don questioned what to believe. The only fact that was certain was he could never trust the so-called official story.

Don thought back to when he first met Beth. It was October 1962 and the world watched and Americans prayed as the United States and Russia were on the brink of nuclear war. There was evidence that Russia had smuggled in and installed nuclear weapons in Cuba, which could easily be launched at any city on the east coast without warning. It was okay that the United States had nuclear missiles close to Russian soil, because God was on our side and the Russians were a Godless society, doomed to burn in hell. It had nearly reached the point where God or no God, the whole world was ready to blow in a nuclear conflagration. Don no longer felt worrying about a promotion was important.

Don went to work that morning wondering if there would be anything left to go home to at 5:00. He was the only person in the elevator bank, which was unusual.

When the doors opened and he entered, he had just pushed the button for his floor when he heard a woman's voice call, "Hold the elevator."

Don instinctively stuck out his arm to block the doors from closing.

A young woman, a few years younger than Don, rushed in out of breath and said, "Thank you. I'm late for an important presentation."

Don smiled and said, "If they push the nuclear button, your

meeting won't matter one bit."

She gave him a remorseful look and said, "I guess you're right."

Don was immediately attracted to her. He only had a few more floors, before the elevator door would open and she would walk out of his life. He took a chance and asked, "If the world is still here at five o'clock, would you like to go for a drink?"

Her first reaction was that guys are so horny, they would use anything, even the end of the world, to try to get laid, but there was something genuine about this huge hulking man standing next to her.

She smiled and replied, "Why not? If I have a few drinks and the world ends, at least I won't have to worry about a hangover in the morning."

The elevator door opened on her floor and she said, "Meet me in the lobby at five."

When the doors closed, he almost hit the emergency button; he was in such a panic. A beautiful woman had just agreed to go out with him on a whim. They did not even know each other's names. He could not stop thinking about this mysterious woman all day. He kept telling himself that she would never show, once she had a minute to think about what she'd agreed to. Don went down to the lobby at 4:55 and anxiously waited.

He expected to walk away at 5:05 alone, but the elevator doors opened and she walked up to him with a confident stride and said, "I bet you thought I wouldn't show up."

Don smiled, "I wasn't sure, but I'm glad you're here. He extended his hand and said, "I'm Don."

She gently shook his hand, but it was lost in the massive configuration of skin, bone, cartilage, and ligaments of Don's hand. "I'm Beth. It's nice to meet you."

Her bright red curly hair dangled over her forehead and down to her shoulders. He was reminded of Shirley Temple. Her face was pure white and flawless. Her eyes were blue and wide. Her nose was short but straight and her cheekbones were prominent when she smiled. She wore red lipstick, which closely matched her hair. She was only five feet four and weighed about one hundred and ten pounds. Standing in front of Don, she looked like a little girl, although she was twenty-three.

    Don did not know how to initiate the conversation, but he blurted out, "So how did your presentation go?"

    "The presentation went well. My boss did the presenting, although most of it was mine."

    "I hope he thanked you for your work."

    "He only acknowledged me when it was time to get everyone coffee and a donut."

    "Sorry to hear that. I bet you did a great job."

    She gave a frustrated look and in an exasperated voice mumbled, "I did. Where should we go?"

    "How about O'Neil's right down the block?"

    A look of discomfort crossed her face and she replied, "No, my boss usually goes there and I'm afraid he might see me."

    Don tried to make a joke and said, "Who is this guy? I don't know him, but I know I don't like him."

    "He's a little twerp with a Napoleonic complex."

    "How come you work for him?"

    "Cause it's tough for a woman to get a good job. No matter how good my work is, I'm still considered his secretary."

    So far, Don was not feeling too comfortable with his elevator woman.

    Don then tried not to sound too desperate when the said, "Let's walk the opposite way and go in the first bar we see."

    "That's the best idea I heard all day." They walked side by side until they found themselves in front of a real dive bar. It was small and three steps below street level. The front window displayed the first three letters of the sign for Slims, barely visible through the grime and lack of light. They both looked at each other and laughed.

    "What do you think?" asked Don.

    "We agreed the first bar, and this is the first bar."

    Don grinned and said, "Well, let's go."

One-Way Elevator

That was thirty-nine years ago and he wondered how his life would have been if he had not been on that elevator that day. *Life is just a roll of the dice*, Don thought.

He agreed with Woody Allen who said, "His life is just a series of different crises."

***

Later that night while lying awake in bed, he continued time travelling in his mind. After that first drink, they relaxed and after a few weeks of dating realized they were in love. They were engaged the next year, but the wedding was much sooner than either had anticipated. When Beth broke the news that she was pregnant, Don did not panic. His first thought was to question. Could he be a good father and always be there for his child? He vowed that he would never allow his child to grow up the way he did, but then came to the realization that many things are outside of his control. His second thought was, "What the hell did I do?" There was never any question that they would be married. They were both Catholic and abortion was not an option. His mother was shocked, but she was also sad, because she knew how her husband would have loved his grandchild. This new life brought back memories of another cut short.

It was a small hastily organized wedding ceremony. The reception was held in the auditorium of the Catholic school across the street from the church. A nearby Italian restaurant catered it.

Beth wanted to have children one day, but that day was much further into the future than five months after the wedding. Father McDermott, the pastor of Our Lady Of Grace Church, absolved them of their sexual sin and agreed to perform the ceremony. Of course, a little extra donation to the parish school building fund by Mr. Sweeney smoothed the way. Martin Luther was probably turning over in his grave, when the transaction was completed.

Beth wanted a career. She did not want to be a housewife with all the connotations and limitations that went along with the title. She wanted to be something different and aspired to a more fulfilling life.

Changing diapers and having dinner on the table, when her husband walked in the door, did not appeal to her. She witnessed how that life had impacted her mother. Now she could understand why her mother drank so much. It was not that Mrs. Sweeney drank because she enjoyed alcohol. She drank to escape the boredom and drudgery of domestic life raising five children. Beth knew there was more to life than what she considered domestic slavery, but when she held her baby in her arms, she knew she would sacrifice anything for her child. If that meant forfeiting a career, it no longer mattered.

When Don first held his son, the years of frustration and loss of not having his father melted away. He dreamed of doing with his son all the things he wished he had done with his father. Marriage alone was a difficult adjustment. Marriage and a new baby made it much more difficult. They hardly had time to settle into their apartment and write the thank you cards for the wedding gifts. They were shopping for a crib before they even had the pictures developed from their short honeymoon. Don was making a comfortable salary, but without Beth's income, it was not that easy to make ends meet.

Beth was a good mother, but Don knew she wanted more out of life. Beth was a good wife, but he knew there was more to life than being there for her husband and child. Beth decided to go to school at night for her teacher certification. She planned to teach high school English. She wanted the older students because she felt she could make more of an impact with them. At least that is what she told herself

It seemed as though he just blinked and his son, Ryan, was three years old and Beth was two months pregnant. Don distinctly remembered it was a Friday night, and Beth felt a slight twinge in her stomach. She thought it was from something she had eaten, but during the night, the pain continued and grew more intense. She noticed a bit of spotting, so she called her doctor, who told her to rest with her feet raised. The next morning, the pain still continued and the spotting increased. The doctor said to meet him at the hospital. Don had a bad feeling as he wheeled her into the examination room.

In a worried hesitant voice, Beth asked, "What if I lose the baby?"

Don gave an encouraging reply that he knew was a lie. "Don't'

One-Way Elevator

worry. You'll be fine."

Don waited while the doctor examined Beth. It was the same waiting room, where he drank several cups of coffee eagerly awaiting the birth of their first son. When the doctor came out, Don was afraid to look him in the eye.

When he heard the words, "She lost the baby," he felt he was nine years old again and the Doctor had on an army uniform instead of a white coat. Don forced himself to remain somewhat calm.

"How is Beth?"

"She's resting. She'll be okay."

"Can I see her?"

"Yes, She needs your support now."

Don hesitated but he had to ask, "Will she be able to have another baby?"

The doctor was both consoling and optimistic, when he replied, "In a few months, you can try again. There's no reason not to. There are many reasons for a miscarriage. It's nature's way of telling that something is wrong."

Don's only response was, "I'm going to see her now."

Don stood alone, while the doctor turned and walked away. He remembered how he felt his whole world was crushed, when the Giants cut him, but to Don, this was infinitely worse. Everything else seemed petty and selfish in relation to this moment When Don entered the recovery room, Beth was crying.

He took her hand and she looked up at him and sobbed, "It's my fault we lost the baby. I was trying to do too much and I didn't rest enough."

Don pulled a chair next to the bed, sat down and said, "It's not your fault. It's not my fault. It's just something that happened."

Between sobs, in an erratic tone she replied, "I'm the mother. I'm supposed to carry and protect the baby. I'm the one to blame."

Don was at a loss on how to console her. He basically repeated what the doctor said about there being something wrong from the start. "This is nature's way. It's nothing you did. It happened early and you're healthy. The doctor said we can try again in a couple of months."

The sobs turned to anger and in a measured voice she said, "I don't want to risk going through this again. I should have had my tubes tied."

It hurt Don to see her this way, but he knew she needed time to process everything. "Just rest now. You don't have to make any decisions about anything right now."

Her eyes shot arrows of anger, her face reddened and her lips trembled. "I just lost a baby. Don't tell me I don't have to make any decisions. How can I ever forget this?"

Don tried to sound firm, but he did not want to further upset Beth. "Remember I'm part of this too. How do you think I feel?"

Her anger quickly turned to understanding. "You're right," she said softly, "We just lost a baby. I just want to get out of here now. I can't stay another minute in the maternity ward."

The doctor discharged Beth and two years later their second child was born.

Emily was a miniature version of Beth. Don was grateful that she did not display any of his traits, because it would not be appealing on a girl. Emily was now married and a successful doctor with two boys of her own, Bill and Kevin. Don hated the thought of being a grandfather, because it was another reminder of how fast time had gone by, but he loved the kids. It almost felt like he had another chance to be a father and spoil them like most grandfathers.

His promise to be there for his children was easy for Don. It was not until the children were older that it was put to the test. Don could never understand why his son never played any sports. Ryan was tall and lanky and was the perfect size for a wide receiver, or a forward on the basketball team, but he was more interested in music and politics. Don found himself guilty of trying to live his lost youth through his son. He tried to use sports to bond, but it only drove them further apart. Ryan could see the disappointment in his father's face. Don tried too hard to be a good father.

Don dreamed of his son scoring the winning touchdown at his alma mater. He could not accept the concept of letting the child live his own life. Don became angry with Beth when she told him to be happy as long as Ryan was doing what he liked. Don felt Ryan was making a mistake not playing sports, and when he did not apply to Notre Dame, that was another slap in the face. Rutgers was a good school, but it did not compare to the prestige and notoriety of the "Fighting Irish."

It all started in his freshmen year, when Ryan began dating a girl he met in his English class. Ryan could not believe she was interested in him. She could have had any guy she wanted. Mika was beautiful and she knew it. She was a petite Asian with shimmering black hair, a flawless complexion, and a perfectly proportioned figure. Her eyes were wide and her smile revealed perfectly straight pearly white teeth. Unfortunately, nothing else about her could be considered straight. On their first date, they went to a party at a house off campus. It was within walking distance from the dorm rooms. After Ryan picked her up and before they had walked two blocks, she lit up a joint and asked Ryan if he wanted to share. Ryan had never smoked before, but he did not want to disappoint this beautiful goddess. They were both flying by the time they reached their destination. Ryan felt his feet were hovering slightly above the ground, and he was accompanied by a drug impaired goddess. He knew his parents and everyone else had drummed into his mind since he was a young child, that drugs were bad. "I've never felt so good in my life. Why did I believe all the warnings about drugs?"

Once inside, Mika led him around and Ryan gladly followed like an obedient puppy dog. She knew everyone, and Ryan wondered why he was not angry or jealous when Mika flirted with other guys right in front of him. He drank a few beers and shoved handfuls of whatever snack he could grab in his mouth. Ryan saw a greasy looking guy hand something to Mika. She gave him a peck on the cheek and sent him away.

Ryan asked, "What did he give you?"

She led him to an unoccupied chair, sat on his lap, seductively smiled and said, "Something that makes everything feel more intense."

Ryan did not know what to say except, "I feel great now. I don't need anything else."

The music was blasting, his world was vibrating and he never felt so enveloped by anything before in his life. Ryan was about to kiss her, when he saw the flashing lights of three cop cars outside. He was still aware that the cops would not appreciate his state of mind and he knew that whatever Mika had was not legal.

He pushed her up and said, "We gotta get out of here now."

Ryan could see the momentary fear in Mika's eyes, when she heard the loud knock on the door. He grabbed her arm and pulled her through the kitchen and out the back door. Luckily the yard was not fenced in and they were able to run though another yard and come out on the next block over.

Ryan came down quickly and his high was replaced by panic. "We could have been busted, and then we would be thrown out of school."

Mika looked at his frightened face, laughed, and said, " True, but we weren't. What a rush."

Ryan could not believe how nonchalant she was about almost being arrested.

"It wasn't a rush for me. I have to admit it was great, until the cops showed up. "

Mika replied coyly, "It can still be great. The night's not over yet."

She kissed him and in her seductive voice said, "We can go back to my room, because my roommate went home for the weekend."

Ryan never expected this on the first date, but then again he never expected to be smoking pot and running from the cops either. Ryan was not comfortable in his drug-induced world, but now it was his male libido taking charge. He wanted her more than anything in the world.

He took her hand and said, "Lead the way."

It was not like any normal first date, where each person reveals some carefully controlled information about him or herself. It usually ends with an awkward kiss and a hope for a second date. When Ryan walked into Mika's dorm room, he crossed into another world where he was no longer in control.

Ryan began to smoke pot with Mika almost every day. They would smoke before class, between classes and after classes ended. Ryan was having a hard time adjusting to college and dorm life, but with Mika everything appeared easy. She seemed to know everyone, especially anyone who could sell or give her drugs. It was not long before she introduced Ryan to other drugs including amphetamines.

Ryan did not select a major, but it was between political science and music. He loved music, but he was not sure what he could do with a music degree other than teach. He did not want to go into the business side of music and he knew the odds of making it big in a band were about the same as being elected president. He did not want to be a music teacher, so he was only taking general requirement courses to bide his time until he had to make a decision.

He had started off full of enthusiasm and wanted the taste of freedom that living away from home allowed, but that freedom also had its limits. He exceeded his limit, when he met Mika and developed his taste for drugs. He began to miss some classes. It was only one or two a week at first, but then it grew to one or two a day. There was a direct relationship between the drugs consumed and the classes missed. He could not concentrate on his studies. He was consumed with Mika and her illegal substances. He knew what he was doing was wrong, but he could not control his chemical or sexual appetites. He had learned all about drug awareness and prevention in school, but now he questioned if he should take what he had learned seriously. When the semester began he would go home on weekends for a visit, but now he rarely even called. Beth was worried, but it was Don who defended Ryan.

"Give him some space and let him enjoy his freedom."

When Ryan came home for Thanksgiving, Don ate his words. Ryan looked haggard. His hair was longish and his usually clean-shaven face was covered by stubble. This was not the same boy, who had left at the end of the summer, Don thought.

Don and Ryan had a tradition of going to the local high school Thanksgiving morning football game, with their rival from the next town. This annual game was the closest Don ever came to sharing his love of football with his son. Don had dreamed of sitting in the stands and watching Ryan catch the winning touchdown pass as the clock expired, but he watched his team lose on the field and wondered if his son was losing off the field.

After the game, the crowd rushed home to forget about the loss by consuming large amounts of turkey, stuffing and apple pie. A little alcohol would also be necessary to fully erase the stinging 42-6 drubbing.

Ryan stood up to leave, but Don said, "Wait a few minutes and let the crowd go. We're in no hurry."

Ryan shrugged his shoulders, sat back down and thought about Mika and how good it would be to smoke some pot before attacking the turkey. After a few minutes, Don stood up and they walked down toward the field and the exit, but Don walked out on the empty field. Ryan followed wondering what his father was doing. Don stopped at the fifty-yard line.

He looked at Ryan and asked in a serious voice, "So tell me what's really going on in school?"

Ryan was not prepared for that question and he gave a quizzical look. "What do you mean?"

With a stern expression Don continued, "I'm asking, because I can tell there's something going on and you're not doing a good job hiding it either."

Ryan was always a bit intimidated by his father, even though he knew he loved him and would do anything for him. He gave a feeble attempt to bluff his way out of the situation. "Things are going good. I have a girlfriend, and I think I'm passing everything."

"Think you're passing," Don scoffed, "That doesn't sound like the Ryan I know."

Ryan attempted to maintain his façade. "It's a bit of an adjustment, but I'll be fine."

Ryan looked to the goal post on his left and then to his right and thought to himself, "If I go one way, I'm losing yardage and headed for a big loss. If I go the other way I may not reach the goal, but at least I'm going in the right direction."

Don looked at Ryan and saw that he was struggling. He decided to force the issue.

"Are you going to tell me what's really going on, or will we have to stand here all day and miss Thanksgiving dinner? Either you tell me right now, or we both get down in a three-point stance and if you can knock me over, you don't have to tell me anything. So you have a choice. Knock me over, or tell me what's really going on."

Ryan looked down and shuffled his feet on the white line

stretching across the field, which reminded him of the white lines of coke Mika snorted at her desk. He decided to come clean, but was unsure how to start.

"You're right, there is something wrong. Now that I've started, I'm not sure how to stop, and I'm not sure I can, even if I wanted to."

Don knew he had to keep calm. "No matter what it is, it can be fixed. The longer you let it go on, the more difficult it becomes. So tell me and I'll do whatever it takes to help."

Ryan could see that his father was sincere, and he knew his father would do anything for him.

He looked his father in the eye and said, "I met this girl, and we've gotten pretty serious, but she's really into drugs."

Don felt as if he'd just had the wind knocked out of him from a vicious block. "Where did you meet her?"

"She's in one of my classes and we went out to a party and we smoked pot before we even reached the party."

Don remained calm. "You know all about drugs and what they can do to you."

Ryan shook his head and said, "I know, but she is so gorgeous, I didn't want to act like I wasn't cool, so I went along with it. I know that's breaking one of the first rules about drug prevention, but I didn't care."

"What other drugs have you taken?"

"In the beginning it was just pot, but then she convinced me to experiment."

Don blurted out, "And from the way you look now, I think the experiment failed."

He regretted his words, but Ryan did not shut down on him. "I did some amphetamines and prescription pain killers, but I never would do any cocaine. Once I started, that's all I seemed to think about, and that was the most important thing to me besides Mika."

Don knew his son was asking for his help, otherwise he would have kept quiet and continued the lie.

Part of Don felt so angry that he felt like dragging Ryan across the field and walking away, but in a controlled voice he asked, "So what can I do to help?"

Ryan looked up into his father's face and said, "I don't know if you can. I know what I should do, but I can't seem to force myself to do it."

Don made full eye contact. "I know it's not easy, and I'm not going to lecture or yell at you. I just want what is best for you. If you need to take time off from school, or transfer to another school, we'll do whatever it takes."

Ryan could see the pain in his father's eyes and hear the sincerity in his voice. Ryan knew he had let himself down, but he had not realized how much he had hurt his father.

Don began speaking again. "I've seen a few players get hooked on pain killers after an injury, and I understand how easily it could happen. I'm certainly no expert, but if you make the commitment, you can stop. It has to be 100%, or else you're only kidding yourself."

Ryan nodded yes, and Don kept on going. "Some players thought football was so important that they risked everything for a game. The game was more important than real life, and it was okay if they needed pills to get by. The reality was they could walk away from football, but not from the pills."

Don did not want to preach too much, because he wanted to keep Ryan's full attention. "You didn't bring any drugs home with you?"

Ryan shook his head and mumbled, "No."

Don smiled. "Good. So that means you have four days without any temptation. We can fatten you up and hopefully get you back on the right track."

Ryan looked up and gave his father a brief smile. "I am going to try."

Don put his hands on Ryan's shoulders and said, "The hard part will be when you go back. I think you know what you have to do."

Ryan spoke with a bit of uncertainty in his voice, "I don't know what's gonna be harder, breaking up with Mika, or stopping drugs."

"Remember it's not one or the other," Don said in a firm voice, "It's both. It's not heads or tails. You may not have a choice, but you're lucky you still have a chance to make things right."

Ryan gave a faint smile. "I know."

"Let's go home; there's plenty of food waiting."

With a wary look, Ryan then asked, "You won't say anything to Mom will you?"

Don knew that Beth would not be very understanding. "No. It will be our secret, but if you relapse, I'll have to."

Ryan held out his hand. "It's a deal."

Don shook his hand and said, "Anytime."

Don walked off the field feeling better than if he had won the super bowl. He knew that this victory was the only one that really counted.

Don could not remember a happier Thanksgiving, or one where he ate more. He dutifully watched the football games on television and as a vote of confidence allowed Ryan to have one beer.

Don still remembered the Thanksgiving toast, when he said, "Let's give thanks for everything we have and always remember that if we are not careful, we can lose it all, before we realize we are going down the wrong path. So let's stay on track and remember what's really important in life."

Beth had a puzzled look and Ryan gave him a nod.

When Ryan went back to school, he broke up with Mika, despite her enticements of sex and drugs. It was close, but he managed somehow to turn her down. He tried to bury himself in his books, and he started running every day to transfer his addiction to something positive. What helped him the most was when he saw Mika kissing another guy outside her dorm. He was a bit jealous, but he hoped Mika would not drag this new guy into the same drug induced world he had just escaped.

Ryan did meet another girl and now he was happily married and drug free with a son who played football.

***

As the time narrowed before his retirement, Don found himself living more and more in the past. He recalled football games when his team won, or when he had sacked the quarterback, resulting in a fumble. He remembered how proud he felt, when the New York Giants drafted him. He thought that was the highpoint of his life, which only proved how little he knew. He also recalled the day his mother died, which was one of the low points in his life. He had called her and in passing she said she felt a bit nauseous. Don said she should go to the doctor, but she insisted that she would be okay. His mother was living alone in the same house he had grown up in. Don knew he should have forced her to go to the doctor, but he was busy with work and the kids. He planned to visit her the next day after work. The following day he was at a meeting in a conference room, when the secretary came rushing in and in a panicky voice, told him to call home immediately. For some reason, he knew what the words would be before he dialed. He rushed to his office, but feared to reach it. When Beth picked up, she was crying. "You're mother is dead. It looks like a heart attack. A neighbor found her on the kitchen floor."

Don felt crushed and could only mumble, "I'll be home as soon as I can."

When he hung up the phone, he quickly grabbed his jacket and rushed home. He was angry with himself for not dragging her to the doctor. He passed a homeless man and wondered why he was still living, while his mother was dead. He felt guilty that she had died alone, but the worst feeling was that he did not have a chance to say goodbye. There were so many things he wanted to say to her, and now he never could. He was in a state of shock, but his guilt overpowered his other emotions. He did not have many memories of his father, but his mother was the most loved and influential person in his life. She'd stood by him and never tried to control him, but in her own way, gently guided him. She never went out with other men, or ever thought about marrying again. In her mind, her husband was dead and that was the will of God. She would never question her faith and never complain about how hard her life was raising a son on her own.

Don made the funeral arrangements and a long line of friends and relatives came to express their condolences. Kneeling in front of the coffin, he stared at her face and never realized how she had aged. She was not the ageless, vibrant woman he envisioned. The years of smoking had finally caught up with her. If he had taken her to the doctor, would she still have had the heart attack? Don knew the last thing she wanted was to be dependent on anyone. Knowing that she did not suffer and linger in a hospital bed was the only positive thought he could generate.

When he stood at the gravesite and looked at all the people around him, he realized that his mother was directly responsible for everything he had. Her love and support was the guiding force. He placed a flower on the coffin and once again was reminded of the fragility of life and the speed of time.

***

One of his happiest days was his daughter's wedding. Emily met Tom a few months after starting her internship at Overlook Hospital. Tom was a resident, and they quickly became a serious couple. Tom was a surgeon and Emily was going into pediatrics. Tom's father was also a successful surgeon. When they announced the engagement, all Don could think about was the cost of the wedding. He had to go all out on the reception, but neither he nor Beth cared, because it was their only daughter who was marrying a great guy. Don thought back that he could have retired two years earlier, if it were not for the wedding cost. It was a beautiful late summer day with a clear blue sky with the temperature near eighty degrees with low humidity. The wedding ceremony and reception were held at an exclusive country club. Don was not a member, but Tom's father pulled a few strings. The bride wore white, but it was the color of money that made it possible.

When he walked his daughter down the aisle, he was floating on air. After he shook Tom's hand and focused all his attention on the couple standing before the priest, he felt that everything was right with the world. When he danced with Emily, he did not want the song to end.

When he gave his toast, he only remembered one phrase clearly when he said, "Tom, I hope one day you can stand at your daughter's wedding and feel as proud as I do tonight."

***

Don was excited and pensive about his fast approaching retirement. What would he do with all his free time? Would he be bored? Would he drive Beth crazy? Would he drive himself crazy? He knew the first two weeks would seem like a normal vacation, but after that how would he fill his days? There were so many places he wanted to travel to, but he could not be constantly travelling. He always wanted to write a novel. He had plenty of ideas, but he never took the first step of putting pen to paper. He questioned if he was too old to begin. He partially consoled himself, thinking that he would probably be dead before he completed the book. Maybe it was his recent bout of nostalgia that triggered the idea, but he decided to give it a shot. He decided to write his memoir. He did not care if it was ever published. He thought it would be a good story and it would keep him busy. He also decided that he would sign up as a tutor for underprivileged kids. He wanted to help the students, who were about to drop out of high school. He thought he could use his size to intimidate them into graduating.

He began to seriously plan his memoir. He thought about signing up for a writing course at the New School or New York University. His first question was when should it begin? He thought about it a long time and decided to begin the day two soldiers in clean, crisp uniforms rang the bell to tell his mother her husband was dead. He could remember that scene as if it were yesterday. He felt the logical end would be his retirement. He had no idea how long it would take, or if he would ever finish, but he felt good thinking about it. The more he thought about it, the more he wanted to write about his life. He decided to keep it to himself and not even attempt to have it published. Who would even buy it? He was not famous or rich and had never committed a serious crime, or anything else special. The only thing he'd done was to survive in a world that had changed so much over his lifetime. If he had been a pro football star, then maybe a few would buy it, but since that never happened, his audience was limited to his immediate family. If he were in some historical event, a publisher may take a chance. He did not want to be famous. His only dream was to spend all his time with his wife and family. He was perfectly content to live out the rest of his days in anonymity and die a happy man.

One-Way Elevator

Chapter 4

John Haddler proudly walked across the stage, accepted his diploma and shook hands with the dean. His parents, aunts and uncles stood up and cheered. His father, Alan, looked at his wife, Joan, and she had tears in her eyes. It was a different feeling than a high school graduation. At eighteen, he was leaving the comfortable world of high school, where he was a big fish and entering into the expanded universe of college. Now leaving college, he was about to enter the real world where even Alan Haddler's cheers could not overcome the harsh economic reality. Alan questioned whether the $100,000 plus cost for an economics degree at Lehigh University was worth it. Now his son had no job and decided to take the summer off before starting his career. Alan attempted to explain to John that it was difficult to find a job, and a good percentage of the graduates were beginning their careers without being too discerning about the position. Alan also pointed out that perception is often more important than reality, and that taking the summer off would not look good, when John went for a job interview.

John did not care. He never had a summer off before, and this might be his only chance. From the age of eight, he had played baseball all summer, every summer. He started in Little League, and then advanced to a travelling team. There was maybe one week or two when the family could go away, but now he finally had a chance to relax. He played ball in high school. He was the center fielder and a good solid hitter. John received a few partial scholarship offers from small schools, but he wanted Lehigh. He surprised a lot of people, including himself, when he made the team. For the first two years, his position was sitting impatiently on the bench instead of center field, but he continued to work hard and play in the summer. In his junior year he became the starting center fielder and continued his solid play. As a reward for all his hard work, he was given a half scholarship for his senior year. John batted a respectable .320 with only one error, but the team finished two games below .500. He made his only error in the last game, and he struck out four times. It was not the way he had expected to end his baseball career. His dream was to play center field for the New York Yankees. His plan was to be drafted by the Yankees out of college, play two years in the minors and then be called up to the big team near the end of the season, make a great impression and start in center for the next fifteen years.

Now sitting back in his seat and watching the rest of the graduates, he felt one door had closed in his face, but another had not opened. "What's three months when you have the rest of your life to work?" he thought.

Alan had to keep reminding himself that he could not control every aspect of his child's life. He has to stand back and let John find his own way. Alan wondered if he made the right decision pushing John to play ball all those years. He encouraged John to pursue his baseball dreams, even though he knew the odds of making it to the big leagues were less than winning the lottery. Now he wondered if the odds with an economics degree were any better.

He was proud of his son and hoped he would be happy in whatever career he followed. Alan knew it was wrong that everything was measured in dollars and cents, but unfortunately that was the society they lived in. How much money you made should not be the measure of success. He was surprised when John turned down offers from other schools to attend Lehigh. Alan did not push him, even though Lehigh was his alma mater. Alan did not want to add up the costs of all the travelling and individual coaching lessons, but when he watched John play, it was all worth it.

With no more college tuition, there would be some extra savings, completion of some long overdue home improvements and even a more adventurous vacation. At least his son was not starting out with a huge college loan to pay back.

***

One-Way Elevator

The commencement speaker was a former Lehigh graduate who spent the last twenty-five years working in the State Department serving in embassies all over the world. He was just about six feet tall and thin with a full head of black hair. He was in his early fifties and distinguished looking. He walked up to the podium, stood for a moment and then after thanking the dean, the parents and the graduates, he began his prepared speech.

"I lived in a small town in Pennsylvania. My parents were not rich, and we never had extra money for any luxuries or fancy vacations. We lived comfortably in my small world, but as I grew older I began to realize how much of the world I had never seen. I worked hard in high school, and I was fortunate to receive a scholarship to Lehigh. If I had not received that scholarship, I might still be in that small town. Going to college opened the door to the world for me. My college education gave me my chance to do things I'd only dreamed about. I hope all the graduates will feel the same way. I know it is quite a shock to finally graduate college. Lehigh is a great college, and I was nervous to leave that comfort zone and go out into the world. The friends you have made, you will never forget, but each person will find his or her own path to follow. My advice to each graduate is not to rush into any job. Remember, you will be working a long time, and I found out the hard way that if you do not like what you are doing, it doesn't matter how high your salary is. If you like what you do, then it doesn't seem like work. It's just like some of the courses you had. The courses you liked, you did not mind the studying and the research papers. The courses you did not like, it felt like a struggle to do the minimum to pass.

When I graduated, I joined the Peace Corps. I had never been out of the Eastern Time zone, and there I was on my way to a small town outside of Caracas. It seemed I could never get out of a small town."

John could sympathize with him. The speaker continued. "I had a limited ability to speak Spanish, but I learned quickly. My job was to help the peasants in that small town organize, so they could sell their hand made products for more money in the markets in Caracas. It seemed that a small group had control over the market, and they made huge profits on the goods, while the workers lived in poverty. I was truly idealistic to think that a skinny white kid would be able to form a union in defiance of the local mafia. "

There was some laughter from the audience. "Well, I survived and the workers did eventually receive more of the profits. It taught me some valuable lessons. First, I realized that even with a college degree, how little I knew about the real world. The second and probably the most important lesson I learned was that if you put your mind to something, you will be amazed at what you can accomplish. I grew up quickly in Caracas. When in school, I complained that some of my professors were unfair, or that an exam was too hard. I saw what was really unfair when I looked into the faces of the workers and saw how hard each worked for very low wages. When I saw the faces of the children, who had no way out, I realized how easy I had it growing up and how much I had to learn about the world.

"Each graduate has made a big commitment and has received a great education at this wonderful school. The parents should also be proud, because you were all such a big part in guiding your child. It is an emotional experience to see your child walk across that stage and receive his or her college diploma. Yes, the student had to work hard, but without the parents, it could not have been done. It's like everything in life. It is a team effort. And the main lesson is that we do not stop learning after college. Our entire life is spent learning, both from our successes and our failures.

"I have lived all over the world in my years at the State Department. I've worked in embassies in Moscow, Lima, and Johannesburg. The societies may differ but basically people are the same. Each person strives for a better life, and I know that each person is basically good. I know each graduate has hopes, dreams and plans for a career, but whatever that career may be, I ask that there be one constant goal for each of you. That goal should be to make the world a better place. You do not have to make millions and contribute huge amounts to charities. You do not have to cure cancer, or come up with some new invention. All one has to do is to make the lives of the people around you better and remember to help those less fortunate in the world. In all the countries I have lived and visited, this country is by far the best. It is not perfect, but if each of you tries, it can become a little less imperfect.

"Now I want to congratulate each of you and wish you the best as you go out into the world and never forget that each of you can make a difference."

***

His girlfriend, Kelly, dominated John's thoughts. She walked across the stage with a swagger that could not be concealed by the gown. John never grew tired of looking at her. She could have been a model, but in September she planned to attend law school at Georgetown. He was not sure when, or if he would ever see her again. They met in freshman year at a party in her sorority house. John hated fraternities and sororities, because of all the phony self-serving, manipulative people they attracted. He went to the party out of boredom. His plan was to have one drink, laugh to himself at the phony girls, and then call it an early night.

His roommate, Paul, so poetically stated, "I'm gonna pick up some drunken sorority, bitch and screw her."

John laughed and said, "So much for chivalry."

The party was already in high gear, when they walked in. The music was blasting, and the sorority house, which was off campus, was packed. Nobody seemed to notice as they made their way to the kitchen to deposit the beer they had brought. John thought to himself, "So much for all the warnings at school about the dangers of alcohol." John scanned the faces in the kitchen and opened a beer. Paul walked into the living room, but John stayed leaning against the side of the refrigerator. Someone tapped him on the shoulder and said, "You don't have to hold up the refrigerator. It won't fall."

John turned his head and could not believe that a beautiful girl was talking to him. She was five feet eight with long blond hair. Her eyes were blue, and they looked a bit glazed over from the alcohol. Her nose was small, narrow and straight and her smile could make anything seem special. She wore a white knit top, which prominently displayed the curves in her slender body along with jeans and black shoes with low heels.

John tried to think of a quick response, but all he could come up with was, "Last party I was at, the refrigerator did fall over."

She laughed a bit too loud and said, "In that case, why don't we move into the living room?"

"That sounds good too me. My back's a little sore from all the weight."

She held out her hand. "I'm Kelly."

John gladly shook her hand gently. "I'm John."

She led him by the hand into the living room. When Paul saw John with a beautiful girl, he quickly came over to see if she had any friends.

Kelly asked John, "What year are you in?"

"I'm a freshman. How about you?"

"I'm a drunk freshman."

Paul tried to barge into the conversation, but Kelly wanted nothing to do with him. Paul attempted humor and said, "So what's a great looking girl like you doing with my roommate?"

Kelly gave him a stern look. "What's it to you? Why don't you go see if you can find someone drunk enough to think you're not a perv."

John didn't believe what he was hearing, and he tried not to laugh. Paul knew he had met his match and excused himself to get another beer.

When Paul left, Kelly felt guilty and in a somewhat remorseful voice said, "I'm sorry I treated your friend like that, but sometimes when I drink, I forget myself."

"Don't worry about it. You definitely read him right. He's a perv."

Kelly said, "Let's not talk about him. So tell me about you."

"There's not much to tell. I'm thinking of majoring in business or economics and I hope to play for the baseball team in the spring."

"So I was right, when I thought you were a jock."

"I guess, but I never thought of myself as a jock."

She leaned closer to him and said, "Well, take it from me. You are. Let's get another drink and I'll introduce you to some of my sorority friends." She then whispered in his ear, "Most of them are bitches, so watch what you say."

John did not know what to think, never mind what to say; but she was so gorgeous he would follow her anywhere.

"Are you going to pledge in any fraternity?"

John shook his head. "I don't want to get involved with any of that."

She laughed. "There's one fraternity I hear that is full of jocks. You should fit right in."

John tried to change the subject. "So where are you from?"

"I live in Roanoke, Virginia. Where are you from?"

"I live in Westfield, New Jersey."

They walked back into the kitchen for another drink. Kelly filled her glass and John reached into a cooler in the corner of the kitchen for another beer.

Kelly took a long gulp and nearly drained her glass. With a slight slur of her words she teased, "So you're a Jersey jock?"

John was still a bit shocked that he was talking to a beautiful girl.

She then asked in a taunting voice, "Does the Jersey jock have a girlfriend?"

"Not at the moment." He wished he had a few more beers in him. It would make this seem like less of an interrogation. John knew she was drunk, but he felt uncomfortable in this situation.

She dragged him over to a group of three girls and blurted out, "Hey everybody, this is John. I just met him, and he's getting me drunk. John, this is Katie, Sally and Sue."

They gave a condescending nod and continued with their conversation. John could now understand why Kelly had said most of the girls were bitches.

Kelly felt embarrassed. "Let's have one more drink and then get out of here."

"I think you've had enough already. You don't want to get too drunk and regret it in the morning."

In a flash of anger she said, "You can't tell me how much to drink. You're just some guy I met at a party."

John felt like she was a lost cause. "No, I wouldn't try to tell you what to do. If you want another drink go ahead."

"Stay right here," she ordered.

John watched her walk away and figured she would not come back. A minute later she returned. "I didn't think you'd be here."

John tried to act offended. " Why would I leave?"

"Cause jocks from Jersey probably don't like drunk girls."

John let that statement slide and said, "I can see what you mean about the other girls."

She suddenly looked sad. "So far I hate it here, and I don't fit in."

"Give it some time. You can fit in anywhere."

She moved her body close to his and said, "Maybe you can fit something in me later."

John was captivated by her, but knew it was the alcohol talking. "Why don't we leave and get a cup of coffee someplace?"

"Okay, as long as we wind up back at my room."

Paul came over to them. "I'm leaving now. I'll see you later. Nice meeting you, Kelly."

John was going to ask Paul to join them, but his baser instincts prevented him from extending the invitation.

***

They walked out together and nobody noticed. The music and the multitude of voices continued. When the cool night air hit, Kelly had difficulty walking. John placed his arm around her waist to keep her steady. John spotted a small coffee shop that was still opened. She did not want to go in, but John almost dragged her inside. They sat at a booth and there were only three other customers, all sitting at the counter. The waitress frowned when she saw Kelly slumped down with her elbows on the table that looked older than the waitress.

"Do you want to see a menu?" she asked in an unfriendly tone. John figured she had probably seen too many drunks during her career.

John quickly answered, "No. Just two coffees."

He looked at his new friend, who was not exhibiting her best behavior.

She smiled. "I like the way you order. I bet you like to take charge in everything. How about in bed? Do you take charge, or are you one of those wimpy submissive guys?"

John could not believe what he was hearing. She must really be

One-Way Elevator

drunk, he thought. Luckily the waitress returned with the coffee, so he did not have to respond.

After the waitress left, John commented, "I hope this sobers you up a bit."

"No you don't," she scoffed. "You just want to take advantage of me, like most guys I meet."

John shook his head. "I would never do that to you."

"You're just saying that until you get me back to my dorm room. My roommate went home for the weekend." Her blue eyes were clouded over and her hair looked as if she'd come in from a windstorm, but to John she still looked fabulous.

They drank the coffee and John paid the bill and even left the unfriendly waitress a nice tip.

She somehow made it to the ladies room and returned saying, "You see I'm not in bad shape."

John just smiled and walked her out. The coffee did not seem to have any effect on her condition. When they reached her dorm room, John was unsure of what to do. Luckily they were able to get by the security, because it was not too late, and John said he would be right down. John removed the key from her bag and opened the door.

"Aren't you going to stay with me tonight? You can do whatever you want." Her hand slipped below his belt buckle.

John reluctantly pulled away. "No. Not tonight. You need to change and go to sleep. You're gonna have a wicked hangover tomorrow."

He pulled down the covers, sat her down on the bad and took off her shoes.

He sat next to her and then he gently pushed her down.

"I knew you were gonna do it," she said in a sexy voice.

He pulled up the covers and kissed her on her forehead.

"Where you going? We have the whole night."

"I'll be right back." John found a pad and a pen on a desk near the window and wrote his name and number and the words, "Call me." He looked back and she was asleep. He left the dorm room thinking that this was one of the best nights he ever had.

The next morning, Kelly called him and was extremely apologetic about being drunk.

"I was up half the night sick as a dog. I usually never get drunk." She was worried about what she may have done, or if they had sex. She was afraid to ask over the phone, so she asked if they could meet later in the cafeteria.

***

Kelly was waiting when John walked in. The cafeteria was fairly empty, since it was mid afternoon. She looked more beautiful today than what he remembered. She was sitting alone with a glass of ginger ale, a sure sign of a hangover.

He walked up to the table. "Good to see you again."

Kelly did not smile. "I guess so."

John sat down and could tell she was more nervous than he was, if that was possible.

Kelly began, "I don't remember much from last night. I hope I didn't make a fool out of myself."

" Not at all. You just had a little too much to drink. No big deal."

She appeared tentative about what to say next.

"I remember talking to you after I introduced you to those three bitches and then I woke up in my clothes in my bed. Everything in-between is gone, or hazy at best. Then I saw your note."

"You want me to fill in the blanks?" John could see the anxiety in her face.

John explained how they left the party and stopped at a coffee shop, but the coffee didn't help.

"I have no memory of letting you into my room."

"You couldn't open the door by yourself."

He saw the concern in her eyes. "You told me your roommate was home for the weekend."

In a panic stricken voice, Kelly asked, "What else did I say?"

John was not sure if he should reveal that to her. He decided that it was best to tell the truth. "You asked me to stay."

"Oh my God!" she gasped. "You didn't. Did you?"

John smiled reassuringly. "No. I didn't stay and nothing happened."

A wave of relief spread across her face. "You're not lying to me are

One-Way Elevator

you?"

"No. I only made sure you were in bed and then I left after leaving that note."

She looked down for a moment. "I feel like such an idiot. Thank you so much for helping me last night. Another guy may not have been as honest as you."

Now that the tension was gone, John said, "You didn't make it easy to leave."

Kelly blushed. "Don't tell me anything else. Can we start over again and try to forget about last night."

John smiled. "That would be great, but on one condition."

Kelly looked puzzled. "What's that?"

John laughed. "Don't call me a jock anymore."

"Oh my God! Did I really call you a jock?"

"A number of times. A Jersey jock."

Kelly shook her head and her face was flushed with embarrassment. "Well, whatever happens, I promise you won't hear that from me anymore." Kelly held out her hand and said, "Is it a deal?"

John took her hand and said, "You bet."

From that day forward they were together, but now each would follow a separate path: Kelly to law school, and John to a rented house down the Jersey Shore.

The night before graduation, they went out for dinner to their favorite restaurant. They both knew what would happen, but neither wanted the night to end. Each felt as if it was the last meal before the execution. Kelly wore a short black skirt with a low cut grey blouse and heels, even though the restaurant was nice, but not very fancy. John wore a beige pair of Dockers and a blue knit collared shirt and sandals. They sat at their usual table for two in the back, but this time it felt awkward. Neither wanted to admit that this was the last time, because it would cloud any memories.

The waitress walked over to take the drink order. "Wow, aren't you guys dolled up tonight. What's the big occasion?"

Sarah had served them the first time they came for dinner and over the years they became old friends. She was in her mid thirties, married with three children. She was about five feet two with black hair and a friendly face. She was thin with no ill effects from childbirth. She had an optimistic disposition, despite having to work as a waitress to supplement her husband's low paying job.

Kelly spoke first. "Remember, this is our last time here. Tomorrow's graduation."

"That's right. How could I forget? Congratulations to the both of you."

"Thank you," John replied, "We're going to miss this place."

Kelly looked up. "This was the one place we felt at home and we always had great food and great service."

Sarah mumbled a shy, "Thank you," and then asked, "So what can I get you for your last meal at this illustrious establishment?"

"I'll have a light beer and Kelly, do you want white wine?"

"Sounds good."

When the drinks arrived, John said, "I'd like to make a toast."

Kelly picked up her glass and looked across the table at the one person, who had always been there for her.

John cleared his throat. "I don't know where the time has gone. These four years have flown by. I have so many good memories, but I'll never forget you."

Kelly put down her glass and said, "That wasn't a toast. That sounds more like a good-bye."

John saw the hurt look in her eyes. "No. What I meant was that out of all the memories, the ones with you were the best."

Kelly looked at John and could sense that he was scrambling to make an attempt at damage control. She decided to let the topic slide for now, so they could enjoy their dinner. "I know what you're trying to say, and I feel the same way too." Kelly then raised her glass, and they lightly clinked glasses, took a sip and stared down at the menus.

They ordered fried calamari as an appetizer and Kelly could not resist having her favorite fillet of sole, while John remained faithful to his shrimp stuffed with crabmeat.

"When are you moving into your house down the shore?"

"Next weekend. It's a dump, but with four other guys it should be fun."

"Is your father still mad about you taking the summer off?"

"I think he is, but he doesn't yell about it anymore. I think my mom is worried about me, but she doesn't let on."

In a supportive voice, Kelly said, "It's only a few months and then you'll have no problem finding a job."

"I'm not worrying about that now. It will be strange not to have to do anything in the summer and know that I don't have to go back to school in September."

Kelly finished her wine. "I'm nervous about starting law school. What if I don't like it?"

John tried a little humor and sarcasm in his reply. "You have nothing to worry about. I'm sure you'll graduate near the top of your class, land a job in a big law firm and be a partner, while I'm struggling in some dead end job."

Each realized how they were talking about separate futures, but attempted to block out those thoughts for now. The calamari arrived, and it was excellent as usual.

"So what will you do with all your free time?"

John perked up. " I'll be on the beach as much as I can. When I'm not on the beach, I'll either be drinking or sleeping."

Kelly forced a laugh. "Sounds like you spent a lot of time formulating that plan and carefully calculated every detail."

John played along. "My plan is no less complicated than the Normandy invasion."

Kelly frowned. "I'm going to miss your weird sense of humor."

John pretended not to read into her last words. "We're both being thrown into the ocean now, but for now I'll just ride the waves and lie on the beach."

The main courses arrived and they adjusted napkins and silverware for a moment.

Kelly took a bite. "As good as ever."

John wiped his mouth and nodded in agreement. "It is a pretty scary world out there. I wish we had another year together."

"If we did, then we would be back here saying we wish we had another year."

"I guess you're right. Enough of this morbid talk. We should just enjoy the meal and not worry about tomorrow."

Kelly nodded and signaled to Sarah for another round of drinks.

The third drink worked like a charm, and they spent the rest of the meal discussing courses, criticizing professors and commenting on what other classmates were doing after graduation.

Sarah came over and said, "In honor of your graduation, dessert and coffee is on me. We do have a new double chocolate cake that is out of this world."

They both thanked her, and John said, "How could we refuse?"

"So what are you both doing after graduation? Are you still going to law school, Kelly?" Kelly nodded her head. "And what about you John?"

John felt slightly embarrassed by his response. "I'm taking the summer off and living down the Jersey shore and then I'll find a job in September."

Sarah knew as a waitress she should not be judgmental, but she had hoped for a different response.

"I'm sure you'll make a great lawyer and John, I'm sure once you start looking, you'll have a number of jobs to choose from. I wish you both the best of luck."

The dessert lived up to Sarah's endorsement, but after all that remained on the plates were a few crumbs and traces of chocolate and the coffee cups were drained, John reluctantly asked for the check. As soon as John and Kelly stood up to leave, Sarah gave each a hug and another wish for good luck. When John took his last look at the restaurant, the cloak of perception was removed, and the walls appeared more drab, the carpeting more worn and the lighting dull instead of intimate. When they walked outside, John felt one door closing forever and was not sure what other door would open.

They slowly walked back to Kelly's dorm room, each a little drunk and each knowing that this could be their last walk together. When they reached her dorm, Kelly invited John in, knowing that her roommate would be out late. They sat down on the bed and she kissed him, but each knew this time was different. John asked the question they had both been avoiding for the past few weeks and especially at dinner.

"Do you think we can have a long distance relationship?"

Kelly acted a bit surprised. "Of course we can. It won't be that hard."

John looked into her eyes, softly questioning. "Is that what you really think?"

She placed her head on his shoulder. "Sure, plenty of people do it."

John stared straight ahead. " But how many of them last?"

Kelly continued her optimistic charade. "I bet most of them do."

"I'm not so sure about that."

Kelly was momentarily startled. "Look we can take turns visiting. Who knows where you'll find a job. Maybe you'll find one in D.C. Wouldn't that be great?"

"It would, but I have no clue where I'll wind up. Probably New York City."

"There are so many law firms there, I bet I could land a job at one of them when I graduate." Kelly was becoming a little upset. "We've spent almost the last four years together and now you sound like it won't go on. Don't you still love me?"

The glow of the alcohol was fading quickly. "Of course I do, but right now I have no idea where I'll be."

Kelly became emotional. "I can't believe what I'm hearing. Are you trying to break up with me?"

John stood up and took a few steps. He then turned and faced Kelly. "That's the thing. I don't know what I want to do. You're the best thing that's happened to me in the last four years. I don't even know if I would have stayed, if it weren't for you. I have to figure out what I'm gonna do on my own. You have everything neatly planned, and I don't see where I fit into those plans."

Kelly's face turned sullen and her voice was raised to near panic decibel level. "Of course you do. How could you say that?" There was resentment in Kelly's voice. "You're more important to me than any law school. I wasn't sure I was going to law school, because I thought we might be engaged by now."

John was shocked. John loved her, but he never thought about getting married so soon out of college. He wanted to be secure before he settled down. "Why didn't you talk to me about it?"

Kelly stood up and walked to the other side of the room. "I tried to, but you never wanted to make any plans for the future. You were happy going along with the way things were."

John now realized how many hints she had thrown, and all of his friends were always asking when he was going to put the ring on her finger? John always laughed it off, and now he saw how wrong he was. "I'm sorry if I hurt you, but I wouldn't even think about marriage until I was able to support myself with a good job."

Kelly was still feeling the alcohol from dinner. "Is that what I am to you? Someone you don't have to worry about and can put off?"

"I didn't mean it that way."

"Then how did you mean it?"

John was frustrated. All of this was coming at the wrong time. Graduation was a major life change. He could not handle another major change at the same time. "I'm sorry. I didn't realize and we could have talked about this earlier. It's the night before graduation, and you spring this on me."

"I didn't spring it on you. If you weren't so pig-headed, you would have realized that you don't stay with someone for four years just for the hell of it. You don't stay, because it's convenient. I'm not like one of your baseball teams, where you have a good season and then say goodbye until next season. Well, there is no next season. My friends said I was wasting my time with you, but I wouldn't listen. I guess I should have."

John could see the tears and watched her attempt to control her shoulders from shaking with the sobs.

Kelly continued, "What did you expect when we graduated, that we would just shake hands and say it's been great and keep in touch?"

John now realized how his non-committal attitude had really hurt Kelly. He walked over to her, put his hands on her shoulders and said, "I never meant to hurt you. You know how good we are together. So, you think I want this to end?"

"No, I think you like things the way they are, and you're afraid to move forward. I know that's the real reason you're taking the summer off."

John knew she was right. He had to admit she knew him better than anyone. With a feeling of guilt and frustration, John said, "Then what do we do?"

Kelly felt the thrill of graduation and the anticipation of law school quickly fade away. She did not want to lose John, but she did not know how to keep him. Tomorrow each had separate plans with family and once out of the dorm, would they begin to lead separate lives? She began to think that maybe John had the right idea after all. Maybe they needed some time apart to determine if each one really wanted to continue the relationship. If each one wanted it enough, they could make it happen, but right now she was fumbling in the dark.

John did not want to lose her, but he did not see any future with each of them going separate ways. He loved her and now realized that he took her for granted. She was always there for him and now after tomorrow, she would be there no longer.

A perfectly good night was ending badly. A perfectly good relationship was being swept away by the incessant movement of time. In baseball there was no time. There were only nine innings and no clock. In baseball, if you lost a game, the next day you started over again. Too bad the rest of life did not follow the same rules.

He had to do something to end this tragedy. In a Greek play some God would intervene and make everything right, but there were no signs of any God in this American saga.

"Maybe we should call it a night," John finally said, "We can talk things through after graduation."

Kelly could not be consoled. She walked up to John, put her arms around his waist, pulled him close and said, "This could be our last night together. Let's make the most of it." She kissed him, and John did not want to pull away, but he felt he had to.

"I want to stay, but I think we both have some serious thinking to do."

Kelly took a step back in shock. "You're leaving now?"

John painfully nodded, yes. "Remember the night we met and I did not take advantage of you? Well tonight is somewhat similar. If I stayed I would feel like I was taking advantage of you. I don't want you or me to wake up in the morning with any regrets. It's better if I make my exit now."

The tears started flowing again and Kelly implored, "Don't you love me?"

"Of course, I do, but maybe we do need some time to figure things out."

"I don't want to have my last day at college ruined with the memory of us breaking up. How could you do this to me?"

John tried to control his emotions. "Let's not call it a breakup. Let's take the summer to work things out. I said, I need to know what I'm doing before I can make any other commitments."

Kelly now sounded angry. "I can't believe it's going to end like this. Once you walk out that door, you're walking out of my life."

John looked down at her and although it hurt, he replied, "That's the chance I'll have to take." He kissed her on her forehead, turned and walked out the door.

Kelly lay on the bed and cried. Tomorrow was to be one of the biggest days in her life, and now it would be marred and the bad memory ingrained forever. Last week her life seemed so perfect. She was graduating with honors, accepted at a prestigious law school, and she was with the man she loved. She felt as if she had lost John, and graduating with honors did not seem so special and the law school not as prestigious. Everything had suddenly changed and she could not wait to get through the graduation ceremony and return home. It will be quite an adjustment, she thought. I hope Thomas Wolf was wrong when he said, "You Can't Go Home Again."

Her father had set her up in a job as a summer intern in a friend's law firm. Right now the whole thought of going to law school seemed like a waste of time. Was she tough enough to be a good lawyer? What field of law would she pursue? She was interested in entertainment law. She could not see herself defending criminals, but then, she thought, there was a lot of law breaking in the entertainment industry. It was just a different type of crime. Even though she had a degree, she felt as if she had thrown away four years of her life on a relationship she did not want to end. She tried to make sense of everything, but the only mistake she could see was that they were too comfortable with each other.

John walked around the campus and he had many good

memories, but tonight would overshadow them all. Did his lack of commitment doom the relationship? He realized he might never know. He had to figure out how to live without Kelly, without school, and without a job.

He did not know how he would like his newfound freedom. It all came too fast, and he was totally unprepared for the future. He really did need the time off to figure out what to do. In class or in center field, he was confident and self-assured, but in a job interview, he was like a rookie, nervous about choking in the clutch.

They saw each other briefly, while lining up for the graduation procession into the stadium.

John stood motionless, while Kelly walked up to him and said in an emotionless voice, "Congratulations. Keep in touch."

She gave him a quick kiss on the cheek and as she turned to walk away, John only meekly mumbled, "I will."

After graduation, they smiled for the pictures with friends and relatives, but each one was only going through the motions. When John's mother asked about Kelly, John answered that she had to go with her parents, and they had seen each other earlier. When Kelly's father asked about John, Kelly only said that he was somewhere with his parents and that they had dinner last night and had seen each other earlier.

***

The next day, John packed up his father's car with all his stuff and settled in for the dreaded ride home. When his father pulled into the driveway, there was a new metallic silver Honda Civic with a big bow on top waiting for the new owner. John could not believe it. He thought he would have to hitch rides with his friends for the summer, but as he opened the door and jumped into the diver's seat, he felt in control.

After a quick check of the interior, he walked up to his parents and said, "You didn't have to buy me a car. That's too much money."

His father replied, "You deserve it. You'll need it down at the shore and who knows where you'll find a job."

"Thank you both." He shook his father's hand and gave his mother a big hug and a kiss.

His mother commented, "Now you can come up from the shore whenever you want and have a home cooked meal."

"There's still a little time until we get the house, so I'll be enjoying your cooking until then."

After he took a quick spin in his new toy, they went inside with his bags. His first thought was to call Kelly with the news, but now he was not even sure she would pick up. When he went up to his room, he unpacked and then lay on the bed, stared at the ceiling and attempted to make sense out of everything. He had reached a milestone in his life, but knew this was not the way it should feel.

The Haddlers hosted a graduation party on Saturday in the backyard with all his relatives and friends. John was not in a party mood, but he knew he could use any graduation money to support his frugal summer. He promised himself that he would ignore any judgmental looks from relatives, when he gave them news of his summer sabbatical. He would cash the check as soon as possible and use the money to drink whenever he wanted. The only rule this summer was if he drank, he would never drive. No more classes, no training schedule, no summer league schedule. There was no schedule at all. He had nobody to depend on and no one depending on him. He was truly liberated, but why did he feel so empty? He knew the answer and he wondered what Kelly was doing. Was she home? Was she with her friends? Was she happy?

***

Driving down the Garden State Parkway to the rental house in Point Pleasant, he felt as if he were hiding from the real world. He laughed to himself and thought he was literally attempting to hide his head in the sand. His friends, Tom and Carl were with him. They were meeting Bob and Stan at the house. Tom and Carl had one more year until graduation. Bob and Stan had graduated and were both working. Bob was a high school math teacher and Stan worked for an auditing firm in New York City.

When they pulled into the driveway, Bob and Stan were already sitting on the porch drinking beer. The porch was about six feet wide, and it extended the twenty-foot width of the house. It was in need of a coat of paint, but perfect for a shore house. Sand and pebbles replaced the grass in the front of the house. The front door opened directly into the living room, which had a beige couch, two brown recliners that had seen better days, and a 32-inch television in the corner. A ceiling fan with a light and one blade slightly bent hung precariously above. The hardwood floors were in pretty good condition and the walls were painted white. The dining area was next to the living room and contained a large table and six chairs. The galley kitchen was small, but there were no plans to prepare any gourmet meals. One eight by ten bedroom was located next to the kitchen with a single bed and a chest of drawers. There was only one window, but it contained an air conditioner. A closet next to the kitchen was converted into a half bath. Upstairs there were three bedrooms, two with queen size beds and one with two double beds. Bob and Stan had picked out the house, and John was pleasantly surprised that the house seemed like a good deal.

John reached for his phone to call Kelly, but he forced his hand to return to his side and once again faced the reality that he was now alone. He had all the freedom he dreamed of but was unsure how to enjoy it. He unpacked and then drove to the liquor store to exercise some of his freedom. While in the liquor store, he observed a girl struggling to carry a case of beer to the counter.

"Can I help you?" John asked.

"Sure. Thank you. I hate beer, but we need some for the party tonight."

She handed the case to John who said, "It must be a small party if all you need is one case?"

"It's only going to be about twenty people. Other people are bringing wine and beer too."

She was about five-feet three inches tall and she did not seem old enough to be in a liquor store. She had short chestnut brown hair and a stunningly beautiful face with a wide energetic smile. Her brown eyes had a sparkle and her skin was bronze as if she had a permanent tan. She was thin, but shapely in her tight white shorts and blue tank top.

"What are you in here for?" she asked.

John placed the case on the counter. "I'm getting a case of beer too, but not for a party."

She gave a quizzical look. "Then what is it for?"

John laughed. "It's for me. I just dropped my stuff off at our house and came here."

She gave a quick smile. "I guess you'll be busy this weekend?"

"I have nothing going on, except this case of beer."

She then extended her hand. "My name is Dawn."

"I'm John."

The clerk came over and said, "Is that it?"

Dawn hurriedly said, "No. I still have to get some wine."

John thought back to how he met Kelly at a fraternity party, when she was drunk. Now he was in another situation involving alcohol with another woman.

John could not believe the words coming out of his mouth. "I could help you carry the wine if you want?"

Dawn smiled suggestively. "Do you always help out strangers?"

"I do, especially if they're pretty and there's alcohol involved."

"Sounds like you like to party."

John brought himself back to reality and felt guilty with his not so innocent flirtation. "If I'm in the mood."

Dawn surprised him, when she asked, "Well if you're in the mood tonight, why don't you come to our party?"

John hesitated momentarily and asked, "Where's your house?"

"We're two blocks from the beach. It's 165 second avenue."

"How many people are in on the house?"

"It's me and five of my sorority sisters."

"I'm staying with four of my friends. No sorority sisters."

"Why don't you bring them with you?"

"Maybe."

"Where's your house?"

"I think we're close. I'm one block from the beach up from Jenkinson's boardwalk."

"You're definitely within walking distance. The party starts at 8:00."

"Are you still in school?"

"Rutgers. I'm officially a senior now. I'll graduate next year. How about you?"

"I just graduated from Lehigh. I'm taking the summer off, before looking for a job."

"Congratulations. That's great."

John frowned and mumbled, "Thanks, but I don't know about how great it is."

"What could be wrong? You're down at the shore. No more school and now you're going to a party."

John tried not to act like such a downbeat. "I guess if you put it that way, it's pretty good."

They picked out four bottles that were inexpensive, but a few notches above rock gut. John carried them to the counter and hurried to get his case. He then carried both cases to the cars.

Dawn spotted the shiny civic. "I see you also have a new car, so how much better can things get?"

John shrugged his shoulders. "I guess they can't get much better than this."

"Well John, it was nice meeting you and I'll see you at the party tonight. Don't drink all that beer before the party."

All John could muster was a feeble, "I won't."

He watched her drive away and felt he had cheated on Kelly. When he went back to the house, he never mentioned Dawn or the party. John and his friends cooked burgers for dinner on the not so clean grill in the small backyard. They hung around and, drank some beer and listened to music. John felt relaxed at last. Maybe this was what he needed, but he knew it would only last for so long. Around 11:00 o'clock his friends decided to invade one of the local bars, but John told them to go without him. He planned to call Kelly and explain more in detail, why he needed a break from everything. He was sitting on the porch with a beer in his hand, listening to Bruce Springsteen sing "Jersey Girl." He was about to press her number, when he realized she never called him.

He thought back to how he had met Kelly at a fraternity party. He stood up, finished his beer and decided not to call Kelly, but go to Dawn's party instead. He took a quick shower and put on a decent shirt, even though he knew nobody would care what he looked like.

John felt nervous walking into a party, where he only knew one person and that person he hardly knew at all. Why was he doing this? Why was he placing himself in a scene, where the odds were that it would turn out bad? Was he going because he was attracted to Dawn, mad at himself, or mad at Kelly?

He could hear the music and the loud laughter, before he could see the house. Dawn said there would be about twenty people, but there were at least twenty outside on the porch and in front of the house. Now that he was there, he once again questioned his decision. He walked with his six-pack underneath his arm onto the porch and looked inside the open door. He could not see Dawn, and he felt like an intruder, so he turned around and walked home. He thought, she probably has a boyfriend and he did not want to be in another awkward situation. He also did not want to get his ass kicked, if her boyfriend was some pumped up muscle head. It was much safer to wallow alone in misery. When he returned home, he placed the beer back in the refrigerator and went to bed.

The next day was sunny and hot, so after lunch, they all went down to the beach. The water was cold, because it usually took until July to be considered refreshing instead of numbing. John was slowly easing himself into the ocean. He stood ankle deep in the surf. In a couple of minutes, he would move a little closer to England and then take the full plunge. He found his thoughts always drifting back to Kelly. He was about to go up to his knees, when he heard the words, "Where were you last night?"

He turned, and it was Dawn in a white bikini, which jolted his mind from any other thoughts. She had a perfect body, and she knew it. She was one of the beautiful women one would see at a fancy resort, or at the pool in Las Vegas, not at the Jersey shore.

"I actually did walk over, but when I didn't see you, I just turned around and went back home."

"You should have looked harder. There were a lot of people there. Way more than we had expected."

"So how was the party, anyway?"

"It was good, but some of the guys there were jerks."

"Well I'm sure your boyfriend wouldn't let any of them bother you?"

She gave John a puzzled look bordering on anger and replied, "I don't have a boyfriend now. Why would you assume that?"

John felt trapped. Why did he always say the wrong thing? "I made the assumption that someone as attractive as you would naturally have a boyfriend."

John knew that was wrong the moment it came out of his mouth. Before Dawn could say anything, he quickly tried some damage control. "I know that came out wrong. I'm sorry. That's why I left when I didn't see you. Saying things like that is one of the reasons, I don't have a girl friend now."

Her expression softened and she said, "What are the other reasons?"

"I just recently parted ways with my old girlfriend from college after graduation. She's on her way to law school in Georgetown and I'm in a dump down the shore with no job."

She gave him a knowing look and said, "So that's it. Your not sure you made the right decision, and you feel guilty even talking to another girl."

With a stunned look on his face, John said, "What are you, psychic?"

"No. I can usually read people pretty good. I can tell you're a nice guy."

John relaxed and said, "Well, I won't argue with you on that one."

She stood next to John and bent down to place her hands in the water. John no longer felt the cold water.

She smiled and playfully commented, "So that's why you're acting so non-committal. I can tell you're not sure about breaking up with your girl friend."

John did not want to talk about it with anyone, especially a beautiful woman in a bikini that left nothing to the imagination.

"I'm sorry if it's that obvious, but I have a hard time with change. That's the main reason I'm here for the summer. I want to take time to figure things out, before I make any type of commitment."

"I can understand. At least I believe you. Most guys I meet have a line and one thing on their mind. You seem different, and I like that."

John smiled and said, "I guess I am, but I've been called a lot worse than different. I don't believe in lying about anything. The truth always comes out in the end."

"Since we're in the truth-telling phase, I recently broke up with my boyfriend, and I'm not one bit sorry that I did. Maybe we can trade stories if you feel like talking?"

"That sounds good."

"Why don't you meet me tonight after I get out of work?"

"Where do you work?"

"I'm the hostess at La Catrina's. It's a fancy restaurant and the pay is good."

"What time?"

"I'm there until 11:00. It's on Ocean Avenue just four blocks down."

"Great. I promise not to act so moody."

"I'll hold you to that. I have to get back now. Last night I hardly got any sleep. I'll see you later."

"Definitely."

When Dawn walked away, John sprinted five steps and dove into the cold water. When he resurfaced, he felt refreshed and relaxed. Maybe the summer won't be so bad after all, he thought. After a few minutes of bouncing with the waves, he returned to his blanket with his hands and feet numb, but feeling content. The rest of the crew was there, and Stan started to kid him.

"So who was the hot bikini chick?"

"Her name is Dawn."

Bob started singing a bad karaoke version of the song by the "Four Seasons" with the same name.

"Dawn, go away, I'm no good for you."

Stan threw his two cents in.

"What did she think, you were lost? Standing there all by yourself with that lost puppy dog look on your face?"

John was a bit embarrassed and angry when he retorted, "What? Are you losers jealous? You're over here squirting suntan lotion on each other and you wonder why no girls come over."

Carl squirted some lotion at John and said, "Does she have any friends?"

"She has a house with a few other girls a few blocks from us. I met her yesterday in the liquor store and I'm meeting her later tonight after she gets out of work."

"I guess she made you forget about Kelly. I'd forget about everything if I had a chance with her."

John sat down in his beach chair and mumbled, "We'll see what happens."

John reached over and grabbed a beer out of the cooler, breaking the no alcohol allowed rule of the beach ordinance.

For the rest of the day, John tried to figure out what to do about Dawn. This was not the way he had expected to begin the summer. He was perfectly content to be alone and mope. He needed some time to determine if things could ever be salvaged with Kelly. Now he had a date, and he felt guilty, but he had to admit that he was attracted to Dawn.

***

He kept staring at the front entrance of the restaurant. He was early, which only made him feel more like a pathetic cheating dog. "Maybe she'll change her mind and sneak out the back door, " he thought. An older couple walked out of the restaurant with Dawn a few feet behind, wearing a short black skirt and a white blouse, which was striking against her bronze skin. When she spotted John, she ran up smiling and gave him a quick kiss on the cheek.

"I wasn't sure you would show."

"I said I would, and I wouldn't stand you up two nights in a row."

In a cheerful voice, Dawn said, "So where do you want to go?"

"It doesn't matter to me. Let's jut walk along the boardwalk for awhile and talk."

"Sure. It's a nice night and it's not too late."

John felt comfortable and he tried to suppress his guilty feelings.

After walking a few silent yards, Dawn asked, "So tell me about yourself. Where you live, what you like etc..."

John shuffled a few steps and looked around, stalling for some ingenious words to suddenly erupt from his mind that would make him sound interesting,

"There's not to much to tell. I grew up in Westfield. I played baseball in high school and college. I graduated from Lehigh with a currently worthless degree in economics and now I'm here taking the summer off."

Dawn laughed, "Yes that was really the abbreviated version."

John retorted, "Well, how about you. Tell me a little about yourself."

Dawn did not hesitate. "I live in Fort Lee. I just turned twenty-one and I'm going into my senior year at Rutgers. I have two older brothers, who are bigger than you and are very protective of their little sister."

John laughed. "I think the little sister can take care of herself."

She tried to sound serious when she replied, "You better believe it. I played on the soccer team and I was on the gymnastics team until I hurt my knee."

"How did you hurt it?"

"It was a dismount from the balance beam and I landed badly and tore my knee up. That ended my soccer career too."

"That's too bad. My dream was to play center field for the Yankees, but there were no offers from any team so my baseball career is officially ended with no injuries except to my ego."

"I bet you have a lot of good memories."

"I do, and I wouldn't trade them for anything."

"So we both have something in common."

"What's that?"

"We're both over the hill athletes, who now like to party down at the shore."

They passed by a club that did not look too crowded, so John asked, "Do you want to stop and have a drink?"

"Sure."

It was a Sunday night, and most of the weekend tourists had left hours ago, driving north on the Garden State Parkway, cursing the traffic, but making plans to do it again next weekend. When they entered, it was spacious, but there was nothing special about the set up. On the right, tables were spread out around a parquet dance floor. A small stage stood in the back with a sign for the men's room on one side and ladies on the other. The bar and kitchen occupied the left side. The house band was not playing at the moment, but there was music from a D.J. John was not sure if he picked the right spot for a first date. Dawn appeared relaxed and in a good mood. She soon confirmed his suspicion that she would not be the one to hold anything back. "It feels good to sit down and not have to seat anyone."

"I bet it does."

"I just started and I don't know if I can last the whole summer."

John replied, "This is my first weekend here and I don't know if I can last the whole summer either."

"Why should you have anything to worry about?"

John remembered he had to sound upbeat. "Let's order a drink and forget I said that."

She agreed, but he knew she would not.

A perky young waitress approached the table. John knew the law was that she had to be over twenty-one, but she looked more like a high school junior.

Dawn ordered a glass of white wine and John a beer. Dawn continued the often-contrived new relationship banter.

"So how does it feel to be a college graduate and not have to go back to school anymore?"

"It's pretty scary. When you're in school, nobody questions you about anything other than your major. If I'm asked what I'm doing now, I have to answer either nothing; or I'm taking the summer off, which is just another way of saying nothing."

"I never thought of it that way, but I can see your point."

The drinks arrived and Dawn proposed a toast. "Here's to a great summer and a great future."

John smiled and felt at ease with Dawn. They lightly clinked glasses and each partook of the obligatory mouthful. He thought back to his last toast with Kelly and felt a twinge of guilt and remorse. He quickly decided not to dwell on the past, but live in the moment.

"What's your major?"

"It's psychology."

John could not suppress a laugh.

In an irritated voice, Dawn asked, "What's so funny about that?"

John turned serious and said, "I've been saying to myself that I need a psychiatrist, and now I meet one."

"I'm a long way off from treating people, but why do you think you need one?"

"Because I can't adapt to change, and I have trouble making a commitment."

"That's not so unusual. The unusual part is that you acknowledge it."

"I could probably be in a case study of people afraid of commitment."

"Is that what happened with your girlfriend?"

"That was a factor, but mostly stupidity on my part. I took things for granted and just assumed they would go on like that forever and I ignored the changes I knew were coming."

"Maybe you both knew it was time to part."

"You could be right."

"Did she try to talk you out of breaking up?"

John did not know how to respond, so he took the non-committal way out by answering, "Not too hard."

"See, maybe I am right. You shouldn't feel so guilty about it. Maybe you need some time apart to figure things out."

John smiled. "You're going to make one hell of a doctor."

"Right now I'm no different than a bartender listening to one of his customers."

At that moment John did feel like a patient on a couch. "For some reason I feel comfortable talking to you about it. I really never even discussed it with my friends."

Dawn finished her wine and said, "Do you want to order another round?"

"Sure. I have nowhere to go until Labor Day."

One-Way Elevator

After the fourth round, Dawn said, "Let's dance."

There was music playing, but the dance floor was empty. John gave an initial protest. "I'm not much of a dancer and we would be the only ones out there."

"So what? You can do anything you want until Labor Day."

In one respect, John was glad it was a slow song, because his dance moves were robotic at best, but on the other hand he felt uncomfortable holding someone else close.

She took his hand and led him to the center of the floor while "Unchained Melody" softly played.

Dawn pulled him close and placed her head against his chest. He forgot about Kelly and enjoyed the moment. He realized how lucky his was to meet a girl like Dawn, but he did not know how to proceed. When the music stopped, she did not pull away. He could tell she was a little unsteady on her feet. She whispered, "Can you take me home now?"

John softly replied, "Whatever you want."

It was one o'clock in the morning when they left. It was a clear, starlit night. The moon was at three quarters, and the sound of the waves and the white foam invading the beach made John feel connected, even though he was only a small speck floating in the infinite universe. The universe had to follow laws of physics in order to exist, and John had to follow a different set of rules in order to exist in his world. At the moment, Dawn was fighting the law of gravity and proving the geometric theorem in a negative way, that the shortest distance between two points is a straight line.

"I'm so glad I met you at the liquor store, " Dawn softly said as she walked with John's arm around her waist.

"I'm glad too."

"I hope we can become good friends, and even though I never met your old girl friend, I hope you forget about her."

John knew it was the alcohol and not Dawn talking, but he replied, "You're making it easy for me."

She stopped, turned, kissed him and asked, "Does that make it any easier?"

John blurted out, "Yes it does," but he regretted saying it so quickly.

She looked up and her only response was, "Good."

When they reached her house, the lights were on and three of her roommates were watching television.

When they walked into the living room, Dawn yelled, "Hey everybody, this is John." She then pointed at the girls one at a time and said, "This is Pat, Jane, and Sarah."

With an embarrassed look, John acknowledged the trio and said, "Nice to meet you."

"We were wondering were you were," Sarah remarked, "And now we know what happened."

John felt awkward and knew the sorority trio was judging him, and it brought back memories of the night he met Kelly. He suddenly felt he had to get out.

He looked at Dawn and said, "It's getting late and I better get going. It's been a long day for you."

"I'm not tired. Why don't you stay?"

"Not tonight. I think you need to get some rest. "

John could not believe the similarities of his first night with Dawn and Kelly. He did not take advantage of Kelly and he did not want to take advantage of Dawn. That was not totally true, because a part of his body was urging him on.

Dawn began to protest louder, but John led her to the couch next to her friends, gave her a kiss on the forehead and said, "Give me your number and I'll call you tomorrow."

She grudgingly agreed and John recorded it into his cell phone bank.

He wrote his on a piece of paper that was on the end table, handed it to Dawn and said, "Goodnight everyone. It was nice to meet you," and walked out the door.

On the way home he was tempted to give Kelly a call, but refrained, because he knew if he did he would say something stupid and regret it. He thought the best course was to go slow and not rush anything with Dawn and see what happened.

After John left, the girls were cackling about him, and Dawn told them all to go to hell and went to bed. The next day around noontime his phone rang. It was Dawn with a cheerful voice.

"Hi John. How are you feeling today?"

"I'm fine."

"That's good. I hope I didn't get too drunk last night and say or do anything stupid."

"No, not at all. I had a great time."

"Can I stop over your house? I'm not feeling that great, but I have to get some air."

"Sure. That would be great. I hope you don't mind seeing a big mess."

After the initial crossing of the threshold, Dawn spent most of her time at John's house and they were inseparable. The intervals between thoughts of Kelly grew longer the more time he spent with Dawn, but they were not entirely erased. The days quickly passed and he related to one of his favorite Bruce Springsteen songs, "Jersey Girl." He loved to sit on the porch at night and listen as Bruce sang,

"Cause down the shore everything's all right
You and your baby on a Saturday night
You know all my dreams come true
When I'm walking down the street with you "
John sang along with one of the verses.
"Nothing matters in the whole wide world
When your in love with a jersey girl."

***

John woke up in a panic. A few weeks until Labor Day and then what was he going to do? He knew he had to start looking for a job, but there were always reasons to delay and procrastinate. It was a beautiful beach day. Dawn was coming over, and he and Dawn were going to continue to use up the world's supply of sunscreen. John was lying in the sand, while the sands of time were quickly draining out of the hourglass. That afternoon while walking together along the beach, John admitted his dilemma.

"I have to look for a job, and I just can't seem to get started"

Dawn beamed a smile and responded in an excited voice, "I was wondering, when you were going to start. I didn't want to ask, because I didn't want to upset you."

"You're so considerate that's why we make such a good couple."

Dawn did not react to John's last statement. "I have an uncle who works in some financial company in the World Trade Center. Maybe he can find you a job?"

John stopped short, grabbed Dawn's arms and said, "You would do that for me? If I got a job there, I would be forever in your debt."

Dawn untangled hers arms and in a playful voice said, "That's the way it should be anyway."

John looked intently at her and said, "This has been one of the best summers in my life so far."

Dawn faked indignation when she replied, "What do you mean, *one* of the best summers. It should be the best summer you'll ever have."

John pulled her close. "It has been the best summer I can remember. I'm so glad we met."

"So am I, but things don't have to end on Labor Day."

They slowly separated and continued walking. John said, "I don't want us to end, but I'll definitely miss being here."

"It will be an adjustment, but I think we can handle it."

John stopped short, and in a panicky voice said, "If I get a job, I'm only going to have two weeks vacation. I don't think I can adjust to that."

"Welcome to the real world," Dawn replied in a sarcastic voice, "But just think of all the money you'll have working in finance."

John sighed. "What good is it, if I don't have any time to spend it?"

"You can always spend it on me."

"So now the truth comes out. You're after me for my money."

"Get out of here! If I was looking for someone with money, I would have ignored you, when I saw you buying cheap beer."

John picked her up in his arms and ran into the water. They were both knocked over by a huge wave, but John did not let her go. A second later when they surfaced, John expected Dawn to be angry, but she was laughing.

***

John was thinking less and less about Kelly, and he knew Dawn was the reason. He still had feelings for Kelly, but he knew he was infatuated with Dawn. He was sitting on the front porch, when his cell phone rang and he froze for a moment, staring at the number displayed.

He answered warily, "Hi Kelly "

Kelly responded in a bubbly enthusiastic tone. "Hi John. How have you been? I missed you."

John forced the obligatory reply. "I missed you too."

Kelly continued as if nothing had happened. "So what have you been doing all summer?"

"Hanging around doing a lot of nothing. It's gone by so fast."

"It sure has. I've been so busy with my job; I haven't had time for anything else."

"When do you start law school?"

"The Wednesday after Labor Day. I'm getting nervous."

"You have nothing to be nervous about. You'll do fine. Me, I'm in a panic now that summer is ending. I have to find a job."

"I'm sure you'll have no problem."

"I got a lot of money for graduation and now it's quickly draining away."

Kelly replied in an energized tone, "I've made a lot of money this summer, but I'll need it for expenses once school starts."

The conversation then turned more serious, when Kelly said, "I feel bad the way we left things the night before graduation."

John had to respond. "I do too. I didn't expect it to go the way it did."

Kelly broke the momentary silence. "I'd like to see you. Maybe we can try to have that conversation again. Maybe this time it will end better."

John was not sure how to respond. He did not want to lie to Kelly, but he hesitated to tell her about Dawn. "I don't know how it would end, if we tried again. I don't want it to end with an argument."

Kelly sounded almost apologetic. "I know it won't. I've replayed that last night so many times in my head, that I'm not even exactly sure what happened."

John did not need an additional complication at this time. "I've thought about it too and maybe it is one of those things that just happened and nobody can pinpoint why. I can't believe three months have gone by."

Kelly continued, "I'd like to see you before I start school."

John panicked. Once again, he could not believe the words flowing out of his mouth. "If you want to come to the beautiful Jersey Shore, that would be great." In the beginning of the summer he felt like he was cheating on Kelly with Dawn, now the roles were reversed. *Why do I make things so difficult*, he thought?

In an excited voice, Kelly said, "Just tell me when you are free and I'll be there."

John attempted humor, which was always his diversionary tactic. "Let me check my busy calendar. I have nothing scheduled for the foreseeable future, so whenever you want to come. It's up to you."

"You'll have to give me good directions. I've never been to Point Pleasant. I'll come next Thursday and stay until Saturday. Then I have to finish packing for school."

John did not like what he was doing; yet he could not help himself. He had loved Kelly and now he was in love with Dawn, or thought he was in love with her, until he heard Kelly's voice again. Dawn would be back at school and then she was going to come down late in the day on Saturday. If things went smoothly, Kelly would be gone by then and neither would know what a creep he was. He wondered if he was capable of the charade.

***

John took a crack at making the place look presentable, but quickly realized the only way it would look good, is if one were actually on crack. He was on his own. There was nobody else to bail him out. What should he say when she pulled up? It was a little easier lying on the phone than face to face. Should he kiss her, shake her hand, or just grab her bag and run in the house? This is no way to live, he thought. He would be better off playing ball, because it was only a game. What he was doing had serious consequences, and whatever he decided would have collateral damage.

It was hot and she was late. John sat on the porch and his perspiring was more from nerves than the heat. A blue Chevy Camaro pulled in front of the house, and when Kelly saw John she beeped the horn. John quickly ran down to the street to greet her. When she exited the car, she gave him a hug and a kiss on the cheek, which solved the first on his problems.

"It's great to see you again," she exclaimed like two old friends who have been apart for a long time. It looks like life on the beach suits you well."

"It's great to finally see you again. You look great. This is the first summer we won't be talking about our schedules for the fall semester."

Kelly faked a frown and said, "I still have a schedule. It's going to take me some time to adjust to law school."

"You'll have no problem. Let me grab your bag and I'll show you the mansion I've been living in."

When he carried her bag inside, he avoided the second and bigger problem by leaving her bag in the living room and not bringing it to any bedroom.

"The place is cute. I actually expected worse."

"This is the American dream. Go to school for seventeen years and wind up unemployed living in a shack down at the Jersey Shore."

Kelly laughed. "I have no doubt that one day you'll be a big success with a big job in New York City."

"I may have to work in the city. That's where the good jobs are, but I don't know how I'll put up with all the noise and congestion. I'm accustomed to the sound of the waves, not the subways. I like a crowded beach, not a crowded street. I like lifeguards, not cops."

"Boy, the Jersey Shore has turned you into an anti-social beach bum."

John smirked. "Yes, Jimmy Buffet is my new hero. It's sad to admit, but he's replaced Mickey Mantle. They both have one thing in common, which is alcohol. Jimmy likes to sing about it, and Mickey liked to drink it."

They had lunch on the porch, which consisted of a sub sandwich John had bought earlier, and a beer.

After lunch John said, "Get on your bathing suit and let's go to the beach. We can make margaritas later and listen to Jimmy Buffet songs."

"I'll go to the beach and drink margaritas, but I draw the line at Jimmy Buffet."

John faked disappointment. "How could you not like Jimmy Buffet?"

"It's easy, if you just listen to a few of his songs."

There was an awkward moment when Kelly asked, "Where should I change?"

John attempted to act nonchalant and replied, "Anywhere you want. It doesn't matter to me."

"What if I want to change right here?"

John quickly responded, "That's okay with me."

Kelly smiled seductively and said, "You haven't changed that much."

Kelly rolled her suitcase to the empty bedroom on the first floor and they both left the sleeping arrangements to be considered at a later time.

Her blue two-piece bathing suit was modest, but she looked great. It was not as revealing as Dawn's, but sometimes the imagination was better than the real thing.

It was a beautiful beach day despite the humidity. The sky was a picture perfect blue with a few white puffy clouds to supply more contrast. The waves were a good size, but the water was not choppy. Kelly loved the water, and she and John did some serious body surfing. When they were sitting in their beach chairs, it was as if they never had separated. John could see that she was enjoying herself.

She looked at John and said, "I can see why you wanted to stay here all summer. If I had known it was this nice, I would have come down sooner and quit my boring clerk job."

"Some people think I'm lazy, but this may be the only summer in my life that I could do this. It's all part of my revised master plan."

"And what is your new master plan?"

"I don't know, but this is part of it."

Kelly laughed and squirted him with the tube of sunscreen. There were a few white gobs on his shoulder and chest.

"So this is how you treat your gracious host?"

She knelt down next to him and said, "Let me rub it in."

John closed his eyes. "I could never refuse that. You know how important it is to have the proper amount of protection from the sun."

She slowly rubbed her hands over his shoulders like a masseuse and then moved her hands slowly down his chest.

John was enjoying her advances, but could not forget about Dawn.

"I bet you never had sun block applied like that?"

John straightened up in his chair. "No, but if you want you could apply it like that even in December."

Kelly pushed him over in his chair and said jokingly, "Just like a guy who's been alone for too long."

Then it clicked. Kelly was attempting to find out if he'd been with another girl in her round about way. Should he tell her now or later?

John decided to kick the can down the road. "I guess so."

The afternoon went by quickly and they went back to shower and change for dinner.

"Do you have any food to cook?" Kelly asked, already knowing the answer.

"What are you kidding? I'm taking you out tonight. You're on vacation. No cooking."

"That's fine with me. What type of restaurant?"

"How about seafood? I know a good place. It's not fancy but the food is good."

John started singing Jimmy Buffet's Margaritaville: "Livin on sponge cake. Watching the sun bake. All of those tourists covered in oil. Strummin my six string. On my front porch swing. Them old shrimp is starting to boil. "

Kelly screamed, "One more verse and I'll put my head in the oven."

When they entered the Neptune Inn, Kelly was feeling no pain due to the bottle of wine she had consumed after showering. He had to worry about what he would do in the future, but his immediate problem was what to do about Kelly. The place was crowded and the service was slow. It was a small restaurant with dark brown worn wooden floors. The tables were close together and the lighting was bad, but the quality of the food more than made up for any lack of ambiance. They ordered the shrimp cocktail as an appetizer, with a glass of wine for Kelly and a beer for John.

Kelly laughed and said, "I hardly drank over the summer."

In a half joking sarcastic voice John replied, "Well I guess you're making up for it tonight."

Kelly gave a seductive smile and in a sexy voice replied, "Maybe we can make up for some other things too?"

She rubbed his leg with her foot under the table. John was torn between Kelly and Dawn. He had to be honest, because he would never be able to have a relationship with two women at the same time. It was hard enough dealing with one. John decided to enjoy the dinner and wait for a more appropriate time, knowing there would never be one.

They each ordered a dinner of shrimp and scallops. The meal was excellent and it seemed like old times.

Kelly remarked, "The food here is better than our old place back at school."

John laughed and said, " If we were living down here, this would be our new place."

Kelly suddenly turned serious, "How come you never called me all summer?"

John was caught off guard, but quickly responded, "I wasn't sure if you wanted me to call."

"Of course I did. Were there other reasons you didn't call?"

Here it comes thought John. Kelly suddenly looked like a prosecuting attorney on the attack.

"No. I just bummed around all summer."

Kelly gave a wary look and replied, "So you haven't met other girls all summer?"

"No. I didn't say that. I said I just bummed around."

Now she was toying with him, but digging for information. "So you did meet other girls?"

John tried to parry the assault with a joke. "How could any girl resist me? A college graduate with no job and no prospects, who has to go home and live with his parents after Labor Day."

The waitress came to the rescue and asked, "Do you want any coffee or dessert?"

They both declined, and John asked for the check.

When they were outside, Kelly took John's hand and said, "I'm sorry if I seem like I'm prying."

"No need to apologize. I often wondered what you were doing all summer too. I figured you probably met someone else and I would fade into your memory like an old picture stuffed in a drawer."

"No. I didn't go out with anyone else over the summer." She then laughed and said, "But this old guy whose been with the firm about fifty years kept on following me around and asking if I needed any help."

"See what I mean. How could I compete with a rich mature lawyer?"

"'Mature', if you mean one foot in the grave."

John decided that this was the appropriate time. "I could never keep anything from you when we were going out, so I'm not going to start now."

Kelly looked puzzled and in a hesitant voice replied, "What do you mean?"

"What I mean is that I haven't told you everything about my summer."

Kelly stopped short. "I don't know if I want to hear this."

John squeezed her hand, and they continued walking with John staring straight ahead. "I met a girl who was renting a house a few blocks away and we've been hanging out most of the summer."

Kelly did not seem shocked, but she had hoped there was nobody else. The alcohol did not make it any easier to speak. "I'm glad you told me. You don't have to feel like you were cheating on me. The way we left it, there were no strings attached."

"It wasn't easy for me to be with another girl after you."

Kelly felt a surge of anger and jealously, but she knew John really did nothing wrong.

"Well at least you told me the truth. Where is she now?"

"She's going back to school."

"Does she know about me?"

"I told her all about us and she understood why I was reluctant to get involved with anyone else."

In a dejected voice, Kelly replied, "But you did."

John suddenly felt guilty. "Yes, but now that you're here, it feels like old times again."

Kelly continued with her woman-scorned persona when she said, "But it can never be the same, and it was stupid of me to even come here to see you."

"No it wasn't. I'm glad you're here." John led her to a bench on the boardwalk looking out at the ocean.

"I was happy to be here until a few minutes ago. Maybe it would have been better if you lied to me."

"That would have been the easy way out, but I couldn't do that to you."

"That's why I can't be mad at you, because you're so honest."

"I have to admit, I didn't plan to tell you until tomorrow, but it doesn't matter now."

Kelly leaned over and kissed him on the mouth and said, "I wish we could turn the clock back. Maybe things would be different now." The memories of how they were came flooding back, but he had to build a dam in his mind to block the flow.

John repeated one of his over-used baseball analogies, "Too bad it's not like a baseball game where yesterday you lost a game, but today you start out with another nine innings."

Kelly stood up. "I'm sick of your stupid baseball comparisons. Let's go back. I'm tired and I know I'm pretty drunk."

They walked home in relative silence. John's mind was racing and he could see that Kelly's stride had no swagger and her steps were a bit unsteady. When they entered the house, Kelly headed straight for the bathroom and then went straight to the bedroom on the first floor. John sat on the couch and stared blankly at the images on the television, while he wondered what to do. He must have fallen asleep, because when he woke up with a stiff neck, it was 1:00 AM. He quickly turned off the television and went to bed. He wondered how Kelly was, but he dared not go into her room. He thought to himself, " I should have known this was a bad idea. It's ridiculous that we haven't seen each other and now that we have, we're both miserable. I guess I can't blame her for reacting the way she did. I feel like an idiot. I forgot how much I really care for her and maybe I shouldn't have started anything with Dawn. "

John slept upstairs, but in the middle of the night he felt Kelly slide into bed and put her arm around his waist. It felt right, but he kept still as if asleep. He wanted to roll over and kiss her, but he fought to control his desire. When he woke up in the morning, the bed was empty. He raced downstairs and the door to her room was open. Kelly was nowhere to be seen. He called her name and walked into the room. The bed was made and her suitcase was gone. He ran outside and her parking space was empty. He suddenly felt alone and angry with himself. "Whatever chance we had to get back together is gone now," he thought. "I think this was worse than our last night at college."

He dejectedly walked back inside. He saw a note on the kitchen table. He quickly picked it up and read.

Dear John,
I was so glad to see you and I guess I was only naïve to think that we could be together like the old days. I guess you moved on quicker than I did. I'm glad you did not lie to me. You were always honest to a fault. Now I can start a new school in a new city with a no strings attached. I was hoping things would have turned out different, but maybe it is for the best. If you're ever in Washington, give me a call.
Love, Kelly

He felt like ripping up the paper and he wanted to be angry with her, but he knew everything was his fault. He carefully folded the paper and placed it in the back of his wallet. He felt like he had no purpose. He wondered if he had blown the best thing that happened to him. He still had Dawn, but it was not the same. It was the end of the summer, and he felt it was the end of the road, even though he was only twenty-two. Very soon he would have to move back with his parents for the foreseeable future. After being away for four years, it would be an excruciating adjustment. His mind was in turmoil, and he felt lost.

"How long will it take me to find a job and be able to move out on my own? I hope Dawn's uncle can set up an interview. That would be great, but then how would that impact our relationship? Why is everything so complicated? Is that all there is to life, one complication after another? Everybody always says I have my whole life ahead of me and I can be anything I want, but what if I don't know what I want? What if I take a job and get stuck there and never find out what I want to be until it's too late and I look back at my life with regret? It doesn't feel like the start of my life. It feels more like two outs in the bottom of the ninth and I have two strikes."

Kelly felt like such a fool. How could she think that John would wait for her? How could she have thought that things could be just as they were, after three months of no contact? Maybe it was not serious with the other girl. Maybe he would realize that he still loved her. The tears streamed down Kelly's face and it was difficult to see the road, even though the skies were clear. Maybe they both tried too hard to recapture the spark, only to watch it slowly extinguish itself. She knew she had her whole life ahead with a bright future, but why did she feel so empty?

***

Before going to the beach, John had worked on revising his resume which he thought was pretty pathetic, but he tried not to let it depress him any more than he already was. He bought the New York Times and The Star Ledger and continued his search for the Holy Grail.

One-Way Elevator

Most of the jobs listed wanted experience, but there were a few management trainee positions that looked promising. He realized that he should have been looking for a job, when several companies held recruitment days near the end of the semester. He'd scoffed at applying, since he was taking the summer off. What a mistake that was. Now the only thing he had to show was a tan that would soon fade away, and the start of a beer belly which would be much harder to discard. He was glad none of his friends were coming until Saturday.

In the afternoon, he went to the beach and mainly slept in his chair under the shade of his umbrella. He tried to sort his mess of a life out. Should he tell Dawn that Kelly had been here? What would she think? After the way Kelly reacted when he told her about Dawn, he decided against it.

"I really like Dawn, but is it only a summer fling? What will happen when she goes back to school? I guess I could be out of the picture. I better not upset her, because she may be the best shot I have of landing a job. I hope her uncle comes through. That would be great to work in the World Trade Center. I was never even inside. I've also never been to the top of the Empire State Building. I haven't seen too many places, because I've spent most of my time confined to the dimensions of whatever field I was playing on, or classroom I was sitting in. The World Trade Center would be a pretty good place to start my career."

He thought of his future retirement date of 2044, jumped off his chair and ran into the ocean ignoring the crashing waves.

***

Dawn returned unexpectedly on Friday night and he was so glad to see her.

After a quick hello kiss, she asked, "So what did you do down here all by yourself?"

"Nothing much. I just hung around and looked for a job after I updated my resume."

His mind was reeling. What would he have done if Kelly had not gone home? They would have teamed up and killed him and covered up the murder. He would now be floating with the ocean currents and food for the fish.

"That's great. I did speak to my uncle about you and he said he'll see what he can do."

John smiled. "I don't know what I'd do without you."

With a gleeful look on her face and in a taunting voice Dawn replied, "Just remember you are gonna owe me big time."

"Am I destined to be your indentured servant?"

Dawn failed at keeping a straight face. "That sounds just about right."

"If that's the case, this better be the job of a lifetime."

Dawn turned serious. "You never know."

The next morning, they went down to the beach, but all John could think of was walking the same path with Kelly. They applied sun block on each other, but John tried to imagine Kelly rubbing his shoulders and back. They went in the water where Kelly had no fear, while Dawn was more cautious.

"I'm all screwed up," John thought. "Why do I feel guilty being with a beautiful girl on the beach? Why can't I just enjoy the moment and not worry about complicated relationships?"

When they returned from the beach, his friends were there and Dawn went back to her place.

"Labor day weekend," Stan mused.

"Don't remind me," retorted John in an irritated voice.

Bob chimed in. "How come you're in such a bad mood? Girl trouble?"

"Nope. Unless I come up with a hit song like Jimmy Buffet, my days as a beach bum are over."

"You're no musician," chided Stan.

"Well, I don't consider Jimmy Buffet a musician and he built a whole career on one stupid song."

"Maybe you can write a book and call it *Lost Down The Jersey Shore*."

"I don't think so. I checked my bank account last week and it's pretty pathetic. Almost all of my graduation money is gone and what do I have to show for it?"

One-Way Elevator

In a joking voice, Stan said, "You have Dawn, even though I don't know what she sees in you."

John did not take the comment as a joke. "Fuck you, Stan. You have a job and some money, but you're a nerd." John stormed off to his room and then to the shower. After the shower John apologized to Stan, but they both knew it was not sincere. Stan knew John was feeling down, so he let it slide although the comment did hurt.

John sat down and once again scoured the want ads and found a few more companies to send his resume. He was reading an advertisement for a bartender's school and was seriously considering applying when Dawn walked in. She could immediately sense that something was wrong, but she was afraid to say anything to John. They'd had a great summer and she did not want anything to ruin it.

In a cheerful tone she asked, "How's it going?"

"Would you still go out with me, if I were a bartender with a college degree?"

"That bad, huh?"

"My hundred thousand dollar degree has done me a lot of good."

"Well I have some good news."

In a monotone voice John replied, "Go ahead. I'm listening."

"My Uncle just called and he knows of a job opening and he can get you an interview."

John immediately perked up. "That's great. When's the interview?"

"My uncle said the guy is away next week, so he set it up for 9:00 on September 11th."

John laughed and said, "That's pretty ironic. My first job interview is on 911. That's an emergency to me."

Dawn was not amused and said, "It's only a date. There's no significance to it."

"There will be, because that's the day I will land my first job and start my long successful career in the world of high rolling finance."

"Don't jump ahead of yourself. Just get the job first."

John had a momentary look of disappointment on his face, but perked up and said, "You're right, but don't be surprised if your uncle isn't reporting to me five years from now."

In a sarcastic voice, Dawn quipped, "Get out of here. Let's go for a walk on the beach. Maybe that will bring you back to reality."

John put his arms around her, pulled her close and said, "I feel great. It will take more than watching a few waves to replace this moment."

Dawn kissed him. "I wish it never had to end."

Chapter 5

It was Tuesday, September 11th. The sky was clear blue and the warmth of the summer lingered, not yet ready to fade into fall. John woke up before his alarm after a restless nights sleep.

"I better not blow this interview, " he thought as he stood in the shower faced with the reality of trekking to the city instead of the beach.

He nicked his face shaving and now wished he had never taken the summer off.

"If I began looking for a job back in May, I wouldn't be in this situation now. I would probably be complaining about my job, but that's ten times better than looking for one. What am I going to say, if I'm asked what I did this summer? I can't say I spent nearly three months in a drunken stupor. I can't say I never even read a book or a newspaper, except for the want ads. Maybe that question won't come up. The only thing I have going for me is that I wasn't arrested for drinking or drugs."

He dressed in a dark blue suit with a red-striped tie. He had his hair cut the day before, and he smiled at himself in the full-length mirror in his bedroom. His face was tanned and the sun had lightened his hair. He'd had a great time that summer, but with the drinking and bad diet, it probably took about ten years off his life. John now resembled a young republican - ready to make a lot of money working for an investment company, avoiding taxes, and complaining about the size of government and all the programs for the needy.

"Life was so much easier down at the shore. The tide went in, the tide went out. If it was sunny, you went to the beach and drank and if it rained, you stayed in and drank. No pressure. I didn't have to impress anyone, unless it was a girl I just met on the beach or in a bar. Now I have to impress some stranger, who knows nothing about me, other than my experience-challenged resume. Instead of responding to the question, "How's the water?" I have to explain where I see myself five years from now. I'd like to answer; 'I have an economics degree not a crystal ball. How the hell do I know?' If I am asked why I chose economics, I'll tell him that Alan Greenspan is my role model and I want to be head of the Federal Reserve one day, because I'd like to talk in vague terms and have everyone think I am a genius like Greenspan, when in reality most of what he said was truly only vague."

John had to catch a 7:30 train that would arrive in Newark at 8:00. He then had to switch to the PATH train, which would deliver him to the depths of the World Trade Center around 8:30, if he made the right connection. He wanted to be in the office fifteen minutes early. He knew it would be ten times worse than sitting in the waiting room at the doctor's or dentist's office.

"I guess it is better than getting my prostate checked or a root canal, but at the moment it's close."

He stood on the platform and watched the regulars read a newspaper, book or stare aimlessly down the track; waiting for the first glimpse of the same train that came at the same time every day to take each person to the same place, until that retirement date down the track and out of sight.

"Is this what I am destined to become? Forty years from now, will some kid my age look at me and say to himself, 'I don't want to end up like that?' Will I continue to perpetuate the pattern of graduating, working, making money and buying things I really don't need?"

He concentrated his gaze on a well-dressed man approximately sixty years old with deep wrinkles in his forehead, thinning grey hair, slumped shoulders and a little paunch pushing his white shirt over his belt. He shuddered to think that he could be that man in forty years. He wondered if the man has a wife and kids. Did he have to struggle to send his kids to college? Did he want to retire already, but could not because he never put enough money in his 401k plan? How many hours had he spent commuting over the years? How many newspapers had he read and how many cups of coffee had he consumed on the train? John had no idea what he really wanted to do with his life, but he did not want to get stuck in a job and be forced to stay because of the bills or kids, and wind up at his retirement party appearing gracious, but wondering what else he could have done.

John turned away and said to himself, "I have to stop thinking like this. I'm only starting out and watching these people only makes me depressed."

John spotted an attractive girl about his age and thought maybe there were some good points to working after all. She was tall, slender with long blond hair and a tan that required frequent trips to the beach or a tanning salon. Her white blouse and beige skirt contrasted nicely with her skin. Her high heels were stylish, but John questioned how anyone could actually feel comfortable in them. He wondered where she worked and if she took the same train every morning. Maybe he could get lucky and sit next to her. He shook his head and suddenly felt like a stalker. He had Dawn, so why was he even looking at another girl? He continued to struggle with thoughts of Kelly, and he felt like a horrible human being. He had to focus on the job interview. He could not let anything else distract him now.

The train pulled in with every seat occupied, but he was able to stand next to her. John wanted to strike up a conversation with his new attraction, but he could not come up with anything that didn't sound pathetic. For some reason, early morning on the train did not seem an appropriate time.

John knew he was looking for anything to distract him from thinking about the interview. He was nervous, uncomfortable in his new shoes, and fearful of entering a new world. The train gently rocked as it sped down the tracks. He closed his eyes and imagined himself on a boogie board bobbing up and down in the ocean. The conductor tapped him on the shoulder for his ticket. John fumbled in his pocket for a moment before producing the proof. The conductor quickly punched it and moved on to the girl, who flashed a monthly pass. A few minutes later the train pulled into Penn Station, Newark, and everyone emptied out to either transfer to the PATH, or to a connecting train to Penn Station in New York City. John could not help but follow the girl at a safe distance. She kept a good pace taking the stairs instead of the escalator and then crossed the main level and again hustled up the steps to the PATH platform. John was breathing hard when he reached the platform; admitting to himself that he was not in real good shape.

The Path started at Newark, and the last stop was the World Trade Center. The platform was filled, and everyone shuffled forward as the doors opened and jockeyed for seats like musical chairs. The one thing John noticed was that women were treated as equals. He watched as a middle-aged man slid into a seat cutting off a woman about the same age. He quickly realized the survival of the fittest started even before one reached his job. John was standing, but after a quick look around the car, he spotted her sitting between two men. She was reading a book, but he could not see the title. He tried not to stare at her, so he looked out the window, but every minute or so he would find her back in his gaze.

"If the interviewer tries to make small talk and questions my commute, I'll have to lie and say it was fine and leave the stalking part out."

The PATH train finally arrived at the World Trade Center. John felt as though he had already finished a day's work with his commute.

"It is going to be tough to do this every day. No wonder everybody appears in a semi-comatose, robotic state. By the end of my first week, I'm sure I'll be a member of the club."

The escalator from the platform to the main floor was a long ride. He lost sight of her, but in a way he was glad, because he did not want to take the steps. If he did he would collapse, before reaching the top. He felt worse when he realized she did the stairs in her high heels.

***

When Nancy awoke on the morning of 9/11, she was nervous and excited. Nervous, because that night she planned to tell her mother and Phil's parents that she was pregnant, and excited, because she was going to the doctor after work for her three month checkup. As long as everything was good with the baby, she would break the news. Would she also announce that she and Phil were going to be married, or save that for another visit? She could feel her body changing in small ways, but anyone looking at her would never guess that she was three months pregnant. She had read about some models, who only gained ten pounds during the entire pregnancy, but that was not natural. All she wanted was a healthy baby and hoped to be able to lose any weight gain. She wanted so badly to tell someone about it, but they had decided to wait until the three-month date. The stress of keeping this secret was not good for her or the baby, but she felt as if she had no choice. She and Phil also agreed to wait to find out the sex of the baby, until it made its grand entrance.

As if being pregnant weren't stressful enough, planning a wedding on short notice was worse than the morning sickness. She did love Phil, but she was not sure how ready she was for marriage. The timing was not right, but the fact that she was pregnant threw all the laws of timing out the window. Phil said he was ready for marriage, but she questioned if he was only trying to do the right thing. Could a marriage based on doing the right thing last? Could a marriage where the baby was due soon after the honeymoon last with all the added stress of a newborn?

The third pillar of stress she was under was the question of who would take care of the baby, when she went back to work? Her company only allowed six weeks maternity leave. She planned to work until the last possible day, so she could spend more time with her newborn. She never thought about how quickly six weeks could go by. It was so expensive to place a child in daycare. Neither Phil nor Nancy could support a family on one salary. Other countries allow up to a year maternity leave, but the richest country in the world, could only afford six weeks. Everyone said that children were so important, yet it was now considered the norm to allow babies to be raised by strangers in often less than ideal conditions. What happened to the American dream? She turned from the philosophical back to the practical. Should she go alone to her mother's, or bring Phil?

When she went in the shower, she did feel a small bump in her stomach. Feeling that little bump and knowing that it was a new life, made it real, and it frightened her. She now was responsible for another life. Was she ready? Would she be a good mother? Her life would never be the same.

When she walked into the kitchen, she was met with a pleasant surprise. Phil had made her breakfast. There were two plates on the table with eggs, toast, and two glasses of orange juice. Phil was about to fill the cups with decaffeinated coffee.

"Good morning to the two of you," Phil said and went back to barista mode.

Nancy smiled. "Now I know that we are going to make a good family. Thank you so much."

"Today's the big day and we both need to start off with a good breakfast."

"Thinking back to when I got pregnant, if we had started off with a good breakfast instead of what we did, then we wouldn't be in this situation now."

Phil suddenly appeared glum. "Is that what you think this is, a situation?"

"In a way it is. I'm sorry to put it that way, but this is just a lot to handle at once."

"Right, but I think we have everything pretty much under control."

Phil finished pouring the coffee and they both sat down.

Nancy slowly sipped her orange juice. " I think my mother and Ronnie are going to freak out when they hear."

Phil could see she was worried. "So what if they do? They can't change anything."

Nancy looked perplexed, but she continued. "I know how old fashioned they are and my mother will feel like it is her fault."

Phil laughed and said, "I don't think anyone will blame her. I think I have that all to myself."

Nancy then spoke in a serious tone, "If they ask us if we're getting married, let's say we're discussing it and we haven't decided yet."

"Why wait? I don't understand."

Phil stood up and brought his plate over to the sink. Nancy could tell he was upset. In a consoling voice, Nancy replied, "A wedding and a baby in one night is too much for my mother to handle."

"To me that sounds worse than saying we are not getting married. I bet she's going to be more upset at the thought of an unwed mother. Your mother can't handle any change. To her daylight savings time is a horrible event. It's up there with a tornado."

Nancy laughed. "Don't mock my mother. She likes you."

"Will she still like me after she finds out I knocked up her daughter."

"Don't say knocked up. That sounds disgusting. I don't know how Ronnie will take the news. You better hope he doesn't have a few drinks in him, because I may be knocked up, but you'll be knocked out."

"If I see he's a little drunk, I'll wait in the car while you tell them. I'll keep the engine running."

"You'd abandon your future wife and baby at the first sign of danger?"

"I think I can take anything else except Ronnie. I admit he can kick my ass."

Nancy felt a little better knowing she would not have to hide her secret much longer. "So should we keep the wedding a secret from your parents? We're not even officially engaged yet. We still have to decide on a date."

Phil swallowed a piece of bacon and replied, "No. I think they'll be happy after the initial shock wears off. You know how they already treat you like a daughter. Don't worry, because I'm working on the engagement piece."

Nancy then laughed and said, "Well, you better hurry up. When we're married, should I call your parents Mom and Dad?"

Phil paused for a moment and then said, "You know, I never even thought about that. Sure call them Mom and Dad. I'll call your mother, Mom and I'll call Ronnie, Weird brother-in-law."

Nancy cracked up laughing. "I think my mother will be okay with that, but you know Ronnie will beat the hell out of you, if you call him weird."

Phil acted serious and said, "You're right. I'll train the baby to call him weird Uncle Ronnie, who lives with his mother."

Nancy threw a piece of toast at him and said, "What do you have, a death wish?"

***

Phil's plan was to surprise Nancy Friday after work and they would drive down to a bed and breakfast in Cape May, New Jersey. The summer season was over and it would not be crowded, yet it was still warm enough for a walk on the beach. Phil intended to propose to Nancy on the beach. He and Nancy both loved the ocean, and Phil could not think of a better place to make the start of a limitless future with the love of his life official.

Phil played the scene over and over in his mind. The sun would be setting and they would be alone on the beach. The only sounds would be the gentle waves and their footsteps in the sand. Phil would kneel down on one knee, take her hand in his and ask, "Nancy, will you make me the happiest man on earth and marry me, so we can spend the rest of our lives together?"

Nancy would be in a semi state of shock. Even though they both knew they would be married, now that it was finally happening she would not believe it was real.

She would look directly into his eyes and softly respond, "Yes. I will do everything to make our lives together as perfect as possible."

He would slip the ring on her finger and feel in perfect unity with the world.

***

Don woke up, but today he was not tired and felt a surge of energy as he showered and shaved before breakfast. One day closer to retirement was all he could think about. The days were dwindling, and the September 14th finish line was now within his grasp. He was slowly cleaning out his office and slowly transferring his work to his other team members. There were a few projects he wished he could finish, but there were others he was glad to kick down the hall.

"What am I going to do without any deadlines? Now the only boss I'll have is my wife. " He thought of that old Henny Youngman line, "Take my wife, please, " and laughed to himself. No more going to bed on a

Sunday night and dreading Monday morning. He bought the New York Times like every other day and did not mind the dinginess of the subway station. He was not even upset, when the same preacher he had heard many times before walked into his subway car and began his standard sermon.

"I was a crack addict, but luckily I found Jesus. If I didn't find Jesus, I would probably be dead right now. Without Jesus you will die and burn in hell for eternity."

The preacher was an African American with short-cropped hair in his late thirties or early forties. He was not much smaller than Jim and he had a deep powerful voice that served him well on the high decibel subway. He wore a pair of black jeans and a white tee shirt with the words, "Jesus Saves," scrolled across the front and back. Deep creases crisscrossed his forehead along with puffiness under his intense, glaring eyes. His clean-shaven face displayed signs left from his past life, which he carried like a cross. He weighed about two hundred and twenty-five pounds and was an intimidating presence in a crowded subway car.

The subway wheels screeched, and the car rolled like a boat hit by a wave, but the preacher kept on preaching.

"Jesus said, 'I am the way and the resurrection.' If you want eternal salvation, you have to follow Jesus. You can't continue to go through your life ignoring Jesus. You think you have everything going for you, but one day it will all be gone and then, when Jesus questions what you did with your life, what will you say? Did you help the poor? Did you help the needy, or did you just try to accumulate all the wealth you could? Remember, Saint Peter denied Jesus three times before the cock crowed. Will you deny Jesus your whole life? Jesus also said to the apostles, when they fell asleep on the night he was arrested, 'The spirit is willing, but the body is weak.' You have to work hard to help others to make the world a better place, because you and all your material possessions can be gone in an instant. You always have to be prepared for the end. The only way to fully prepare is to follow Jesus. He is the way and the light."

The high-pitched screeching of the wheels could be heard as the subway rounded the bend and pulled into the World Trade Center stop. The doors opened and unleashed the thundering herd from the confines of the subway car to the confines of the office cubicle. Don walked in front of the preacher while exiting and the preacher gave Don a knowing nod. Don instinctively nodded back briefly making eye contact, which was usually something he avoided in the subway.

***

Jim woke up in a bad mood. For some reason Tuesdays were always his worst day. The glow and the memories of vacation seemed like years ago. Mondays never felt that bad, since he was coming off a weekend. It was Tuesday with the reality that there were four full days remaining until the next break. He knew it was not a healthy way to live, but as of right now he did not have much choice. He listened to Howard Stern on his Sony Walkman and forgot about things while Howard and Jackie the Joke Man made stupid jokes like some high school kids, but making more money than most people listening.

People listened because they wanted a diversion from the daily mundane grind. Terri thought he was disgusting, but Jim thought he was really smart. How many people can be paid millions for making sex jokes, bullying people and flirting with the occasional porn star? Yesterday on the show, there had been a man whose sexual perversion made him want a naked woman to puke on him while he was lying in a small, unfilled plastic pool. Jim found nothing erotic about that, so he changed to the classic rock station and listened to, *Stairway To Heaven* for about the three hundred thousandth time.

Jim thought it was ironic that on one station a woman was puking on some pervert, while on another station Robert Plant sang "There's a lady who's sure all that glitters is gold."

***

The main level of One World Trade Center was bustling. John slowly merged and followed the flow. He passed by the many stores and watched as some carried their cups of coffee as if they were sacred

One-Way Elevator

chalices. He had some time, so he walked slowly with no desire to reach his destination. He wanted a job, and yet he was afraid of rejection. He wanted to make money, but did he have the confidence to sell himself like a politician during a campaign? It was only an entry-level position in an investment company. If offered a job, he would take it. Any job and money was more than he had now. The World Bank would have to wait a few years.

Would he go for his M.B.A.? The best approach would have been to continue now, but he could not ask his parents to continue paying. John did not want to be $60,000 in debt for another degree without a guarantee of a job. It would take him at least ten years to pay it off and he would be working for next to nothing. How could he afford his own apartment or anything else with that much debt? Being a bartender and living near the beach looked pretty good at the moment. A sign for one of the stores caught his eye, and he stopped to investigate. "The Store of Knowledge" displayed telescopes, globes, and replicas of the solar system in the window. In addition, there were books on astronomy and various games. It looked like a great place to browse.

John laughed to himself. "If I ever get stuck on a problem at work, maybe I can come down here and find the answer." He looked at his watch and it was 8:35.

He walked to the security desk and nervously mumbled to the guard, "I have an interview at 9:00 with Jason Manning. My name is John Haddler."

The guard called to confirm. Once confirmed, a photo was taken, and then he was given a temporary ID. He looked at the photo, and there was no smile and a look of fear in his eyes.

John asked the guard, "Which elevator bank?"

The guard could sense he was nervous, but he smiled and said, "You just go around the bend and go straight. You can't miss it. Remember, you have to wear your ID at all times while in the building."

"Thank you."

"Good luck on your interview."

John forced a smile. "I'll need it."

It was 8:43 when he turned the corner and headed for the elevator. There was a crowd of people waiting in the bank. A man about forty years old carrying a folder looked agitated and punched the elevator button a few times. He was obviously late for some meeting, or his boss was waiting and probably pissed off.

"Good way to start the day," thought John.

Finally two elevators touched down and opened together. After the few people exited, the waiting mass pushed in. John glanced at his watch and it was 8:45. The elevator was an express. John secured his small patch of space and looked straight ahead waiting for the doors to close. After a few seconds, John glanced at his watch and it was 8:46.

***

For some reason the preacher's words played in his mind. Don had spent his entire life working hard, and now he was about ready to reap the rewards. The words "Everything you have could be gone in an instant," made him suddenly think back to his father. Suddenly the exuberance he felt earlier about retirement, faded away. He walked into the North Tower elevator bank, and watched as some guy hit the elevator button over and over. When the elevator finally came, he was standing next to some young, nervous looking kid, who, Don thought, had so many years ahead until he took his last elevator ride into retirement.

***

When Nancy came out of the subway, she walked around outside the World Trade Center before going to her office. It was warm and the sky was a deep blue with only a few white misshaped clouds. She sat down on one of the benches and stared in awe at the white tower looming over her. From her vantage point, it appeared to go on forever. She felt small and insignificant in its shadow. She had the same feeling, when she stood on a beach with the waves lapping at her feet. She knew she was no longer insignificant with a new life

One-Way Elevator

inside her. Everything else seemed insignificant to that new life. Her appreciation of how much her mother had done and sacrificed for her grew. Her understanding of why her mother was so protective also grew. She now regretted how harshly she sometimes treated her mother. She would try to remember that tonight, if things did not go smoothly. Nancy suddenly glanced at her watch. It was 8:44, and she was late for work. She quickly stood up and walked to the revolving doors and entered her infinite tower. The elevator bank was crowded, and each person was fixated on the elevator doors. Finally one opened and the crowd pushed in. She looked at her watch. It was 8:46.

The doors were about to close when a man came running and yelled, "Hold it please."

Nobody moved, but Nancy reached out to stop the doors, but she was too late. She looked at him and mouthed the words, "I'm sorry," as the doors closed. She wondered why some people were always in a rush. There will always be another elevator.

***

Jim was walking toward the security turnstile, when Art Finch from sales stopped him and asked, "How's Janice?"

Janice was a coworker, who was fighting cancer and undergoing chemotherapy.

"She's hanging in there," Jim responded, "She has a treatment today. She's a fighter."

Art grinned and said, "I know from some of the meetings that's she's tough."

"I'll tell her you were asking about her," Jim said, and swiped his ID badge.

He turned the corner to the elevator bank and saw an elevator door about to close. Jim yelled out, "Hold the door," and lunged forward in an awkward attempt to dive into the nearly overflowing box. Nobody moved, but a young woman stuck out her arm to try to prevent the doors from closing. They hesitated momentarily, but then continued to close.

The woman quickly pulled her arm back and mouthed the words, "I'm sorry."

Jim stood helplessly still as the elevator doors closed, but he could not forget the young woman's apologetic face. "What am I getting upset about? There will always be another elevator."

Suddenly, before the next elevator arrived, the whole building shook. His first thought was a bomb. He remembered the 1993 bombing. How could it be another bomb? They really improved security. Maybe there was a gas explosion in the cafeteria on the 44th floor, but it would have to be a large explosion to shake the whole building.

People were running from the lobby to the outside, where there was a big commotion. All of a sudden one of the elevators crashed to the lobby, the doors flew open and flames shot out. A man standing a few feet away was caught in the flames. Jim pushed the man down and attempted to put out the flames by rolling him on the floor. Jim beat the flames with his briefcase. The man screamed in agony as the flames were extinguished. The man's face and arms were badly burned. The smell of burnt flesh and smoldering cloth permeated the air. A security guard rushed to help as Jim led the man away from the elevator bank. The man was in intense pain and was screaming for help.

Jim tried to calm him down. "They'll get you to a hospital as soon as possible." The man just stared blankly at Jim and groaned.

Another Security Guard rushed over. "We'll take care of him," he said, "You get out of here!"

Jim put his hands on the groaning man and said, "You're gonna be okay," and walked toward the revolving doors.

When he walked outside and looked up, the flames were pouring out the side of the upper floors, and debris was falling and people were scattering.

***

It was about 9:20 when Phil finished cleaning the kitchen and reading the paper. He had worked a double shift and was tired, but he was too

One-Way Elevator

excited to sleep. He walked into the living room and flipped on the television. He was about to sit down, when he heard the reporter's words, "The first plane hit the North Tower at 8:46 and the second hit the south tower at 9:02." He took a panicked step forward and watched in terror as the towers blazed on the screen. He immediately thought of Nancy and as if in a bad dream, he watched the replay of the second plane slamming into the South Tower. His heart pounded as the flames shot out of the towers and the sound of the crashing plane reverberated in his ears.

Now he understood why he heard all the sirens in the background. He dialed Nancy's number at work, but she did not pick up. He quickly dressed and ran outside. He had to make sure Nancy was all right. How could this happen? Who would fly a plane into a building?

He knew he would never get close with his car, so he hailed a cab that was parked near his building and yelled, "Get to the World Trade Center as fast as you can."

The cabbie said, "I can't go down there. Everything is stopped."

"My wife's in that building," Phil shouted, "I have to make sure she's okay! Get me as close as you can."

The cabbie, who was a middle-aged African American said, "I'll try, but I'm sure she's okay."

Phil tapped on the front seat. "Let's go!"

The cab pulled out and sped toward the towers via the Brooklyn Bridge. The traffic was heavy with mainly fire engines and emergency vehicles all heading to the same location. To Phil, it felt like everything was moving in slow motion, but his mind was reeling at warp speed. *She's on the 65th floor. I think the plane hit above her. What about the smoke and the elevators? What if she's trapped?*

"Can't you go any faster?" Phil yelled.

The cabbie knew what Phil had to be going through and replied, "I'm trying. I'll do whatever I can."

He pressed his foot on the accelerator and began weaving through the traffic. A light was about to change from yellow to red, but he floored it and zoomed through the light and onto the bridge. He followed close behind a fire truck with its siren blaring. When the fire truck stopped two blocks away from the towers, Phil grabbed two twenties from his wallet, handed it to the cabbie and took off for the North Tower.

The cabbie yelled, "I hope you find your wife!" He was not even going to charge him for the ride, but he took the money and stuffed it in his shirt pocket.

***

The sound of the phone awakened Alan Haddler in his hotel room in San Francisco. He wearily answered and immediately recognized the hysterical voice.

"Planes have crashed into both World Trade Center towers and I haven't been able to get in touch with John!"

"How could that happen?"

"Turn on the television and see!"

Alan quickly obeyed the order and watched in horror as the flaming towers consumed the screen and the video of the second plane smashing into the South Tower was replayed.

"What time was John's interview?"

"Nine. He was probably in the building when the first plane hit."

"Do you know what floor? The plane hit the upper floors. If he was on a lower floor he should be okay."

"I've been calling, but nothing is getting through."

Alan was about to attempt to convince her that everything would be okay, when the South Tower collapsed. He was frantic and felt helpless three thousand miles away.

"I'll take the next plane I can get."

"All flights are cancelled. No planes are allowed in the air!"

"Goddammit!"

He sat down in a chair and felt as though his heart had been ripped out. The last words he had spoken to John were, "Good luck on your interview." He had to get back home. He had to be there for John. He had to do something.

"I'm going to the airport as soon as I pack. I'll make sure I get on the first plane out."

"I can't handle this by myself. I need you home. I'm going to wait for his call. I'll call you as soon as I hear anything. I love you. Hurry home.

"I love you too. Don't worry. John's probably trying to get back home now."

Alan quickly packed and took one last glance at the flaming screen and rushed to the lobby.

***

Ronnie was working on a building in Jersey City directly across the river from the World Trade Center. He was on a coffee break when the airliner slammed into the North Tower. He saw the flash and the flames shoot from the top floors.

"What the hell was that?"

He thought of Nancy and the cup fell from his hand. His coworkers all stared at the inferno. Ronnie broke into a cold sweat and for one of the few times in his life, did not know what to do.

He heard the words, "Hey Ronnie, doesn't your sister work there," but he was too fixated on the scene and it took a few seconds to respond.

"I've got to get over there to see if she's okay."

***

Dawn was walking across campus when her friend Amy ran up to her.

"Did you hear what happened at the trade center?"

"No. I had an early class. I just got out."

"Each of the towers was hit by a hijacked airliner."

"You gotta be kidding."

"I'm not. There still on fire and a lot of people are trapped."

"Oh my god! John had an interview and my uncle works there!"

She immediately tried to call John, but there was no service.

"What time did the planes hit?"

The North Tower was hit first about a quarter to nine and the South Tower about twenty minutes later. It's on all the channels."

She began to panic. "John's interview was at nine and he was probably in the building!"

"A lot of people were evacuated. I'm sure he's fine."

Dawn did not appreciate Amy's attempt to sound positive. She tried John's house, but still could not get through. She ran back to her room and turned on the television. When she saw the screen she fell back on her bed. She did not hear the words from the commentators. She only saw the flames and the smoke and felt her stomach churn and the room sway with the flames. She thought of John jumping into the waves and would not allow herself to picture him trapped in the flames. She had to find out if he was safe. She had to see him. She had to hold him in her arms. She cold not stay in her dorm room and wait. She raced to her car and sped up the New Jersey Turnpike to his house.

***

Police, firemen, fire trucks and emergency vehicles surrounded the entire area. When Phil looked up, he saw how bad it really was. The flames and smoke were clearly visible in the bright blue sky. He saw what could possibly be white handkerchiefs or flags waving from the top of the World Trade Center. They must be trapped, he thought. Suddenly he saw what he first thought was debris falling toward the ground, but it was a body. He followed the path and was shocked to see the remains of two bodies. Each had chosen what he thought was the least painful way to die. As an experienced fireman, Phil could understand the decision. He tried to get inside, but an officer stopped him.

Phil was not deterred, "My wife's in the building and I have to make sure she's safe."

"You can't go any closer. The firemen will take care of everything."

"I'm a Fireman," Phil yelled. He pulled out his wallet with his picture ID and flashed it in front of the policeman's face.

"Go ahead, but you won't be allowed to go up."

It did not matter what he said. Phil pushed his way forward until he was in the lobby, which looked like a bomb had hit. He saw people exiting a stairwell and started to run over, when there was a huge

One-Way Elevator

rumbling sound like an approaching tornado. After several seconds the rumbling stopped, but the outside was dark as night as the sun blocking dark dust cloud from the collapsed South Tower enveloped the entire area.

He reached the stairwell and began his ascent. The people streaming down and the firemen lumbering up in full gear slowed his climb. By the time he reached the twentieth floor, the muscles in his legs were burning and he was breathing heavily, but he would not stop. On the twenty-fourth floor he heard someone call his name. He turned around and it was Brian, a fireman he knew from another firehouse.

"It's pretty bad. What are you doing here?"

"Nancy's on 65. I have to get to her."

"She probably outside by now."

Phil could not slow down to talk. "I have to be sure." Phil continued his sprint. When he reached the fortieth floor, all of a sudden the fireman ahead of him stopped and turned around. He blocked the stairway.

"Get out of my way," Phil yelled.

The fireman stood his ground and said, " We just got orders to evacuate the building. They think it's gonna come down."

Phil's heart skipped a beat and his flushed face turned white.

"I have to get to sixty-five. My girlfriend is there!"

"She's probably out."

Phil pleaded. "I'm a fireman too."

His colleague said, "If you go up there, the chances are you won't walk back down. What if she's outside waiting for you?"

To Phil it was like Sophie's choice. He had to make a quick decision. He decided to play the odds and turned around and retraced his steps.

When he reached the lobby, the devastation was worse from the debris and dust from the South tower. It looked as if an asteroid had hit, and it was the end of the world. It was the end of the world to Phil, if he could not find Nancy. As a fireman, he felt that he should be helping more, but his prime concern was finding Nancy. He stood still unsure of what to do, or where to go next. He watched the cops and

firemen all trying to insure that everyone possible is evacuated.
A cop yelled in Phil's face, "Get out of here now!"

***

Jim stood about three blocks away from the burning towers and wondered how this could have happened. It did not seem real, because it could not register in his mind that a commercial aircraft flew into each building. He could not find anyone from his company and he stood around not knowing what to do, or where he should go. He did not have a cell phone, so he could not call home. He wondered how many more people were still in the buildings. How many were trapped in the upper floors? How many had been killed or injured?

He slowly worked his way through the crowd back toward the building. He looked up to the top, and after a moment realized what he saw were people hanging halfway out broken windows. He then watched in horror as a body came spiraling down. He knew how close he was to catching that elevator. He froze, when he thought of the young woman, who attempted to hold the door for him. He hoped that she had escaped, but then the scene of the elevator doors opening with flames shooting out made him sick to his stomach. The sirens were blaring, and he wondered how anyone could fight a fire near the top of the World Trade Center. Were firemen rushing up the stairs carrying equipment? What about anyone in a wheelchair, who could not make it down the stairs? Maybe the fire would burn itself out. The jet fuel should burn quickly, but he had no idea about the furniture on the floors. From where he stood, he could see both towers and wondered how long it would take to reopen? He could not even begin to speculate the damage to the other floors.

A thunderous crashing sound erupted mixed with frightened screams. His eyes were locked on the South Tower as it began to collapse from the top down. The sound intensified as the floors collapsed. It was coming straight down like some of the buildings he had seen on television brought down with controlled demolition.

Everyone around began to run. Nobody knew if it would continue straight down, or suddenly fall on its side. Jim stood transfixed. He

One-Way Elevator

could not take his eyes off the building. When it reached the ground, a dark swirling cloud like the inside of a tornado erupted and began moving out in all directions from the impact zone. Jim began to run, but the vortex of dust and smoke engulfed him and he stood behind a tree in an automatic evolutionary reaction for self-preservation. The black cloud obliterated the deep blue sunny sky. The clean fresh air was transmuted into a hot, eye-stinging, lung-piercing black cauldron of destruction. He stood motionless rooted to the tree. It took a few minutes before he could see clearly enough to move. He stepped away from the tree and through squinted eyes gazed at the smoldering pile of debris, that was once one of the most famous buildings in the world.

His uncle, Paul, had been one of the workers on the building. He was a crane operator, who would maneuver the heavy steel beams into place. His uncle had passed away the year before, but he would have been so upset to see what had become of his beloved towers. Now one had crumbled like a house of cards. Jim stood there unable to move and unable to take his eyes away. How could the building collapse? It was one plane. A building that size should be able to withstand a hit from more than one plane. How could the South Tower collapse so soon? It was hit after the North Tower. Jim then wondered if the North Tower would be next.

***

Terri was teaching her class, when a few teachers, who knew Jim worked at the World Trade Center, interrupted her.

Her friend Joan came in and asked, "Have you heard from your husband?"

Terri replied, "No. Why is something wrong?"

Joan tried not to worry her too much as she replied, "There's been some kind of accident at the World Trade Center. A plane hit the building."

Terri froze for an instant.

Pam, another teacher rushed in. "Call your husband now. I'll watch your class."

Terri became nervous. "What kind of plane?"

"I don't know. Just try him now."

Terri went down the hall to the teacher's lounge and dialed. The phone rang, but there was no answer. Her anxiety grew. She turned on the small television and felt her world come crashing down, while the towers burned before her eyes. She began to shake uncontrollably. A close friend, Bill Bowan, who was the gym teacher walked in and attempted to console her.

"A lot of people have already evacuated. I'm sure Jim is a few blocks away by now." Terri began to cry, "What if he's trapped and can't get out?"

Bill spoke calmly and tried to sound hopeful, "There's all sorts of firemen and rescue squads there. They'll get everything under control quickly."

"How can anyone be rescued from that high? It will take hours." Her gaze was fixated on the small screen.

Bill continued his well-intentioned optimism. "They have sprinklers, and they run drills just like we do here."

Terri sobbed and replied, "But we have two floors here. He's in a towering inferno."

Terri screamed as the South Tower collapsed on the small screen. At that moment she did not know which tower was collapsing. Her whole world was disintegrating before her eyes.

Terri ran out of the office and into the hallway. Several parents with spouses, who worked at the trade center, came to bring their children home. She nearly ran into the principal, who told her to go home. She wondered if Keith knew anything.

Jim did not have a cell phone despite all her complaints that he worked in IT and yet he was against any new technology. "He's going to get one now," she thought, but then stopped herself. She could not let herself complete the sentence "If he's still alive."

It was a five-minute drive to pick up Keith from school. She gripped the steering wheel like a vice, in order to prevent her hands from shaking. When she turned the corner and pulled in front of the school, Keith was standing near the entrance with a few of his friends.

She ran out of the car, but before she reached him, Keith asked in a shaky voice, "Did you hear from Dad?"

She could only shake her head, no. Keith's face was ashen and his shoulders were slumped. Keith let her give him a hug, even though he was in front of his friends. They slowly walked to the car together.

When they pulled away, Keith said in a voice laden with desperation, "I just know Dad's all right. He's a good runner and he could get down the stairs faster than most people."

Terri smiled and attempted to sound convincing, "If anyone could get out, it's your father."

When they arrived home, there was no message and the earlier faked optimism was replaced by thoughts of the worst-case scenario. She could not bear to watch television or listen to the radio, so she puttered around the kitchen and made a batch of corn muffins to take her mind off her nightmare. When she placed the tray in the oven, she thought of the burning buildings. Keith sat alone in his room, worrying and praying.

***

Ronnie ran to his car and headed toward the Holland tunnel, but the traffic was barely moving and by the time he was near the tunnel it was closed. He made an illegal turn out of the traffic jam and drove to his apartment in Hoboken. While driving he was shocked when he heard on the radio that the South Tower had collapsed. He feared the North Tower would not be far behind and prayed to god that Nancy was out. He pulled over and called Nancy's cell phone, but there was no service. He called her landline at her apartment, but only heard her voice on the answering machine. He parked in front of his apartment and ran up the stairs feeling helpless, but knowing he had to do something. When he flung open the door, his mother was sitting at the kitchen table crying.

"Did you hear anything from Nancy," she sobbed.

"No, but I bet she's walking over the Brooklyn Bridge by now."

"I couldn't go on if she's gone."

Ronnie's face was flushed, his fists were clenched and his voice shaky.

"Don't even say that. I can't look for her, because everything is closed. They say it was terrorists. I'd like to fucking kill them all for what they did."

Jane slowly pushed her chair back and stood up holding onto the table for support. She stared at the recent picture of Nancy standing with her cap and gown and moaned in agony. Ronnie quickly held her tight and attempted to appear strong.

"We'll find her. I bet she's with Phil."

"I think we should go to church and pray that she's okay."

Ronnie released her hug. "If that's what you want."

They slowly walked the three blocks to Our Lady Of Grace and entered the solitude of the church.

***

Jim's eyes burned and it stung when he took a breath, but he was alive. His dark pants were covered with dust and everything around him was also coated in destruction. The only direction he could go was away from the devastation, away from the death, and dark cloud of terror. He began to walk uptown. His ears no longer heard the sirens, even though they continued to wail. He did not see the others covered in the white dust, although he walked among them. He was in a state of shock, but he realized that this one act would change the world.

After walking for a while, he stopped in a bar to try to make a call home. The bar was crowded and the television was on. He ordered a soda to clear his throat of all the dust particles he had inhaled. He took a napkin from one of the tables and wiped some of the dust from his forehead. He looked back at the television and watched a replay of the South Tower collapse. He looked back at the napkin and saw the grayish smear and felt the sting in his eyes, which were slightly watering.

The coverage then returned to the North Tower. He heard the reporters say that the order had been given to evacuate all police and firefighters. He moved closer to the television. The North Tower began to collapse just like the South Tower. Although he was safe in a bar blocks away, he felt as if he were watching from where he stood when the South Tower collapsed. The crashing sound reverberated in his mind. He felt consumed by another cloud and he wanted to run, when he saw the cloud billowing across the screen.

The phone booth was located in the back of the bar and there was a long line. When he finally had his chance, he could not get through. He knew Terri and Keith would be worried. He walked out of the bar and continued uptown. The further away he walked, the more normal the city felt. He spotted a bank with an ATM, so he went inside and withdrew two hundred dollars, because he was not sure how he would get home. When he finally arrived at Penn Station at 34th Street, the building was closed and a large crowd was milling around. Barricades were set up to control the crowds. After waiting a few minutes, Jim walked up to the Port Authority building to try to get a bus, but all the tunnels were closed and no buses were leaving. He was standing next to a man with a cell phone, so he asked if he could make a call.

The stranger replied, "Sure. No problem. Some calls are now going through."

He wasn't sure if he could connect with his wife at her job, so he called his home phone and left a message. "Hi it's me. I'm okay. I was in the lobby when the plane hit. Now I'm up at Port Authority trying to get home. I just want to get out of the city and try to make sense of what happened. Love you. See you soon."

He returned the phone to the Good Samaritan and said, "Thanks a lot. I was lucky to be able to leave the message."

The man in his early forties, said, in an angry voice, "It was those fucking Muslim terrorists who did this."

Jim shook his head and replied, "Who knows how many people were still inside, when it collapsed?"

His thoughts turned to his fellow workers, but the face of the young woman in the elevator flashed in his brain.

The man continued, "We should go over there and nuke them all. Then they'll think twice about fucking with us."

Jim said, "We won't let them get away with this," and began walking back down to Penn Station.

***

Phil walked briskly to the exit and went out to the plaza and then to Broadway. The police were forcing everyone as far away as possible. He tried to think of where Nancy would go. Maybe she was sitting in a coffee shop with her coworkers. Maybe she was near him now. Maybe she headed home. He did not think she stayed around.

She always said, "I can't look at a fire, because it reminds me of what a dangerous job you have."

Phil zigzagged as fast as he could through the crowds up and down the surrounding blocks, but there was no sign of Nancy. With panic-stricken strides, he covered several blocks of the Hudson River Park, but it was nearly impossible to find anyone in the scrambling mass of people.

He turned around when he heard the rumble and the screams. He watched in horror as the North Tower collapsed. He was surprised at how quickly it came down. In a matter of several seconds, the once majestic North Tower with the large antenna on the top was now a pile of rubble. He stood still, while others ran from the cloud of dust and debris hurtling toward him. It was as if a piece of him had crumbled when the building fell. He had a strange feeling that Nancy was still in the building. If she were, then his life was over too.

He stood firm and tragically thought, "If her body is part of the dust particles in that cloud, then let it wash over me. If I will never see her again, the last thing I want to do is run away. The last thing I would want to do is hold her and say that everything is going to be okay. " He closed his eyes as he was enveloped by the cloud and pictured Nancy standing beside him, holding his hand.

***

The doorbell rang and Terri ran hoping it was Jim, but it was Jane from around the block. Jane was retired, but was the full-time neighborhood gossip, who had no qualms about asking anyone any question. Nothing was off limits. Her hair was dyed an unnatural shade of reddish black and she had some major reconstruction on her face. Jim always used his favorite line, which was, "She should just go to *Home Depot* and buy a can of spackle for $5.99 along with some sandpaper, instead of all the shots, surgeries and creams." She was tall, still thin and always dressed up, even if it were only to walk her little yappy poodle that she never cleaned up after.

"Have you heard from Jim?"

Terri tried to control her emotions and only shook her head from left to right.

"I'm sure he's okay."

Terri forced a phony smile and said, "That's what everybody keeps telling me."

Jane stood up on her ever present soap box and said, "I can't believe those crazy Muslims attacked us. We should shoot them all."

Jane was a member of DAR (Daughters of The American Revolution). She was not the most tolerant person in the best of times. She would be perfectly happy with a few slaves to maintain her house and walk her dog. Terri's only concern was Jim's safety. Whoever was responsible, did not matter at the moment. Terri's good friend Carol pulled up in front of the house and beeped the horn. Terri gratefully excused herself and ran down to the car.

Before Carol could ask, Terri said, "No word yet. I know it's hard to get a call though now, so I hope he's wandering around the city away from the buildings."

Carol turned the car off, exited and stood on the sidewalk. Terri looked back at the house and Jane was walking down the block, probably annoyed that someone else had usurped her.

Carol gave Terri a hug and said, "I can't believe this is happening, but there was a lot of time before the North Tower collapsed and I believe that most people were able to get out."

Terri, knew that was a line of bull, but she knew her friend meant well.

"Do you want a cup of tea? I could use some company?"

"Sure. I'll stay as long as you like."

They walked slowly up the stairs and Terri put the kettle on. She glanced over at the phone and the message signal was flashing. She quickly hit the play button and never felt so relieved in her entire life when she heard Jim's voice say that he was okay.

There were tears in her eyes, when she turned to Carol and sobbed, "I never thought I would hear his voice again. Now I can breath."

She yelled upstairs to Keith, "You're father's okay."

Keith came running down the stairs, smiling and full of nervous energy.

"I knew they couldn't get him."

Terri gave Carol a wary look and said, "Let's just be glad he's alive for now."

"How come you didn't answer the phone?"

Keith looked down and softly replied, "I was afraid. I thought it might be bad news."

Terri gave him a hug and said, "I understand."

Terri turned off the kettle and replaced the teacups with two wine glasses. She happily walked to the wine closet and grabbed the first bottle she saw. She quickly popped the cork and filled the glasses. She took a long sip, emptying half the glass and began sobbing.

"What about all the other wives and husbands who still don't know? How many never had a chance to say good-bye?"

She finished her glass and started to refill, but stopped.

"How can I drink during this tragedy?"

Carol who had been silent said, "You're allowed to be grateful. There's nothing to be ashamed of."

***

When he opened his eyes, he could barely see anything. Unsure of what to do, Phil headed home, still hoping that when he opened the door, Nancy would be sitting on the couch. She would jump up and tell him all about her escape from the building and he would tell her how he had searched for her. She would yell at him for taking such a big risk. He would tell her that he didn't care. He only wanted to find her because he loved her.

She would give him a big kiss and say, "I love you too."

Phil pushed the door open and called out, "Nancy, you there?" The only sounds were the sirens in the background. He checked the

One-Way Elevator

messages and there were several from his parents and several from Nancy's mother and one message for him to report for duty as soon as possible. He called Nancy's mother, but she had not heard from her. In a daze, he turned around and headed back to work. He had not prayed in a long time, but he did not know what else he could do. He could not imagine life without her.

***

The realization that he was almost killed started to fully register in Jim's mind. He knew he should feel lucky to be alive, but all he felt was anger. Why did he make it out alive? Why did he miss that elevator? If he had arrived one minute earlier would he be here now? Was that woman alive? What would happen to Terri and Keith if he didn't make it? The 93 bombing paled in comparison to today, but lives were also lost on that day. He went back over his day from the time he woke up until the moment the building was hit. He tried to pinpoint the reason why he was late for the elevator, and although there were numerous possibilities, it all came back to being asked about his good friend Janice. "Did her misfortune and sickness, save my life? Was there some sort of predestined reason why the doors closed in my face, or was it all a crapshoot?"

He stopped in a pizza place with a long counter and several booths and tables. He ordered a slice and a diet coke.

When he went to pay, the manager at the cash register asked, "Were you at the World Trade Center this morning?"

Jim pulled a twenty-dollar bill out of his walled and replied, "I was lucky."

The manager spoke in a serious tone, "Whoever did this is gonna pay. Put your money away. A slice of pizza is the least I can do."

"Thanks."

"We have a restroom in the back if you want to wash some of the dust off."

"I guess I do look a mess."

Jim put his tray down at a booth and walked to the men's room. He turned the water on and looked at his face in the mirror. His hair and eyebrows were a shade of white. His dark blue shirt, pants, and shoes had remnants of the destructive cloud of death. He splashed water on his face and arms, but he suddenly felt unclean. He stared in the mirror, but he only saw the buildings collapse. He fought the urge to vomit. He fought the urge to feel alive. He returned to his booth, but he could not eat. He left the pizza, picked up his cup of soda and went back outside.

When he arrived at Penn Station, the barricades were still up, but he heard a few people talking that some trains may soon be allowed to leave. Jim wandered around and then he saw what looked like a semi-orderly line snaking along the barricades, so he followed it until he reached the end and hoped for the best. The line began to move in intervals. The crowd would shuffle for five minutes and then wait another twenty before moving again. Jim could not understand that on one hand he wanted nothing more to be home, but on the other hand he felt like he did not deserve to go home. He had cheated death by seconds and he could not reconcile that fact in his mind.

When he finally shuffled inside Penn station, it was once again an unorganized mass of humanity, each one searching for a train that went anywhere near his or her home. The big electronic board in the center of the station displayed several trains. He took the first train he saw with a stop in Newark. If he reached Newark, then he could switch to his Raritan Valley Line, which he hoped was running. The train leaving Penn Station was packed. He stood in the aisle and grabbed the overhead horizontal steel bar. He closed his eyes and suddenly felt exhausted. The train slowly went through the dark tunnel. When it came out into the bright sunshine in New Jersey, there were audible gasps from the passengers. Jim opened his eyes and immediately understood why. The smoldering fires from the twin towers were clearly visible.

Jim almost screamed out, "Those goddamn mother fuckers. If I could press the button, I'd nuke them all."

He felt like hitting something or someone. He had no idea how many people were killed, but it must be thousands. *We are going to war against whoever did this, and it better be a quick war.* Jim felt helpless that all he could do was stare and curse.

When the train pulled into Newark Penn Station, he went to the other side of the building for the Raritan Valley line train to his safe house. Luckily he only had to wait a few minutes, but the relentless crowd crammed into every available space. It was a short ride, but he was unable to see out the window and felt anxious and claustrophobic. He slowly walked the seven blocks from the station to his house. When he walked up the steps to his front porch, the door flew open and his wife and son were there to greet him.

Terri gave him a big hug and kiss and bust into tears. "I'm so glad you're okay. I was going crazy not knowing. Then I heard your message, and I was so relieved."

Jim forced a smile and said, "I was one of the lucky ones who got out. Do they know how many were killed?"

"No, but the estimates are in the thousands."

Keith attempted to act nonchalant and said, "I knew they wouldn't get you. I wasn't worried like Mom."

He gave his father a hug and held tight, not knowing what he would do without him. Terri did not let on that she had heard him crying in his room earlier. Keith attempted to act like a tough guy, but it was all an act. A few neighbors and friends came over to see if everything was all right. Jim did not want to be the center of attention. He wanted to be alone and go to sleep. Maybe he would have a pleasant dream to replace the nightmare of reality.

As soon as everyone was gone, he took a shower. He turned the water pressure as high as it would go to wash away any evidence of the day's destruction. He closed his eyes under the warm soothing water, but all he saw were the buildings collapsing, the giant dust cloud and the young woman's face. When he opened his eyes, he could see the grayish soot swirl at his feet before disappearing down the drain. He coughed and wondered how much dust, smoke, and debris he had inside his lungs. He stayed in the shower longer than usual, because the curtain protected him from the outside world and the sound of the pulsating water momentarily drowned out the sounds of destruction.

He finally turned the water off and stepped back into reality. When he went downstairs, the television was on and every few minutes he saw the towers tumble again. The phone rang, but Jim was in no mood for any calls, so Terri answered.

"Hi this is Amy. Can I speak to Jim? I'm one of the volunteers calling to check if everyone can be accounted for."

Terri relayed the message to Jim and he reluctantly picked up. "This is Jim. I'm fine. Did everyone get out? "

Amy responded in a non-committal voice, "We just started calling people a little while ago, so I don't know."

"Okay. I don't want to hold you up. Thanks for the call."

Before hanging up, Amy said, "I'm glad you're safe and at home."

The phone did not stop ringing that night. Everyone he knew was calling and he had to repeat the same story over and over. He was glad when it was time to go to bed, but as soon as the lights were off he stared at the blackness and felt as if he was back inside the dark thunderous cloud. He wondered how many had died. How many families were shattered? How many people would never be the same? The estimates were in the thousands. Then he thought about himself. What would happen to his company? Where would they relocate? Would it remain in lower Manhattan? Could he work in another skyscraper? Could he even get on an elevator again? Would there be other attacks? Would the country go to war?

A day that had started out with clear deep blue skies had been transformed into one of the worst days in America's history. He thought back to what he had learned about Pearl Harbor and how little he thought about the December 7th anniversary. Years from now would it be the same for September 11th?

The next morning he called a few people from work and the word was spreading that thirteen from his company had died. At lunch, Terri asked if he was okay.

"I'm fine," Jim snapped, "Why do you have to keep asking the same question?"

He stormed out of the kitchen and plopped down on a chair in the TV room. He flipped through the channels and most had coverage of the World Trade Center. He saw volunteers searching for survivors and replays of the plane going into the South Tower. When he watched the buildings collapse again, it felt like the black cloud was about to come into his TV room.

Jim knew he should be glad to be alive, but all he felt was anger - anger at whoever was responsible, anger at how many had died, anger, because he had been unable to do anything, except to feel anger, and anger that everyone was concerned about how he felt. He was alive. What did it matter what he felt? What about the thousands who were gone? Later that night on the news, he watched the crowd standing, many with candles in hand, hoping that a loved one would somehow miraculously be found amid the smoldering rubble. When he saw mothers, wives, and husbands holding photos of the missing, he felt so guilty that he had survived. He wondered if anyone was holding a photo of the woman in the elevator. He wondered if she was married, or had any children of her own.

The next morning Jim went out for a long walk with his eight-year-old golden retriever. He watched as Libby happily sniffed and enjoyed the walk. He wished he could be oblivious to what had happened. Nothing seemed to matter anymore. All he knew was that he wanted revenge on Al-Qaeda and Osama bin Laden. How could anyone murder innocent people? Jim knew most of the thirteen who had died in his company. Most had families, and one young woman was recently married. Each life had been cut short because of hate. How could they pull off a plan to hijack four planes and three of them hit their target? How could the Pentagon be hit, when Washington was supposed to be one of the most protected cities? It all made no sense, and the more Jim thought, the more his anger grew.

The following week, there was a show on the History Channel detailing why the towers had collapsed. Jim watched as the simulation demonstrated how the insulation around the beams was loosened, or knocked off by the impact on the plane. The heat from the full tank of fuel on the plane caused fires that melted the steel of the then-naked beams. Once the top floors collapsed, the weight of the floors continued to cascade downward. The lower floors could not hold the weight. It all made sense now that it was explained in detail. One did not need a degree in physics, engineering or architecture to understand.

Jim suddenly remembered Tony whom he had met in St. Martin. Tony worked on the 93rd floor. He hoped Tony was home yelling at his screaming kids. Jim felt a deep sorrow knowing that someone whom he had only known briefly may have died a horrible death. The next day he received an email that announced that on September 17th, there would be a memorial service in a midtown Manhattan church for the 13 in his firm who had died.

Chapter 6

Dawn stood clutching a candle in a sea of candles; knowing that the darkness could not be penetrated, no matter how many candles there were. Dawn was consumed by guilt.

"I was the one who had my uncle set up the interview. Luckily he survived. I'm the reason John's dead now. I only wanted to help him. I loved him, and I know he loved me."

She looked at the pictures of husbands, wives, and sons and wondered if any would be found. The first thing she thought of when she heard about the attack was John. She'd had the greatest summer of her life with John, and now it would only be a memory and a longing for an unfulfilled future. If she had not met him in the liquor store that day, he would still be alive. She would gladly give up the summer with John, if it meant he would still be here. John was afraid to make a decision about what to do with his life. Now it no longer mattered. She spotted a young pregnant woman holding a picture of her missing husband and cursed the people responsible for the attack. The woman's eyes were glazed over and she held the photo like a cross with unsteady legs buckling under its weight.

Dawn felt like taking the semester off and she desperately needed a place to hide from reality. John found his refuge down the Jersey shore, where everything appeared safe, simple and predictable. She remembered back to the day when they were walking on the beach and she said that her uncle might be able to set up an interview at the World Trade Center. John said he would be in her debt for life. He never imagined if would cost him his life.

***

Kelly stood on campus in the afternoon sun, holding a picture of John taken a few days before graduation. He was standing in front of the dorm with his cap and gown. He was smiling, and the future looked bright that day. Now she clutched the photo hoping by some miracle that he was still alive, but not ready to accept any other answer. Kelly was shocked when she received the phone call from Mrs. Haddler. She knew she had made a mistake separating at graduation. She still loved him, even though he had moved on. She had held out hope that they would one day get back together, but now that hope was crushed and turned to dust. If only she had convinced him to find a job in Washington, where they could be together, he would still be alive. If only she had not waited so long to call him. She kept on playing numerous "WHAT IF" scenarios in her mind, knowing that the past could not be changed, and a life could not be lived based on "WHAT IF."

***

Alan Haddler stood in his two-car garage with the door closed and stared at the car he had bought John for graduation. He pictured John sitting in the driver's seat with a big smile on his face and a bright future. Now, Alan felt like turning on the engine, because he did not see how he could go on. He opened the door and sat in the driver's seat. He realized John was right, when he described how simple life was down at the shore. Alan looked at the few grains of sand on the floor mat and banged his hand against the steering wheel in a fit of rage. How could his only son be gone? He never had a chance to live. How could killing innocent people be justified by any God or religion? Alan felt guilty that he had allowed John to take the summer off. If he forced John to look for a job earlier, he would still be alive today. He put the key in the ignition and attempted to steady his shaky right hand. He thought of his wife, Joan, and how much she needed him now. He slowly withdrew the key and realized that he could not take the easy way out and leave his wife alone.

One-Way Elevator

***

Phil sat alone in his apartment questioning why his whole world was crushed along with the towers. He wondered how his life would have been with Nancy. He opened the box with the engagement ring and replayed that imaginary scene on the beach again in his mind. He wondered if his unborn child was a boy or a girl. The more he thought, the deeper he descended into depression.

How could he continue to try to save lives, when he could not save the one that meant the most to him? How could he extinguish another fire, when the fire of his love was extinguished, while he stood helplessly watching? He sat in front of his computer composing his letter of resignation from the fire department. He would never forget Nancy, but he wanted his memories to be of the good times. He did not want to be reminded of her every time he raced to a fire. He would find another job in another field and at the moment it did not matter.

His next letter was to his landlord stating that he was breaking his lease and acknowledged that he would cover any monetary penalties. He could not live in the apartment, when every time he opened the door, he would expect to hear Nancy's voice. He had to purge her from his physical world and only retain the memories in his own mind. It was too painful to remain in the past, but he was unsure if he could live in a future without Nancy.

***

Mrs. Anderson could not accept that her smart, beautiful daughter who was the light of her life was gone. When her husband left her, she felt that nothing else could be as bad, but now knew she was wrong. It was hard enough when Nancy moved out. She did not know if she had the strength to handle her passing. Ronnie tried to appear strong for his mother, but all his anger poured out on some unsuspecting guy who had too much to drink and caused a scene.

Ronnie dragged the unlucky guy outside the bar and it took three others to pull Ronnie off the now bleeding drunk, who would have a lot more pain than a regular hangover in the morning.

***

Beth could barely force herself to leave her bed, but she could not sleep because of the pain of loss and the terror of reality. She had spent the best years of her life with Don and just when they were planning to spend a long happy retirement, it was wiped out by hatred. He worked his whole life and now everything was gone in an instant. Beth had planned to read and edit Don's retirement speech one final time before his big day. Now the speech would never be delivered and the big day was never to arrive. Now, all the future trips and the life of leisure would sadly be added to the long list of unfulfilled dreams. Don never had a chance to play the fourth quarter of his life; never had the chance to walk off the field one last time knowing that he gave it his all; never had the chance to simply say good-bye.

Beth felt a longing that she could not control and an emptiness that she knew could never be filled. She had assumed the days would continue until each of their lives completed its circle.

Beth remembered the words of the priest on Ash Wednesday, "Remember, thou art dust and to dust thou shalt return."

Ryan could not believe that his father, who was his idol and loved so much, could be gone. Ryan thought back to all the good times and how he was always there for him. He immediately flashed back to the time, when he convinced him to stop taking drugs. He remembered that day standing on the fifty-yard line, and knew the one who had turned his life around from a destructive path was now gone. Ryan thought how his grandfather had died in the Normandy invasion, which was the turning point in the ending of one war and his father was killed at the beginning of a different type of war. One where there were no countries, only hatred and fanaticism.

One-Way Elevator

***

Jim arrived about a half hour early for the memorial service. He saw his good friend Joe, whom he had worked with for nearly twenty years, standing at the top of the steps leaning on the railing.

Jim hurried up the stairs with his hand extended and said, "Hey Joe, good to see you."

Joe shook his hand and with a rapidly fading smile replied, "Whoever would have thought anything like this would have happened?"

Jim looked Joe in the eye and in a cold emotionless voice said, "I know. I don't care if I'm standing in front of a church, I hope they kill every mother fucker who was involved."

"So do I. I was coming out of the cafeteria, when the plane hit. At first I thought it was a gas leak in the cafeteria. I went up the escalator to the elevator bank on the 44th floor, even though the escalator was swaying. When I reached the elevator bank, there was a dark cloud of smoke coming down the corridor. People were throwing their trays and running to the stairs. I had a cup of tea and a bagel, but I held onto them. I didn't want anyone to trip over my cup of tea, so I carried it all the way down. I feel guilty that others carried out people on their backs and all I carried out was a cold cup of tea."

Jim could see the pained look on Joe's face. He paused for a moment and then asked, "How was the stairwell?"

"It wasn't bad, but it was slow. The other floors below were emptying out too, so it took a long time."

"Was there any smoke?"

"There was some when I got down to the lower floors and there was some water from the sprinkler on the stairs. Nobody was panicking, because nobody knew how bad it really was."

"Did you meet up with anyone going down?"

"No. I did see a guy in a wheelchair on the landing around the 27th floor. He was with his friend. I stopped and asked him if he needed help. He said no, the firemen would come and get him. He didn't want anyone to carry him down, because it would only slow everyone else down."

"Do you think he made it?"

"I don't know, but as I continued down I saw a lot of firemen running up the stairs with all their equipment. I hope they brought him down."

"I hope so too, but we'll probably never know."

Joe then asked, "How did you get out?"

"I was in the lobby and I just missed an elevator, which is probably the luckiest thing that ever happened to me. It closed in my face, but I can't seem to forget one young woman's face who tried to reach to open the door, but wasn't quick enough. She mouthed the words, "I'm sorry,' as the doors closed."

Jim heard his name called. He looked at the bottom of the stairs and there was Janice. He met her halfway up the stairs and she gave him a big hug and a kiss on the cheek.

"I'm so glad you're okay. I worried about you so much."

Janice and Jim both started working for the company on the same day. They both had come from different insurance companies and were hired as analysts for the same project.

Jim smiled and said, "Don't worry about me. How are you feeling?"

"I'm holding my own. I was knocked out from the chemo, but I almost had a heart attack when I saw what happened."

Jim gave Janice a look of concern and continued. "I was lucky. That's the only explanation I can give."

Jim did not want to tell her that she was the one who saved his life. He would leave that for another time.

Janice was five years younger than Jim. She was five feet two, slender with long brown hair. She was attractive, but not a beauty. Her complexion was fair and her eyes were set deep. If her face was studied closely, most people would correctly guess that she'd had a nose job. Her most prominent feature was her smile, both genuine and caring. She had an eleven-year-old son, but was raising him alone after her recent divorce. Jim never could understand why anyone would cheat on her, but over the years he had leaned not to be surprised about anything.

In a somber voice, Janice said, "Let's go in and take a seat. This will be tough to get through."

Jim said, "I think you're right."

When Jim, Janice, and Joe walked into the church, there were booklets distributed to each attendee, giving the schedule of speakers and a page with a picture and details about each of the victims. They sat in the fifth row of pews. Jim opened the booklet and his anger grew. His hatred of those responsible increased with each turn of the page. He looked up at the crucifix and knew he could never forgive or as Jesus said, "Turn the other cheek."

Jim also took it personally that someone tried to kill him.

The church was old, but neither the years nor the countless ceremonies had diminished its grandeur. Jim felt more comfortable sitting in a Protestant church next to a Jewish woman, than when he made one of his rare appearances in his local Catholic church. There were approximately four hundred employees present, and the atmosphere was somber.

After the minister said a few solemn words and gave his blessing, the C.E.O. slowly walked to the pulpit. He looked nervous and unsteady, which was in direct contrast to his usually outgoing flamboyant, arrogant manner. Carl Joiner was in his late forties. He was six feet three and an imposing two hundred and ten pounds. If someone just met him in the street and had to guess his profession, the most likely choice would be ex football player. Some might guess mob enforcer, but not C.E.O. He had a full head of black hair with the ornamental touch of grey on the sides. His dark eyes were penetrating, and his smile did soften his appearance, but in a sinister way. He was animated when he spoke and a bundle of energy ready to explode at any given moment. His tirades in the boardroom were legendary like the fictional Gordon Gekko on steroids, but he treated the employees with respect no matter what level. This morning he was somber and subdued.

The church fell into silence and he began to speak, "I don't know how to begin. I don't know how to react. I am still in a state of shock after the tragic events of September 11th. I'm sure many of you feel the same way. Our country attacked. Our company attacked. Our citizens killed. Our employees, co-workers, and friends killed. I can't explain why it happened, but one thing I know is that our country is strong, our company is strong, and our employees are strong.

"Today we are here to honor the members of our family who did not make it. I used the word 'family', because that is what we are. Each of us probably spends more time at work than at home. It is a shame that it sometimes takes a tragedy to realize what is most important in life. John, Darlene, Paul, and Kathy left their families that day not knowing they would never return. It was a perfect late summer day, and look what happened. The four of them were on their way to a meeting on a new project. It was going to save the company over one million dollars a year and now that number seems meaningless. Among them, they had seventy-four years of experience. Each was married with children. My heart goes out to the spouses and children.

"Another big loss was Joe Kelly, who was only with us two years. He started right out of college and from what his manager and coworkers said, he had a bright future with the company.

"I can't begin to tell you how guilty I feel, because I was out of town that day. I felt so helpless watching the buildings fall. I felt so angry at those responsible. I know we can come back as a nation and as a company, because we are strong and determined. It will take time for us to heal as individuals and time to recover as a company, but we will. We can never forget our fallen employees. We are scrambling to find new office space, but that seems petty right now. Today is about remembering our coworkers, to celebrate each life and the contribution each has given to the company. Now one person for each of the thirteen who perished, will come up to the pulpit and share some thoughts."

Jim watched as each life was appreciated and summarized in a few short minutes. How many hours had each spent at work? How much money had each made for the company? He looked at Janice and watched the tears slowly following the laws of gravity and wondered what she must be thinking.

Janice's face was drawn, and she had lost some weight, but not in a good way. She knew the odds of ovarian cancer, but she was a fighter. Jim knew her son was a big reason for her determination. She had hit the five-year mark from her diagnosis. For some reason, five years was a big tracking date in the cancer world. The odds and time were not in her favor, but she still worked with the same enthusiasm as when they began working together.

At the end of the ceremony, the company senior vice president said a few words and reiterated that there should be rental space available soon and until that time, laptops will be available for those who could log on and perform their jobs from home.

After the ceremony, most of the employees stood around in small groups discussing where each one was that day and what would happen to the company.

When Jim explained how he just missed the elevator, he left out the reason. Jim was glad to see his coworkers, but he knew the company would never be the same again. He knew the country would never be the same again. He knew he would never be the same again.

At home, he was fixated on any special program about September 11th and watched them all. One program detailed how the towers were built, while another explained how they came down. The one thing that bothered Jim was that whenever he watched the towers collapse, it reminded him of a controlled demolition. He remembered watching the news when a huge hotel in Vegas was demolished to make way for new construction. When the timed explosives ignited and the building imploded, it looked similar to the World Trade Center. The hotel came nearly straight down, and there was a huge cloud of dust when it crumbled to the ground. His other infatuation was reading the obituaries of the nearly three thousand victims. The New York Times was printing several each day. He knew his picture should have been included. It was so random. A flick of the wrist and the plane could have hit a lower floor and then many more people would have been trapped and died. A few seconds later and he would have been on an elevator. Jim looked each day and wondered if he would see the woman from the elevator?

Jim picked up his laptop and began working at home. It was a big adjustment. He worked in Information technology and anything he could do in the office he could do at home, except print a document. If he had to print anything, he would send an email to his Hotmail address and walk to the other side of the room and print it out on his own printer. Meetings were held using a company dial-in conference number. It was a new way to work.

He missed his office and coworkers, but the way he felt now, he did not want to be around people. The company also had an instant messaging system that had been annoying when he was at the World Trade Center, but was more annoying now. His days were now spent on conference calls, while two or three people pinged him on instant messaging. In addition to the constant pinging and conference calls, there were the never-ending emails. It was impossible to keep up with everything and concentrate on anything. The only advantage was that it briefly took his mind off the tragedy.

He was going through his daily ritual of obituary reading when he turned the page of the New York Times and he saw a picture of his friend, Tony, from St Martin. Jim stared in disbelief at the photo even though it only confirmed what he already knew. Tony was only forty-one with three children, who no longer had a father to take them on vacation and a wife now without a mate. He slammed the paper down on the table and he quickly dressed and went out for a long run.

In the first week of November, the company found office space on east 26th street in Manhattan. Office space was hard to find, but a company had declared bankruptcy, so the law of supply and demand continued to work. In the world of business nothing ever changed. It was always survival of the fittest. When Jim left for work the first day, he walked the same route to the train station and boarded the same train, but he knew it was different. It was like a dream where everything appeared real, but something did not feel right. It was walking the same route, but winding up in a different place.

He had been having strange dreams lately. They were not nightmares of the buildings collapsing, but he was sure that was behind his recurring predicaments in his dream world. In the more

One-Way Elevator

frequent scenario, he was walking back to the Port Authority building late at night. He turned down a block, and there were no streetlights and all the stores were closed. He found himself in a dark alleyway. He knew he was being followed. He reached the end of the alleyway and there was no exit. The footsteps drew closer. His heart was pounding, and his palms were sweaty. He was afraid to turn around, afraid of what he might see. The footsteps stopped, and he could hear breathing, but not his own. He was expecting to be hit, stabbed or shot. He had no choice, so he slowly began to turn around. Before he turned, he sat up in his bed, shaken and sweaty, but not happy to be alive.

    He had another dream, with two variations. In each one he was in a race. It could be a short five-mile race or a marathon. In one case he would arrive late and everyone was already out of sight. He would try to catch them, but he never could, no matter how hard he sprinted. In the other episode, he was in a race and the runners were spread out. There was no one around him, but for some reason he took a wrong turn and went completely off course. He found himself running alone, not knowing where he was going. He tried to retrace his steps back to where he turned, but he was completely lost. He was so exhausted that he could no longer run and began to walk. He was on a road that was flat with no traffic and no signs, other than, "SPEED LIMIT 60." The sun was disappearing over the horizon. He began to panic and started running again. He was drained and thirsty and all he wanted to do was find out how he wound up on a lonely deserted road. He looked up and saw a truck speeding straight toward him. The road was only one lane and on either side was a sheer drop of at least two hundred feet. He closed his eyes, as the truck was about to flatten him and woke up.

***

It was an old building in the middle of a block containing other old non-descript buildings. The lobby was small, and there was one security guard, who casually checked identification cards. There was one elevator bank with two elevators on either side. He was alone in the lobby and when Jim pushed the button, he flashed back to the World Trade Center lobby. He could not watch the red dots on the wall between the elevators, tracking each elevator's ascent and descent from the sixth floor to the lobby. He closed his eyes, heard the elevator crash and saw the doors burst open and the flames shoot out. His mind flashed to the young woman in the crowded elevator and he walked back to the street for a few minutes.

The noise, the traffic and the people, all scurrying to reach some destination, gave him some sense of reality. He walked down the block into a small bodega and ordered a cup of tea and a bagel, since there was no cafeteria in the new location. This is what he needed. He desperately needed to be in a routine. There had been no real structure to his life since 9/11. He paid the cashier and walked back into the building with a momentary sense of purpose. This time there were three other coworkers in the lobby. It was John, Barbara, and Jerry. Barbara was the secretary and John and Jerry were both analysts. They entered the elevator together for the short ride to the fourth floor. It was the first time Jim had been on an elevator since September 11th. He was glad he was not alone.

When the doors opened and they stepped out and surveyed their new surroundings, Jim said, "I guess it really must be hard to find good office space. I hope they got this place cheap."

Approximately seventy-five desks were arranged in small clusters, with no cubicle walls to allow for any privacy. The work area was small with the desktop computer taking most of the space. There were two drawers under the work area to the right for storage. The ceiling was high, but there were exposed pipes running across that were probably for water and heat. In one corner, a small conference room with a glass wall across the front contained a white table and six chairs.

"I hope this is temporary," Barbara remarked in a sarcastic voice. , The rest rooms were along one wall with desks situated directly outside. Jim's momentary enthusiasm was waning quickly. Jim was fortunate to have an office, but it was in a corner without any windows. It was more like a large broom closet, and when Jim entered, he immediately felt claustrophobic.

His desk was metallic grey, and the walls were white. There was no carpeting and the small grey cloth-backed chair on wheels had over time left grooves in the floor tiles like a slowly melting glacier inching across the flat hard land. There was a monitor and a docking station for his laptop on the desk. He did have a separate three drawer metal filing cabinet in the corner. Jim set up his laptop, logged on, and began his meaningless welcomed drudgery. He was not very productive the first morning, since everyone kept coming into his office complaining about the accommodations. Jim felt like locking his door and shutting out the complaints. "What are these people complaining about?" he thought, "They should be glad that they are alive. What am I complaining about? I was seconds away from death. I should be thankful for every day. So how come I'm not? Why am I still angry at everything? How come I don't allow myself to enjoy anything? Why am I punishing myself?"

Jim had read some articles and heard some rumors that upset him. He read that a few of the suspected hijackers were found alive and the government was not 100% sure, who exactly was on the planes. There were rumors that some people knew about the attacks beforehand. It was also alleged that some people were warned not to go the World Trade Center that day and there was also some suspicious trading on the stock market. Jim did not know what to believe. He tried to move forward, but he stored that data in a secret compartment in the back of his mind.

Jim went to lunch with his friend Bill, who was a programmer. They walked around the area and found a pizza place where the prices were cheap, and the pizza greasy but edible. Jim looked around and most of the tables were filled.

"I guess nobody died yet from the grease," Bill said and took a big bite. Some of the grease dribbled down his hand and stopped just short of his shirtsleeve.

Jim carefully picked up his slice and said, "A steady diet of this will put you in an early grave." He quickly changed the topic, because he did not want to talk to anyone about the subject of death, even if it were only a joke. "So what do you think of our new luxury accommodations?"

Bill took a drink of soda. "I think it really sucks. There's no privacy and I sit outside the men's room, which is worse than sitting in the last row on a plane."

Jim laughed. "I would definitely ask to have my seat changed."

"Maybe I'll get used to it, but at least we can still work from home one day a week."

Jim wiped his hands with a few napkins. "That's pretty good. One less day to drag myself into this hellhole of a city."

After each had finished his second slice, they took a different route back to the office. What bothered Jim was how normal everything seemed, if anything in New York City could be considered normal. It was as if nothing had happened. Everybody was rushing around, but then, Jim thought, "Who knows what each person is thinking about?"

Jim did not read the *New York Times* on the way in, since he was too anxious about the first day back, so he opened it up on the train going home. He scanned a few articles and then went to the section of the 9/11 obituaries. He just finished reading about a man who had died and left behind a wife and four children, when he saw her. Jim felt like he had lost one of his best friends. When he read that Nancy was pregnant and planned to marry, he was devastated. He wondered if her baby was included in the official death toll. When he read how young she was and with a bright future ahead, his guilt returned with a vengeance. He could not imagine the pain her mother and fiancé must be going through. Jim knew he and Terri could never be the same, if they lost a child. Jim knew he could never be the same just for surviving this tragedy.

Jim knew thousands of people had survived and he wondered how many were having the same guilty feelings. "How could the pilots let them into the cockpit? How come not one of the planes signaled that there was a hijacking? How could this elaborate hijacking be planned in another country?"

When the train pulled into his stop, he rushed out of the car rudely brushing against anyone in his path. The walk home through the quiet streets of his neighborhood calmed him down. His wife was in the kitchen, when he opened the front door. She called out, "How was your first day back in the office?"

"It's a dump and I hate it."

"It can't be that bad."

"What do you know? You weren't there."

Terri turned away and stirred one of the pots on the stove. Ever since 9/11 Jim had been angry. The only variation was the degree of his anger. Any little thing would set him off. It did not matter if she said it or Keith. She did not know what to do. She tried to console him, but Jim did not want any consolation from anyone.

Jim knew he was wrong, but he could not control himself. What really made him mad was that everyone around him was looking for signs that he was upset and constantly asking if he was okay.

Jim thought, "I normally have a temper anyway, so it is no big deal if it is a little worse. I don't need any help. I'll work it out myself." He knew she did not deserve that, so he attempted to force himself to remain calm.

He sat down at the table, remaining silent for a moment.

Jim was irritated at the way he acted, but he was no longer in full control of his emotions. He wondered how he would have acted, if Terri were at the trade center and he were home waiting.

He was able to check his anger enough to give the perception of normalcy. He forced himself to settle into his new routine and pretend that there was meaning to his work and fake his interest in life. He could not stop feeling that he should have been crushed under the rubble and his remains scattered with the dust that erupted over the area.

On a Friday in November, he received an email that Janice was in serious condition. He wanted to go see her, but he knew her family would be there and did not feel it was his place to intrude. He worried all weekend and on Monday he received the dreaded email that she had passed.

Jim's anger about the cold blooded killings on September 11th overshadowed all other emotions, but when he read the email, he broke down and cried in his windowless office with the door closed.

He knew it was coming, but that did not make it any easier. He thought of her son, who meant everything to Janice. Jim wondered what would happen.

Jim remembered, when Janice was pregnant how he would joke that she could not reach the keyboard, because she was so fat. Jim was surprised, when she told him her marriage was in trouble. Jim thought about how he has been treating Terri and promised not to let that happen to his marriage. It struck him that now Janice was helping him again.

The service was the next day at a synagogue on the Upper East Side. It was a damp, raw day with a gusty wind; a reminder that winter was just around the corner. Janice was very religious and she could never understand why Jim rarely went to church. When Ben proposed to her, one of the conditions was that he had to convert to Judaism. It took a number of months of classes and at the end; Ben had to be given a ritual bath by two Rabbis.

When she told Jim, his only comment was, "He must really love you to let two guys give him a bath."

Janice's parents were standing in the small vestibule when Jim entered.

He slowly walked over to them and said, "I am so sorry that Janice is gone. She was one of the best friends I ever had."

Mrs. Stein forced a smile that redirected a few tears around her mouth. "Janice always spoke very highly of you. She told me how close you both were. In fact, there was a time when I thought she had a crush on you."

Jim knew she was right but replied, "We were just good friends and that was enough for both of us. I thought she was going to beat it, but she gave it her best."

Mrs. Stein continued, "She was a good daughter and mother, but I wish she never got divorced. Now it may be difficult to see our grandson, since he's going to live with his father."

"I know Ben. I'm sure he'll let you see him whenever you want."

Mr. Stein spoke up, "If Ben doesn't, he knows that I'll go after him." He had a glazed look in his eyes and an angry scowl that accentuated the many wrinkles in his face. He was a big man and even though he was in his late seventies, he still looked as though he could handle himself in any situation.

The synagogue was filled with family, friends, and coworkers. It was a nice service devoid of the structure and rituals of the Catholic Church. Near the end of the service, the Rabbi asked if anyone would like to say a few words about Janice. A few relatives said that she was a wonderful person and mother and would be missed by all. The Rabbi then asked if anyone else would like to say a few words. Jim was not prepared, but he suddenly walked up to the alter and stood in front of the microphone. He was nervous, because he never liked to speak in front of an audience, but he had to speak about his good friend. After the ritualistic clearing of the throat, Jim began.

"Janice and I both started our jobs on the same day. I don't know if we liked each other at first. We both had the same title and reported to the same boss. She sat in a cubicle in front of me. The first few days we had this thick training manual to read. We complained to each other how boring and what a waste of time it was, and that's how our friendship began. My first impression was that Janice was a little cold and distant, but I could not have been more wrong. She was really one of the most outgoing and kindest friends I ever had. We really worked well together, and we kind of kept each other in check. If she was upset over a project at work, I would calm her down with a joke or a look, and she would do the same for me. She was always there to talk about anything. Anyone who knew Janice knew she had a temper. Sometimes at meetings, when I could see her becoming angry, we would instinctively go into our version of good cop bad cop. It worked most of the time. When Terri couldn't reach me the day she went into labor with our first child, she called Janice. Janice didn't care about any meeting. She just ran in all excited and said, "Go home now. You're about to become a father. I would always joke with her when she was pregnant, because she was so self-conscious of all the weight she gained. She was such a good mother, who tried her best to balance work and home life.

"When she was first diagnosed, she was in a state of shock, but that didn't last too long. She was a fighter, and she gave it her best. She rarely took any time off work and she always had a positive attitude. Janice had this inner strength that kept her going."

"She was always there for me. She was always ready to help

anyone, anyway she could. She was even there for me on September 11th, although I never told her. She never knew that she saved my life, but I have no other explanation. I was about to enter the World Trade Center lobby, but someone asked me how Janice was doing. I stopped for a minute and said she was having chemo, but she's holding her own. When I reached the elevator bank, I just missed the elevator and the doors closed in my face and the plane hit before another one came. If it weren't for that brief conversation, I wouldn't be here now. So that is what I mean, when I say that Janice was there for me to the end. I will never forget all the years we knew each other and I will always be grateful for having known her."

Jim walked back to his seat knowing that another part of his life had crumbled away and turned to dust. That night he watched on television as two blue beams of light shot up to the heavens, one for each tower. The light cut through the night the way the destruction cut through his heart. The two beams only shed a light on the anger he had seething inside.

Jim had read that many of the survivors had nightmares about the tragic event, but he never dreamed specifically about it until one night after watching another special on the History Channel. In his dream, he woke up and found himself back in time on the Path train heading to the World Trade Center on September 11th. He looked out the window and saw the bright blue sky and gazed in horror at the passengers, who were riding on a death train. Jim did not know what to do. When the doors opened underneath the trade center, he rushed out and dialed 911 on the emergency phone near the escalator.

When the operator answered, he yelled, "There are two hijacked planes going to crash into the towers. The North Tower will be hit at 8:46 and the South tower at 9:02."

The operator said, "How do you know this?"

"I came back in time from the future and I can prevent the tragedy."

"Is this some kind of prank call?"

Jim panicked and knew he would not get anywhere. He ran to the security desk in the North Tower and cut in front of the line of people waiting for security clearance and screamed, "A plane is going to hit the building in about ten minutes! Everyone run!"

The people in line gave him strange looks as if he was some kind of nut. A security guard came up to him and asked, "Are you okay, sir?"

"Listen to me," Jim yelled, "A plane was hijacked and is headed here. If you don't evacuate, thousands of people will die!"

A second guard came over, and Jim was becoming more irate. Both guards thought Jim was nuts.

One of them firmly grabbed Jim's arm and said, "Let's discuss this further outside."

Jim could not argue, so he walked though the doors out to the plaza.

"Can I see some identification?"

Jim was frazzled. "Don't waste time with that. Help get everyone out. Call the police and have them call the Air Force to intercept the plane."

"Okay sit down and I'll call." The one guard stood over Jim, while he sat on a bench near the fountain and the other called his superior.

"It's almost time. You have to believe me," Jim screamed.

He looked at his watch. It was 8:45. He broke away and began screaming, warning everyone not to go into the building. He suddenly stopped, when he heard the roar of the engines. He looked up and saw the plane coming straight at the tower. He closed his eyes as it knifed through the building and exploded in flames. When he opened his eyes, he was sitting up in his bed.

Chapter 7

It was a late afternoon in the spring of 2002, and Jim was stuck in his windowless office on a conference call, when the lights went out, the phone died, and his monitor went blank.

"Goddamn piece of shit office," Jim mumbled as he opened his door. When he looked out, the entire floor was without electricity. Everyone was standing in small groups.

Marty noticed that the traffic light was out, and the sign over the pharmacy across the street was dark. "It must be a blackout," he yelled out.

Marty was a programmer, who had been with the company about ten years. He was very intelligent and had recently obtained his MBA in business. Jim wondered why he continued as a programmer. He could have easily found a higher paying job. Jim thought that Marty was too comfortable in his position and was afraid to make a move that would involve risk. He could totally understand. If you are the only source of income in a family, it is difficult to make a career change and have to prove yourself once again.

Jim walked over to Marty. "I wonder if it's just around here?"

"I hope it's only local" Marty responded, "It better not delay the trains."

Jim continued, "It'll probably be back on in a few minutes. If I had to, I could walk up to Port Authority and take a bus."

A security guard came around and told everyone to leave. The whole city was out, and he heard it was also some other states. Jim remembered back to the first big black out in New York City in 1965 where everyone helped each other and there was no violence or looting. The blackout in 1977 was totally different with rampant looting and overall chaos.

It was after 4:30 when everyone began to leave and attempt to reach home. Jim left the office and began walking to Penn Station

One-Way Elevator

hoping that the blackout would soon be over. The streets of New York were chaotic with electricity, but without power it was a sea of turmoil. It was light, so there was still a party atmosphere. People sat outside the bars and restaurants drinking beer, before it would succumb to the heat and taste like warm piss.

It was difficult to cross the streets with no traffic lights. In the 1965 blackout pedestrians directed traffic. In 2002 it was every man for himself. Jim's hopes dimmed slightly, each block he walked. The streets were jammed with people with everyone leaving work at the same time. The traffic was stop and go, and most of the intersections were blocked. The horns honked and the people shuffled up the streets and zigzagged though the maze of traffic. When Jim reached Penn Station, there was a cop directing traffic, so there was some semblance of order. The famous marquee in front of Madison Square Garden was dark and the Empire State Building loomed in the background, majestic with or without light. Of course no trains were running in or out, so Jim decided to try his last option and walked to the Port Authority Bus Terminal on 40th and Eighth Avenue. It was the same path he had walked on 9/11.

It appeared that many other people had the same idea. The streets going uptown were also clogged, and it was slow moving. When he reached Port Authority, there were no lights and no buses. He heard that there was a ferry leaving from the far west side that would go to Weehawken, which had power. If he could reach Weehawken, Terri could drive there and pick him up. The sidewalks were overflowing with people and many were forced to walk in the street. Everyone was rushing to the ferry and between the cars and the people; he felt as if he were stuck inside a giant video game.

A petite young woman walked up to Jim and asked, "Can I walk with you to the ferry?"

Jim was surprised, but recovered quickly and replied, "Sure, I can use the company."

She extended her hand and said with a noticeable eastern European accent, "I'm Irena. These crowds make me nervous."

He shook her hand and replied, "I'm Jim, and I hate these crowds too."

They began walking together, and Jim started the conversation by asking, "Where do you work?"

"I work for Macy's. I'm the manager of the cosmetic department."

Jim glanced at her closely as they walked. Irena was in her early thirties with blonde hair in a pageboy cut. Her skin was perfect, almost like fine porcelain. He could not tell if it was the makeup or her natural skin. Her eyes were blue and her face was angular but very attractive. She was about five feet two without the two-inch heels she was carefully balancing on. She could not have weighed more than one hundred pounds, but she had the curves of a full-grown woman.

"Where 's your office?" she asked.

"It's on 26th street. It was in the World Trade Center, but we moved there after 9/11." Jim attempted to lighten the conversation. "This is nothing compared to 9/11. A few lights, out no big deal."

Irena gave him a somber look and said, "I lost my husband on 9/11."

Jim almost stopped short. He felt like an idiot. What could he say now to make amends for his stupidity? "I'm so sorry. I shouldn't have mentioned 9/11."

She did not appear to be upset. "You had no way of knowing."

In an apologetic voice, Jim grumbled, "I guess so, but I still should have kept my mouth shut."

"It's good for a change to hear someone actually talk about it. All my friends and family feel like they can never mention it. It's a taboo subject."

"I guess you're right. I think about it all the time, but I don't talk about it too much. The only reason I'm alive is that I stopped to talk to someone for a moment and then the elevator door closed in my face. I would have been on the elevator when the plane hit."

She smiled. "I'm glad you survived."

Jim made it his mission to protect Irena from the crowd and see that she arrived home safely. She had to be a strong person to move on with her life after such a loss. Jim wondered what Terri would have done. He tried not to think about it and focused his attention on Irena.

When they arrived near the pier, there were thousands of people waiting in a long line about ten persons wide and three blocks long. They stood in line, but there was little movement. Everyone was becoming more restless and irritable as time moved forward. At the current speed, it would be hours before they would be able to squeeze onto a ferry. The sun was sinking in the sky, and pretty soon the moon and the stars would be the only light. There were all sorts of rumors spreading through the crowd. Someone said the whole east coast was out. Someone said it started in Canada. Another theory was that it was terrorists. Jim had a bottle of water in his bag. He was thirsty, but he was hesitant to drink too much because then he would have to go to the bathroom. He offered some to Irena but she refused, probably for the same reason. They talked about anything that came to mind. It turned out Irena was a big baseball fan. Even though she liked the Mets instead of the Yankees, Jim thought that if he had to be stuck, he was lucky to be stuck with Irena. The latest rumor meandering through the weary crowd was that some buses were leaving Port Authority.

"So what do you think?" Jim asked. "Do we stay here, or try for the buses?"

Irena looked nervous and replied, "I don't want to be in this crowd when it gets dark."

Jim nodded in agreement and said, "Okay, let's see what happens." Jim was like an offensive tackle blocking and leading Irena through the scrimmage line of bodies. They began walking east up 40th street knowing that they had to get on a bus soon. It was dusk when they were about two blocks away. The empty buses were coming up 40th street and then making a left onto Eighth Avenue and loading at the corner of 41st, between the old and new Port Authority buildings. Barricades were set up to control the lines. Jim heard that once each bus was filled, it would go to the Meadowlands in East Rutherford. That is where The New York Giants Football Stadium and the New Jersey Nets basketball arena were located. There was a huge parking lot, so it could easily accommodate all the buses and cars picking up the weary travelers. Jim and Irena walked to 41st street, but the line was worse than at the ferry. It was now dark and people were in the street and the buses were turning the corner, which made for a dangerous combination. Jim would have carried Irena if he thought she would have let him. He held her arm at the bicep and kept her as close as he could. The line stretched back down 40th street, where the empty buses were idling, waiting to make the turn. People began banging on the doors for the bus driver to let them on early. The drivers refused, but some began banging harder and cursing at the drivers. The only lights were from the buses and cars.

Jim was amazed at how quickly the order and civility was replaced by survival of the fittest instinct. One driver opened his door and the crowd rushed in filling every seat and available standing room. Once the other drivers saw what happened, their doors opened and the restless crowd streamed in. The people who were following the rules and waiting in line would never get a seat. Once they saw the buses come around the corner filled, people pushed through the barriers and went out on the street to jump on the first available bus. Jim thought the best thing would be to walk back down 40th street and hope that a bus would open its doors. They carefully meandered through the crowd that had turned ugly. Jim put his shoulder into someone who was too close to Irena. He could see the look of concern in her eyes.

"Don't worry. We will get a seat on the bus."

"I hope it's soon."

They turned the corner and walked back down 40th until the crowd thinned out. When Jim saw an empty bus turn the corner, he jumped in its path and flagged it down.

The bus stopped short and he ran over to the driver's window pleading, "Can you let us on here?"

The driver opened the window and said, "My orders are to pick up in front of Port Authority."

Jim remained calm and said, "I know, but it's chaos up there. There are no lines and it's just a free for all. Can you let us on?"

The driver looked at Irena and said, "Okay, hurry up."

The door opened and Jim and Irena hustled on. Once the door was opened, it was like a beacon for the desperate travelers. It felt so good to sit down. They had been standing or walking for a little over four hours.

Irena looked at Jim and said, "Thank you so much for staying with me."

"I'm glad I could help, even though I really didn't do much."

"I don't know what I would have done without you."

One-Way Elevator

Jim felt embarrassed, and it was hard for him not to be attracted to this beautiful woman. "I can't believe how quickly things just fell apart."

"It was pretty frightening," Irena softly replied.

The bus made the turn and then sat in stop and go traffic on Eighth Avenue. At the corner of 42nd and eighth, there were cops directing traffic. Jim would not feel safe, until the bus was in the Lincoln Tunnel on its way to the New Jersey Meadowlands.

Jim said, "I always heard that quote from Karl Marx who said, 'No country is more than three meals away from a revolution.' In America it's no more than three hours without electricity."

Jim called Terri and they agreed to meet right in front of the Net's arena. It was about a twenty-minute ride for Terri.

"If you can't get a ride, my wife is picking me up and we can drive you home."

"Thanks, but you've already done so much for me. Let me see if I can get a ride."

Irena called a friend, who agreed to pick her up. Luckily Irena lived in Lyndhurst, which was close to the Meadowlands.

"When you went to work this morning," Jim joked, "I bet you never thought you would be on a bus with some guy you met in a blackout."

Irena smiled briefly and with a hint of sadness in her eyes. "The way things go, I shouldn't be surprised at anything anymore."

Once again Jim felt he had tried to make a joke, but only dredged up bad memories.

Irena then said, "Let me give you my cell phone number."

"I was just going to ask you for your number."

Irena knew everything always came back to that day. She closed her eyes for a minute.

Jim watched her and wondered what she was thinking. It was a welcome sight to see lights. When the bus pulled into the Meadowlands, it was almost as crowded as a concert or a football game. When Jim and Irena arrived at the meeting spot, Irena's friend was waiting. Irena ran up and gave her a big hug.

Irena grabbed Jim's hand and said, "This is my body guard, Jim. I don't know what I would have done without him tonight. Jim, this is Ann, who lives on the same block as me."

Ann was in her mid thirties, tall, and slender with long dark wavy hair and straight bangs across her forehead. Her eyes were wide and deep set. Her nose was angular in perfect proportion to her face. Her smile was inviting, and her lips were full.

When they shook hands, Ann held on a bit too long and there was a moment of embarrassment, but Irena continued. "You should have seen the crowd and how everyone was pushing to get on the buses. I've been thrown under the bus before, but this time I was afraid it was actually going to happen."

"I wouldn't let that happen," Jim said.

Terri stood at the bottom of the stairs and saw Jim talking with two very attractive women. Terri looked at her sweat pants and baggy tee shirt and felt intimidated. She slowly, almost hesitantly, walked up the stairs to the landing.

"Jim," she called. "I'm so glad you made it." She gave him a hug and a big kiss. Jim quickly said, "This is Irena, who I met in the city, and her friend Ann, who is here to drive her home. Irena, Ann, this is my wife Terri."

"I don't know what I would have done if your husband didn't help me," Irena said, "I would still be over there, and it was getting dangerous."

Terri gave Jim a look. "Oh, Jim will give anyone the shirt off his back."

"Jim, how come you never mentioned you had such a beautiful wife?" Irena teased.

Jim's face flushed and he felt Terri's stare. "We were in a blackout. I guess I had other things on my mind."

Irena went up to Jim and gave him a big hug and a peck on the cheek. "Thank you for everything. I'm so glad we met."

Jim tried to act nonchalant. "I'm glad everything worked out tonight. It was nice meeting you." He then said to Ann, "Nice meeting you too. Drive safely."

Terri said an emotionless goodbye and walked toward the car with Jim. After a few steps, Jim turned and took one more look at Irena. Terri stomped her way to the car with Jim following a few steps behind. She was silent until the car was on the highway. "So you pick up a younger woman in a blackout?"

"I didn't pick up a woman."

"Well it sure looked like it to me."

"She asked if she could walk with me, because the crowd made her nervous."

"Oh come on. If she wanted protection, she could have found someone bigger and tougher looking than you. You're no bodyguard."

"It wasn't like that at all."

"I saw the way you looked at the two of them back there. What were you thinking about, a threesome?"

"What the hell are you talking about? I'm not looking to cheat on you. You are way out of line on this one."

"I don't think so."

"The reason I stayed with her and made sure she was safe was because her husband was killed on 9/11," Jim shouted, "I kept on thinking how you would be, if I had been killed that day."

"I'm sorry," Terri said in a subdued voice, "I guess I jumped to the wrong conclusion."

Jim calmed down and said, "How would you have known."

Terri continued with her apology. "Do you know how I feel every day when you leave the house? I'm afraid you won't come back. I'm afraid something will happen and I'll lose you. When I saw you standing with Irena, I said to myself, you survived 9/11 and now I don't want to lose you to anyone else."

Jim never thought of the stress on Terri. He was only looking at things from his own point of view.

Jim placed his hand on her shoulder. "Don't worry. You won't lose me."

Terri smiled. "I want us to grow old together. I love you."

"I love you too."

The next morning he went to work, but he could not concentrate.

He took out Irena's cell phone number and was going to call to see how she was. He began to dial, but hung up before it rang. Was that the only reason he was calling? He sat for a minute staring at the piece of paper with the number. He crumpled the piece of paper in his hand and threw it in the trash.

One-Way Elevator

Chapter 8

By the time 2003 rolled around, Jim's anger remained, but at a subdued level. Jim had learned like most Americans to move on with his life, but the nation was on the road to war with Iraq. Jim followed the events closely, but to him it appeared to be a forgone conclusion. He watched with interest how the pieces of the puzzle were forced into place to frame Saddam Hussein as a madman with weapons of mass destruction.

Jim wondered why the government was suddenly so concerned about how Hussein had treated his people. Yes, he had used poison gas in the past, but where was the outcry at that time? Where was the outcry, when it was the United States who supplied the chemical weapons to Iraq in the first place?" The links being reported between Hussein and Al-Qaeda just seemed too convenient. Jim saw photographs on the news of suspected sites where the weapons could be hidden and he could not tell if they were from Iraq or Newark.

Jim thought back to the Gulf of Tonkin in Vietnam. He remembered President Johnson stating that an American ship had been attacked and that was the justification to pass the Gulf of Tonkin Resolution, which greatly expanded the Vietnam War. It was later proven that there had been no real attack, but it was too late to save the thousands of U.S. soldiers and at least one million Vietnamese, who died in the war that the U.S. should never have been involved in.

When he heard the Secretary of State Condoleezza Rice talk about Yellowcake allegedly procured by Iraq that would be used against the United States, Jim wondered if that was true, or if we were being sold another bill of goods. He listened to General Shinseki, who said it would take almost half a million troops to invade and occupy Iraq. He watched Donald Rumsfeld state that the invasion could be successful with only 125,000 troops. Who was telling the truth? Did Rumsfeld know that with the lower troop estimate he could obtain approval from congress? With the war in Afghanistan still going on, using the lower number could show that the army would not be stretched too thin. Once the war had started, he could always ask for more troops.

Colin Powell neatly wrapped up the package when he spoke at the United Nations and displayed new photos of suspected sites for the weapons of mass destruction.

In college, Jim had protested the Vietnam War, but now he felt that any protest would be futile. Maybe he did not have the energy to protest, or maybe he had become apathetic. He felt the country was going to war based on a pack of lies, and most Americans either believed the media, or felt protesting was as pointless as attempting to patch the leak on the Titanic.

Jim watched his television screen light up as the bombs exploded over Bagdad. He watched the tanks and armored vehicles roll across the Iraqi dessert. He watched the statue of Saddam Hussein topple. He was tired of hearing the words, "Coalition Forces," when it was mostly American forces with some support from England with its long history of colonization, conquests and the manipulation of borders. George Bush and Tony Blair held many press conferences together. They appeared to be friends and presented a united front.

Jim wondered what would have happened if Al Gore were President. Jim felt that Al Gore had won the election in 2000, but the Supreme Court handed it to George Bush, for reasons he could never figure out, other than outright fraud. Jim no longer trusted anything he read in the papers or watched on the network news. He did not feel that the war in Iraq was a fight for our freedom, but that our freedom had been eroded since September 11th with the passage of the Patriot Act as the foundation. How could anyone be against the Patriot Act? That would be unpatriotic. The title was good, but it was the content that was questionable. It was similar to believing diet soda was healthy, until one read the ingredients listing all the harmful chemicals.

***

Keith was in his senior year and had to make a decision on college. He was an above average student, but his scores on the College Boards were only average. Keith was into film and music. His weakest subject was math, which was why his scores were not higher. He was not in many clubs and he had almost given up on sports, because he wanted to concentrate on music. It was quite a surprise when he was accepted to Drexel, American University, The School of Visual Arts in New York City and Berklee College of Music in Boston.

"Where do you think I should go, Dad?"

Jim felt proud that his son had been accepted at every college, but he was more proud that Keith was asking him for advice.

"I think you have to do what is most comfortable for you. Don't go by what others tell you alone. You can take their advice, but in the end you have to live with the decision you make. Remember, if you don't like a school, there's no reason you can't change. Don't let yourself get locked into one thing. You don't have to decide what you want to do with the rest of your life now. College is a big decision, but it's only one in a long list that you'll have to go through."

Keith did not want a lecture. He needed a push. He looked down at the floor and said, "I have to make a decision pretty soon."

Jim could see that Keith was struggling. "If you really like music, take a chance now, because if you don't do it now, you'll always wonder what would have happened if you did. You can always change your major or switch schools. Whatever you decide, your mom and I will support you."

"What would you do if you were me?"

"I've always been too conservative. I wished I had taken a few chances."

"What chance did you want to take that you didn't?"

Jim took a moment to compose his story. "I had a friend who lived in Hoboken back in the mid seventies. He told me about how the brownstones were selling for about $50,000 and you also received a low cost mortgage from the government. At that time Hoboken was pretty run down. Most brownstones had three floors and a basement apartment. The only catch was that you had to live there for five years and fix it up. If I rented out the other floors and the basement apartment, it would have more than paid my mortgage. I wish I had taken that chance."

"How come you didn't do it?"

"I just couldn't bring myself to live in Hoboken, no matter how cheap. Now I'm kicking myself, when I see how it has changed so much for the better. The brownstones are going for at least a million dollars and the rents are outrageous. I could have been a rich man. But you never know what's going to happen. If I had bought it, maybe I wouldn't have met your mother and you wouldn't be here right now. I wouldn't trade you or your mother for anything."

Keith grinned. "So I'm worth more than a million dollars to you?"

"No, you cost me more than a million dollars and still counting." He gave a playful tap to the side of Keith's head.

Keith faked a left jab. "You wouldn't know what to do with all your money if I wasn't around,"

Jim turned serious. "You're probably right. If you want my opinion, I would try for Berklee. If you graduate and can't make a career in music, you can always work for an insurance company."

Jim felt like that was a memorable moment in their relationship.

***

"I've made my decision," Keith announced one week later.

Jim and Terri stopped what they were doing. "Okay, let's hear it."

Keith cleared his throat. "I've decided to go to Drexel and major in communications."

Jim was confused. What happened to his talk about taking a chance? "That's great. Drexel is a good school. What made you pick communications?"

"I'm not sure what I want to do, so I picked communications until I figure it out."

Jim was dismayed. *He took my advice of having a backup, but he left out the taking a chance part.*

Terri said, "That's good news. Drexel is a highly rated school, so no matter what major you pick, you'll get a great education."

Terri was relieved that Keith did not go to Berklee, because it was so hard to make it in music. He had to come out of college with some marketable skill.

Jim could sense that Keith was not fully committed to his choice. At eighteen, it was difficult to make a life altering decision. Jim's only consolation was that Keith was not going into the army with the wars in the Middle East.

Chapter 9

By June, 2006, The 9/11 Commission had long ago released its report stating that Al-Qaeda was responsible for the terror plot, but Jim often wondered if this was just another white wash. Was it more of a political document than a factual one? He was browsing the aisles in *Barnes and Noble,* when he came across a book stating that 9/11 was a government conspiracy, and The 9/11 Commission Report was full of lies and did not reveal the full story. Jim had heard rumors of a conspiracy before, but he had ignored the stories and kept his own questions locked away in his secret compartment for another time. He tried to block out that day from his memory, because he found that was the best therapy. When he did that, he was not as angry and he could move forward with his life and concentrate on his family and career.

He thought back to the questions he'd had about the Kennedy assassination, and the Gulf Of Tonkin resolution and wondered if he could fully believe anything the government said. But then how could the government kill three thousand of its own people?

He thought of the Iraq war, which he felt was based on lies. The government had sent thousands of soldiers into battle, knowing that many would die, so it could be conceivable that civilian deaths would not be off limits.

Jim stood frozen in his thoughts for a moment and then marched up to the register to pay for the book. Driving home, he vowed to read the book with an objective mind. He would need real proof that could be verified, before he would believe anything.

When he arrived home, Terri was in the kitchen making a cup of tea.

When she saw the bag she asked, "What did you buy?"

Jim pulled out the book and once she read the title, she scoffed, "You're not one of those conspiracy nuts, are you?"

"Not yet. I just want to see if any of it makes any sense. I'll let you know when I finish."

"Sit down and have a cup of tea and forget about crazy conspiracies."

Jim was a little annoyed by her condescending tone, but he kept his cool. "It doesn't hurt to question. I'm not someone who believes everything the government says. Just because it comes from Washington doesn't mean it's true."

"You sound like you already believe it's a conspiracy, before you even start the book."

"No, it's just like you tell your students, 'Just because it's on the Internet doesn't mean it's true.' Well, my comment is, 'Just because it's from the government doesn't mean it's true' either."

"Now you're acting like one of my students."

Jim kept his composure. "Sometimes the teacher learns from the student."

Terri smiled and said, "You're right," and ended the mini sparring match in a draw.

***

While brushing his teeth before bed, Jim thought back to the moment when he saw the South Tower collapse. The fact that stayed with him was how fast it came down. He knew the official explanation was the impact of the plane knocked the insulation from the steel beams. The fires then were so hot that the steel melted and the beams all gave way and the floors collapsed upon each other.

Jim also thought back to a *New York Times* article he had seen a few weeks after 9/11, which stated that several of the names listed as hijackers were incorrect and the alleged hijackers were found to be alive and well. Jim had originally thought it was an honest mistake, but after spitting out the last of the toothpaste and watching it swirl around the sink before disappearing, he began to wonder.

From the start, this did not appear to be a book written by someone with an unbelievable, crazy, far fetched theory. According to the Preface, 42% of the population believed that the government and

The 9/11 Commission concealed crucial evidence. A Scripps Howard/Ohio University poll stated that 36% believed that federal officials either participated in the attacks on 9/11, or took no action to stop them, because they wanted the United States to go to war in the Middle East. Jim never realized so many people felt that way. If so, then why wasn't a new investigation started into what really happened? He read that there was a 9/11 Truth Movement, so he decided to check out the website.

According to the author, there were many professionals and intellectuals, who proved that the official story of 9/11 was false. Jim felt he was entering a new world where the blinders were removed, and everything would become clear.

Jim remembered how foolish he felt when he'd played, "Three Card Monte," on Seventh Avenue a number of years ago. He saw a small crowd gathered around a young man standing behind a small folding table. Jim watched as the man showed the two black cards and the one red card and after turning each face down, began moving them around.

The dealer yelled out like a carnival barker, "Pick the red card and you win. Put ten or twenty dollars and I'll match it if you pick the right card."

Jim watched and one guy was betting and winning. Then another man bet forty dollars and Jim thought he was going to win, but when the card was turned over, it was black. The loser was angry and stormed away. Jim saw that the red card had a slight bend so he followed it closely as the three cards were moved around face down on the table. Nobody was betting and every few seconds the dealer would show the red card and continue to prod people to bet.

Jim watched and followed the bent card and when the dealer stopped, he threw twenty dollars on it.

The dealer asked, "Are you sure this is the red card?"

Jim smiled and nodded.

The dealer continued, "Okay. Let's see."

He turned the card over and it was black. Jim was shocked. How could he be so stupid? He knew the cards were switched, but he was staring closely and he did not see anything. The guy who was winning was probably working with the dealer. He was angry at how easily he was manipulated. He was angry with himself. He knew the truth, but he was enticed by the thought of easy money. It all seemed so simple, but he missed the crucial point of the switch. Jim wondered if the government was running a "Three Card Monte" scheme on the public. See the pictures and hear the easy explanation, but miss the obvious. His mind was racing too much to read anymore that night.

The next night, when Jim entered the 9/11 Truth Movement website, he was overwhelmed by the amount of information available. How could he determine a valid question from a theory with no basis? Since he was neither an architect nor a physicist, he might believe things that he read, that were way off base. He reminded himself that he was a systems analyst, who had learned to gather information and make recommendations based on the analysis of the data. This was how he made a living. He would treat his research like a project. The objective was to determine if there were sufficient unanswered questions to warrant a new, independent investigation. He was now beginning the data collection phase. He would try to use as many sources as possible. He would then analyze the data and make a recommendation based on that analysis. It would be hard not to come to a conclusion before the analysis was complete, but that was no different than most projects. The big difference was that with this project nearly three thousand people died, and Jim was almost one of them. It would be difficult to remain detached. Was the motive as simple as the government line, "They hate us because of our freedom"? Or was it some hidden agenda only known to a select few? He planned to follow the yellow brick road and see if there was someone pulling the strings from behind the curtain.

One of the first questions was, how were the planes able to be hijacked and flown into the building without being intercepted? For background information, Jim read about the standard operating procedures for the air traffic controllers and the Federal Aviation Administration. When a plane loses radio contact, it is not immediately considered serious, but when a flight is significantly off course, it is considered a real emergency, because it could collide with another plane. When American Airlines flight 11 lost radio contact at 8:14, no calls were made, but when the flight went off course around 8:21 the procedure was to call the Northeast Air Defense Sector (NEADS).

The emergency procedure was to intercept the flight as quickly as possible. If the procedure was followed and the call made to NEADS, then the fighters would have been scrambled no later than 8:27 and the hijacked aircraft intercepted no later than 8:37, which was several minutes before the North Tower was struck.

For some reason the FAA did not notify NEADS until 8:40, which was too late. The question was, why was the procedure not followed, or if it was, was the time of the call covered up, because of a stand down order?

This was the first time Jim had considered that the hijackings could have been allowed to happen. He found it hard not to be judgmental and jump to conclusions without all the facts.

It was uncovered that the military knew at 8:43 that United Airlines flight 175, which crashed into the South Tower, had been hijacked. Why did it take until 8:52 for the fighters to take off? Jim also wondered why the fighters were not scrambled from McGuire Air Force Base in New Jersey rather than Otis Air Force Base in Massachusetts. No wonder they did not have time to intercept the hijacked planes! There appeared to be inconsistencies in the timeline presented by The 9/11 Commission and various other reports.

He became angry again, because he fully understood that if what he read was true, the planes never should have hit the towers.

In the beginning of his research, Jim was depressed, because it brought him back to that dark time in his life, but it soon became his mission to find out the truth. The more he read, the more vital the mission became. His day job no longer seemed essential. His other interests were put aside, and his relationship with his wife was once again strained similar to the time directly after 9/11. Terri noticed the change and at first was not concerned. All Jim wanted to talk about was 9/11, but she usually found some way to change the subject, or make some excuse to leave the room.

Jim was up late one night on the computer reading articles on various websites about different aspects of the conspiracy while Terri was reading in bed with her eyes closed. Her open book had fallen in her lap with the bookmarker on her chest.

Jim ripped the blanket down knocking her book to the floor and said in a low, almost maniacal voice, "Those mother fuckers did it, and they should all be hanged by the balls."

Terri awoke from her deep sleep, stunned to see the look of anger in Jim's eyes. She rolled over and said, "Forget about your conspiracy and go to sleep. It's late."

"Do you really understand why the towers fell?"

"Will you stop reading all that crap?" Terri pleaded, "We can talk about it some other time."

Jim did not like being dismissed. "You won't even listen. What are you afraid of? Are you afraid if you found out the truth, it may upset your little world? You can't bring yourself to believe that your government could be behind it. You don't think the FBI or the CIA could pull it off with a little help from some other agencies? You don't think that a lot of people knew it was going to happen? You don't want to admit that The 9/11 Commission was no better than the Warren Commission? Yes, some of the stuff I read is crazy, but a lot of it makes sense. I haven't read enough to be fully convinced, but now that I've started, I'm not turning back."

When Jim looked at Terri, she appeared to be fast asleep on her side in a fetal position. Jim turned off the light and quickly fell asleep.

Terri opened her eyes when the light went out and was wide-awake, with her mind racing and worrying about Jim.

***

The next and most obvious question was, why did the towers collapse? There were a lot of alternative theories, but the one thing Jim found was the official explanation did not make logical sense and also violated the laws of physics.

The National Institute of Science and Technology (NIST) said that the towers were not built to withstand the impact of a Boeing 767. At the time the trade center was built, the largest plane was a Boeing 707. A 767 was 20% larger, but the analysis was based on the 707 travelling at 600 miles per hour. The 767 that hit the North Tower, was travelling at 440 miles per hour. The energy released from the impact of a 707 at 600 miles per hour was greater than a 767 travelling at 440 miles per hour. That fact was conveniently ignored.

The 9/11 Commission also ignored a statement made earlier by John Skilling, who was responsible for the structural design of the twin towers.

He said, "There would be a horrendous fire and a lot of people would be killed, but the building structure would still be there."

Jim wondered why the designer was not consulted.

NIST also said that the planes sliced through several core columns and stripped off the insulation. Then the question was, if the fires weakened the steel, why did the South Tower, which was hit after the North Tower, collapse first? Jim's data gathering only raised more questions.

In order to begin to melt steel, the temperature had to be 1,000 degrees Celsius. The steel framework of each tower was 90,000 tons and since steel was a conductor of heat, it would have taken fires burning at 1,000 degrees Celsius many hours before the steel would weaken. The time it took each tower to collapse was measured in minutes, not hours. The duration that the fires may have reached their highest temperatures was about fifteen to twenty minutes after impact.

Jim was stunned that all this information, which seemed plausible, was not even considered. It began to appear that if the data did not fit the official theory, then according to The 9/11 Commission, it did not exist.

There was no direct evidence that any steel column either in the perimeter or in the core ever reached 1,000 degrees Celsius. Jim felt like an investigative reporter, even though he was reading what others had already investigated. He found no satisfaction in realizing all the inconsistencies, but felt a sickening feeling in the pit of his stomach that the country had been fed a bunch of lies about 9/11.

Jim thought back to the famous movie, "The Towering Inferno," where a fire burned in a high rise for many hours, but did not collapse. There were no critics stating that it was unrealistic for a steel-framed building to burn for hours without collapsing. Was a fictional Hollywood movie more realistic than the government's story?

Jim found information about other fires in steel high-rise buildings. There was a fire in the Meridian Plaza hotel in Philadelphia that burned for 19 hours with no collapse. In May of 1980 the Interstate Bank Building in Los Angeles burned for more than three hours with intense flames. After the fire was extinguished, the fire inspector reported that there was no damage to the main structural members and only minor damage to one secondary beam and a small number of floor panes.

Jim watched a few shows he had recorded on compact disc and timed how long it took the buildings to collapse. The 9/11 Commission said that the upper floors above the impact zone gave way and the lower floors could not hold up under the massive weight. It sounded logical to Jim until he read about Sir Isaac Newton's Law of Physics called, "Conservation Of Momentum." The basic principal was that the undamaged steel and the undamaged floors below would slow down the fall of the building. It was impossible that the building could collapse at that speed, unless the resistance below was somehow removed or compromised. As the mass increased, the speed of the fall should decrease, unless by some miracle the twin towers were not subject to the natural laws of physical science. Jim thought it was just another way of explaining a controlled demolition. The lower floors suffered no damage and should have offered resistance. It was a question that should definitely be answered by a qualified physicist and not some corporate politicians controlled by political strings.

It was estimated that the towers fell in approximately 16 seconds. In a vacuum it would take 9.2 seconds. The conclusion was that in order for the towers to fall that fast, the floors below had to be pulverized. Jim's own inaccurate timing had it at about thirteen seconds. And it definitely was not a vacuum.

Neither NIST nor The 9/11 Commission explored the possibility of controlled demolition. As long as nobody questioned the data, there was little need to back up the data with facts. If people could accept the magic bullet theory brilliantly conceived by Senator Arlen Specter, the collapsing towers seemed like a slam-dunk.

If the towers' fall violated a law of physics, then what other evidence was ignored or manipulated? Jim did not have to do too much research on that one. It all came back to the phrase, "Controlled Demolition." Not only was scientific data ignored, but also eyewitness descriptions of explosives in 118 of the 503 oral histories of 9/11 were rendered irrelevant. The information was released in August 2005.

One of the witnesses was *Wall Street Journal* reporter John Bussey, who said, "I looked up out of the *Wall Street Journal* office window to see what seemed like perfectly synchronized explosions coming from each floor. One after the other, from top to bottom, with a fraction of a second between, the floors blew to pieces. "

William Rodriquez, a janitor in the North Tower, on the morning of 9/11 heard and felt an explosion in the first sub level at 8:46. NIST was contacted with the information, but again it was ignored and discarded.

Jim also read that two firefighters, Chief Otto Palmer and Fire Marshal Ronald P. Bucca had a plan to fight the fires on the 78th floor of the South Tower.

Part of the transcript read, "We've got two isolated pockets of fire. We should be able to knock it down with two lines."

Jim questioned, "Why would there even be a plan to fight the fires, if they were as intense as The 9/11 Commission Report stated?"

It did seem to be a classic example of "Lies Of Omission" because it was also known that some sections of the perimeter steel columns were ejected horizontally and flew over 500 feet. Further proof of horizontal ejections was supported by the fact that over 700 bone fragments were found on the roof of the nearby Deutsche bank building.

Auxiliary Fireman Paul Isaac, spoke about bombs in an interview with Internet Reporter Randy Lavello. Isaac said, "Many other firemen knew there were bombs in the buildings, but they were afraid for their jobs to admit it, because the higher-ups forbade discussion of this fact."

Jim could not understand how all of this evidence, if really true, could be ignored. How could it not be thoroughly investigated? Even a member of the NIST team, who did investigate, said that the burning jet fuel did not melt the steel.

His anger was becoming more intense than in the days after 9/11. He constantly thought about his initial findings and the magnitude of the implications. When he read a *New York Times* story from 2002 by James Glanz and Eric Lipton, he felt like punching a wall.

The article stated, "Perhaps the deepest mystery uncovered in the investigation involves extremely thin bits of steel collected from the trade towers and from 7 World Trade Center. The steel apparently melted away, but no fire in any of the buildings was believed to be hot enough to melt steel outright."

Why wasn't there a public outcry?

He sat down in the TV room while Terri was watching "American Idol." He watched the judges criticize a performer for not being true to himself in the interpretation of the song he sang. He listened as the audience disagreed with the stinging words coming from Simon Cowell, stating the performance was listless, off key, and unimaginative. The young performer hung his head as he was warned that he might not make it to the top ten, unless he has a strong performance next week.

Jim could not believe how millions of people watched every move and carefully scrutinized every note of each performer, while the facts about something that was actually important were left untouched. Was it easier to worry about the fortune of a dozen fame seekers, than the reasons for the loss of nearly three thousand? Jim wished he were a scientist, chemist, physicist, or an architect so he could better understand the implications of what he was reading. He did not know how to design a building or fully comprehend the laws of physics, which could not be violated like any man made law. He sat in his office, stared at the walls, and imagined the steel columns behind those walls holding up the entire building. He had just read that the steel had thinned due to sulfidation. He was not familiar with that term, but now fully understood the impact of when sulfur is mixed with thermite. The effect was to greatly lower the temperature at which steel melted. The result was that a one-inch column could be reduced to a half inch with razor sharpness. It seemed so obvious that this was why the buildings collapsed, but the site was never tested for explosives by NIST. Was the reason for not testing, because they knew what the results would be? The bigger question was, "Who were 'they'?"

Was NIST ordered not to perform any test for explosives and was The 9/11 Commission ordered not to pursue that line of investigation?

Stephen Jones studied dust samples from the site. As a physicist, he knew that iron-aluminum rich micro spheres were produced in thermite control reactions and that was exactly what he found.

To Jim that was the most damning piece of evidence and yet why was this not being reported in the media and why wasn't anyone investigating who did it? People had been convicted of murder on less evidence! Jim wanted an expert to verify Stephen Jones's findings, which would be a good first step. If verified, the next question would be, "How were the explosives planted in the building?"

One night, he took a slight detour on his walk back home from the train. He stood in front of the small 9/11 memorial and shook his head and clenched his fists as he read the names. He tried to imagine his name carved in that cold stone and wondered what would have happened to his family, if he had not survived. He knew how much he loved his family and he knew that they loved him, but the very event that should have moved them closer was now pulling them apart. Terri was against his research, and Keith did not like to hear them argue. So far Keith had not taken sides, but Jim hoped it would not come to that.

He read in bed while Terri watched the Tonight Show with Jay Leno. While Leno made jokes about George Bush's intelligence and mangling of the English language, Jim read that two of Bush's relatives were in the same company that was in charge of security at the World Trade Center. There were reports that over the weekend before 9/11, the power was off in the South Tower and many workers were coming and going. Also in the North Tower, the passenger elevators were out of service on the west side of the building and crews were supposedly working to restore.

Jim also read that Scott Forbes, an employee in the South Tower reported that on the weekend of September 8th and 9th, floors 50 and above had the power off for 36 hours, because the electrical cables were being upgraded. Of course, this was not investigated. Jim felt it was something that could be easily checked. Jim had no idea how much thermite would be necessary to bring down each of the towers, or how explosives could be set without detection, but they were questions that should be answered. Jim wondered how many other things were left out of The 9/11 Commission Report, when it did not even mention the fact that a 47-story building also collapsed. It's not like it was an oversight or a typo. When 7 World Trade Center collapsed, it was the first time a steel framed building had collapsed from fire alone, but did someone order that it be excluded from the report? There was more controversy when an American Idol contestant inadvertently left out a few words from a cover song.

Jim became more cynical about politics and the wars in Iraq or Afghanistan. When he heard the president or any politician state that our troops were fighting the terrorists to keep us free, he was sure he would throw a left hook, if that politician were in front of him. He thought of all the soldiers fighting and dying not to protect our freedom, but to foster someone else's agenda.

He wasn't totally sure of the old expression, but the words, "I have met the enemy and it is us," came to mind.

He wondered if this could be the biggest cover up in United States history.

Chapter 10

The more he read about the collapse of 7 WTC, the more he became convinced of a cover up. Two New York City officials stated there were explosions early in the morning. Michael Hess was the city's corporate counsel and Barry Jennings was the director of the Emergency Services Department of the City Housing Agency. Neither would have any reason to lie or to make up a story, especially about 9/11. They were both on the 23rd floor, which is where the Office of the Emergency Management Command Center was located. There was no one else there and all the power was out, so they began to walk down the stairs.

When they reached the sixth floor, Jennings said, "The landing that we were standing on gave way – there was an explosion and the landing gave way. The explosion was beneath me."

Jennings knew it had to be an explosion and not from one of the towers collapsing on the building because he said, "Both buildings were still standing."

A Daily News Reporter said, "There was a rumble. The building's top row of windows popped out. Then all the windows on the thirty-ninth floor. Then the thirty-eighth. Pop! Pop! Pop. Was all you heard until the building sunk into a rising cloud of gray."

There were other reports of explosions, but they were ignored. There was also a reporter from the BBC, who announced the collapse of 7 World Trade Center, while it could still be seen in the background.

Jim was incredulous. If what they said was true, then how come it was never reported in the media, even if it were left out of the other reports? It was theorized by others that 7 WTC was meant to come down at the same time as the twin towers, but something went wrong. Jim agreed with others in the 9/11 Truth Movement who called for a new investigation. Jim wondered if the same people who restricted and manipulated the evidence, would also fight to defeat,

One-Way Elevator

delay or defer a new investigation?

Jim found another website that also listed many of the statements from the Oral History of 9/11. What he read was compelling and added additional evidence that it was not the planes that brought down the towers. He became enraged as he read the different quotes:

Frank Critters – Chief (FDNY) Citywide Tour Commander
"There was what appeared to be at first an explosion. It appeared at the very top, simultaneously from all four sides, materials shot out horizontally. And then there seemed to be a momentary delay before you could see the beginning of the collapse."

Jim wondered why there was nothing covered in the news or The 9/11 Commission.

Kevin Darnowshi – Paramedic (EMS)
"I heard three explosions and then we heard like groaning and grinding and tower two started to come down."

"Sounds like a bomb to me." Jim scrolled down on his MAC desktop computer.

Thomas Fitzpatrick – Deputy Commissioner for Administration (FDNY)
"Some people thought it was an explosion. I don't think I remember that. I remember seeing it. It looked like sparkling around one specific layer of the building. My initial reaction was that this was exactly the way it looks when they show you those implosions on T.V."

Jim was livid, "These individuals would have no reason to lie and make up a story. It seems the only one fabricating a story was the government." He continued:

Joseph Meola – Firefighter (FDNY) Engine 91
"As we are looking up at the building, what I saw was it looked like the building was bowing out on all four sides. We actually heard the pops. Didn't realize it was the falling. You know, you heard the pop, explosions of the building. You thought it was just blowing out."

Jim thought about the traces of nano thermate and the molten steel and muttered under his breath, "You goddamn lying mother fuckers. The whole thing was a set up, and almost everybody bought it."

He could not stop himself from continuing down the page.

Kevin Murray - Firefighter (FDNY) Ladder Company 18
"When the tower started – there was a big explosion that I heard and someone screamed that it was coming down, and I looked away and I saw all the windows domino."

Daniel Rivera – Paramedic (EMS) Battalion 91
"At first I thought it was, do you ever see professional demolitions when they set the charges on certain floors and then you hear, 'Pop, pop, pop, pop, pop?' That's exactly what – because I thought it was that."

Albert Turi – Deputy Assistant Chief (FDNY)
"And as my eyes travelled up the building and I was looking at the South Tower, somewhere about halfway up, my initial reaction was there was a secondary explosion and the entire floor area, a ring right around the building blew out."

Gary Gates _ Lieutenant (FDNY)
"So the explosion, what I realized later, had to be the start of the collapse. It was the way the building appeared to blowout from both sides. I'm looking at the face of it, and all we see is the two sides of the building just blowing out and coming apart like this. As I said, like the top of a volcano."

Jim logged off and decided to go for a long run to try to sort things out. He knew if he continued, he would probably find more evidence of a cover up. He always had the option to stop and just carry on with everything the way it was and count himself lucky to be one of the

One-Way Elevator

survivors. He knew he could not quit, because he would be miserable and feel like a coward. But what could he do with this information? None of what he was finding was original. It was all from others who had done the research. The people who were trying to expose the conspiracy were the ones who should be considered patriots instead of constantly being marginalized.

He thought of his original objective to see if a new investigation was needed. He began to believe that he really could try, when he had enough information collected. Maybe he could help to inform the public, so everyone could make his or her own decision and hopefully start another investigation and bring those involved in the cover-up to justice.

Jim had run six miles and he felt he could have run another ten.

Unfortunately, the feeling did not last long. After a few more weeks, Jim was so distraught and disillusioned; he decided to take a short break from his research. He made an attempt to go back to his normal routine of watching television and falling asleep during the late night television shows, but he found that the mindless dribble emanating from the small screen could not drown out the call to seek the truth. He watched the news and saw reports on the death toll of American troops, which only reignited his anger. He knew that the entire war on terrorism was based on the fact that 19 hijackers flew planes into buildings because they hated our way of life. Was that just propaganda? There was no link between Saddam Hussein and Al-Qaeda other than what the government reported. There were no weapons of mass destruction other than what the government reported. If the government lied to justify a war, what would stop or prevent lies about 9/11? If the government was willing to send hundreds of thousands of troops to invade a country knowing that many would die, what was a mere three thousand innocent civilians? What about the innocent Iraqi civilians killed in the bombings, or as a result of the crippling sanctions? Maybe the people wanted to be free from Saddam Hussein, but how many were willing to die in the process?

Jim saw a news report about a disabled veteran who had his legs blown off in a roadside bomb thanking God that he was still alive and stating that he was proud to serve his country. Jim had tears in his eyes as he watched the young man take his first steps with his new prosthetic legs. Jim was torn. How could he support the troops, but oppose the war? How could he tell someone who was injured, or had a son or daughter die, that the war was based on lies and not to protect our freedom?

Jim thought, "It is ironic that our Commander in Chief, who gave the orders to start two wars, never even fulfilled his service in the Texas Air National Guard."

Jim wondered how Bush could even look at himself in the mirror.

Jim found that he could not abandon his research. He once again contemplated whether 9/11 was just an excuse to launch the war on terror and the wars in Afghanistan and Iraq. If it had been an unexpected terrorist plot, then Jim could understand the call for revenge. He was amazed at how almost the entire country came together to denounce the terrorists and wave the American flag of freedom. Whoever was behind the attacks knew the country would be consumed with fear and revenge, instead of asking questions.

Jim scowled and thought, "They waved the flag, while they covered their tracks and hid behind the veil of patriotism."

Jim pictured Bush, Cheney and Rumsfeld sitting in Washington and then tried to imagine how a hijacked plane could fly around the Capital and crash into the Pentagon without being detected. "Why weren't the fighter jets at Andrews Air Force base used instead of scrambling jets out of Langley Air Force Base 393 miles away? Wouldn't there always be fighter jets on alert to protect the White House, the Capitol Building and that other important building called the Pentagon? With all the billions of dollars spent on defense each year, how could a jet airliner just fly in, do a loop around the city and then crash into the Pentagon without being intercepted or shot down? From January 1, 2001 to September 10th, there were 67 intercepts carried out by NORAD, how could there be none on September 11th?"

Jim also read theories that it was not a plane that hit the Pentagon. There was an eyewitness account from April Gallop, an administrative assistant at the Pentagon, who worked in the damaged area. She reported, she heard a loud boom and debris from the ceiling fell on her.

When she ran outside she said, "I had no jet fuel on me. I didn't see any airplane seats. I didn't see anything on the lawn. I didn't see luggage or metal pieces. "

There were other reports from witnesses who thought they heard a bomb, but it was never fully investigated. Another interesting fact was the reported smell of cordite in the air, which is used in bombs. The smell is completely different from jet fuel. Just like the traces of thermite at the World Trade Center, it was also ignored. Jim could not understand why the offices of Rumsfeld were not targeted. Why were the financial/audit offices on the first floor a target?

A few weeks later Jim stumbled upon a possible answer. At a press conference on September 10th, The Secretary of Defense, Donald Rumsfeld, stated that the Pentagon was missing 2.3 trillion dollars. The old saying, "Follow the Money," could apply. Jim was baffled and thought that theory was a bit of a stretch. If the purpose was to cover up the missing money and it was a bomb, then what happened to the plane? What happened to the people on the plane? What happened to the money? But if there was no evidence of a plane crashing and the radar showed that the plane was over Washington, then how could that be?

If it was a plane that hit the first floor of the Pentagon, an inexperienced pilot could not have maneuvered a commercial airliner to a direct hit without resulting in any damage outside the Pentagon, or wreckage from any parts of the plane, or at least a piece of luggage. Did it all magically disintegrate?

A Boeing 757 was 155 feet long with a wingspan of 125 feet. The height of the plane from the bottom of its engine to the top of the tail was 45 feet, while the fuselage was 13 feet in diameter. The impact hole at the Pentagon was between 15 and 20 feet wide. The height of the hole was approximately 25 feet, which is 20 feet too low to accommodate the tail. The F.B.I. reportedly confiscated all the surveillance video in the area around the Pentagon. If there were not something to hide, why wouldn't they release the video?

The biggest question still was, if it was not a plane that hit the

Pentagon, then what happened to the plane? Jim developed a migraine trying to figure that one out. One other possibility was that like the World Trade Center, the bombs might have been placed to insure that the job was complete. This raised the same questions as to how the bombs could be planted and who had access?

There were more questions than Jim was ready to deal with. Jim also never heard anything further about the missing 2.3 trillion dollars. Even if the offices and all the computers were destroyed, Jim could not comprehend that all the data would not be backed up at some off-site location. Why wasn't there a full investigation into the missing money?

***

By Christmas Jim knew that the only way he could enjoy the holidays was to put his research on hold until after New Year's Day. He went shopping, watched all the incessant commercials on television, decorated his house, put up the tree in the living room next to the fireplace, and organized the Christmas village on a small table in front of the living room window. The glad tidings of the season could not completely overshadow his lingering questions about the real story of 9/11. In the village there was a one-story schoolhouse that he placed on one side with an open area covered with fake snow. He stood in front of his tiny village and imagined that it was Washington D.C. He picked up a miniature sled and held it above the city like a plane. He maneuvered the plane over the village post office, church, and firehouse. He circled his sled close to the schoolhouse that he pictured in his mind as the Pentagon and slowly executed the 330-degree spiral dive that flight 77 allegedly followed and straightened out at ground level, and flew into the schoolhouse without hitting the snow. Jim realized how impossible it would be for a commercial jet liner to perform like his miniature sled. He did it again, this time placing a miniature street sign, like the light posts that were obstacles to flight 77. The maneuver was even harder. The alleged pilot of the plane that crashed into the Pentagon reportedly had trouble even flying a small Cessna. If that was true, how could he execute that pattern? Jim was angry.

He said to himself, "So the most protected village in the world with anti-aircraft batteries and under constant protection allows a sled to circle the village, fly over City Hall and crash into the school house after executing a flight pattern that even Santa Claus would have trouble with. I don't think so. Where would the pieces of the sled go? What about the presents in the sled? It would have been much easier to fly into the back where the principal's office was located. It just made no sense at all."

Jim walked out of the room and into the kitchen, where he poured himself a large glass of Bailey's, even though it was early afternoon.

On Christmas Eve, he followed the town tradition and placed Luminaria down his front walkway on either side and along the front of his property. The entire block was lit and with a clear, crisp night it was like a postcard. He followed the tradition of attending midnight mass with his family, even though he no longer believed. He had lost his faith before 9/11, but he still enjoyed sitting in church and listening to the carols. When the choir sang, "Silent Night," he thought about the two wars going on in the Middle East and how the cradle of civilization was more violent than ever. He watched the parishioners sing, oblivious to the death and destruction across the world, but safe in the serenity of the brightly lit church.

On Christmas morning they exchanged gifts and Jim found himself reminiscing about earlier Christmas mornings, when his son believed in Santa and he was chasing after Keith on a riding truck instead of chasing after conspiracies. He would sit on the floor and patiently help Keith put together a puzzle of a city with its streets and buildings, instead of trying to fit the pieces together to explain why the buildings had crumbled.

He surprised Terri with a pearl necklace, which cost a lot more than he had planned on spending. They gave Keith a few shirts, pants, and an acoustic guitar and case, which was more than the necklace. Jim found that he no longer worried about saving as much for the future, because he was already living on borrowed time. He was happy and grateful for his family, but he could not help thinking about all the other families trying to fill a void that was especially deep during the holidays.

Jim put on a good front for everyone, but it was a strain to keep his emotions bottled up. Terri and Keith gave him a new digital camera with all the bells and whistles. It was a nice day together. They were invited to dinner at his sister-in-law's house, which was within walking distance. Jim was glad, because it meant that he could drink and not worry about driving. Amy was the younger sister and was always trying to outdo Terri in anything and everything. Amy's house was bigger. She drove a BMW instead of a Honda. She had two kids to Terri's one. Her husband Paul, a stockbroker on Wall Street usually received more in his annual bonus than Jim made in two years. Jim made an effort to like her, but no matter how hard he tried, there was something about her like fingernails on a blackboard, that turned him off.

Amy was pretty and full of energy. She kept herself in good shape by spending hours in the gym each week and she had no stress from the pressures of working. She stood five feet three inches and weighed no more than one hundred and ten pounds. Her skin was tan all year, thanks to rotating like a rotisserie chicken in a tanning booth when she was not jogging on the treadmill. Jim knew it was only a matter of time before her skin would wrinkle, wither and peel off like a snake molting. Her long blond hair was not its natural color and could be the true reason for Jim's attitude. There was nothing about Amy that was real. And Jim did not like cover-ups.

Amy's husband, Paul, was a likeable guy, and Jim could not understand how Paul managed to stay married to her. Maybe the extra hours in the office helped. Paul was only forty years old, but the long hours and the stress of the job, had taken its toll. Paul was an even six feet tall, but about twenty pounds overweight. The wrinkles on his forehead were not the result of a tanning salon. The ashen look of his complexion screamed that he never entered a tanning salon and rarely saw the light of day. His hair was thinning, and the grey hair was quickly overtaking his original remaining black. Paul had an engaging smile, but he also had nerves of steel to make a trade worth millions of dollars as coolly as another person would buy a loaf of bread. Jim remembered when Paul had tried to explain to him how the new credit default swaps worked. Jim understood enough to know that it sounded too risky, and he wondered how it all could be considered legal.

Amy was a great cook, despite her semi-anorexic appearance. The turkey was moist with a golden brown skin. Jim wondered if frying her own skin helped her with cooking the turkey. The stuffing was moist, and the sausage gave it just the right zest. Jim would have to run a few extra miles to make up for his overindulgence. Amy would probably spend the next twenty-four hours on the treadmill.

Everything was going great, and Jim was in a festive mood. There was good conversation, and holiday music played in the background. Nothing could spoil Jim's mood. Even Amy did not seem quite as annoying, which could be considered a Christmas miracle. After dessert, Paul opened a bottle of Bailey's. Jim usually only drank beer, but he did like an occasional glass of Baileys during the holidays.

Paul filled the glasses and said, "Let's have a toast." Everyone raised a glass, whether it contained alcohol or water. Paul continued, "Here's to a merry Christmas and a happy new year to everyone."

Jim took a long sip and felt the smooth rich chocolate liquor warm his bloated stomach. As soon as Jim was finished, Paul refilled his and Jim's glasses. Paul was a (currently drunk) conservative republican, who supported George Bush and his two wars. He was all for the tax cuts and free trade as long as it helped the market go up.

Jim knew better than to ever talk politics with him, and he had no intention of breaking that rule until Paul said, "I don't know why some people are protesting the war. We ought to bomb all those Muslim terrorists and just take their oil."

Jim tried to ignore the comment, but Paul continued, "Osama bin Laden killed three thousand Americans, and he should pay."

Jim commented, "It wasn't only Americans, who died that day. There were many from other countries."

"They should hang Osama bin Laden and all his terrorists. They're nothing but murderers."

Jim took a gulp of his liquid courage and remarked, "Nobody knows for sure who was flying those planes."

Paul looked stunned for a moment. He quickly recovered and in a condescending tone remarked, "There were nineteen hijackers. Who else would fly the planes?"

Jim did not hold back. "It wasn't the planes that brought down the buildings. It looked more like a controlled demolition."

Paul gave him a look laced with contempt. "I thought you were smarter than to believe all that conspiracy crap that's out there."

"And I thought you were smarter than to just blindly believe the government's story," Jim retorted.

Terri walked in from the kitchen and gave Jim a look that said, "You better keep quiet."

The three children walked in from the living room to check out what was going on. Paul's face turned a not-so-jolly shade of red. "The planes knocked off the insulation, and then the fires melted the steel, and it collapsed."

Jim remained calm, which only irritated Paul more. "Then why were there eyewitnesses who heard explosions and there were huge steel beams ejected out the sides of the buildings?"

"There were no explosives and the people who thought they heard them were just hearing the building collapse."

Jim stood up. "Well there were 118 people who made the same mistake then. That's how many reported explosions. They were mostly firemen, who should know the difference."

"Why do you get involved with this garbage? It's just a way for people to make money, and anyone can say anything on the Internet."

"First of all it's not garbage," Jim said angrily, "and I'm not 100% convinced of anything, but I do know there are a lot of questions that need to be answered."

"And who's gonna answer the questions?" Paul asked, "You?"

Jim felt like smashing the bottle of Bailey's over Paul's head.

"Why are you guys arguing on Christmas?" Terri interrupted.

Paul seemed to calm down "You're right. Let's change the topic. It should be peace on earth and all that good stuff."

Jim seemed to morph into another person. "I guess if you can go along with all the phony Christmas crap, then you can believe anything the government tells you about 9/11. I think it's more probable to think that Santa flies his sled all over the world in one night than to believe the terrorists were in control of the planes."

Paul started to say something, but stopped. Keith looked at his two cousins and shrugged his shoulders. He felt embarrassed for his father.

Amy broke the silence and said, "Paul can you help me in the kitchen?"

"It's getting late and it's been a long day," Terri announced, "We should get going now."

Jim realized he had ruined the holiday. He knew he should have kept his mouth shut, but he could not understand how others could go about without giving 9/11 a second thought. It was an awkward departure and the walk home was in silence, with no relation to the song, "Silent Night."

The remainder of the holidays were tranquil and without incident. Jim did make a New Year's resolution, which he kept to himself. It was to become active in the truth movement and try to do what he could to help spur interest in a new investigation.

Chapter II

Jim searched for details about the alleged hijackers. In his research, he came across statements made by George Bush and Donald Rumsfeld that were lies.

Bush said, "Had I had any inkling whatsoever that the people were going to fly airplanes into buildings, we would have moved heaven and earth to save the country."

Donald Rumsfeld said, "I knew of no intelligence during the six plus months leading up to September 11th to indicate terrorists would hijack commercial airlines, and use them as missiles to fly into the Pentagon or the World Trade Center towers."

Jim was enraged when he read that even one of The 9/11 Commission members said, "The concept of terrorists using airplanes as weapons was not something which was unknown to the U.S. Intelligence community on September 10th, 2001."

Prior to September 11th, NORAD had plans to simulate in an exercise a simultaneous hijacking of two planes in the United States. There were also exercises using airliners as weapons to crash into targets and cause mass casualties.

As early as 1998 Richard Clark was in charge of an exercise where a group of terrorists hijacked a Lear Jet in Atlanta, loaded it with explosives and flew it toward a target in Washington, D.C.

In early 2001, the Fox Network had a pilot show of a series called, "The Lone Gunman," which was eerily similar to the September 11th attacks. In the episode a secret faction within the U.S. government plotted to hijack and fly a remote controlled Boeing 727 into the World Trade Center. The plot was foiled at the last second, when the autopilot system was deactivated. Jim wondered if the only difference between the television show and reality was that the remote control system was not deactivated?

One of the first facts discovered by Jim was that one of the alleged hijackers, Waleed al-Shehri could not have been on the plane, because he was alive and well in Morocco. Jim thought that could just be a mistake, because of the different spelling of the Arabic and Muslim names, but it did raise doubts.

There were two brothers Ameer and Adnan Bukhari, who were supposedly on Flight 11. It was physically impossible, because Ameer had died a year earlier and Adnan was still alive on September 12th. Was the mix up the result of confusion in the turmoil after 9/11, or was it something else? If the identities of all the hijackers were not known, then it should have been reported. Why would it be so important to cover up identities?

There were also reports of a few of the hijackers drinking and going to strip clubs, which was contrary to the behavior of any devout Muslim. Jim wondered how he would have reacted if he knew he was going to die in a few days. Would he say the hell with everything and go out and have a good time; or would he pray to a God for strength? Then he read a report that Mohammed Atta had lived with a stripper in Venice, Florida in early 2001. Atta did not fit the definition of a devout Muslim. Most people would consider anyone who lived with a stripper, drank heavily and frequented strip joints a sleaze ball no matter what religion.

The list of the hijackers was modified a few times. What Jim found disturbing was that Hani Hanjour's name was not on the original list.

David Ray Griffin the author of, "The New Pearl Harbor," commented that since Hani Hanjour was a last minute substitute, it might explain why flight 77 was piloted by a person who could not fly. It was also reported that one of the hijackers, Hamza al-Ghamdi, had booked later flights to and within Saudi Arabia. Apparently he did not believe or know it was a suicide mission.

Jim also found some other disturbing material. It appeared that several of the alleged hijackers had received training at military installations in the 1990's. Atta had trained at the International Officers School at Maxwell Air Force Base in Montgomery, Alabama. Abdulaziz Alomari attended the Aerospace medical school at Brooks, Air Force Base in Texas. Saeed Alghamadi had been to the Defense Language Institute at Monterey, California. Three of the nineteen trained at Pensacola Naval Station in Florida also in the 1990's. Why wasn't this brought up in the 9/11 investigation? What was the purpose of the training?

Jim did not know if all he was reading was true, but it did raise questions, which should have been answered. He also read that the FBI reported finding the passport of one of the hijackers, Satam al-Suqami, at the World Trade Center. That did seem to be a bit of a stretch, if it was true. With all the deaths, fires, building collapses, and pulverization of desks, bodies, file cabinets, computers, walls, bathrooms, this one passport somehow miraculously appeared intact?

So now the FBI could say they had solid proof that he was one of the hijackers. It was a little too coincidental. Maybe that would work on a soap opera, where people were constantly coming back from the dead. Jim thought again and determined it was even too unrealistic for a soap opera.

Jim also read that the original flight manifesto did not have the names of any of the nineteen hijackers. The names were added later after a few modifications. The inference was that there were no hijackers on the planes at all. Jim could not accept that without definite proof. He thought back to the Fox series Lone Gunman and thought it might not be so far fetched after all.

There was another nagging question that Jim wanted answered. He always wondered why none of the pilots on the four hijacked planes signaled that there was a hijacking. There is a four-digit code (7500), which takes a second or two to enter into the transponder that alerts the air traffic controllers of a hijacking. There were a total of eight pilots and not one had a chance to enter in the code? To Jim that was almost as unlikely as finding the passport at the WTC.

"If all of this is true, then why isn't there a new investigation?" Jim asked himself. "Why aren't people protesting in the streets to find whoever was really behind the attacks? Where are the investigative reporters? Where is the news media? How come I can read about these things in a book, and yet if I talk about it with anyone, I'm looked at like some kind of kook? We don't know who was on the planes, but we know the final ten on American Idol? We can't explain how a building could collapse when the fires weren't hot enough to melt steel, but we're proud when we know the answer to the final *Jeopardy* question? Maybe I'm just wasting my time. Maybe the fact is, only a few care."

Jim continued to doubt his quest. If it was a conspiracy, imagine how many people were involved and still had to keep quiet? It would be difficult to do, but not impossible. Jim remembered back to how easily everyone, including himself was manipulated to believe the official story of how the towers collapsed. He thought about the blatant lies told about weapons of mass destruction and links to al-Qaeda with Saddam Hussein, and Jim thought maybe it was not as difficult as he first thought.

Jim continued to find out additional information about the men the government said were the hijackers. Jim read about an operation known as, "Able Danger." It was a Department Of Defense data mining operation to identify terrorist cells operating in the U.S. *The Times Herald* (Norristown, PA) published a story, which stated that two years prior to the September 11th attacks, U.S. intelligence linked Mohammed Atta to al-Qaeda and also identified him as a member of a terrorist cell in Brooklyn.

The 911 Commission Chairman, Thomas Kean, said there was no evidence anyone in the government knew about Atta before September 11th. Jim was ashamed that the former governor of his state was even involved with The 911 Commission. For some reason the information was never supplied to the FBI Counterterrorism agents and the Able Danger operation was shut down. In addition to Atta, three of the other alleged hijackers were also identified.

Lieutenant Colonel Shaefer claimed that he contacted the FBI about Atta, and the terrorist cell and was ignored. He also spoke to Philip Zelikow, who was the controller of The 9/11 Commission, but he did not pass any information to the other members. There was a congressional investigation into Able Danger and 9/11 held on September 21, 2005. Representative Curt Weldon, who was Vice Chairman of The House Services And Homeland Security Committee, initiated it. Shaffer was ordered not to testify by the Department of Defense.

Why was he ordered not to testify? What information did he have that they did not want made public? Could it be the truth?

Weldon later stated that he was no longer sure that it was Atta who was identified. One possibility floated was that there might have been two Atta's.

Jim was really frustrated. What could he believe? Everything he read was later contradicted by something else. There were people who were supposed to be dead who turned up alive. There were mistaken identities, ignored information, and data destroyed. No wonder there were conspiracy theories. Was it even possible to find out the truth?

Jim was convinced of some type of cover up on Atta when he read about a newspaper article in Portland, Maine, where a librarian stated that she had seen Atta a few times in April 2000. When she saw his photograph as one of the terrorists, she recognized the face.

One of the most puzzling pieces of information Jim came across was that Osama bin Laden was never formally charged with the attacks on 9/11. The F.B.I. did not have enough hard evidence to bring charges in a court of law, but the Bush administration said there was enough evidence to go to war.

In December 2001, the government released a video where bin Laden admitted responsibility for the attack. The tape was found in a house in Jalalabad, Afghanistan. Jim did not see the tape, but read that the bin Laden on the tape was a poor excuse for a double. There were reported differences in skin tone, a facial feature and weight between this latest video and other videos of bin Laden. The man in this video also appeared much healthier, unless Osama was on steroids. How could the government make a fake video? Wasn't that too risky? Jim made a note to try to find a copy of the video.

On September 16th, bin Laden told Al Jazeera television, "I would like to assure the world that I did not plan the recent attacks, which seem to have been planned by people for personal reasons."

Jim was also surprised to learn that most of the information linking bin Laden was obtained through the use of enhanced interrogation techniques (torture) and could not be considered reliable evidence.

One-Way Elevator

Jim continued with his research into the alleged terrorists. Mohammed Atta and Marwan al-Shehhi enrolled in the Huffman Aviation School in Venice, Florida. Ziad Jarrah went to the Florida Flight training center also in Venice. The owner of Huffman Aviation said his school only taught how to fly light aircraft, not commercial jetliners. Jim wondered how legitimate these schools were. Jim read that Atta and al-Shehhi had one session on a flight simulator and it was for a Boeing 727 not a 767. He did not know how they did, but he did uncover that each one flunked a Stage 1 Rating Test at Jones Aviation, which was a basic course. "I guess they are not the Muslin version of TOP GUN, " Jim mused.

Jim knew nothing about flying, but he wondered how someone with no experience could maneuver a large commercial jetliner and understand all the controls? He thought back to when his father taught him to drive a car. Although he had sat and watched from the front passenger's seat, when it came time for him to take the wheel, it was a totally different experience. The first few times, he could not go straight and his foot was too heavy on the gas and brake. He had difficulty making a turn, because he could not judge how fast to go, or how far to turn the wheel. This was only a little Dodge Dart and not a Boeing 767. He was only going about thirty miles and hour and had trouble steering. Imagine flying a huge aircraft over 500 miles an hour.

Jim read a story about a flight instructor named Don Goalos, who was a professional pilot for twenty years. On 9/11, he was working at a training facility in Phoenix, Arizona. Using the flight simulator, he had his class, which included some experienced pilots attempt to crash a 737 into the World Trade Center. It turned out that none of the students could do it, until they slowed down to near landing speed. Jim questioned how these alleged terrorists could do it. Jim tried to rationalize the possibilities. Either each of the pilots was extremely lucky, had the hand of Allah guiding him, or he was not in control of the plane. If Jim had to pick one, he would pick the latter. Jim thought back to the Kennedy assassination and Lee Harvey Oswald. Did he really fire the shots, or was he just the fall guy? Was history repeating itself?

There was another pilot named Rob Balsano, who said it took him five times on a Microsoft flight simulator program to hit the Pentagon at the same angle as flight 77. Mr. Balsano became one of the founders of Pilots for 9/11 Truth. Jim also read a similar theory that the flight instructions were only a diversion and the alleged terrorists were merely patsies in a much larger plot.

Jim wanted to prove what he had read was true, so the next week he made an appointment to speak to a flight instructor at a flight school near Teterboro Airport. Jim set up the appointment on the premise that he wanted to enroll in one of the programs. Driving to the school, Jim imagined what it must have felt like to be one of the terrorists who believed he was training to die a martyr; or was each one no more than a willing dupe?

***

The school was located about a half mile from the entrance to the airport. An old abandoned firehouse had been converted into a modern flight school. Jim was pleasantly surprised, when he entered the building. The old brick façade was a perfect contrast to the clean modern interior. The floor was a dark grey tile, and one of the walls was painted fire engine red as a reminder of days past. Photos of the old firehouse and the brave firemen, who once protected the small airport and the surrounding community, were proudly displayed on one of the walls. When the airport expanded, it included its own fire department and when the community expanded, a new firehouse was constructed a few miles away leaving the one hundred year old building vacant and without purpose. A few ex-pilots came together with a few investors hoping to fill the need for flight training in a fairly affluent area.

Jim walked up to the receptionist's desk and an attractive woman in her early twenties directed Jim to the second floor to meet with Ted Simmons, one of the founders and instructors. Before he could proceed, he had to fill out an application with all the usual questions of age, where one lived and worked etc. It also requested the reason for taking the lessons. After the brief delay, Jim proceeded to the next leg of his journey.

Jim knocked on the deep mahogany door, which was partially

opened, and an authoritative voice responded, "Enter at your own risk." He took the risk and entered with a smile, but from the facial expression on the man behind the desk, Jim knew he was expecting someone much younger. He was in his late forties with short black hair, a pale thin face with sunken cheeks and a large nose. When he stood up to shake Jim's hand, he was two inches taller than Jim and without an ounce of fat. His long arm stretched across the desk and his handshake bordered on crushing.

"I'm Ted Simmons. Welcome to the Fail Safe Flight School."

"I'm Jim Winters."

"So what brings you to our school?"

"Well, I'm thinking about learning how to fly, and your school has a good reputation." Jim handed Ted the application form.

"Yes, we run a good school. We've been here about six years and haven't lost a student yet."

Jim gave an obligatory laugh at the cheesy joke that Ted probably told hundreds of times.

"Have a seat."

Jim sat down and Ted asked, "Do you own a plane?"

Jim replied, "No, but I've always wanted to see how it feels to fly one. I don't have to go that high or that fast. I just want to be up in the air in control."

Ted quickly glanced at the application. "That's great. I'm sure we can get you up and back down safely. What type of plane do you plan on flying?"

"Something small, like a Cessna. That shouldn't be too hard to control."

"It's not, but there's a lot to flying a plane," Ted said. "There are many regulations you have to follow to get a pilot's license, especially after 9/11."

Jim had an opening, but decided to wait. "How long does it take?"

"Let's not worry about that now."

"Is it as bad as a driver's license?" Jim joked.

Now it was Ted's turn to force an obligatory laugh. "If flight school was like motor vehicles, those hijackers never would have made it in the air."

Jim could not wait any longer and asked, "Do you also have flight simulator training?"

Ted smiled. "We're a state of the art school. We have all the latest training. We offer simulator training on all types of aircraft including commercial jetliners. You can pick your aircraft, plug in the starting location and destination and it's just like flying the real thing."

"That's amazing. Maybe after I pass my pilots test, I'll try the flight simulator."

"I just want you to be aware that it's a bit expensive to try just for kicks," Ted warned.

Jim turned serious. "It's not just for kicks."

With a puzzled expression on his face, Ted asked, "What do you mean?"

Jim leaned forward in his chair and decided to tell the truth. "I was in the World Trade Center on 9/11, and lately I've been doing some research about the terrorists."

Ted's expression changed to concern.

Jim continued. "I read how the flight instructors said most of them were incompetent pilots, and they questioned how they could have flown the planes at that speed and hit their targets. I also wondered why none of the pilots punched in the code to signal a hijacking."

"What have you been reading, all that conspiracy garbage?"

Jim did not want to have a debate. "I have been doing some research, and I'm not sure if I agree. That's why I'm here. I read about a former commercial jet pilot now a flight instructor, who said it took him a few tries to hit the trade center and another flight instructor who reported none of his students could hit the Tower at nearly five hundred miles an hour. The one guy started the Pilots for 9/11 Truth."

There was a look of disdain on Ted's face. "I don't believe any of those stories. They're just urban myths."

"I don't think the guy had any reason to lie. Did you ever try your simulator to fly a plane into the World Trade Center, or to do the 330 degree loop and then hit the first floor of the Pentagon without damaging anything in front?"

Ted's face reddened. "I've got better things to do than to play conspiracy games. This is a serious school. If you're not here to really learn how to fly, then you should try another school."

One-Way Elevator

Jim stood up and said, "Haven't you ever thought about how these guys were able to do it? I'm trying to keep an open mind and you should do the same. If you don't want my business or care about what really happened on 9/11, I'll find someone else who does. Thank you for your time." He turned around and walked out of the office.

***

Later that afternoon Ted had some free time, so he went into an empty lab with a flight simulator. He did have a nagging feeling in the back of his mind that what Jim had said could conceivably be true. He found an old flight simulator program from 2001, punched in the coordinates for the World Trade Center and began his approach. He increased the speed of the 727 to five hundred miles per hour and focused all his attention on hitting his target. It was difficult to guide the large aircraft, which was a bit smaller than the 767 flown by the hijackers. He had to maneuver between the large buildings, which were a real challenge at that speed. He had difficulty on his first approach and was shocked when he passed to the right of the WTC. Ted swung the plane around and tried another approach. This time he was sure he would not miss. He had fifteen years experience as a commercial pilot. He flew in all types of weather and made many difficult landings. How could he miss? On the second approach he increased the speed to five hundred and fifty miles per hour, but he overcompensated and missed again. Now he was angry. He turned the plane around again and this time slowed to three hundred and fifty miles per hour and crashed into his target. Instead of a sense of accomplishment, he felt a wave of nausea pass.

***

Jim was reading a report in his office, when the phone rang.

"Hi Jim, this is Ted Simmons. I want to apologize for the way I acted yesterday."

"No apologies are needed. I didn't mean to get you upset, but I had to tell you the truth about why I was there."

"I appreciate that. I have something to tell you. After you left I was angry, but also curious about what you said. I went down to one of the labs and found an old flight simulator. I tried to crash into the World Trade Center, and it took me three tries to finally hit it."

Jim could not believe what he was hearing. "Now I have actual proof that the official story could be a lie. I don't know how to thank you."

"Don't get carried away here. Just because I missed doesn't mean there's a conspiracy. It just means there are questions."

Jim returned to reality. "You're right. It doesn't prove anything except that the odds of two planes hitting both towers flown by two inexperienced pilots are pretty slim."

"So where do we go from here?" Ted asked.

Jim paused momentarily before replying. "I don't know. I never thought I would be involved in finding evidence to back up what most people call a crazy conspiracy theory."

Ted commented, "Maybe I should check out that Pilots for 9/11 Truth?"

"I think you should. I also want to do some additional investigation on the plane that hit the Pentagon. There are a lot of theories. If you can use your simulator to follow the same path of the plane, maybe it will give additional proof."

"Call me whenever you want to come in."

"That sounds good. You know, when I walked out of your office yesterday, I never thought I would hear from you again."

Ted gave a short laugh. "As soon as the door closed, I tossed your application in the trash, but there was something nagging me in the back of my mind about what you said. I went to the simulator just for the hell of it. I have to admit I've never pulled an application out of the trash before."

"I'm glad you did."

"So am I. Let's keep in touch."

When Jim hung up the phone, he was too excited to do any work. He went to the coffee shop down the block and sat alone in a booth with a cup of tea and his thoughts. Everything had changed. Up to now, he was never sure about what he was reading, but Ted had no reason to fake his flight simulator tests.

Jim remembered an article he had read about former Senator Max

Cleland from Georgia, who was a decorated hero from the Vietnam War. He was a member of the commission, but resigned after serving one year. The reason for his resignation was that he felt he did not have full access to all the information.

It was reported he said, "It is a national scandal. One of these days we will have to get the full story, because the 9/11 issue is so important to America. But the White House wants to cover it up."

Chapter 12

Jim went back to review everything he had gathered in his research. He began with flight 77, which hit the Pentagon, and its alleged pilot, Hani Hanjour. To Jim it was inconceivable that a hijacked plane could fly over Washington and hit the Pentagon without being intercepted.

The Capital of the world's most powerful country, which spends more on defense that the next twelve or thirteen countries combined, allowed its military command center to be attacked by a commercial jetliner piloted by someone who could barely fly? How could the plane go undetected?

There were stories about another plane flying over Washington. A few witnesses identified it as an E-4B, a command military aircraft that could communicate with the military all over the world. It had all the latest electronics and surveillance equipment. If that were true, than how come it could not detect Flight 77? Or did it know all about the flight and allowed it to continue? The 9/11 Commission reported that the military only had one or two minutes warning before the Pentagon was attacked. Jim knew that if the E4B was in the air, then someone was lying.

Jim was also concerned about the lack of physical evidence of a plane crash at the Pentagon. There was a small piece of the fuselage displayed as evidence, but it had no soot or fire damage. It could have been planted, which reminded Jim of the passport found at the World Trade Center.

Hani Hanjour had flight training at Cockpit Resource Management in Scottsdale, Arizona. It was alleged that he was told to leave and not come back, because he was such a bad student. Jim also read how weeks before 9/11, Hani Hanjour and Ziad Jarrah attempted to rent a plane from Freeway Airport in Maryland. Before renting the plane, they had to prove on a test flight with an instructor that they could handle the plane. The instructor, Marcel Bernard, refused to let them rent the plane because neither one could even handle a Cessna.

Jim kept a detailed record of all his findings. He spent many hours organizing the information, so he could readily access and keep track of all the questions raised. Whenever he re-read his files, it only led to additional questions. When he read about, "Global Hawk," in light of what Ted's flight simulator proved, he was even more convinced. Global Hawk was the name of the aircraft that on April 23, 2001 flew from Edwards Air Force base in California to Edinburgh Air Force base in South Australia, a distance of 7,500 miles. It was significant, because it was a totally unmanned flight from takeoff to landing. Jim knew it did not take a rocket scientist to understand that if an aircraft could be remotely controlled and travel 7,500 miles, a trip from Boston to New York would be a piece of cake.

Jim searched for information on how the controls of an aircraft could be taken over from a remote location. He read that aeronautical engineer Joe Vialls stated that the government had the ability to take over the controls of an aircraft. There was an initiative called, "The Defense Advanced Research Projects Agency," whose purpose was to recover hijacked aircraft. The purpose was not to prevent the hijacking, but to take control of a hijacked plane and land it at an airport, where the police would be waiting to arrest the hijackers. He also read that Boeing allegedly installed this backdoor control override device into its computer design for its 767 and 757 commercial airliners.

If that could be proven, then it did not matter if Hani Hanjour could not even fly a kite. He wondered why there had been no investigation. This would go a long way in explaining how the planes hit their targets. Jim came back to the same question - Were the terrorists, who thought they were on a mission for Allah, merely patsies in a larger plot?

Jim was at a crossroads in his investigation. He had more questions than answers and no end in sight. He had some theories about how the planes hit their targets and how the buildings fell, but he needed to find out about Flight 93,which did not hit its target and crashed in Shanksville, Pennsylvania.

Jim read some of the theories and even with an open mind, he had to question whether he should even consider them in his research. When he first read about the problem with the official story about the cell phone calls from flight 93, Jim thought it was a ridiculous theory to state that the calls were faked. The core of the theory was that high altitude cell phone calls in 2001 were virtually impossible, because the technology was not available. It was not until 2004 that Qualcomm announced it had developed new technology, which allowed passengers to receive and place calls as if they were on the ground. Jim now had a plausible explanation for the theory, but if cell phone calls could not be made, then how come there were reports of several calls? It made no sense. Wouldn't the passengers know they could not make a cell phone call? Jim continued his reading and then was more disturbed when he read about "Voice Morphing Technology." Voice morphing is where a call could be morphed into sounding like someone else was on the line. That was too way out for Jim to even consider, but then he read about a report from The 9/11 Commission, which stated that only two calls were received from flight 93 when the plane was down to an altitude of 5,000 feet. Both calls were at 9:58. Jim decided to drop the theory of faked or morphed phone calls for the moment.

Jim's curiosity was peaked when he read what one reporter said about the crash site for flight 93. "There was just a big hole in the ground. All I saw was a crater filled with small charred plane parts. Nothing that would even tell you it was the plane. You just can't believe a whole plane went into this crater. There were no suitcases, no recognizable plane parts, and no body parts."

There was an additional problem with the official story. Flight 93 would have had thousands of gallons of jet fuel and yet there was no evidence of contamination, or smell of jet fuel. Jim tried to digest this latest information.

He mumbled to himself, "Most plane crashes do not dive straight into the ground and basically disappear. So now we have steel buildings collapsing for the first time in history and plane crashes at the Pentagon and here in Pennsylvania, where one plane disintegrates inside the Pentagon and one disappears into the ground. If it disappeared into the ground, why was debris from flight 93 found eight miles away? How could a one-ton section of the engine be found over a mile away? Where were the bodies? Something isn't right, but I have no idea what, except that the official story needs to be examined."

Jim also read other theories about how flight 93 was shot down and the discrepancies in the exact time of the crash between the official time and the time based on a seismic study, which said the time was at 10:06 and not 10:03. There was also an alleged three minutes missing from the cockpit voice recorder. If little was found at the crash site, then how could anyone know what was missing from the recorder? Who even found it? The number of questions raised seemed overwhelming and almost inconceivable.

Jim found an article from the *Philadelphia Daily News* dated September 16th, 2001. In the article, there was no clear explanation for the three-minute discrepancy. One theory is that it was an electrical failure or a circuit breaker could have been pulled to cut off the cockpit voice recorder.

Jim reread the paragraph, which stated, "Numerous witnesses in the Shanksville area have told the *Daily News* and other publications that a mysterious low flying unmarked white jet, military in nature circled the area at the time of the crash. The F.B.I. has claimed this was a business jet that had been asked by air traffic controllers to inspect the flight 93 crater."

The explanation did not seem logical to Jim. Why would a civilian plane be asked to do an inspection, when the military should be in charge? That was like asking a guy on a fishing boat to examine an oil spill off the coast of Florida. Jim would have these witnesses, the air traffic controllers and the pilot of the business jet contacted in any new investigation.

Jim was in a quandary. At times he thought what he was reading was true, and then he read something else, and it did not fit. He wondered if he should just go back to watching mindless television and wasting time on video games?

The one fact that kept nagging in the back of Jim's mind was how the military could not know of the hijacking right away? He read that General Larry Arnold who was the commander of NORAD'S U.S. continental region stated that he knew about flight 93 at 9:24. If the military knew nearly forty minutes earlier, there was plenty of time to have the airliner shot down.

How can anyone search through all the conflicting data and find the truth?

To quote Shakespeare, "There's something rotten in Denmark," or in this case, Shanksville.

Everywhere Jim turned, there were pieces of information that did not add up, but was it proof of a conspiracy beyond a shadow of a doubt? Some evidence was very damaging to the 9/11 report such as the way the buildings came down, the temperature of the steel, the thermite found in the dust, and the eyewitness reports of hearing explosives, but there were also many aberrations of behavior or outright contradictory statements that could not be ignored.

Jim read a report that said the Pentagon held an evacuation exercise about a month before 9/11 in which the Pentagon was struck by a plane.

Jim's anger was once again resurrected, when he thought back to what George Bush had said: "Had I had any inkling whatsoever that the people were going to fly airplanes into buildings, we would have moved heaven and earth to save the country."

He knew using airplanes as weapons was not a new idea. What about the Kamikaze pilots in World War 11? What about the Tom Clancy novel, "Debt of Honor," where a hijacked Boeing 747 was flown into the Capital Building?

Jim continued to reread some of his data.

Donald Rumsfeld told the 9/11 Commission, "I knew of no intelligence during the six plus months leading up to September 11 to indicate terrorists would hijack commercial airlines, use them as missiles to fly into the Pentagon or the World Trade Center towers."

He found a quote from Condoleezza Rice made under oath to the 9/11 Commission.

"This kind of analysis about the use of airplanes as weapons actually was never briefed to us."

Jim was disgusted about all the lies that he read from government officials. The 9/11 Commission also stated that there was no evidence that the government knew about Atta before 9/11.

Jim scoffed and thought, "You mean to tell me that if I could find out about Able Danger, The 9/11 Commission with all its power and influence did not? I wonder if the commission could figure out who pardoned the turkey on Thanksgiving at the White House?"

***

Jim had previously dropped the theory of the faked phone calls from flight 93, but then he read again where the FBI in 2004 said that it no longer confirmed that there were any high altitude phone calls. He wondered if there was really something to the theory of morphed calls. He still could not understand why that would be done. He wondered if the faked calls were used as a cover for the plane being shot down? The passengers could be hailed as heroes and once again it would all be wrapped up into one nice neat package for public consumption.

He had to take a break from his research and read a piece of fiction, even though he now considered much of The 9/11 Commission report a piece of fiction. Out of all the books available in his bookcase, he picked up and old copy of George Orwell's, "1984" that had been unopened for years. As he read, he drew comparisons between Orwell's fictional society and America after 9/11. Jim shuddered, when he read the slogans from Big Brother

"War is Peace.
Slavery is Freedom.
Ignorance is Strength."

He thought of the Patriot Act, which supposedly was drafted to strengthen our country, but it was at the expense of our freedoms. He thought of *Newspeak*, which was used by Big Brother to rationalize an action or redefine a meaning. How could anyone vote against an act called, "The Patriot Act?" It would be considered un-patriotic. When he saw how quickly people relinquished their rights to secure the American way of life, the words, "Slavery is Freedom," echoed in his mind. When he thought how quickly most people accepted the official explanation of 9/11, the words, "Ignorance is Strength," reverberated in his mind. When he saw how quickly the country united behind the president invading Afghanistan and going against Saddam Hussein, who was portrayed as the epitome of evil the words, "War is Peace," seemed appropriate.

Jim was not much of a gambler, and he only bought one stock on his own, but he did have a 401k plan with money in a few stock funds. He invested three thousand dollars in a gold stock when gold was going up in value, and the following week it took a plunge. He had received a tip from a guy he once worked with, who said the stock would double in value in a few months. Jim knew it sounded too good to be true, but greed was a more powerful force than logic. The last time he'd checked, the shares were trading at sixty–three cents. He reminisced about his stock investment, after reading about some unexplained buying and selling of stocks leading up to September 11th.

According to the investigation of Don Radlauer, United Airlines had a 9,000% increase in Put Options between September 6th and September 10th. A Put Option was a bet that a stock would decline in value in a specific time frame. American Airlines had a 6,000% increase in Put Options compared to the usual average. That time honored phrase, "Follow the Money," played in Jim's mind again. There was also a much higher volume of five year U.S. Treasury Notes, purchased right before 9/11. U.S. Treasury Notes were considered a safe and secure investment. Jim wondered why this was not fully investigated by the Commission. Jim was quickly learning that there were no real coincidences, only cover-ups and diversions.

***

Jim was a big fan of television crime series. He grew up watching cops and private investigators, who always solved the crime and never wavered in the pursuit of justice. The one practical piece of advice he learned from all those hours in front on the T.V. was that for every crime there was always a motive. What was the true motive for 9/11? How could he hope to help solve a crime without establishing the true motive? Perry Mason, Baretta, and Columbo would be disappointed in his methods so far. He would be an embarrassment to any CSI investigation. Jim made a promise to his imaginary heroes, to find a plausible reason why this would be allowed to happen. Was it money or power or both? Who would benefit from such a tragedy? These were the questions to be answered in another investigative phase.

Jim was surprised when he read that Hamid Karzai, the current president of Afghanistan had been on the payroll of Unicol. He also discovered that Unicol was involved in a proposed pipeline project that that would cross Afghanistan. If the United States occupied Afghanistan and installed a friendly leader, once the project was completed, there would be a reliable steady source of oil. Jim added oil to his list of possible motives. He would need to do a lot more digging to see if it were a credible reason.

He also read from a few different sources that the U.S. wanted control over not only oil, but also other raw materials. Was oil also behind the invasion of Iraq? He read in Bob Woodward's, "Plan of Attack," that George Bush began the planning sixteen months before the invasion of Iraq, but Richard Clark said the administration began with Iraq on its agenda.

Jim felt a special affinity to the main character in "1984," Winston Smith, when he said, "I know the how. I don't understand the why." Winston Smith was tired of all the lies about the present and rewriting of the past. He was no longer sure what was real. He had his one tiny alcove, where the ubiquitous Telescreen could not see him. With the government now listening to domestic phone calls and scanning emails, Jim understood the next step was not far behind.

Was 9/11 the excuse needed to launch the War On Terror? There had been an enormous effort to link Hussein to Al-Qaeda, but there were no real links, so the administration resorted to lies. The government was not much different from a person who finds the more lies he tells, the easier it becomes.

Jim thought, "What's a few more lies, when three thousand people have already been killed?"

Was 9/11 the New Pearl Harbor needed to bring the country together against one common enemy? It did not matter that there was no hard evidence that would hold up in a court of law linking Osama bin Laden to 9/11. He was the enemy. He was just like Saddam Hussein, who became the epitome of evil, even though our government had supported both bin Laden and Hussein in the past. It now appeared totally logical that the government did not want to capture bin Laden. It could explain why he was allowed to escape from the mountains in Tora Bora even though he was trapped. It explained why he was allowed treatment in a hospital in Dubai, even though he was wanted for the bombings of the USS Cole and the Embassies in Tanzania and Kenya. The only evidence against bin Laden was obtained by torture and the 9/11 Commission did not question the validity of the information.

Michael Ratner, who is the president of the Center for Constitutional Rights remarked, "Most people look at The 9/11 Commission Report as a trusted historical document. If their conclusions were supported by information gained from torture, their conclusions were suspect. As a mater of law, evidence derived from torture is not reliable, in part because of the possibility of false confession. At the very least, they should have added caveats to all those references."

As evidence to back up that statement, Jim read that Khalid Sheikh Mohammed had confessed to a number of atrocities and attacks. He allegedly said he was responsible for planning an attack on the Plaza Bank in the state of Washington. It sounded legitimate based on his other confessions, until one realized that the bank was not built until after he had been imprisoned.

There were many across the world, who also doubted the official story of 9/11.

Adrew von Bulow, a former West German State Secretary of Defense said, "The planning of the attacks was technically and organizationally a master achievement. To hijack four huge airplanes within a few minutes, and within one hour to drive them into three targets with complicated flight maneuvers is unthinkable, without years of long support from secret apparatuses from the state and industry."

The Pakistani President, Pervez Musharraf said, "I didn't think it was possible that Osama, who was sitting up there in the mountains, could do it. Those who executed it were much more modern. They knew the U.S. They knew aviation. I don't think he has the intelligence or the minute planning. The planner was someone else."

Jim found some additional information to corroborate his "Follow The Money," line of investigation. The Miami Herald stated, "A preliminary review by German regulators and bank researchers, showed there were highly suspicious sales of shares in airlines and insurance companies along with major trades in gold and oil markets before September 11 that suggest advance knowledge of the attacks."

Jim once again thought, "How many people actually knew about the attacks? How could it be kept a secret?" He remembered that old saying, "Two people can keep a secret if one of them is dead."

Jim read about three studies which concluded that there was enough statistical data on the, "Put and Call," options prior to September 11th to prove it was consistent with insider trading. In August 2003, FBI agents briefed The 9/11 Commission on insider trading, but it was glossed over like so many other important facts.

Jim was stunned when he read that one of the alleged insider traders, Wirt Walker, was a distant cousin of President George W. Bush. It was reported that Wirt Walker purchased 56,000 shares of stock in Stratesec, a company providing security at the World Trade Center. The stock gained $50,000 in a few days. Jim also read that millions of dollars were pushed through on transactions while the planes hit.

Jim found additional evidence that conflicted with the official report of flight 93's crash landing. So far there had been no credible explanation of the time difference, or if it even meant anything. The fact that the time difference had not been accounted for led to some theories Jim thought were off the wall. They ranged from a shoot down with a missile to high intensity radiated fields, which could cause an airliner to go into an uncontrolled dive.

Jim found information on a radio frequency weapon called, "Transient Microwave Device," that released a single, powerful pulse of energy similar to an electrostatic discharge, with the same deadly results. If an independent commission answered the questions, would it resolve all the speculation? There were reports by local residents of the lights flickering right before the crash, but the cause was never fully investigated.

Jim was perplexed by all the conflicting stories. The one fact he did obtain was that the radar showed that there were no other planes in the vicinity of Shanksville, although some residents reported spotting a plane. This was in direct conflict with other information he had read.

Jim also found further evidence, which could help validate that the planes were remotely controlled. If flight 175 had started the turn into the North Tower just one second sooner or later, the aircraft would have missed the tower (Assuming a speed of 799 feet per second). He uncovered some supplementary data about other flight management systems that could override the initial flight path of a plane that were available on 9/11. Jim still wondered why this was never investigated, but he knew that the commission report raised enough questions to fill another book. That night while he continued reading, "1984" he had an enlightened moment. A few simple words brought everything about 9/11 into clarity.

One of the main characters, O'Brien, said, "Who controls the past controls the future. Who controls the present controls the past."

Jim thought of all the lies and omissions in the official story and then he read on the next page, "Whatever the party holds to be truth is truth. It is impossible to see reality, except by looking through the eyes of the party."

Not too much difference between 9/11 and 1984, Jim thought. If the party says the towers came down because of the planes and subsequent fires, then that must be the truth. If the party says two plus two equals five, then it must be true, even though one knows it is false. In the book it was called "doublethink". In the real world it was called controlling the message. Jim did identify with Winston Smith who was the main character being tortured and brain washed into believing in Big Brother.

After one of his torture sessions, Winston asked O'Brien, "How soon will they shoot me?"

"It may take a long time," said O'Brien. "You are a difficult case. But don't give up hope. Everyone is cured sooner or later. In the end we shall shoot you."

Chapter 13

Jim knew he would never be able to schedule a meeting with his congressman, if he said the purpose of the meeting was to investigate a 9/11 conspiracy. The only way was to lie, so he said he was the representative from a local community group concerned with flooding and overbuilding in his town. The group wanted the Army Corps of Engineers to determine if any flood controls could be established. The town mayor was in favor of more building, because it meant additional tax revenue. It really was a legitimate concern, but Jim was more concerned about who was responsible for 9/11 than some water in his basement. He first sent an email to Congressman Green, detailing the flooding issue. When he did not receive any response after one week, he called his office and was able to speak to one of his aides. The aide happened to live fairly close to Jim, so he played up the issue with the congressman, and Jim had his meeting scheduled for a Friday afternoon.

The office was located in a professional building in the nearby town of Westfield. Jim was tense when he entered. It reminded him of the waiting room in his doctor's office.

He walked up to the receptionist and said, "Jim Winters. I'm here for a three o'clock with the congressman."

The receptionist was a young girl, who Jim thought was most likely a college intern, majoring in political science. Jim thought it was ironic that the politics seemed to ignore the science in everything involved with 9/11.

She checked the calendar, looked up, smiled and said, "Please have a seat, the congressman should be with you shortly."

Jim nodded politely and found an empty seat next to the coat rack near the door.

On the other side of the room there was a group of four elderly women. Jim speculated they were lobbying to make sure nothing happened to their monthly social security checks or Medicare benefits. A young man in his early twenties walked in, glanced nervously at the old ladies babbling away and took a seat next to Jim. He was thin, and his eyes were lifeless and his cheeks sunken. He had short hair, and his pants and shirt hung loose around his tall thin body. He looked at Jim, but quickly turned away when their eyes met.

Jim could sense that he wanted to talk, so he broke the ice and asked, "Have you ever met Congressman Green before?"

The young man was a bit startled but he replied, "No. I know nothing about him. I didn't even vote, since I was busy over in Iraq. I didn't care who was elected."

"Glad you made it back safe."

The vet smirked. "A lot of good it did me. Now I don't have a job and I'm having trouble getting a loan to go back to school. That's why I'm here."

In a reassuring voice, Jim said, "I'm sure he can help with whatever the hold up is."

"After two tours, I couldn't wait to get out. I may be safe, but this isn't what I was fighting for. I put my life on the line, and now I feel like once the uniform is off, I don't matter anymore."

Jim felt sorry for the young man and kept his own views on the war in check. "This country is lucky to have someone like you to fight for its freedom. The government should do more to help the vets." Jim held out his hand. "I'm Jim Winters. It's nice to meet you."

The young man smiled, shook Jim's hand, and replied, "I'm Tom Crane. It's nice to know that someone appreciates the vets."

The conversation was interrupted, when the receptionist called out, "Mr. Winters, the congressman will see you now. Go straight back. His door is open."

Jim stood up and said, "Best of luck to you, Tom," and took the most important steps so far in his quest.

Congressman Green was a democrat, and Jim had voted for him. This was his fourth term, and Jim liked the way he'd spoken out against the war in Iraq and against the way the civil liberties were being curtailed in the name of national security.

Jim knocked lightly on the half open door and walked in. Congressman Alan Green stood up and walked to the front of his desk with an outstretched hand.

Alan Green was taller in person than he looked in his photos. He was at least six feet three and slender. He had a pale complexion, a thin, straight nose, slightly indented cheeks and a wide smile. His jet-black hair was parted on the side and combed back. It was at that perfect length that usually occurs at the midpoint between haircuts. Jim figured it was meticulously kept that length permanently. Alan Green was in his early forties with a wife and two kids. He was an ambassador of the American dream, which to Jim was now covered by the dust from the World Trade Center. He was concerned with the environment, which was another reason Jim chose his subject for the meeting.

"Alan Green. Nice to meet you, Mr. Winters."

Jim shook the outstretched hand and wondered if his right arm was longer than his left from reaching out and shaking so many hands.

"Thank you for taking the time to meet with me."

Alan seemed confident and full of energy. He flashed a quick smile and said, "Have a seat and tell me about your issue."

Jim was concerned about the flooding issue, so he was not being totally duplicitous. "My concern along with many in my town is the problem with flooding. It just seems like every available piece of land is built on and there is nowhere for the water to go."

The Congressman nodded and Jim continued.

"It's not only in our town, but the cities and towns upstream. The big joke around town is that we have the 'Hundred Year Flood,' every few years."

Congressman Green smiled and replied, "I don't know what I can do about all the building."

"Can't you have a study done by the Army Corps of Engineers to see what can be done to reduce the flooding? I know people who have been flooded out twice in recent years. The property values go down and nobody can sell his house."

With a pensive look, Alan replied, "I understand how serious this is, but it is a tough issue, because like you said, it involves other communities. Any solution would have to be a regional one and that would be difficult."

With a look of frustration on his face and a hint of resignation in his voice, Jim said, "Are you telling me there's nothing you can do?"

Congressman Green went on the defensive like any good politician. "No that's not what I meant."

"Then what did you mean?"

"What I meant was that it will be difficult to get all the towns and cities involved to agree on any plan."

Jim sighed. "I know what you mean. What about the Army Corps of Engineers?"

In a somewhat remorseful voice, the Congressman replied, "I could try, but I doubt they could be finished before the next flood."

Jim saw an opening and asked, "What if a Commission was set up to find out all the facts and present a report? Something like The 9/11 Commission. Except this time find out and present all the facts and answer all the questions, instead of leaving a lot of things unanswered"

The Congressman gave Jim a puzzled look. "What do you have against The 9/11 Commission?"

Jim smiled to himself and answered, "I don't think The 9/11 Commission Report gave the real story. It was more political than factual. It left more questions unanswered and ignored or intentionally left out a lot of facts."

The Congressman gave a short laugh. "I thought you were concerned about flooding. I didn't know you were also into conspiracy theories."

Jim restrained his rush of anger at the somewhat condescending tone. "I wasn't, until I started to do some research."

Alan appeared interested and asked, "Where did you find your information?"

"I found it from multiple sources. From books, newspapers, CNN, the Internet and from Tom Kean and Lee Hamilton, who both reportedly said they were deceived by the CIA."

In a more respectful tone, Alan remarked, "There are a lot of theories out there and some are really out there."

"You're right, but I think there are enough unanswered questions and laws of physics broken to justify creating a new independent commission. This time there should be experts in science and architecture, instead of politicians."

The Congressman seemed reluctant to continue. "I thought we were here to talk about flooding, not who was behind 9/11."

"I don't think there are any conspiracies behind the flooding," Jim said glibly, "but now that the subject has been brought up, I would like to know what you think of the commission report."

Alan gave a typical political response. "I think it was a good report. I don't know if everything can ever be in one report. Why are you so concerned?"

Jim hesitated for a few seconds and then responded. "Because when somebody tries to kill me, I get angry."

A look of surprise came over the Congressman's face. "I'm sorry. I had no idea you were there."

"I'm only here now, because I missed an elevator in the lobby of the North Tower."

"I'm glad you missed the elevator."

"Thanks, but sometimes I wonder if I was supposed to be on it and I just cheated death for a while."

"It wasn't your time. Don't think you cheated death."

Jim had to remember his objective and not become confrontational. "Now that I've found out all this new information, I'm hurt and angry again."

"I can understand how you feel, but you don't know for sure if everything you're reading is true."

Jim forced a smile. "That's where you come in."

"How can I help?" the congressman asked in a serious voice.

"You can start a new congressional investigation into what really happened that day."

Alan felt that he had lost control of the meeting. "It's gonna take a lot to get that started. There has to be some pretty convincing evidence, or questions raised in order to justify even bringing up the subject."

"If I can convince you and show how many important facts were left out, witnesses not questioned or ignored, then you can make up your own mind if it's worth it. I understand if you don't want to take the risk politically, but you're part of the government that may have been involved with murdering its own citizens."

Alan stood up, took a few steps toward the window. "That's the first question I have. Why would the government be involved?"

"I'm not sure of all the reasons, but 9/11 gave the government the excuse to launch the global war on terror, invade Afghanistan and Iraq, and increase defense spending by billions of dollars. There's also the whole issue of oil and also the minerals in Afghanistan."

"How could the government keep this a secret?" Alan countered, "So many people would have been involved."

Jim was ready for that point. "I'll answer your question with a question. How could a small group of people some in caves in Afghanistan with cell phones pull off the largest terrorist attack in history?"

Alan smiled "I never questioned how they pulled it off."

Jim stood up and in an exasperated voice said, "I'm not asking you to put your political future on the line. If you can just read a few of the articles I have and check out the websites, maybe we can talk again."

Jim placed the small pile of his research material on the desk.

A look of relief came over the Congressman's face. "I promise I will look into this and keep an open mind. If I think a new investigation is warranted, I may need your help."

Jim shook his hand. "That's all I can ask for. I'll give you any help you need."

Alan laughed. "And I thought you were just another constituent complaining about a local issue."

"I was serious about the flooding issue too."

When the door closed, Alan looked out the window and tried to figure out what had just happened. Jim did not fit the profile of what he thought was a conspiracy theorist. He seemed intelligent and well spoken. He did not seem like someone, who would believe any wild theories.

Jim drove away believing the meeting was a success and a

possible big step forward. His fear was that the Congressman would not really read the material and would just write him off as a World Trade Center survivor with a chip on his shoulder. In a moment of panic, Jim wondered, what if he agreed to look into a new investigation? Would he be able to convince others in Washington that it should be done? Would he be treated like an outcast? Would he be painted by others as a conspiracy theorist and maybe jeopardize his political career? It would be easy to portray him as unpatriotic just by raising the questions. Jim could understand why even if he did agree, he could not do it. If he were truly patriotic, he would want the truth and anyone involved brought to justice.

Before the 9/11 Commission started, Tom Delay said, "A public commission investigating American Intelligence in a time of war is ill-conceived and irresponsible." He wondered what the senator would say about a new commission?

***

That night the Congressman read a few of the articles while lying in bed. What he read shocked and disgusted him. He never thought about why none of the pilots in the four planes signaled that there was a hijacking. He never considered that the reason for pools of molten steel in the rubble could have been from nano-thermite and not the fires. He never knew that Osama bin Laden never said that he did it and was never formally charged. He never knew that the flight instructors who trained one of the terrorists failed him and said he could not even control a small plane, never mind steer a large commercial airliner at nearly 500 mph into a building. He put down the folder and tried to sleep, but his mind was in turmoil. He planned to finish the material and not make any hasty decisions.

The one thing he failed to mention to Jim about 9/11 was that a good friend of his died in the North Tower. He had known Bobby since fifth grade. They played baseball and basketball together. Bobby went on to play high school and college basketball. They went down different paths, but always kept in touch. The kid who had blocked so many of Alan's shots on the basketball court jumped from one of the top floors to escape the flames. Alan tried to remember Bobby running down the court, on a fast break, but the image of his death overshadowed his thoughts. He thought of Bobby's wife and two young children and felt a surge of anger, but before he could do anything he had to be fully convinced that the questions and issues raised were legitimate.

The next week Congressman Green returned to Washington. The first night back he went out to dinner with two other congressmen. Congressman Rand was from Colorado and Congressman Keller was from New York. Congressman Rand was in his seventh term and a conservative republican without the compassion. He was in his early fifties with thinning grey hair and a protruding stomach, the result of stuffing his face at too many fundraisers. He wore black-framed glasses, which contrasted with his pasty complexion. He was only five feet seven and had a Napoleonic complex. Alan wondered why he had invited him out to dinner. Alan was sure it was not out of the goodness of his heart, because to Alan he was heartless.

Congressman Keller was also a republican, but he was more reasonable and pragmatic. Walt Keller was in his third term and had aspirations of running for Governor. He was the same age as Alan, but still retained his boyish looks with his blond hair and lack of wrinkles. He was a lean one hundred and seventy pounds and six feet tall. They were friends and Alan thought he would make a good governor. Congressman Rand was the head of the Appropriations Committee, which meant he wielded a disproportionate amount of power. If a congressional district needed money for a project, it had to go through him, so if he invited you to dinner the offer could not be refused.

"So how are things in your district?" Congressman Rand asked after they had been served a round of drinks.

Alan stirred his rum and coke. "Things are pretty good, but we do have some problems with flooding in some areas."

"It's just the opposite in my district," Congressman Rand bellowed back, "This damn drought seems like it will never end."

"In my district it's job loss that's the biggest problem," Walt Keller chimed in.

One-Way Elevator

Phil Rand continued, "It's always something and now that idiot from California has introduced a bill to ban assault rifles."

Alan suddenly knew the reason for the dinner invitation. Alan considered Congressman Cole a friend and definitely no idiot. Alan kept his mouth shut, because he knew he would need Rand's backing for any investigative committee.

They ordered the entrees and for a brief moment the attention was food instead of politics.

Congressman Rand continued his rant. "There will never be a ban on any guns while I'm in congress. They can strip away any other rights, but not the right to bear arms."

Congressman Rand turned to Alan. "You're pretty quiet. What's on your mind?"

"In my district the people are more concerned with flooding than guns right now. I think the only way to solve the problem is to have a regional solution and have the Army Corps of Engineers make a recommendation."

Congressman Rand grunted. "You'll be under water before those useless idiots can make a decision."

Alan knew Congressman Rand was not interested in a little flooding, so he said, "I'm going to recommend that a study be done and we'll see what happens."

"That's fine, but I need your vote against the assault weapons ban."

Alan never cared for the so-called give and take of politics. The deals never seemed worth the price. Principals were sacrificed for the privilege of taking back a few crumbs to the constituents. He tried to stall. "I haven't made up my mind yet. I don't see why anyone needs an assault weapon. There are too many guns out there to begin with. I do support the second amendment, but at the time that was written you had to reload after one shot."

Congressman Rand glared at Jim. "I certainly hope you do come around. Remember, banning an assault weapon is like that old saying, 'The tip of the camel's nose in the tent.' Do I like assault weapons? No, but I don't think the government should be allowed to ban them."

Alan never liked to be bullied. "There is no use for any civilian to have that kind of weapon. It's certainly not for deer hunting or self-defense. There's just too much violence in our country."

Walt broke his silence. "I think most of the people will support an assault weapons ban in certain parts of the country, but the NRA is a pretty powerful lobby."

Congressman Rand smiled. "That's right. It's a losing battle to vote against it. You have to know what battles to fight and when to accept reality."

Alan swallowed a piece of steak in disgust and nodded in agreement, knowing that he could face a real battle in the very near future.

Once Congressman Rand assumed he'd made his point, the subject was changed to sports and steroids.

Alan waited for an opening. It came during a lull in the conversation during dessert. "A few weeks ago a guy came into my office and brought with him a bunch of material stating that 9/11 was a conspiracy. He said there were a lot of unanswered questions and a lot of information was left out of the 9/11 Commission's report."

"There are a lot of loonies out there with some pretty ridiculous stuff," Congressman Rand sneered

"True, but this guy who was in the North Tower that day has a lot of questions that sound legitimate. He thinks explosives and not the planes brought down the towers. He said there were traces of nano-thermite, which cuts through steel, and that the government was somehow involved. He said the reason the towers came down so straight was controlled demolition."

Alan could see the flash of anger and a moment of concern in Congressman Rand's eyes.

Congressman Keller also noticed and tried to lighten the subject. "I had one guy come into my office and tell me that aliens had taken over the planes and flew them into the towers."

Everyone laughed, but it was a forced nervous laughter.

Alan thought he should drop the subject for now, but Congressman Rand asked, "So what does your 9/11 survivor really want?"

"He wants an independent commission set up to investigate what really happened. He wants it to be filled with experts in architecture, engineering and physics with investigative journalists instead of politicians."

Congressman Rand scoffed. "Do you realistically think that in Washington there could ever be a committee without politics?"

Alan was not going to be overridden by this political windbag. "Actually he really wants it treated like a murder investigation."

Congressman Rand's face reddened. "Why did you even give this guy any time? Everybody knows what happened, and it was a tragedy, but why continue to chase after ghosts? There are still people running around saying Oswald didn't kill Kennedy. After all these years nothing has ever been proven that it was someone else."

Alan gave Congressman Keller a knowing glance. "You're probably right, but this guy was so sincere, I couldn't brush him off."

"Then tell him you tried and nothing can be done. Tell him to go back to his job and thank the government every day that he is safe from the terrorists."

Alan pretended to submit and replied, "I'll meet with him and let him down easy. I guess he focused all his energy into believing some of the theories as a way to cope."

Congressman Rand seemed appeased. "There are better ways to cope than listening to crazies."

Alan knew he would have to navigate around him and find another way to establish the committee. He would have to be careful, because it was political suicide to be on Congressman Phil Rand's enemies list. The remainder of the dinner went well and they all shook hands and parted like three close friends, which in politics could not be further from the truth.

Driving back to his small apartment in Georgetown, Alan was dismayed and depressed about the situation.

"The function of government is to protect the people, not kill them," he thought to himself. "Maybe some of the conspiracy theorists should be considered patriots instead of kooks, weirdos, or troublemakers. Is it patriotic to lie to the public and send young men and women to fight an unnecessary war? Is it patriotic to take away the rights of the citizens and justify the actions under the cover of protection from terrorism?"

 Alan wished he could change his vote on the Patriot act. He now understood he had sacrificed his principles in order not to be labeled as unpatriotic. He wondered what Thomas Paine would have thought of his vote. He wondered what the founding fathers would say, if they were able to see George Bush as president. They would probably rip up the constitution and beg the Queen of England to take back the colonies.

***

As the weeks went by, Jim wondered if he would ever hear from his congressman again. He knew it was a long shot going in, but he had to try. If he did not succeed by himself, he would do whatever he could to help the 9/11 Truth Movement. He was no expert in any field, but he was like a dog with a bone on some issues. He continued his research and he came across another book about the collapse of 7WTC on 9/11. It was a good refresher course on the material he had already read. He had almost forgotten about how strange it was, because it did not collapse until 5:21 p.m., hours after the other two towers. There was little publicity about the collapse and even less written. The 9/11 Commission basically ignored it. The official reason for the collapse was due to damage and fires caused from the debris from the other towers, which to Jim was just an outright lie. What made the collapse unique was that it was the only steel framed building in HISTORY to collapse from fire. When he read those words again, his anger returned.

 Jim reread the official story that the fires burned so hot for so long, that the steel was compromised and weakened. That caused the building to pancake similar to the two towers. "What a coincidence?" Jim thought. Each fact Jim uncovered seemed to strengthen his belief that there was a conspiracy. Jim reviewed some of his research findings.

 In one of the books, David Ray Griffin examined the evidence logically. There were so many questions that should have been investigated, and they were all ignored for some reason. The first big

One-Way Elevator

issue raised was the eyewitness accounts of bombs exploding in the basement of 7 WTC around 8:30 in the morning. The accounts of Michael Hess and Barry Jennings were detailed in the book. Mayor Rudolf Giuliani's Office of Emergency Services was located on the 23rd floor and for some reason was empty at the time of the most horrific tragedy in the city. The fact was, the damage from the towers was not extensive. It was nothing like an airliner crashing into the building. The fires never burned hot enough to melt the steel, because there was insufficient combustible material on the floors. The firemen who heard explosions were never interviewed. That should have been one of the first priorities of any investigation. It was a murder scene that was not treated like one. Even the cops and detectives on television could have conducted a better investigation.

Another important fact confirmed in the book was in order for the building to collapse the way it did, all the steel columns would have to give way at the same time, which was highly unlikely. The building could not have fallen as fast as it did if it followed one of the proven laws of physics.

Jim's bitter thoughts resurfaced about the collapse of the first steel building from fire and a law of physics broken on the same day.

"What are the odds of that? Probably the same as hitting Lotto two times in a row."

What Jim could not fully grasp was how whoever orchestrated this event could have so little regard for human life. If the planes hit an hour later, there would have been many more people in the buildings. If the planes hit twenty floors lower, there would have been many more trapped. Were the time and the floor location part of the plan?

Jim could also not comprehend why more people were not outraged about the unanswered questions. It was all neatly wrapped up in a simple package with one simple message. The terrorists did it and now we have to do everything to stop or eliminate them and prevent it from happening again. Jim understood that life was pretty cruel and messy at times. It was easier to accept the explanation than to raise a question. It was analogous to that saying used when something could not be explained - "God works in mysterious ways." Jim always thought that was a cop out, and now he also believed that total blame on the terrorists was also a cop out.

    Jim was frustrated that there was no word from his congressman. The more research he did, the more he felt that it appeared to be a conspiracy. The evidence was pointing more to the government as the guiding hand behind the mass murder and the terrorists used as pawns in the global game of world domination. All Jim wanted was the truth. There was nothing unpatriotic about the truth. It was still a government by the people and for the people, even if others had a different opinion.

***

There was a local cable show on every Wednesday night called, "Residents Speak Out." It provided an opportunity for residents to express views on local issues, from neighborhood crime to garbage collection. It was a fairly popular show and there were several times when the local government took action after a problem was discussed on air. Since his ploy had worked with the congressman, he decided to use it again. He called the program manager and asked if he could appear on the show to discuss the flooding problem, the impact on the town, the resale value of homes and the increasing dangers if left unchecked. The program manager agreed and a fifteen-minute segment was scheduled with Jim as a member of a panel of three. Jim hoped that if he had some publicity, other local residents might support him, which would lead to more pressure on Congressman Green to initiate an independent investigation. He knew it was a long shot, but the only thing he had to lose was his standing in the community. He accepted the risk of being labeled a kook and his wife embarrassed to go to the local supermarket.

    The station liked to have upset residents speaking out. It was like a modified "Jerry Springer Show" without the fighting and extra marital affairs.

    Before the show, Jim spoke to the moderator and said, "If I go off topic a little and it's interesting, will you let me continue?"

Chris, who was a lifelong resident and also an adjunct professor at Montclair College, gave an uncertain look. "I won't have a problem, but the station manager may."

Jim said, "I promise that if you get in any trouble, I'll explain everything to the manager."

Chris figured it really didn't matter much who said what. "I hope it's good."

Jim smiled. "I promise it will be."

Chris was just over six feet tall and had a slender build. His black hair was showing sings of premature grey, but it only seemed to accent his boyish face. His full time job was an insurance agent and he had a fairly good business in town.

The show was live in a small studio with a small stage. There was no live audience, which Jim felt was advantageous. The backdrop was a large picture of the center of town, with the Town Clock in the center, city hall on the right and the train station on the left. The flood issue was the first segment; followed by a discussion about building a skateboard park. Not exactly "Face The Nation," but Jim thought it would have to do for now.

The other two guests were the town engineer and a local realtor. Andy, the town engineer was a hulking man in his mid forties, who looked as if he spent his time sampling the local restaurants instead of concentrating on the flood issue. He knew the routes between restaurants better than the flow of the floodwaters. Sarah was a successful realtor, who would try to spin anything to make a sale. She would not say that the flooding was a problem for the house she was trying to sell, but state that it was a good price for waterfront property.

The moderator did not discuss anything with the guests before the segment, which Jim found strange. Jim knew that on most shows the questions and answers are discussed beforehand in what is called the pre-interview.

Jim thought to himself, "I guess there is still free speech after all."

The moderator sat with the Town Clock at his back. Jim sat in front of City Hall and the other two guests sat in front of the entrance to the train station.

Chris opened up the show by saying, "Welcome to Residents Speak Out," your local station where you have the chance to speak out on the issues that impact our community. Tonight we have three residents, who are here to discuss the persistent problem of flooding in our community. We have Andy Castaldo, the town engineer. Sarah Williams, a prominent realtor and Jim Winters, who has lived through a few floods."

The camera briefly focused on each as the moderator spoke.

He then continued. "Why don't you start us off Andy? What do you feel is the main reason for the flood problems?"

Andy looked nervous. He shifted in his seat, cleared his throat and replied in an uneven voice, "I think it is a combination of things, but if I had to pick one reason, I guess it would be the fact that the state environmental regulations make it nearly impossible to dredge the river. If we didn't have all the regulations, that would solve a big part of the problem."

"Why is dredging an environmental problem?"

"Because when we remove the junk from the bottom along with the dirt, there is no place to put it," Andy replied, "Everything is so much more controlled than in the past."

Jim chimed in. "Yes, everything is more controlled except the flow of the river. I think the flooding causes more environmental problems than a controlled dredging."

Andy gave a look, which said, *Who are you to cut me off?*

The moderator commented, "That's a good point Jim." He then turned to Sarah and asked, "How has the flooding impacted home prices?"

Sarah sounded like every other realtor Jim had known. "The home values are good. This is a great town to live in and raise a family. The schools are good and the taxes are stable. I think the home prices would be slightly higher if there were no flooding, but I don't see it as a major issue."

One-Way Elevator

The moderator then asked Jim, "Do you agree with Sarah?"

Jim found that he liked being on television, even if there were only a few people watching. "I agree we have a great town and I have a lot of friends and I have no plans to ever move, but the flooding is a big issue. It's nice to take a canoe ride down the river, but not down your street. It seems we now have a hundred year flood every few years. We're not going to solve the problem alone. We need a regional solution and help from the Army Corps of Engineers. Since we've built on most of the available land there's nowhere for the water to go except down everyone's basement."

Andy jumped in. "The Army Corps of Engineers will take years to write a report, and the recommendations probably won't work anyway."

Jim could see that Andy felt insulted that anyone else could fix the flooding problem. He did not want to argue, because he still had his main objective to speak about.

In a voice filled with a bit of pleading and a sense of urgency, Jim looked at Andy and said, "You may be right, but the point is we have to do something now. I think we're passed the talking point. We've reached the tipping point."

The ever commission-minded Sarah said, "Yes we have to do something, but I don't want people to go into a panic that their homes will be swept away any time soon."

Jim could not contain his reply. "It won't be any time soon, because it's not hurricane season yet."

Sarah shot Jim a look of disdain, while Andy held back a smile, and the moderator reveled in the entertaining debate. The moderator broke the momentary silence and said, "It's too bad but we're running out of time and we need to wrap this up. I would like to thank each of you for a lively discussion on an important subject."

Jim raised his hand slightly and the moderator said, "Go ahead Jim, but make it quick."

Jim cleared his throat and began. "I have another topic that I wanted to discuss. I do not want to offend anyone, but it has to be addressed. I was there on 9/11 and I am thankful that I survived, but many others were not so lucky. I am still angry at whoever was responsible. I guess it's only natural to be upset, when someone tries to kill you. We just mentioned the Army Corps of Engineers coming in and doing a study on the flooding problem. Well The 9/11 Commission conducted an investigation and the report left a lot of unanswered questions and evidence that was ignored along with witnesses that were never interviewed, questions like: How could the steel columns melt when the temperatures of the fires never reached the melting point of steel? How come eyewitnesses saw steel beams ejected from the towers and land 500 feet away? How come there was nothing mentioned about the traces of thermate found in the dust? Thermate is an explosive that cuts through and can melt steel. Nobody actually knows who even flew the planes. It's also strange that not one of the planes signaled that a hijacking was in progress. I'm not an expert. I'm a systems analyst who studies the flow of information. To me, there is definitely something wrong with the flow of information about 9/11. A new independent study is needed, performed by scientists and experts in the field of architecture, instead of politics."

Chris now understood what Jim meant when he said it would be entertaining. He did not want to interrupt him. The next segment could be a little shorter.

Jim continued, "If the experts complete the study and it upholds what The 9/11 Commission found, then it should satisfy everyone, and the conspiracy theorists can go back to the Kennedy assassination, the moon landing, or Area 51. But the exercise should be done, because this was the worst act of murder on American soil, and we should know all the facts. I have met with Congressman Green and hopefully he can help with establishing the investigative committee."

The moderator stood up and said, "That's all the time we have. I hope you have your questions answered."

When the camera was off, Jim turned to the moderator and said, "Thank you for letting me talk. I thought I would get cut off."

Chris shrugged and said, "I thought about it, but then what you said made a lot of sense and what harm could it cause to have another investigation?"

Sarah looked angry and said, "So you are both loonies. What did you have this all planned? You're lucky not too many watch this stupid show anyway." She gave Jim a look like he had leprosy and stormed out of the studio.

Andy shook his head and remarked, "You can investigate all you want, but I still think it was those Muslim terrorists who did it."

Jim calmly replied, "All I want is the truth."

When he returned home, Terri was sitting on the couch with the cordless phone in her hand. Jim asked in a jovial tone, "So what did you think?"

Terri stood up and in an irritated voice, bordering on shrieking said, "What do I think? I think you're nuts! Why did you have to do that on television? Now you've embarrassed me and made a fool of yourself."

Jim was stunned. "What do you mean? I made a fool out of myself? I thought I was good."

Terri frowned, and in a sarcastic voice said, "You were until you went crazy at the end and started spouting all that conspiracy crap."

"It's not crap. They're all legitimate questions. We do need a new investigation."

Terri was angry. "Maybe you inhaled a little too much of the dust at the WTC. I think it affected your mind."

Jim was angry now. "You have such a closed mind. You accepted the government explanation like all the other sheep."

In a high-pitched angry voice, Terri said, "Well a number of the sheep have called and you should hear some of the things they're bleating."

"I don't care. After the investigation, they'll understand."

"You think another investigation will ever be allowed? Nobody wants to bring up those memories again. Now I'm embarrassed to leave the house. Everybody will be talking behind our backs."

Jim stomped to the kitchen. "So that's the real reason. You don't want to be embarrassed. It doesn't matter that the biggest mass murder in American history may be a lie. All you care about is that you might be embarrassed!"

Keith came running down the stairs and said, "Hey, Dad, you rock.

Nobody wants to admit that it was an inside job, but you called them out."

Jim turned to his son and replied, "At least somebody in this family appreciates what I'm trying to do."

"I hope there is an investigation," Keith added cautiously, "but you better watch your back, because whoever was responsible is still out there, and if you get too close, you may be added to the victim list."

Although Jim had thought about the consequences of his action, he was momentarily stunned, hearing those words from his son.

Terri's red face went white. "That's another reason you should stay out of it. It's not worth taking a risk. You were lucky to survive 9/11. Let's keep it that way."

Jim opened the refrigerator and pulled out a bottle of beer. He twisted the cap off. "Don't worry about me. If they get me, then you won't be embarrassed anymore."

Terri stood up, walked up to Jim, gave him a hug and said, "I'm sorry. I guess I deserved that. I don't ever want to lose you, even if you're crazy."

Jim smiled. "Don't worry about that. I'm not going anywhere."

***

The next day, Jim received a call from a representative from the Star Ledger, who asked if he would agree to an interview about his views on 9/11. Someone from town had called the paper and explained how Jim had hijacked the discussion from floods to 9/11. Jim had to work, so he called the reporter from his office during lunch. Jim was nervous. He was never interviewed by a reporter and wasn't sure how his answers would sound. He had no idea whether the reporter would be a supporter, or try to make him look like a fool. Jim dialed the number and hoped for the best.

A gruff voice answered, "Tom Sullivan here."

"Hi. This is Jim Winters."

In a more pleasant tone, he replied, "I appreciate you calling on such short notice."

Jim tried to picture Tom Sullivan on the other end. Was he young or old? Was he short, tall, heavy, or thin? Was he a democrat or republican? Did he know anyone who died on 9/11?

After the usual background questions about Jim's family, where he worked, etc, Tom began the real interview. "So I hear you caused quite a stir on your cable channel?"

A few seconds of silence passed, and Jim asked, "Before I answer, what kind of article are you writing? Will it be a big story, or something small in the back pages?"

"That all depends on your answers."

Jim did not like playing games, but he went along, although he knew that old saying, "Any publicity is good publicity," did not apply to his cause. "I'll try to answer any question you ask."

"Did you plan to bring up 9/11 before you went on the show?"

"Yes I did. I know there are a lot of conspiracy theories out there, but I wanted to show that there are a lot of unanswered questions. Maybe some of the theories are way out, but a lot of the questions are not."

"How did you become involved with 9/11?"

"Well I was in the elevator bank in the North Tower that morning, and the only reason I'm here now is that I missed the elevator right before the plane hit."

"But why are you raising questions five years later?"

"I bought the official story at first, but I always wondered about how the towers came down so straight and how none of the pilots signaled that there was a hijacking. I also read that some of the terrorists named were not even on the planes. Right after 9/11, I was so angry that all my focus was on revenge. It wasn't until I was in a bookstore and picked up a book that questioned the official 9/11 story that I began to rethink everything."

"So you read one book, and you believe everything you've read?"

"No. Not at all. The truth is, after reading several books and going on the Internet, I don't know what to believe."

"Then why pursue it?"

"Because I want to find out the truth. Everyone should know the truth, especially the families who lost loved ones."

"Did you speak to your congressman about it?"

Jim gave a short laugh. "Yes, I used the same ploy of discussing the flooding problem in our town. I then started talking about 9/11 and all the things The 9/11 Commission left out or ignored."

"What was his reaction?"

"I don't think Congressman Green appreciated being ambushed like that, but he didn't throw me out. He listened."

"Did you ask him to do anything about it?"

Jim answered with a slight bending of the truth. He did not want to cause any embarrassment to Congressman Green. "I did ask for his help and said that a new investigation should be started."

"Did he ask you for any proof?"

"He did. I gave him some material. I also told him that there were traces of the explosives found in the dust at the World Trade Center and how the fires never burned hot enough to melt steel. I told him there were firemen who said they heard explosions, but were never interviewed by The 9/11 Commission. I questioned how the alleged pilots, who were barely able to fly a small plane, could maneuver a large airliner into the twin towers and the Pentagon."

"How did he react?"

"He didn't let on. I think I made an impression when I told him the country has to know who did this, because if it wasn't the terrorists, then whoever was responsible is still out there, and it could be done again. The one thing I did ask was that he keep an open mind."

"Who do you think is responsible?"

Jim had to quickly form a response. "I'm not sure. I have my suspicions, but I'll wait for the results of the new investigation to answer that."

The reporter pressed the issue. "If you had to guess, who would you say?"

"I just think it was too big of an operation to be planned and executed without any help."

"By 'help' do you mean the government?"

"I don't know. Possibly a faction within the government, but hopefully, I'll let the new investigation answer that question. I do wonder how a few terrorists, one in a cave, planned and executed one of the most complex mass killings in history. It just doesn't seem possible."

"One last question. Did you hear back from the congressman?"

"No, but I've learned to be patient and persistent."

"I can tell that you are. I wish you luck and hope you find what you're looking for."

Jim did not feel that he was sincere, but he chose to be gracious in his reply. "Thank you. So do I."

Jim quickly discovered that not everyone was happy with his fifteen minutes of fame. He was able to listen to and erase several phone mail messages before Terri or Keith heard them. There were one or two of support mixed in with others that were laced with profanity and threats of physical harm.

"What happened to my nice quiet town?" Jim lamented.

When the article came out, it was on the bottom of the front page. The article did not display the opinion of the reporter. It was neither supportive nor dismissive. It was word for word from the interview. The only negative statement made was the fact that any new investigation would only serve to open up old wounds and memories that are better left untouched.

A few days after *The Star ledger* article, Congressman Green received a call from Congressman Rand who said, "So I see your constituent has been pretty active with his 9/11 wacko stuff?"

Green had not seen the article or heard about the cable show. "What do you mean?" he asked.

"Your constituent hijacked a talk show and started saying that 9/11 was a conspiracy and a new investigation is needed. He also was interviewed for an article in *The Star Ledger*."

Alan briefly smiled to himself and replied, "How did you find out all of this? I didn't hear anything."

"You need to spend more time on what's going on in your district. I got a call from a friend who knows somebody at the paper."

"I've been so busy on my committees that I haven't had much time for anything else."

"If you democrats would just go along with us, then everything would be a lot smoother and you'd have more time."

Alan laughed, "I think it's the other way around. You guys won't compromise on anything. No wonder our approval rating with the public is so low."

Alan could picture the face on the other end, becoming flush and the vein in his fat neck expanding.

Rand made no effort to hide his irritation. "You better contact your boy and tell him there's no way he's gonna get a new investigation."

"I'm not saying anything until I know that's true."

"If I say there's no investigation," Congressman Rand screamed, "there's no investigation."

Alan would not back down. "I'm trying to serve the interests of my constituents and if enough of them want an investigation, it is my obligation to try to make it happen."

In a voice laced with threats, Congressman Rand said, "You're up for re-election next year and if you upset some people, it will make it a lot harder to raise any money. Also, a lot of money could be raised against you. You know the drill."

Alan would not let any threat change his mind. "If I get a few other congressmen and find out something during the investigation, I won't have to worry about money. I'll have all the support I need. And I won't have to bow down to a congressman, who only won his last election because of gerrymandering." Alan could feel the negative energy directed his way.

Congressman Rand had only one short comment. "Be careful what you wish for." He pressed the END button on his phone.

***

Jim received an email from a representative from the 9/11 Truth Movement. Jim could not believe how far his little television charade had gone. He read the email slower the second time.

Dear Jim,
I received a video of your appearance on your local cable station. I was impressed with the way you presented the argument for a new independent investigation into the murders on 9/11. I also read the

article in the Star Ledger. With your voice people can now see that the questions are not being raised by a bunch of conspiracy nuts. When they see an intelligent person with a good background who was there that day, it does lend an air of realism. Everyone can see that you are not out for the publicity and would not raise the issue unless there were legitimate reasons. There is a conference scheduled for September 11th in New York City and I'd like you to sit on one of our discussion panels. The mainstream media generally ignores our meetings. Maybe you can help us with that. Also, if we can have more publicity, then maybe your congressman will be forced to give you an answer instead of delaying any longer. I am an architect, and there is no way that building came straight down without a little help. I guess something went wrong with the explosives in building seven, which is why it did not fall until later that day. I bet there are people who will do almost anything to stop any new investigation. It has all been wrapped up in a neat package and sold to the country. Almost everyone bought it, but luckily there are some who knew it was a lie from the beginning.

I hope you will attend the conference. If you are interested, please respond and I'll give you all the details. I hope to hear from you soon.

Your fellow patriot, Ray Vega.

Things were happening a little bit too fast for Jim. He never wanted to be in the spotlight, but now he was knowingly stepping into the light. He could not turn back, because he needed to know and so did the rest of the world. He knew he was no hero. He felt he was living on borrowed time and he now attempted to get the most out of every day.

Chapter 14

A few days after the argument with Congressman Rand, Congressman Keller walked unannounced into Alan's office and closed the door.

With a look of surprise, Alan said, "I didn't think you'd want to risk being seen with me after that enjoyable meal with that piece of garbage, Rand?"

Walt grinned. "I'll take my chances. We're not in a total police state yet."

"Not yet, but it's getting close. So what brings you here on a Friday afternoon, when you should be relaxing?"

The smile changed to a look of concern. "I spoke to my brother in-law, who is an architect, and I asked him about 7 World Trade Center. He never heard about it, but when I told him it collapsed like the other two towers on 9/11 he could not understand how it could have happened."

"It seems like there are a lot of things we don't know about that day," Alan commented, "I guess there are a lot of people out there with questions."

Walt continued. "I found a video on You Tube of the collapse, and my brother in law said that if he did not know it was building seven, he would have thought it was a controlled demolition. He also questioned how a steel framed building could collapse from fire."

Alan stood up and walked to the window. "The more I find out, the more questions I have."

"Do you think the government could be behind it?" Walt asked

Alan shrugged his shoulders and replied, "I don't know. Maybe a part of the government? Maybe the NSA or the CIA?"

"If there are others behind it," Walt commented, "they must be pretty powerful to pull this off."

"That's for sure. Imagine the planning that went into it and how many others were involved."

Walt sat down and in a voice filled with a mixture of fear and uncertainty said, "Remember, whoever was behind it killed three thousand and if anyone gets too close, adding a few more to the list would not be a problem."

Alan was a bit shocked by the accusation, but he knew Walt was right. He sat down behind his desk. "I never thought about that, but there are a lot of people out there making all these charges about a government conspiracy, and I don't hear of anyone getting killed."

Walt smiled nervously. "That's because the media has portrayed them as nut jobs, even if they do have a lot of valid points. I don't know what would happen if someone started to get close and somehow managed to get a new investigation."

Alan thought about Jim and wondered if he should even continue to help. Jim was a World Trade Center survivor and he wanted to keep it that way. Alan asked, "Where do we go from here?"

"Good question. Maybe some things are better left alone. It could throw the country into turmoil. It would be so hard to prove anything and it would paralyze the government."

Alan was quiet for a moment trying to process all the information. Then he stood up with a look of determination and said, "It could be dangerous. It could upset the entire government and country, but if we do nothing it could happen again. I had a good friend of mine die that day, so I want to know for sure who killed him."

Walt paused momentarily before stating, "If you're in, I'm in. Who says both parties can't work together?"

Alan grinned and in a sarcastic voice remarked, "Why couldn't we be working together on something simple like global warming?"

With a look of concern, Walt replied, "We have to come up with a plan to get the investigation going and keep it under the radar until we're ready."

"You're right. Washington's a small town and it's tough to keep a secret when you don't know who you can trust."

***

Congressman Rand walked out of the meeting understanding what had to be done. He disliked being summoned almost as much as he disliked taking orders without displaying any signs of disagreement. He was powerful in congress, but he realized that in the scheme of things, he was merely another pawn. A good soldier obediently completing his mission, even if deep down he knew it was wrong. He wished he had never been involved. He knew nothing beforehand, but found himself privy to some disturbing information after the fact. Once involved, there was only one way out, but the Congressman planned for a long retirement, so he checked his conscience at the door and soldiered on. He had his orders and now he had to complete the mission to control the message and keep the information that would jolt the country more than 9/11 itself suppressed and out of the public eye.

Alan could not believe Congressman Rand wanted to see him in his office as soon as possible. Alan scheduled a meeting for the next day. When he walked in the office at precisely 10:00, Congressman Rand greeted him like a long lost relative.

They shook hands and Rand said, "I appreciate your coming over on such short notice."

"No problem. It was good timing, since I was free this morning. So what is this all about?"

Congressman Rand replied, "After our last conversation, which I know did not end well, I've been doing some serious thinking about this new investigation."

Alan suppressed a grin. "So you agree that a new investigation is needed?"

Rand seemed to back off a little. "I didn't say that, but I've heard about your guy getting a lot of publicity and how a lot of others are agreeing with him. I guess it's because he seems like a normal guy."

"That's what I told you from the beginning."

"I would like to talk with him and see if he can convince me."

Alan was skeptical of his sudden change of heart so he asked, "Do

One-Way Elevator

you think The 9/11 Commission left a lot of unanswered questions?"

Congressman Rand frowned and remarked, "I never read the whole report, so I don't know. Your guy seems to think so, and if he can convince me, then maybe we can start the ball rolling for at least a preliminary hearing."

Alan listened, but he felt that something was wrong. The words were not convincing, and why did he want to speak with Jim alone?

"If my guy agrees to meet with you, I want to be there along with Congressman Keller."

Rand hid his resentment. "No problem. I want to see for myself if he is legit and if he can stand up to some tough questions. I don't want to be embarrassed, if he can't handle the pressure."

Alan was still not sure, but he figured it was worth a shot. "I'll give him a call and I'm sure he'll agree to come down."

Rand suddenly appeared a bit irritated. "I'm giving you want you want, so I'll expect your support in the future."

Alan suppressed the words, "Go to hell, asshole," and replied, "I guess nothing is ever done in Washington without an ulterior motive."

Rand was serious and said, "Well, can I count on your support as payback for this favor?"

Alan knew he had to play the game, so he responded, "If that's what it takes to get this investigation."

***

Jim was sitting in his office when the phone rang. He saw the name on the caller ID and quickly answered, "Congressman Green. How are you?"

"I'm fine. I'm sorry I didn't get back to you sooner, but now I may have some good news."

Jim felt his heart begin to race and he sat up straight in his chair. "That's great. So what's the news?"

"When can you come down to Washington?" Jim jumped to his feet, excited. "When do you want me there?"

"Congressman Rand wants to meet with you. If we're ever going to get anywhere, we have to convince him."

"That's fine with me."

Alan continued. "I don't trust him at all, but without him it would be difficult to start any investigation. I was going to try to get around him, but he suddenly changed his mind and agreed to meet. I can't figure out why, but it doesn't matter now."

Nothing could diminish Jim's excitement. "I don't trust anyone anymore, especially in government, except you," he said in a jovial voice.

Alan laughed. "That's good, because this guy is a real arrogant slime ball. I'll set up the meeting for next Friday. You can drive or take the train the night before and stay in a nice hotel on my tab."

Jim's mind was racing. "That would be great. I didn't think you would call back. I can't believe this. There are a lot of people out there asking for a new investigation, but for some reason we may be the ones who actually get it done"

Alan replied, "Sometimes things happen that can't be explained."

When Alan hung up the phone and thought about what might happen, he remembered a quote from Edmund Burke, "All that is necessary for the triumph of evil is that good men do nothing."

***

When Jim boarded the train to Washington late in the afternoon for his meeting the next day, he did not know how he should feel. Should he feel happy that he was on the path to find the truth about 9/11? Should he feel disloyal, because he was basically accusing the U.S. government of mass murder? Should he feel vengeful and hope that the people behind the attack might finally be identified and sent to jail? The only thing certain was that Jim did not feel good. Now that he was in reach of his goal, he questioned if his quest for the truth was worth the potential costs.

Deep down he knew that if the government could do it once, they could do it again. He was concerned if there were another event, it would be harder to protest, now that the government was watching everything, listening to cell phone conversations and reading everyone's emails. The world had changed since 9/11 and not for the better. Most people were willing to sacrifice rights for security, but to others it seemed like a choice between lethal injection and the electric chair. Was he really on the right path, or was he foolishly following the yellow brick road in an attempt to find out who was behind the curtain?

He had all his documentation and evidence to make a strong case for a new investigation. Jim reminded himself that even Tom Kean and Lee Hamilton, who headed The 9/11 Political Commission, admitted that information had been withheld. Jim's biggest fear was that he would be portrayed as just another crackpot conspiracy theorist. He was careful to make a logical case and not accuse anyone directly. He would let the professionals first prove why the buildings really came down. If the evidence was strong enough then the next step would be to identify who was behind it. He let his imagination take off and dreamed he would announce at the 9/11 Conference that a new independent investigation was starting. He realized he was jumping ahead and putting the cart before the horse.

He stared out the window at the scenery flowing by and suddenly felt insignificant. He was one man going up against the most powerful government in the history of the world. He knew there were many covert operations involving the FBI the CIA and the NSA, but he hoped that one middle-aged guy from New Jersey would go unnoticed for now. Jim realized he was deluding himself into believing he was living in a spy novel, where his every move was monitored by sinister agents. He looked around the nearly empty car and the man across the aisle was sleeping and the two young girls in the seat in front of him were each divulging too much information about their boyfriends. Nobody was paying any attention to him, except the conductor who punched his ticket.

When the train pulled into Union station at 7:00 p.m., it was still bustling. He was just another faceless traveler as he slowly walked by the stores and the crowded fast food restaurants. He watched the people innocently eating and thought back to the innocent people sitting in their offices, or eating in the cafeteria on 9/11. His anger returned and he clutched his briefcase tighter and walked a little faster.

Once outside the station he hailed a cab. Jim sat in the back seat and watched the cab weave through the justifiably maligned Washington traffic. When he walked into the hotel lobby, he did not feel like a tourist. He certainly did not feel like a lobbyist. If he were, he would have cash in his briefcase instead of documentation that could implicate the highest levels of government in the worst tragedy on American soil.

The lobby was large and the registration desk was in the center against the back wall. To the right was a piano bar with several small tables and low lighting. To the left were the elevator banks.

Jim walked up to the clerk and said, "I have a reservation. Jim Winters."

The clerk punched a few keys and said, "Welcome, Mr. Winters. We have you here for one night in room 332. Will you need one key or two?"

"Just one key. I'm alone and I'm not expecting any company."

The hotel clerk handed Jim the key card and said, "Let me know if you need anything, or have any questions."

Jim liked the young affable clerk. "Thank you. Do you know a good restaurant close by?"

"I do. There's a great Italian restaurant, Angelina's. Make a right out the door and walk down two blocks. They have the best eggplant parmesan in the entire east coast."

Jim exclaimed, "That's my favorite dish. I'll just drop my bags in my room and I'll give it a try. Thanks."

"Enjoy your stay with us."

Jim turned toward the elevator and replied, "I will."

A few feet away, a man browsing the rack containing brochures about sight seeing looked up when Jim walked away. Jim pushed the elevator button and waited. After 9/11, he never pushed the button more than once, because he was superstitious and knew that he had cheated death by one push of the button. There were eight floors in the hotel, which was recommended by his Congressman who was also picking up the tab.

The unassuming man removed a few of the brochures and walked outside. Once outside, he made a quick cell phone call. The only

One-Way Elevator

words he said were, "Three thirty two." Congressman Rand listened on his untraceable cell phone and quickly hung up.

The room was a small suite. The living area contained a couch, wing chair, coffee table, and a large screen television. There was a desk in one corner and a separate bedroom with a large bathroom with a Jacuzzi and shower. He placed his bags on the bed and then went back downstairs in search of an eggplant parmesan dinner.

Jim felt self-conscious eating in a restaurant by himself, but in Washington it was a common occurrence with all the travelers passing through with government business. The eggplant was good, but he had better in New York. He drank one light beer with dinner and skipped desert. He was anxious to get back to his hotel room and prepare for tomorrow's meeting.

It was a clear night and pleasant temperature, so he suddenly changed his mind and decided to take a detour.

He walked to the Washington Mall. He stood and stared at the great expanse of land and the light of the Capital Building. He thought back to Martin Luther King's "I have A Dream Speech," delivered in front of the Lincoln Memorial and how it impacted a nation. He now stood in the same place where thousands had stood, placing their hopes and dreams in one man's words. He wondered how much more Dr. King would have done, if he had not been shot. Jim wondered if it was the man who pushed the movement for civil rights, or if the movement had been inevitable. He walked to the Lincoln Memorial and thought what a great man Lincoln was. He wondered how much more he could have done, if he had not been shot. He then contemplated if Lincoln had not freed the slaves, was it inevitable.

He thought of John and Bobby Kennedy and how different the world would be, if they were not both shot. Jim then questioned whether human progress was inevitable, or whether it was controlled by chance events or specific people. He thought about George Bush and the wars in Iraq and Afghanistan and wondered if that was progress, or a step backward. Jim was leaning heavily toward a step backward.

Were the ugly scars of racism now being replaced by religious intolerance? Were the freedoms that so many sacrificed and died for now eroding like a beach in a storm in the name of national security? He thought how easily the media manipulated everyone. 9/11 was explained and wrapped in neat package that could readily be understood and then each person could go back to his or her own life.

There was no criticism of the government spending billions on national defense, but if the cable bill went up five dollars, or the subway fare was raised a quarter, there was a public outcry. How much did the government care about its citizens, when it may have let three thousand die on 9/11? How much did it care about its soldiers, when it was willing to let thousands more die in Iraq, which had nothing to do with 9/11? Did we really care about the Iraqi people, when almost a million died due to the sanctions imposed and then by the violence of war? Leading up to the war, the politicians kept on stating how Saddam Hussein had used chemical weapons on his own people. How come there was no outcry at that time, but it was only used, as a justification for war? How come there was no outcry that the U.S government supplied the chemicals in the first place? What if it was determined that some faction of the government was behind 9/11? George Bush stated that he wanted to bring democracy to Iraq, while he basically stole the 2000 election from Al Gore and then with the Patriot Act was turning the country into a police state, where the government was almost given free reign in the name of security.

Jim did not think George Bush had anything to do with 9/11. It had to be planned before he even took office. He also thought Bush was too stupid to plan anything so sophisticated. The only part he was given was to read the children's book, "My Pet Goat," to a class of small children in Florida.

Suddenly, Jim did not feel good about his country. He once again felt small and insignificant and questioned whether he had only wasted his time with all his research and accusations. Would he have been better off just going along with everything and watching American Idol and Jeopardy? He wondered if the 10:00 meeting tomorrow would turn out to be meaningless.

Jim was now a full-fledged conspiracy theorist. He had multiple copies of all his documents on three flash drives. The first he gave to Keith with instructions, if he did not make the meeting and was found

One-Way Elevator

dead, it was murder no matter what the official report said. Jim also instructed Keith to contact *The Star Ledger* reporter, Tom Sullivan, and ask him to investigate. He also gave another copy to his friend, Joe, at work and told him to contact *The 9/11 Truth Movement* and have them ask for an inquiry.

The last thing he did was to prepare a video to be uploaded to You Tube, describing why he went to Washington and how if he was murdered that would be another fact proving that it was a conspiracy. Keith was worried, but Jim told him it was just a precaution and he was not in any real danger. Terri was against the trip, but Jim did not divulge any of his concerns or precautions taken to her.

It was 10:30 when he walked back into the hotel lobby. The same clerk was at the front desk. Jim waved on his way to the elevator and said, "The meal was great. Goodnight." He stood in the lobby and waited for the elevator. When the doors finally opened the elevator was empty, but for a brief moment he pictured the crowded elevator on 9/11 and the young woman's face. He shook his head, walked in, pushed the button for his floor and closed his eyes. He opened his eyes when the doors opened and felt that he had once again cheated death. He walked down the corridor, inserted the key in the security lock and walked into the darkness.

***

The next morning, the three congressmen waited impatiently in Alan's office.

Congressman Rand said, "Well, where's your guy? If he has so much information about a conspiracy, then why isn't he here?"

"Don't worry," Alan said, "he'll show." He took out his cell phone and dialed Jim's number, but it went to voicemail. He then called the hotel to see if Jim had checked out.

When the hotel clerk answered, Alan said, "I'm trying to reach Jim Winters, can you tell me if he checked out yet?"

There was a pause and then the clerk said, "I have some bad news. Mr. Winters was found dead this morning, when the maid went to clean his room."

Alan was stunned and he began to yell, "What do you mean he's dead? How did it happen?"

Congressman Rand turned away, walked to the window and stared at the overcast sky without any reaction.

The female clerk was clearly nervous and her voice was uneven and shaky. "I don't know any of the details."

In a shocked angry voice, Alan said, "I'll be right down."

"I don't believe this," Walt exclaimed.

Congressman Rand said in a sympathetic tone, "How could this happen? Why would anyone want to murder him?"

Alan was bewildered by his statement. "We don't know if it was murder. He could have had a heart attack, or fallen in the bathroom and hit his head. I'm going to the hotel now. Are you coming with me?"

Congressman Rand forced a solemn look and in a measured, remorseful voice commented, "There's nothing I can do. I'd only get in the way. Let me know as soon as you find out what happened."

When Alan and Walt arrived at the hotel, they went to the front desk and were allowed to go up to the third floor. When they walked down the corridor, several police officers and detectives were outside the cordoned off room.

Alan rushed up to one of the detectives. "I'm Congressman Green. He was supposed to meet me at my office at ten this morning. What happened?"

The detective frowned and it was clear he did not want to divulge any information. "We don't know for sure. It could be anything."

"Any sign of a struggle?"

"No, nothing obvious."

Alan felt that it was his fault. After all, he had agreed to meet with Jim, and now he was sorry he hadn't ignored him. He should have known better than to get involved in any conspiracy.

He then asked the detective, "Was there a briefcase in the room?"

"No. Just a small suitcase. It doesn't look like there was a break-in or robbery. His wallet and cash were on the night table."

"It seems the victim liked to party," a young police officer interrupted.

"What do you mean?" asked Alan with a look of disbelief.

"It appears there were a few people in the room based on the number of glasses and at least one of them was female. We'll have to see if the lipstick on the glass matches the lipstick smear on his pants near his crotch."

Alan was in a state of shock. "I don't believe this. He was nothing like that. When I first met him, I thought he was straight and a bit of a nerd."

"Sounds like a wacko to me," the officer commented.

Alan could see the initial negative reaction in Walt's face. He raised his voice in anger and said, "Who the hell are you? You know nothing about this man. He was here to try to help with an investigation!"

The young officer acknowledged the look from the detective and replied in an apologetic voice, "I guess you didn't know him as well as you thought."

The young officer walked back to the room. "I know him well enough to know that this is not how he would act," Alan lamented to the detective, "He was down for one night to go to a very important meeting. Why would he risk partying?"

The detective sighed. "I guess sometimes you never know. Maybe he didn't plan it, but he could have met a woman and they went back to his room, and she had some drugs and they started drinking, and he could have overdosed or something like that. It could have been another hotel guest."

Alan shook his head. "Something like that."

Alan was beginning to question whether Jim had been set up, or whether he did like to party. Then he thought, "Why would anyone set him up, other than to silence him? If someone was trying to silence him, that could only mean that he was right, and it could be a conspiracy." When he agreed to meet with Jim, he had no idea if this would go anywhere. Now he felt it had gone in the wrong direction.

Alan asked the detective, "Do you know who saw him last?"

"The clerk at the desk. He's on his way here now to give a statement."

"Can we see him with you?"

The detective hesitated, but then agreed. When the hotel clerk arrived, the detective and the congressmen went to the lobby to question him. The young man appeared nervous and fidgety.

"I'm Detective Jenkins and this is Congressman Green and Congressman Keller. Mr. Griffin, do you mind if we ask you some questions about last night?"

"No. No. Not at all," he stammered. His eyes darted around the lobby unable to look at his questioners directly.

"You were on duty last night?"

"Yes. I worked until midnight."

"Did you see Mr. Winters?"

"Yes. He checked in around 7:45 and asked me if I knew a good restaurant."

"Did you recommend one?"

"I did. Angelina's, an Italian restaurant, which is close by. He went to his room and then came back down a few minutes later and went to the restaurant."

"Did you see him come back?"

"It was about 10:30."

"Was he alone?"

"Yes. He said the restaurant was good."

Alan then asked, "When was the last moment you saw him?"

"I was walking across the lobby, when I saw him push the elevator button and that was the last I saw of him."

The color drained from Alan's face as he flashed back to Jim's story on 9/11 and how he had just missed the elevator.

References

New Pearl Harbor Revisited – David Rey Griffen

9/11 Synthetic Terrorism – Webster Tarpley

The 9/11 Mystery Plane And The Vanishing of America – Mark Gaffney

1984 – George Orwell

Black 9/11 – Mark Gaffney

New York Times - May 21, 2002

Purchase other Black Rose Writing titles at www.blackrosewriting.com/books and use promo code PRINT to receive a 20% discount.

BLACK ROSE writing™

CPSIA information can be obtained
at www.ICGtesting.com
Printed in the USA
FFOW01n1917270115
10603FF